# JACOB JERLOW AND THE NEPHILIM

Lance Peltier

# DEDICATION

This book is dedicated to all of the Christians that have been killed and tortured this past year by people filled with evil.

# ACKNOWLEDGMENTS

I would like to thank my family and wonderful wife for all their support. As each strand of string is bound and intertwined together to make the strongest of ropes, so is our family. I would also like to thank Noelle Freeman. She is an 8th grade student of mine that drew the book cover for JACOB JERLOW AND THE NEPHILIM. She is as bright as her future. Lastly, I would like to thank Michael "DJ Bash" Bashford for his tireless efforts in the help of editing this book. Behind every writing masterpiece is a masterful editor, and he has fulfilled this calling in the highest of standards. I truly appreciate his hard work.

# TABLE OF CONTENTS

# CHAPTER 1

# HIGH SCHOOL

School arrived quickly for Jacob and Bina that fall. It wasn't that the summer ended any more quickly than previous summers, but their adventure-filled summer seemed to fly by. Three international trips will do that for anyone, let alone a couple teenagers who were looking forward to their first year in high school. As unforgettable as the summer might have been, they walked together, talking about some of the fishing they had done recently to ease the tension of their first day of high school.

In the previous school year, they had finished the 8th grade at Sulley Middle School, and Jacob discovered his angelic heritage, which started the whirlwind of a summer of his personal quest to learn more and to find the missing pieces of the Dalet or angelic doorway. On this day, however, they were just two teenagers who were now entering the 9th grade at St. Charles Catholic High School. Their new school would not be a change in location for them because it was connected to Sulley Middle School, but it would definitely be an adjustment.

Students who found themselves at the bottom of the social ladder entering the 6th grade at Sulley Middle School would work themselves up in status through the 8th grade

1

only to find themselves back at the bottom of the hierarchy entering the 9th grade. For some students, it was nothing out of the ordinary, but for others, it was an emotional roller coaster filled with mood swings, sweaty palms, and anxiety attacks. Putting a stop to "bullying" was always at the top of the list for the school's administration, but every year the incoming freshmen heard rumors of hidden upper classmen preying on unsuspecting new high school students with their "toilet swirlies" and "purple nurples." These tales were terrifying for some freshman, but compared to the nearly deadly ending of their summer at St. Paul's tomb in Rome, Jacob and Bina found them only mildly scary and unnerving.

"As much as I love school, I must admit that I would rather be heading to the river to go cat fishing with you than facing my first day as a freshman," Bina said and then smiled as they walked slowly toward St. Charles.

"I agree, totally." Jacob's voice cracked, smiling back at Bina as he recalled the last couple of weeks and their times at the river.

Ever since her first day of fishing with Jacob's Granddad in Alaska, Bina had grown addicted. If she didn't have a book in her hands, Bina had a fishing rod. The two friends had enjoyed solitude and safety in their last days of summer break so much since their trip to Italy that they hadn't even discussed the angelic Dalet doorway, which was hidden in the Hokmah cave. Though it had been a truly unforgettable summer, each of them let the quiet, normally dull end of summer in North Dakota melt away the bad memories while they enjoyed the simple pleasures of their friendship and fishing to avoid remembering all that had happened, especially the deadly battle in Rome.

Jacob and Bina approached the crowded sidewalks of the high school, briefly looked at each other to be reassured, and slowly entered the large, cold, steel doors that separated them from the new, less deadly, but just as scary adventure ahead.

"It's nice we both have the same schedule again this year," said Jacob, walking up to his locker.

"Yeah. It's nice we have Mr. Wolfe again for religion too," Bina replied. The small talk seemed to lessen the nerves.

Because Sulley Middle School and St. Charles High School were adjoined, many of the teachers taught classes for both middle schoolers and high schoolers. This meant that Mr. Wolfe, Mr. Matthews, and some of their other teachers from the previous year would be their teachers again. This also meant that they didn't have to worry about having to get to know new teachers on top of all of the other worries and anticipation that came with being freshman.

While opening their lockers, they were approached by a Catholic priest that they hadn't met before. He was a tall, serious-looking man who had little hair left atop his head. Having received a letter in the mail the previous week, Jacob and Bina had learned that the school's chaplain, Father Fiddle, was new this year. They expected this to be the man.

"Hello, children. My name is Father Fiddle," said the priest a bit more enthusiastically than either of them expected. "And who might you two be?"

"My name is Bina Feldman, and this is Jacob Jerlow," answered Bina, smiling in her easy going way.

"Ah yes. I hope to remember that. I try to remember all of my flock's names. I pray you both will have a blessed year — well, I must be off for now. I'll be seeing you both in weekly Mass, and occasionally in religion class." Father Fiddle slowly walked away, with his hands carefully folded together behind his back, and introduced himself to the next nearest set of students.

"Seems like a nice guy. Don't try saying his name three times really fast though — Father Fiddle, Father Fiddle, Father Fiddle." Jacob snickered.

Bina rolled her eyes and grabbed her textbooks for first

period science class with Mr. Matthews from her locker, which was only a few lockers away from Jacob's. Jacob and Bina then struggled to walk down the high school's hallway while being bumped and shoved by much larger upper classmen.

"Do you think they realize that they are running into us, or is it just some kind of cruel payback for what they had received when they were our age?" asked Bina through the crowd.

Jacob was trying to hear what Bina had just said, but couldn't, as he was squeezing between three large football players who were blocking the passageway. After struggling his way through the group of boys, Jacob noticed why they were congregating in the middle of the hallway. The older boys were at Felix Matthews's locker, listening to him tell a story about catching a touchdown pass in their recent football scrimmage. As usual, Felix was making friends quickly. At their school, only Jacob, Bina, Mr. Lazarus Wolfe, and Mr. Jonas Matthews, knew Felix's dark secret of being a descendant of fallen angels — known as a Tenebra – the enemies of Jacob's descendants – known as Veritas.

"Hey guys, this here is Jacob Jerlow," said Felix putting his hand on Jacob's shoulder. "He's the one I was telling you about that loves to play with frogs."

All the boys laughed. Jacob jerked his shoulder away as hard as he could and quickly walked away. Memories of throwing-up all over the classroom the prior year, because of the disemboweled remains of a frog floating in his drinking water, infiltrated his mind.

"Don't pay any attention to those muscle heads, Jacob," Bina comforted. "If they knew what you had done this summer to help save their sorry rear ends they…"

"But they don't! And they never will, Bina!" Jacob snapped before rushing off ahead of Bina to enter the science room.

Bina followed closely behind.

Mr. Matthews glared at both of them as they took their seats. It was no secret that he disliked children, and Jacob and Bina were probably at the top of his list.

"Sorry, Jacob," Bina said sincerely, a look of concern pinching her brow.

"No, it's not your fault. It's mine. I'm sorry." Jacob apologized. "I shouldn't let him get to me."

Mr. Matthews was eavesdropping on the conversation and couldn't resist interrupting. "You know what you two? Ya both just need to just stop talking because I'm getting all teary-eyed over here," he said sarcastically, in his low raspy voice.

Just as the bell rang, Felix Matthews calmly entered the classroom. His father, Mr. Matthews, managed to push his plump cheeks back into a fulsome grin as his son took his seat in the back of the room. He was very proud of his only son becoming a full-fledged Tenebra — while at the same time breaking their family's curse of generations of only Slugas, who have no angelic powers.

"I hope you all had a relaxing summer, with plenty of mommy-daddy time because now it's time to get back to work," Mr. Matthews barked. "And I know it's of utmost importance for most of you to get your prayer and God time at this school, but remember, when you step foot in my classroom, calculations and scientific methodology rule." He continued about rules of the class, and of course, his favorite topic, disciplinary action. All of the freshman students had Mr. Matthews as their science teacher the year before, so it wasn't like they hadn't heard all of his legislation before, but they also knew to act interested in his words to prevent reprisal. All of the students, that is, except Felix. His head was nodding back for a quick nap.

After science, Jacob and Bina rushed excitedly to their next class. They knew this would be their favorite hour of the day. It was religion class with Mr. Wolfe.

"And good morning to you both." Mr. Wolfe greeted

them at the door. "I hope your school year is off to a good start."

"Well, we did just come from science class, so I wouldn't call that a good start, but I'm sure it'll get better now," Jacob joked.

Mr. Wolfe chuckled while carefully maneuvering his long goatee into a presentable position. He slowly limped to the front of the room with the help of his old weathered cane while the students took their seats. All of the students at the school knew Mr. Wolfe as a kind old man, who, by the looks of things, could barely walk, but Jacob and Bina knew him as much more. Behind the quiet and docile demeanor of this teacher was a ferocious fighter and the leader of the righteous angelic descendants—the Veritas.

"Hello, class. I think you all know my name, but if you had an extremely long summer and have forgotten, my name is Mr. Wolfe, and this is freshman religion class. I hope by the end of this school year you will understand three very important points. First, nothing has changed in the Bible's message since the beginning of Christianity, only people's perceptions of themselves and the world. Second, it is our decisions and corresponding actions that determine the outcomes and products of our lives and we have ourselves, and no one else, to thank or blame for the choices we've made. And lastly, you are a child of the one and only true God, so act accordingly." He paused for a moment. His gazing eyes had a way of both uplifting and nurturing. "Now—please stand for a prayer."

Mr. Wolfe led the class in prayer and, as usual, captivated the students with stories of God's love for them. At the end of class, Mr. Wolfe stopped Jacob briefly saying, "I'll see you tonight, Jacob."

"Yes, sir." Jacob smiled. He was excited to see his leader return to his people.

Their third period was music and band. Because of Bina, Jacob had decided to sign up for this class for the first time.

He had been taking private lessons for the trumpet since he could remember, but this was going to be his first time playing his instrument in the school or around other classmates. He was nervous what the other students would think.

The music teacher was Mrs. Rubis. She wore somewhat crooked glasses that no matter how she repositioned them on her face, they would quickly fall back down with a slight lean to the right. Some students thought it was because her right ear was much lower than the left, while others focused not on how straight they were, but rather the thickness of the lenses. Mrs. Rubis could hear one note go afoul amongst a singing class of 60 students, but, if a student fell off the back row, it would be a miracle for her to have seen. Many of the students didn't know, but she didn't take roll by the students' faces, but by their voices when they answered her calling their name at the beginning of class.

With the introduction of students' names, Mrs. Rubis instructed the class to either sing a few lines of their favorite song or briefly play their instrument after stating their name. Bina was the first to give her name, and she sang the first verse of her favorite song in Hebrew. All of the other students followed suit and sang a short song or played a little tune – all, except Jacob.

"I've heard everyone introduce themselves except one," Mrs. Rubis said, holding her student list a few inches from her face. "Ah yes, Jacob Jerlow. Are you here?

"Um, yes ma'am," Jacob replied.

"Well then, are you going to sing or play an instrument?"

Jacob's voice trembled. "I—I will play my trumpet." Cold metal met hot, sweaty lips, and Jacob let out a high pitched screech through his horn that made many students throw their hands over their ears. He turned bright red when many giggled. He looked over at Bina for assurance and regained focus to try again. This time Jacob played beautifully, actually shocking many of his peers.

"That was wonderful, Mr. Jerlow. I'll be keeping my eye and ears on you." Mrs. Rubis smiled.

As the first day of school passed by, Jacob and Bina started becoming a little more comfortable in their surroundings. They were thankful that physical education was before lunch, but they marveled at the PE teacher, Mr. Colby, and how much his rumored nickname of "4x4" fit him to a tee. The lunchroom was the same shared lunchroom or Commons area they had used in the middle school because the two buildings were adjoined, but it now *felt* different – almost foreign because of their status as freshman and the addition of all of the new social groups and cliques who would sit together *pushing* the non-members to wherever there might be room at other tables. Each new class brought a new challenge and a new part of the building that both of them found intriguing, especially Bina. After lunch, they had English together with Mrs. Strand. Jacob had always found English a bit boring, but Bina's passion for reading seemed to make the books come alive for him ever since they had met. Jacob's lifelong love of history and his father's travels in search for artifacts made sixth period history with Mr. Ramstead an intriguing class for him. Mr. Ramstead was an older, severe looking and stern man who demanded the best of his students and their respect for all that history had to offer, but Jacob and Bina sensed he was actually only gruff on the outside and a warm, caring man inside. Bina was especially excited for seventh period Latin because of her curiosity and desire to learn what was to many a dead language, but what would for her bring to life many ancient texts and conversations with her mother, who was a biblical scholar. Finally, both Jacob and Bina looked forward to having study hall eighth period in the library because they knew they would need the early start on homework or, more importantly, the extra time to research and learn more about Jacob's new world of the Veritas and Tenebras and the secrets of the Dalet.

After school, and upon returning to their homes, both of their mothers welcomed the new freshman with a barrage of questions about their first day of high school. Bina's mother, Rebecca Feldman, eagerly asked about what she had hoped would be Bina's favorite class – Latin and its teacher Brother Jeffries, whom she had worked with in the past on some translations. Meanwhile, Jacob's mom, Sarah Jerlow, anxiously listened to him describe the odd feeling of the lunch room and his favorite classes of religion and history, and she smiled proudly at how passionate he seemed to be about subjects that her late husband had been so passionate about. Maybe living out old high school memories through their children had something to do with it, but Jacob and Bina thought that their mothers were more excited than they were.

After dinner at the Feldman home, Rebecca asked Bina, "Would you like to go tell your father about your first day of high school?"

"Most definitely!" Bina stood up quickly from her chair and helped clear the table. After she cleared the dinner dishes, Bina grabbed the Bible that she enjoyed reading to her father and left for the psychiatric clinic with her mother.

Arriving at the clinic, Bina and Rebecca were somewhat startled when they were greeted at the front desk by the lead psychiatrist because this wasn't normal practice.

"Bina and Rebecca, it's good to see you both," the doctor said hesitantly, his brow somewhat furrowed as if unsure what to say next. "It's been a few months since we've spoken."

"Is everything okay, Dr. Armstrong?" asked Rebecca, suddenly looking concerned.

"Well… there have been some changes," Dr. Armstrong said worryingly. "Follow me." He said the last two words in a rushed fashion as he turned and led Bina and her mother to his office, entered the open door, and then closed it quietly and quickly after Bina crossed the threshold. "Your husband, Levi, has made some...vast changes in the past 24 hours, and...we were just getting ready to call you."

"What kind of changes?" Bina asked a bit worried by Dr. Armstrong's need to close his office door, but even more worried by the odd look of confusion, worry, and hopefulness on his face.

"He is speaking, but...," Dr. Armstrong started.

"My father is speaking... but that's good, right? He hasn't spoken in years!" Bina shouted excitedly.

"I wish it were good, Bina," he started, placing his hands gently on Bina's shoulders, crouching down to look her in the eye. "But...your daddy is...not quite himself." He paused again, straightened up and continued more to Rebecca than Bina, "Perhaps you should wait outside Bina while your mother and I discuss this further."

"Continue Dr. Armstrong. Bina is old enough to be a part of whatever news you have for us about her father," Rebecca said, looking reassuringly at Bina.

"Well, it's almost like..." Dr. Armstrong glanced quickly at Rebecca to confirm that it was alright for him to continue discussing the situation with his patient's teenage daughter present. "Well, it's as if Levi's not the one speaking...when he talks," Dr. Armstrong said, shaking his head as he rounded his desk and sat heavily into his chair. "I know this is difficult to understand. It's difficult for me as well, but when he talks it doesn't sound like the voice is coming from Levi." He suddenly sighed in frustration both with how what he was saying sounded and with his own inability to grasp what he was trying to explain. "It sounds, and I know this is hard to believe, but it sounds like it's someone talking from within him."

Dr. Armstrong shook his head wearily and looked towards his degree from Harvard on the wall in dismay. There was an awkward silence for a moment while Bina and Rebecca stood stunned right where their feet had landed just inside the now closed door. Their minds were attempting to soak in the totally unexpected news.

"I wish to see my husband," Rebecca said, gingerly.

"Rebecca, I don't know if you want to see him right now. I'm not sure you want Bina to see him, he is…"

"Dr. Armstrong, it is ok," said Rebecca. "I appreciate you wanting to protect us, but I think seeing Levi is the best for all of us right now."

"I understand. But I'll have to have a male nurse stand at Levi's door for your safety." Dr. Armstrong rose weakly from his chair and paused again midstride toward the door. "There's something else… Levi is no longer sitting in his wheelchair staring out the window like you are accustomed to seeing. He's inconsistent in his behavior. Sometimes he's seated in his bed rocking back and forth, and at other times he paces from one corner of the room to the other, seemingly chanting the same names and phrases."

The awkward silence returned for a moment, and then, Rebecca nodded her head in understanding while trying her best not to look frightened in front of Bina.

Dr. Armstrong led Bina and Rebecca to Levi's room, stopping briefly to give instructions to one of the male nurses on staff. After looking through the small observation window in the door to Levi's room, Dr. Armstrong unlocked the door and opened it to allow entrance. The door closed, the long hiss from its compression piston ending with its cushioned thud and the metallic click of the latch, leaving Rebecca and Bina in the room and the male nurse watching intensely through the small pane of tempered glass.

"I was wondering when you would arrive," Levi said knowingly. He sat cross-legged on his bed, facing his wife and daughter, but his eyes were closed, as if they had interrupted him during meditation.

Rebecca and Bina looked at each other in bewilderment.

"I see my husband's mouth moving, but the voice that I hear is not his. Who are you?" Rebecca demanded calmly but sternly.

Levi stood up from his bed, turned his back on them, and looked out the window into the black of the early fall night. "Good question. Who am I? Who are you? Who are we all on this miserable planet? I guess, I can be anyone or anything that you want me to be." His tone was mocking and sarcastic, and his voice was not the voice of the loving husband and father that Bina recalled from her childhood.

"Do you have a name?" asked Bina, her voice quivering in fear and worry for her dad.

Levi spun on one heel so quickly both Rebecca and Bina were startled into stepping backward. He glared menacingly from daughter to mother and back to daughter, slowly raised his hand, pointed at Bina, and smiled sinisterly. "I've killed many who have asked such a question." He hesitated for a moment to consider his actions as he drew his hand back to his side. "My name is Baal."

Because she was a Christian historian, Rebecca was very well versed in scriptures of old, especially the Bible. "I've heard your name before. You've been around for many years, Baal, servant of the devil," she said as confidently as she could to reassure her daughter.

In a flash of light, Baal was inches from Rebecca's face, breathing down her neck. The male nurse stormed through the door only an instant later. "Is everything okay?" he asked urgently.

Baal smiled wickedly again, still staring into Rebecca's eyes. "I don't know… Is everything OK, Rebecca?" he whispered, his hot breath washing over her face and flooding her nostrils from just a mere inch away.

The smell of decaying flesh emanated from Baal's mouth, making Rebecca's knees weak. "Yes… yes, everything is fine," she replied as she waved the nurse away while keeping her gaze locked with the demon inside her husband. "We'll call for you if need be."

Bina was biting her lip, trying not to cry. The whole

ordeal of seeing her father act in such a manner was difficult for her to watch. The nurse cautiously backed out of the room, let the door hiss closed, and returned to his limited view through the small portal.

"If you ever call the master and lord of this world the 'devil' again I will rip your tongue out and shove it down your pretty little daughter's throat!" Baal growled his anger and frustration through clenched teeth so that the nurse could not hear. "Don't ever disrespect his name again. He's the true light of this world, and as such, should be called 'Lucifer.'"

"I'm sorry. I meant no disrespect." Rebecca spoke slowly and clearly as she struggled to regain her courage and the strength to stand so close to such evil.

"You – are – path – e – tic!" Baal spat on Rebecca's face with each spoken syllable, droplets of stench filled saliva dribbling down her left cheek.

Bina's voice rang out suddenly, tearing Baal's attention from her mother, and she started reading Psalm 40:1-2 from the Bible she always brought with to read to her father, "I waited patiently for the Lord; he turned to me and heard my cry." Her voice shook with fear for the first few words, but she grew more confident with each passing syllable. "He lifted me out of the slimy pit, out of the mud and mire; he set my feet on a rock and gave me a firm place to stand."

Baal laughed uncontrollably as he stepped back casually, waving his hand dismissively at Bina. "Why do you read such garbage? It's outdated history and a faith that your world has grown too unaccustomed to."

Bina snapped her Bible closed, and her mother jumped a bit at the loud noise. "Are you going to tell us why you're inside my father?" she demanded angrily but warily.

"The angel that was in this shell of a body before me wasn't strong enough," Baal said as he shrugged.

"Angel?" Rebecca's voice remained steady as she drew Baal's attention from her daughter in the way any mother protects her young. "Don't you mean demon?" She emphasized the last word, knowing that it might provoke Baal to focus on her.

Baal stepped slowly toward Rebecca, his breathing increasing as if he were running. "Do you, you hairless ape," Baal's voice seethed with hatred and anger as he extended one finger and poked Rebecca's chest with each word he spoke. "Do you intend to tell Baal what he does or does not mean? I said angel and I meant angel." Rebecca winced, either in response to Baal's poking her chest or in anticipation of another face full of his nauseatingly disgusting spit.

Baal spun around on one heel again and walked toward Bina to continue. "He…the angel," the demon turned to glare at Rebecca over his shoulder. "He meant well, but couldn't speak through a human as a Dominion can. So, yesterday my lord sent me. He knew that I would do his bidding," Baal hissed confidently as he turned suddenly, sprang up onto the bed, and sat down again cross-legged, facing away from them into the depths of the night beyond the window. "Now—leave, for you're beginning to bore me." He waved his hand again dismissively. "Next time, bring someone with a little more…*flavor*."

Rebecca turned hurriedly, the strength returning suddenly to her legs. She reached for Bina and placed a firm but loving, guiding hand on her daughter's shoulder to lead her from the room. Just before Bina turned to follow her mother from what had been her father's room, Bina was certain that the eyes of the reflection in the window blazed briefly with a hellish light from within. Bina exited the room quickly with her mother. On their walk home, they cried, held one another, and shared a great deal of emotion from the turn of events—while they discussed the next action to take.

"What did he mean by bringing someone with a little more 'flavor'?" Bina asked between sobs.

"I'm not exactly sure," replied Rebecca, trying to be strong in front of her daughter. "Maybe you could talk to your high school's new priest tomorrow and see if he would be willing to come to your father's room. What was his name?"

"It's Father Fiddle," Bina responded as she wiped her eyes. "I will ask him tomorrow at school." Her voice took on a tone of determination, and with the hope of action, her eyes dried as she looked back toward the hospital that had cared for her father but now only housed his body, which played host to a demonic force.

Though now a high school freshman, Bina asked to sleep with her mother that night after they had both showered to clean themselves of Baal's stench. Neither Rebecca nor Bina fell asleep quickly or comfortably as Baal's words echoed in their dreams. The demon's evil, which had shined through the eyes of Rebecca's husband as he glared hatefully into her eyes from only an inch or two away, burned like embers at the back of her mind. Those same eyes flashed fiery from the reflection in her father's window into Bina's dreams, warping what should have been the nightly escape of fantastical imagining into nightmares of her searching a blazing cavern for her father's soul amid the shrieks of numerous other suffering souls.

## CHAPTER 2

# HELL'S WRATH

In the deep, dark castle known to all who entered as Muerte Palace, there was great unrest among the Tenebra people because they hadn't retrieved the Dalet. Their leader, Prince Muammar, had been having sleepless nights in the few short weeks since his trip to the Vatican in Rome and the first open confrontation between his Tenebra elites and the Veritas. He smiled at the thought of what the first battle between the angelic peoples in over three millennia signified, but his grin quickly returned to a frown as he gritted his teeth to keep them from chattering. He was scared, for he knew he had to personally deliver the report to his lord that he had failed to retrieve the angelic doorway. The Dalet, which angels constructed at the beginning of time to travel among humans, would have been a perfect pathway by which Lucifer could have entered Earth in bodily form—to rule forever. If he could have escaped his imprisonment and brought his angelic body to Earth, Lucifer's powers would have grown exponentially and made him unstoppable. But the "what ifs" were not Muammar's primary concern at the moment. What truly made Muammar frightened was the lack of immediate reprisal or punishment from his lord. Though his lord had not entered Earth, increased his power, or become unstoppable, Lucifer possessed plenty of power to punish failure, but it had been weeks of silence since Muammar's failure.

Because he didn't have the Dalet, Prince Muammar knew his master would be furious. Prince Muammar paced his chamber back and forth, stopping occasionally to wipe a bead of sweat from his brow; he thought anxiously of what he would say to explain his failure. His bodyguard, Bodach, stood nervously in the corner of the room with all four of his arms crossed and his red skin wet from anxiety. Bodach would occasionally push his tongue out of his mouth to lick the healing burn on his lips – his own painful reminder of their failure – the result of a thrown fireball during the battle between the Tenebras and Veritas in the tomb of St. Paul beneath the Vatican. Yelkie, the wilderness gnome was to thank for that, and Bodach eased his own worrying by imagining how he would thank the runt.

"Bodach, leave me," Prince Muammar commanded. "I will go alone."

Bodach gladly left the tension of the room quickly, thankful to avoid accompanying his master to visit their lord. Prince Muammar sat in front of his large fireplace, which roared with a fresh fire on a pentacle that was carved into the wooden floor. The flames jumped and danced, lapping at the stone encasement, singing the worn stones to a sooty black, but their heat had no effect on either the pentacle or the wood that rested at the bottom of the pit. He closed his eyes, crossed his legs, and folded his arms. The heat from the nearby crimson coals made Prince Muammar's body sweat even more profusely. The flames grew larger and larger, changing from red, orange, and yellow to blue, green, and violet, eventually erupting from the stone pit and encircling him. As the flames licked his perspiring skin causing the droplets of sweat to bubble, hiss, and evaporate, Prince Muammar was deep in meditation, bringing him to

Hell's gates.

The Prince opened his eyes and saw a deep, boundless abyss with cold, black steel bars in the form of a gate in front of him. There was what once was a man lying on his belly near the entrance. He was extremely disfigured — with no legs, no hands, and barren eye sockets from some unremembered punishment; it was obvious that this creature had seen great torture and torment. Prince Muammar shivered beneath his cloak at the sight of what could be his immediate future and then slowly approached the gate. He could feel the intense temperature and pressure coming from the other side of the gate that increased as he drew closer. There were no visible flames, but just an eerie black darkness that gave off such heat that it felt as if his skin and flesh was going to melt from his body's bones.

The creature used his handless arms to force himself upright. He smelled the visitor through what had once been his nose and said, "Muammar, I hope for your sake, you carry good news for the master?"

"I bring news," Prince Muammar answered. "This should be adequate for entrance."

The creature struggled to laugh, but what came out sounded more like a dog choking on a bone. "Hopefully, you fare better than I with your news to the master," he said, waving his arms before him, indicating his missing hands that had been ripped viciously from the limbs.

On the other side of the gate, a demon flashed into view. He wore a dark black robe that was similar to the ones worn by Tenebras. He didn't have one hair on his body and spoke with a deep croaky voice. "Chad, you may open the gate," he said. The creature, having heard his command, coughed vigorously and made a key emerge from his throat. He held the key carefully in his teeth, put it into the lock on the gate, and turned his head to unlock it.

The gate opened, and Prince Muammar threw his hands over his ears trying to block out the screams that burst forth from within. The open gate was letting out the voices of the lost souls of Hell who were crying in agony. The horrifying sound was absolutely deafening. Pain and despair were so thick in the air that it made even the leader of the lost and evil Tenebras shudder. He forcibly threw his hands down to his side and regained his composure.

"You would think you'd never been here before," said the demon, laughing. "I don't even hear their weeping and gnashing of teeth anymore."

"Indeed, Vomul," Muammar announced, essentially ignoring the demon's comment. "I've come to see our lord and master."

"We know why you have come, Muammar. Follow me," Vomul replied as he turned toward the screams that emanated from the inky depths of the abyss, which glowed eerily as the sky does in that last moment before true light of dawn breaks across the horizon.

Vomul led Prince Muammar down a series of stairways, which couldn't be seen because of the darkness, and into a deep corridor. The hall was dimly lit by a chain of fire pits that just barely revealed that the *ground* they were walking on was actually the skulls, bones, and ash held together by the lost. The desperate souls tugged at Muammar's robes and begged for release as he walked toward an immense wall of fire that broke the seemingly endless black of the pits of Hell.

Vomul bowed, tilting his head towards the fire. The flames of the massive wall of fire grew and began spewing sparks onto the gruesome surface before them. The sparks built upon one another from the bottom upwards, forming themselves into a demon made purely of fire and brimstone. The angel of darkness stood barely noticeable against the burning wall of fire behind him. All that Muammar could distinguish was the demon's pitch black eyes and mouth.

The demon of flame approached Prince Muammar and smelled at him saying, "You reek of human stench." He continued to walk slowly in circles around the guest, stopping periodically to look Muammar up and down.

"Fumor, Muammar is here to see the master," Vomul instructed. "It would be best not to eat him — until after." Vomul relished Muammar's torment.

Prince Muammar felt his hands begin to tremble.

Fumor was Lucifer's personal protector of the doorway into the inner sanctuary. No one, or anything, had ever made it past him uninvited. "Very well," Fumor snarled, waving his hand at the wall of fire. The flames suddenly split, dividing them down the middle, making a safe passage through. "Enter."

Prince Muammar began walking through the entrance and looked behind to Vomul asking, "Are you coming?"

"The master would like to see you alone." Vomul's jagged teeth and lengthy canines reflected the light from the wall of flames as he grinned evilly.

Prince Muammar stepped carefully through the wall of fire, extremely aware and protective of what little remained of his mortality and entered another area. The entire area beyond the fiery door took on a more refined structure than the abysmal cavern he had traveled through to get to his master. The features of the walls were no longer roughly hewn rock, but they were finely cut stone and mortar. The crude pits of fire were replaced by grandly constructed fire pits fit for any palace and decorative sconces that securely held torches along the walls. The new chamber he entered was much brighter than the rest of Hell, and to Muammar's temporary enjoyment, the screams of agony and heartache could no longer be heard. That pleasure quickly passed as he remembered why he had come. The shaking of Muammar's hands now spread to his entire body. The sweat, now dripping and running into his eyes, was clouding his vision, but he could see off in the distance his master seated upon a raised throne.

The walls were laden with the most precious jewels and

stones of the world — sapphires, rubies, diamonds, emeralds, jade, and jasper. The pathway that led to the throne was covered in gold and to the left and right angels of Hell laid prostrate, chanting praises to their lord. The air was filled with a floral bouquet that was pleasing to the senses. Lucifer loved riches and beauty. Ever since leaving God's kingdom, he surrounded himself with his own idea of Heaven.

Prince Muammar nervously knelt down in respect before his master, bowing his head slightly, hoping it would not be removed from his shoulders before he could explain how his Tenebras had failed him and his lord. A nearby angel whispered into Lucifer's ear the news of Muammar's arrival.

"Muammar, good and faithful servant, approach my throne," Lucifer said in an even, almost sincere, tone.

Prince Muammar stood and advanced along the path to the throne. While he walked, the angels that were giving praise on either side of him never broke their chant or concentration in praises to their master. As he drew closer to the throne, Muammar noticed a beautifully adorned wooden altar that was at the foot of the throne — covered in blood from a recent sacrifice. Muammar knelt again in submission before the altar.

Lucifer was flawless. From his hand sewn black silk suit to his luxurious leather shoes made from young seals, he didn't have one defect. His hair was blond and combed back with precision. He was, after all, the most beautiful being ever created by God. To his left and right were silver mirrors so that he could admire his beauty whenever he saw fit, and to each side of these were beautiful women dressed in the scantiest of clothing. He loved to be surrounded by lust — for himself and women. Lucifer wasn't just beautiful though; he was brilliant and cunning in every way.

"What news do you bring me of my Dalet?" asked Lucifer.

Muammar struggled to speak, but he suddenly found himself without words.

"Your silence is not reassuring." Lucifer lifted his hand and Muammar started to rise off the ground. Muammar frantically grabbed at his throat, struggling to breathe. As he writhed, Muammar began to kick madly. Prince Muammar was strong, but he was no match for the powers of his master. "I knew you had failed, Muammar. I probably knew before your petty little mind had processed it. My servants on Earth had reported to me your incompetence long ago. How you didn't expect that friend of Jesus to come to their aid is beyond me."

Prince Muammar's face began to change from bright red to pale and then blue, and his attempts to wrestle free from the unseen force that continued to strangle him began to weaken. A searing pain burst from his chest with every slowing heartbeat, sending waves of fiery pain through every artery and vein in his dying body. Muammar's yellowing eyes rolled back into their sockets and his tongue shot out of his mouth like a blue worm breaking through ashen soil. Muammar's mind played and replayed the battle in the catacombs beneath the Vatican faster and faster before his mind's eye, the colors blurring into shades and streaks of colors against a bright screen, which seemed to shrink with each moment, threatening to blink out forever.

Lucifer arose from his throne and gestured toward the nearly lifeless body of his primary minion that floated limply in the air, its right foot twitching and convulsing in a last death dance.

Just as Prince Muammar was certain he would awake from death to find his soul holding together the skulls, bones, and ash along the path beneath which Vomul paced in anticipation of his lord's next visitor, he gasped and inhaled so strongly that it hurt nearly as much as when he was unable to breath. The pinpoint of light in the dim grayness that had been the replaying loop of his failure grew quickly as if he was flying through a railway's mountain tunnel toward the welcoming light of the surface at its end. His eyes rolled back to their intended position and his vision returned to him in a flash. As he gazed upon the wrath of his master, Muammar actually wished he had died.

All six of Lucifer's wings burst forth through his suit, sending ebony silk in all directions as they spread out wide, showing his glory and might. The menacing glare of Lucifer's eyes forced Muammar to look away in shame and terror. The women and servants that were standing close by Lucifer fell to their knees in fear, and for a moment…a seemingly endless moment to Muammar…the chanting of prostate angels in the throne room fell silent. In that moment, in the heart of Hell of all places, Muammar felt a chill run down his spine, raising the hairs on the nape of his neck.

In his mind, Lucifer knew he had a good servant in Muammar, so he didn't wish to kill him at this time, but he needed to send a message—and he had done just that. "The Dalet that I had helped to construct would've been an easy doorway to bring my body back to Earth, but you failed me. Let this be a warning—a one and only warning to you. Do not fail me again! For now, it's lucky for you I am brilliant and have devised an alternate plan to release me from this imprisonment. In the past few days, I sent a legion of my angels out onto Earth to inhabit weak willed, sinful people. They will help you in your quest."

Just then an angel descended from above. His skin was so dark and wrinkly he looked as if he had been severely burned, repeatedly. "This is Adramelech, the leader of most of my legions. He will walk you to the outer gate and tell you of our plans." Lucifer folded his wings back out of sight and took his seat upon the throne of Hell and gazed admiringly at his reflection in the nearest mirror. The prostate angels immediately returned to their chanting while Lucifer's servants and angels ran about seeking to quell their master's anger.

Prince Muammar was grateful to be leaving Hell with his head still attached, but seeing Lucifer and all of his might only nurtured dreams of more rule and power inside his heart. There was an unfathomable emptiness inside of Muammar's soul that needed to be filled, and supremacy was his way to fill it.

## CHAPTER 3

# REVIVAL IN HELDAGO

That same night, as the Feldmans slept fitfully and Muammar nearly crossed the threshold of death at the hands of his master, Jacob excitedly returned to Heldago, the house, school, and sanctuary of all Veritas, while he slept. Under direct order of his rabbi, Jacob hadn't been to Heldago since retrieving the last corner of Dalet from the tomb of St. Paul. The leader, or Rabbi, of the Veritas people had not been seen for many years. For some unknown reason, he had gone into seclusion. Not until that fateful night, under the obelisk, in St. Peter's Square at the Vatican had the Veritas known what had happened to their leader. It was there that Jacob's teacher, Mr. Wolfe, revealed himself as not only the leader of the descendants of God's heavenly angels but also the young man known as Lazarus, whom Jesus had raised from the dead 2000 years ago.

At Heldago, Jacob walked up the castle's stairs and approached the two gate-keepers, Laborc and Raman anxious to enter and catch up with his friends and classmates. He was especially curious about and concerned for Jacques, who was called "Jack" by many of his friends, because he had lost a hand during the battle in St. Paul's tomb. Laborc's and Raman's lion heads atop their human bodies were a grand sight to say the least and brought

Jacob's focus back to entering the grounds of Heldago, but he was curious why they suddenly took a knee as he approached because they had never bowed to him before. Then, he caught the motion of someone coming up from behind. It was Lazarus, their leader.

"Rabbi, it's been far too long," said Laborc and Raman in unison.

"I have missed you as well, my friends," replied Rabbi Lazarus as he stopped before the kneeling guards of the gateway to Heldago. "Your steadfast service to our people is to be thanked. Please rise and open the gates."

The gates were opened, and Lazarus stood motionless — eyes slowly moving, absorbing all of the surroundings. He and Jacob entered the grounds together. All that walked and flew just inside the walls of the Verita sanctuary stopped and stared at them both. It was eerily quiet. Jacob momentarily struggled to breathe.

"Good day to you. Grace, mercy, and peace from God the Father and Christ Jesus I bring to you," Rabbi Lazarus shouted to anyone within earshot.

The people and creatures from within had heard of Lazarus's return, but most hadn't seen him yet. "I will believe it when I see him for myself," many had said.

Jacob became worried for a moment because he didn't know what everyone's thoughts were. *Are they mad at him because he left them without any word,* he wondered to himself.

Maribel, the tiny pixie, broke from the motionless group of onlookers by quickly flying over to Lazarus. She landed on his shoulder and hugged his neck saying, "I have missed you, Rabbi. Welcome home." Her act of kindness and forgiveness moved others, and in moments, Lazarus was surrounded by his people, many wishing to touch his robe and grab his hands to prove to themselves that he had truly returned.

After many greetings, Rabbi Lazarus calmed the crowd of greeters and onlookers, and he made an announcement,

"My people and friends, I wish to speak to you all in our upper corridor. Triple E, please send out a call to all of our people around the world to come to Heldago tonight. Let ALL Veritas meet in one hour in the Great Hall. Tell them their Rabbi wishes to speak to them tonight."

Triple E, the castle's curator, quickly left the area for the Peddle Room. In this secret corridor that holds all of the return points of the Veritas to their homes, Triple E sent out a message using the Rabbi's station. A message that is sent from the Rabbi's station can be heard in the minds of all Veritas throughout the world, whether at Heldago or not and whether awake or in deep slumber. Triple E knelt and went into meditation at the station and called upon all Veritas across Earth's great circumference to come to Heldago immediately and report to the Great Hall.

Within minutes, there were over 200 Veritas filling the inner foyer meadow of Heldago. They were all congregating, speaking anxiously about the sudden and unexpected gathering, and making their way up the steep stairs to the highest point of the castle and the Great Hall.

During the ascent, Jacob soon met up with Jezebel Flores, his good Bethal friend from Mexico. "Hola Jacob! It's so good to see you," she said in her heavy Mexican accent. "I have great news! I've passed my level of Bethal and am now a Clevan. I did it just last night."

Both the Veritas and the Tenebras have a class system that places their people into a specific level of training in which to better learn—much like a school has grade levels. The orders, or classes, from beginning to end are Bethal, Clevan, Moldan, and lastly, Elder. When students are ready for the next level, their instructors test them to see if they qualify.

"Jezebel, that's fantastic!" Jacob exclaimed, hugging her. "I'm sorry I missed your test. I needed to be away for a little while."

"It's okay. I knew you were with me in spirit," Jezebel

reassured her good friend. "So, Rabbi is going to give us a speech, huh?" Jezebel looked around with a look of curiosity to see if she could spot Rabbi Lazarus.

"Yeah, I think he wants to answer some questions and set some things straight," Jacob replied. "Say, I need to find Jack to find out how he is doing after Rome…have you seen him?"

"No, I haven't seen Jacques recently," Jezebel replied. "Maybe we will see him at the meeting. Let's go."

They continued walking up the stairs with the multitude of other Veritas toward the Great Hall. Jacob had only been to the Hall once before. That was when Triple E read the letter from Rabbi Lazarus warning of a Verita inside Heldago that was working for the Tenebras.

Jacob stopped outside the main doors and stared at the eight statues of Rabbis of old. From the first leader to their leader now, there had been a total of nine Rabbis throughout history. Lazarus was the ninth, but his statue wasn't constructed yet because the statues are sculpted after the death of the Rabbi.

Jezebel tugged on Jacob's arm to help him regain focus. "Vamonos!...Come on," she said.

The Great Hall had tables that were carefully situated on different levels according to their respective orders. The Bethals' tables were on the lowest level in the center of the room, and the Clevans' tables were adjacent and just slightly higher. The Moldans' tables were a little higher yet and were to the left and right of the Bethals and Clevans. The Verita Elders sat upon the top level of the hall. Finally, on the upper most level with the rest of the Elders, seven large chairs sat facing all of the tables in the Great Hall. They were beautifully carved oak pieces that had soft red velvet seats. The chair in the middle was slightly larger than the other six. These seven chairs were that of the Patriarch Council — with the largest one in the middle reserved for the Rabbi.

Seated in the seven chairs at the front of the Great Hall,

from left to right, sat Master Kang, the martial arts and body control instructor. Next was Don, the instructor of Powers, and then Sarge, the instructor of Swordsmanship. In the middle seat was Rabbi Lazarus and to his left sat Shir, the instructor of Fine Arts; Triple E, the castle's curator; and lastly Father Santiago Rivera, the Veritas' High Priest.

On each side of the Patriarch Council sat the oldest and wisest Elders, and as the tables got further away, the ages decreased through the other Elders. At one of the tables near the Council sat Shawn, Jacob's good friend. Jacob was quick to notice him and lifted his hand to wave hello. Shawn winked back.

Lazarus was admiring all of his people from his seat when he began to think back to a time, almost 2000 years ago when he was a very young man with Jesus.

****

Under Jesus's direction, Lazarus had fled the area shortly after Jesus had raised him from the dead because Jesus and his disciples were sure that a group of Jews was going to kill him to cover up any kind of a miracle from Jesus. Lazarus hadn't seen Jesus for more than a year and was beginning to have sleepless nights worrying about his friend. He then heard from a passerby that Jesus was in Capernaum, so one night, while his sisters slept, he snuck out of his hiding place and walked to the Sea of Galilee where Capernaum was located. The walk took the entire night, and he reached his destination at sunrise. Jesus was easy to find because there was a multitude of people sleeping on the ground outside his tent.

Well beforehand, Jesus knew that Lazarus was coming, so he had risen from his sleep to meet him before he entered the large group of sleeping people. "Lazarus, my son, peace be with you," he said. "You've walked far this night. Come, let's go to the well for water."

Jesus and Lazarus walked side by side. Just being next to Jesus brought such joy and comfort to Lazarus that his previous worries left him. He was so content he never wanted to leave Jesus's presence. The smell of grain from the freshly cut harvest in the nearby fields was refreshing and would stick with Lazarus his entire life — he didn't know it yet, but this would be the last time that he would see Jesus before his crucifixion.

"I've been fearful for your life," said Lazarus, when they reached the well. "I've dreamt what they will do to you. I can't sleep at night." He began to cry.

Jesus hugged Lazarus and wiped the tears from his eyes. "I know you love me, as I love you, but you must understand that there is man's will, and there is my Father in Heaven's will. Do not rely on your own understanding, but search out the will of God through faith. Lazarus, you have such a bright future ahead of you. You will touch more lives and souls than you could ever imagine. So be of good strength and courage, because God didn't give you a spirit of fear, but of power, love, and self-discipline."

"I understand. I will have faith," replied Lazarus obediently, the feeling of calm and contentment returning and bringing an end to his fears and tears.

"Lazarus, my time is near, and the scriptures are being fulfilled," Jesus explained, placing his hands upon Lazarus' head. "I must give to you the Helper called the Holy Spirit of God, so that he may guide you all of the days of your life. With him, you may be a light in a darkening world... My Father in Heaven, I pray for your Holy Spirit to come into Lazarus, through your power and glory, amen."

Jesus closed his eyes. Lazarus felt his heart rate increase and his eyes widen. For a moment, it was as if fear, doubt, and worry were absent from the world.

"Now — think boldly, act prudently, and always remember you are a child of the one true God," Jesus encouraged. They hugged, as a father does with his son.

****

Lazarus felt the selfless love that came from Jesus once

again run through his body and mind as he came back into focus of the Great Hall and the Veritas that sat before him.

The last Veritas were taking their seats when Triple E approached a circular stone on a stand that was used for voice amplification. "My fellow Veritas," he started. "It's good to have all of us together on this joyous day, for this day our Rabbi has returned."

All in the room stood from their chairs and took a knee in respect to their leader. Triple E did the same. Lazarus slowly hobbled with the aid of his withered cane to the voice amplifier and said, "My friends, please take your seats, for it is I that should kneel. You are the ones that should be thanked because it's you that have done so many good deeds in the name of God. It is you that should be thanked for keeping our people together and strong during my absence. And it is you that should be thanked for bringing back into your house and forgiving a confused, old man."

Lazarus knelt onto one knee in admiration and paused for a moment. He struggled to pull himself to his feet, pulling with both arms on his cane. "It is of utmost importance that I explain myself and my actions to start the healing process," he said. "Many of us here today have fought side by side in battle—losing good friends along the way." Some of the older elders struggled back tears from memories. "My actions of leaving you, though at the time I thought were right, now, I see were selfish and did nothing more than increase fears and strengthen evil.

"As you all know, I am first and foremost a Verita, but I was born a Jew, and with this heritage I hold a great love for the Jewish people. In the early 1900s there were many Jews living in Germany without any inclinations of what was going to happen to them in their near future. In 1940, with the help of a Verita spy, we learned that Prince Muammar was found to have infiltrated the mind of Adolph Hitler, the leader of Germany. Adolph's mind was so completely warped with greed, hatred, and sin that his mind was easily taken over by the Tenebra leader. Muammar was looking to send a message from Lucifer to Heaven that God's chosen people, the Jews, were going to suffer." Lazarus paused, reflecting on the plight of his people at the hands of the evil Tenebra leader.

Jacob loved history, but this was a history he had been ignorant about. He wondered if there was even more history that concerned his Verita heritage that he would one day learn about that would rewrite the textbooks he had previously learned from in his human schools.

"I was informed of Muammar's intentions from our spy, and I began to keep a secretive watchful eye over Hitler's actions. In early 1941, Hitler made the order to begin the murder of the Jewish people. Many were to be sent off to concentration camps to be tortured and gassed. Others would be placed in cruel experiments to further the good of the non-Jew. It didn't matter if they were men, women, or children—they were all to be exterminated like unwanted insects. I physically took part in witnessing Jewish people being rounded up and stuffed into train cars like cattle. The cries of the women and children still haunt me to this day." Lazarus felt a surge of anger and noticed that he had clenched his hands into white knuckled fists. He paused a moment to calm himself and relax his hands.

"I was filled with anger and rage for what was happening to my people. I didn't care about the safety and secrecy of the Veritas. I wanted revenge and Jewish freedom. On my way up to the Heldago gates, the very night that I would raise up Veritas to kill Hitler's army, I was stopped by an angel of the Lord God. 'Lazarus, chosen leader of the Veritas, what is it that you are about to do?' he said. 'I am going to gather our army and defeat Lucifer's plan of killing God's people,' I said. 'You are not to change the destiny of the Jewish people, so sayeth the Lord God,' said the angel."

The Great Hall, previously silent as a tomb, erupted into whispers among the Veritas in response to what their Rabbi had just divulged.

Lazarus paused a moment for the wave of whispers to subside, and he continued, "'Certainly God doesn't wish for the Jewish people to be helplessly slaughtered?' I said. 'What you wish and what God wishes are not the same,' he said. 'Your ways are not his ways. Do not confuse faith with pride.' He left shortly after. I was furious. I couldn't understand why God would want to let the Jewish people be killed when the Verita people could put a quick end to such an atrocity. I stared at Heldago's gates for just a moment and I left—not to return until just a short while ago, some 70 years later." This time Lazarus had to pause to allow the cheers and applause in response to his long anticipated return to die down.

"I had let my pride and personal views outweigh God's overall plan for the world. I shut myself down for many years, taking meaningless jobs to pass the time. About 14 years ago, the same angel of God that had visited me during World War II visited me once again, and he helped to redirect my life into what it was meant for—service to God. You see brothers and sisters, it's not possible to have true faith without good acts of service, and just simply living is nothing, but living simply is the first step in good will."

The Great Hall, which had just erupted into cheers for the return of their long absent Rabbi fell silent as a tomb as the Veritas present sat in awe at what their Rabbi had the strength to admit.

"So, I look back at these years after World War II, and I see the Jewish people regaining their strength and rebuilding their great nation of Israel, and I ask myself, how could I ever have doubted God's plan? My views and thoughts are definitely not His. Who was I to second guess God? My brothers and sisters, I have had to learn the hard way, that it is *adversity* that builds a stronger bridge between your faith and God. When we are weak, God makes us stronger. When we fall, He lifts us up. When we are broken,

He mends our wounds. When we slip, He catches our fall. It's only when we hit bottom and are humbled before the Lord that we totally realize God's love and His plans." Lazarus's voice faltered at the recollection of his own fall. "Pride – pride is the thickest wall that can be built between God and us. It's not until we tear down this wall of pride, brick by selfish brick, that you and I can see God's glory." Lazarus paused again to scan the faces of as many of his Veritas as he could see well in the great gathering to see if they would acknowledge that what he said was true.

"My friends, I come before you now, tearing down this wall of pride that I've created to ask for your pardon and forgiveness in my selfish ways. I know now that it's not by my will that I stand before you, but God's. He has called me to be a leader, and as such, I should be fulfilling his holy obligations. Since my absence, I've heard that the religion classes here at Heldago have stopped. Well, starting tomorrow, they have restarted because a wanderer without any light to shine on his path will most certainly fall into a dark hole." Again, the Great Hall remained silent. For many Veritas the knowledge of their lost faith and falling away from their core values brought shame and embarrassment, which resulted in many looking away from any possible eye contact, and Lazarus found that many were sheepishly looking at their feet as his gaze scanned the hall.

Rabbi Lazarus's tone changed to inspiration and intensity. "Friends, I have foreseen great trials, evil, and battles in our near future. The very people and way of life that our world has known for so long is at risk. With so many humans lost and looking to fill the void left behind where there should be love for mankind and their God, they will undoubtedly be susceptible to demon possession and the powers of evil. I sense Lucifer is amassing his angels as we speak. He is searching for a way to return to earth and defeat any path set forth for the return of Jesus Christ and his second coming. Now! Now is the time to be steadfast and strong, because God did not create you to be fearful, but to be warriors for goodness and purity. So, I say rise up — brothers and sisters! Rise up with me! Rise up and fight the good fight!"

Everyone in the Great Hall stood, cheered, and celebrated. Many Veritas gathered around Rabbi Lazarus to embrace him and show their love.

After giving Lazarus a hug, Jacob and Jezebel were walking out of the Great Hall when Jacob saw the now familiar man named Michael standing in a nearby hall. Michael made eye contact with Jacob and turned to walk away.

"I'll catch up with you later, Jezebel," Jacob said as he walked in Michael's direction. "If you do see Jack, tell him I am praying for him," Jacob yelled over his shoulder, remembering his hope to see Jacques when he returned to Heldago and to see how his injury had been handled and healed. Knowing that Jezebel would get the message to his injured friend, Jacob focused again on his current mission, and he began to follow and catch up to Michael. "Hello, Michael," he said. "How are you?"

"I'm good, Jacob," said Michael. "You've taken in some good rest these past couple of weeks, and you now have Lazarus back in Heldago. These are good things?"

"Yes, sir. I've been curious when I would see you next," Jacob said as he caught his breath from trying to catch up to Michael. "How do you come and go, and why am I the only one who is able to see you?"

Michael laughed. "Have I talked to you and seen you numerous times, yet you don't know who I am or where I am from?" He paused for a moment to think. "I am but a wanderer, trying to find his path. And you, who would you say you are, Jacob?"

"I—I don't know, I guess," Jacob stuttered. "I am just a teenager, trying to find his path, I guess."

"Hmm, I GUESS we are both trying to find our way,"

Michael said. "Only God has all the answers."

"Yes, sir."

"I've come today to give you warning and to expand upon what Lazarus just told you and your friends. Your world, which has grown in darkness for so many years now, is going to see times of unimaginable evil, and you, Jacob Jerlow, will be needed. You will be needed in stopping this great evil."

"Me, why me?" Jacob asked.

"It's your destiny and why you were born into this world. Since your ancestral mother and father of long ago had a child, you were predestined for this journey. Go to the library in the Udall tower of Heldago, and you will find something of great importance to you in your journey. There is a book that contains secret scriptures that were kept hidden to prevent being printed in the Bible — for the safety of mankind. In the east wing of the library, you need to locate a symbol for God. It will lead you to this book of old that I have mentioned."

"But, I have so many questions…," Jacob started.

"I have already said too much. Your destiny is not mine, nor is it my place to disclose it to you. Goodbye for now." Michael vanished into the darkness of the hall.

While he walked to his Powers class with Don, Jacob thought of the Udall tower in Heldago and how he had yet to explore it. He was excited to visit the library but decided it could wait until the next day.

# CHAPTER 4

# THE EXORCISM

The next day at school, Jacob met Bina at her locker and could tell immediately that something was troubling her. She wasn't her talkative, cheery self. "Is everything ok?" he asked. "Did something happen?"

"Jacob..." her hesitation made Jacob even more concerned. "It's my father," she said softly.

"Is he all right?"

"Well, it's difficult to explain, but I think my father is possessed by a demon," Bina mumbled, her face reflecting her own shock at hearing her admission out loud. "Yesterday, my mother and I visited him, and he was walking around for the first time in a very long time, and... Well, another man's voice came out of his mouth." Bina's hands trembled as she tried to gather her textbooks and notebooks for the day.

Jacob didn't know what to say. His mouth opened, but nothing came out. *What does one say to the announcement that a friend's parent might be possessed?* he thought to himself, his jaw hanging open during his hesitation. In his stunned silence, Jacob recalled Lazarus's speech the night before, and how he had said that there would be more demon possessions and greater evil spreading throughout the world. Jacob suddenly became very nervous and anxious for his best friend and her father. Thankfully, Bina was so overwhelmed with the bizarre reality of her father's situation that she didn't notice Jacob's inability to respond while she finished gathering her things. As she closed the door to her locker, their eyes met, and she found some comfort in the pained look on Jacob's face. Somehow, just having said out loud what her mother and she had been discussing the night before and seeing Jacob's obvious concern replaced the need for Jacob to say anything at all. Meanwhile, Jacob noticed that Bina's eyes were puffy and red from what must have been hours of crying. Jacob reached out and placed a comforting hand on Bina's shoulder, nodded as if to confirm he was there for her, and they turned to head to class in silence.

Their feet seemed to guide them unconsciously to Mr. Matthews's science class as they walked, consumed by their personal thoughts while the hustle and bustle of high school students roared around them in a blur. When they entered the room, Jacob's self-induced trance and concern over his friend's terrible suspicions were broken when he noticed that Mr. Matthews was not himself. Mr. Matthews hadn't spewed any of his spite in either his or Bina's direction when they entered the science lab. It was the fact that Jacob and Bina had made it to their respective seats without any comment from Mr. Matthews whatsoever that had made Jacob take notice and glance to see if Mr. Matthews was even in the lab, but Mr. Matthews was standing near his podium next to his half-unpacked grading bag, staring intently at the Rudiger anatomy model human skeleton. His face was pale and his eyes had a certain darkness to them that was eerie. Mr. Matthews's stare passed slowly from the skeleton to the back of the lab and crossed to Jacob himself. Just as their eyes met, Mr. Matthews frowned sourly, mouthed a few words to himself, and went back to unpacking his bag. Mr. Matthews did not say a word out loud until after the bell rang at which point he started his lesson with an extremely

monotone voice and seemed to look right through the
students when he faced the class. Many of the students
picked up on his behavior and whispered rumors that he
was on some type of drug. In light of Bina's news that
morning, Jacob wondered if his science teacher wasn't really
his science teacher anymore at all. A chill ran down Jacob's
spine at the thought, but when he looked toward Bina to
give her a look of curiosity to see if she had noticed Mr.
Matthews's odd behavior he found that Bina was pretending
to be focused on taking notes, even though the page that her
pencil rested on remained blank.

After class, Jacob and his classmates went to religion
with Mr. Wolfe. When they entered the classroom, they saw
their new chaplain, Father Fiddle, at the front of the room
talking with Mr. Wolfe. Everyone took their seat as the bell
rang. "Good morning class," Mr. Wolfe started. "Today we
have a special guest. This is Father Fiddle, our new chaplain
here at our school. Let's all give him a warm welcome."

The class applauded warmly.

"Thank you, students," Father Fiddle said. "It's so good
to be here at your school. Let us start with a prayer. Father in
Heaven, please grant us your wisdom and strength to search
out your heart through love for our fellow man through
your son, Jesus Christ. In the name of the Father, Son, and
the Holy Spirit. Amen."

"Well, I hope to get to know you all in the upcoming
weeks, and I hope you can reciprocate the gesture in return.
As Mr. Wolfe said, my name is Father Fiddle, and our
bishop recently assigned me here as the school chaplain for
Sulley Middle School and St. Charles High School," Father
Fiddle's voice had a strong tenor tone, but it was comforting,
and he spoke with the pleasant cadence that most students
at a Catholic school grew to expect from their priests and
chaplains. Jacob felt certain that he would grow to like
Father Fiddle during his freshman year as Father continued,
"Before coming to North Dakota, I had been studying at the

Vatican in Rome, and it was a great honor to be there. So, have any of you been to the Vatican?"

Jacob and Bina looked at each other knowingly as they and a few other students raised their hands.

"Well, that's fantastic! It's just beautiful, isn't it?"

Jacob looked at Bina again, and Bina grinned despite her preoccupation with her worries about her father. They both grinned, recalling the sites and experiences they had in Rome during their last summer trip. It was the first smile Jacob had seen on Bina's face that day, and at that point, Jacob knew that Bina would be alright...if they could find a way to help her father.

"I was honored to stay there and learn under great teachers of the Holy Catholic Church," said Father Fiddle. "Do any of you have any questions for me?"

Jeffrey Johnson, a larger than average boy with a thin mustache, raised his hand and asked, "Did you meet the Pope?"

"Why yes, young man," Father Fiddle paused as he searched his memory for the recently learned name.

"Jeffrey Johnson, Father," Jeff interrupted the awkward silence, anxiously hoping that the chaplain's tale might take up more of the class time so that he might not have to take any notes.

"Thank you, Jeffrey. Yes, on many occasions I met him and took communion from his hand at Mass. He is an extraordinary person," Father Fiddle continued with some excitement.

Some in the class became a little star struck for a moment, but not Bina. She had been wondering all morning long why the demon, named Baal, had called himself a Dominion, and she needed answers. "Father, have you ever heard of a Dominion?" she interjected.

The awed silence of the class broke into a couple of whispers and one giggle at the abrupt change in topic. Many looked at Bina as if she had come to school dressed in a banana costume, and Jeffrey Johnson smiled in satisfaction while he put his head down on his desk, knowing that Bina had ensured that the discussion in class would take up much more time than either Father Fiddle or Mr. Wolfe may have intended.

"A Dominion, you say." Father Fiddle paused for a moment and glanced at Mr. Wolfe. "That's an unexpected but inquisitive question, Bina," Father Fiddle responded hesitantly, caught a bit off guard.

Bina smiled because Father Fiddle had remembered her name, and she waited expectantly for his explanation.

Father Fiddle smiled and relaxed before continuing, "Well there are different levels, or classes, of angels, and a Dominion is one of them. Everything is not explained in the Bible about angels, but I will explain what we do believe about angels thanks to the meditations and writings of St. Thomas Aquinas and others." He turned and walked to the white board and grabbed a dry erase marker, gesturing to Mr. Wolfe for permission to proceed, and Mr. Wolfe nodded.

"At the top level of the angels are the Seraphim," Father continued as he wrote Seraphim at the top of the board and turned back to face the class. "These angels have six wings – two cover their faces, two that cover their feet, and their final two are for flying. The Seraphim are guardians before God's throne." He looked around the room and was pleased to see that he held all of the students' attention...all except for Jeffrey Johnson, whose drool had begun to form a small pool just under the right corner of his mouth as he breathed deeply. Mr. Wolfe was already halfway down the aisle to touch Jeffrey gently on the shoulder rousing him from his cat nap.

Father Fiddle turned again to write on the board. "The second highest group of angels is the Cherubim. These angels are double winged and symbolize God's power through their praises of Him." The word Cherubim took its place just beneath Seraphim as the chaplain continued, turning to write each level or caste of angel in their place on the board as he gave an explanation for the class, "Like the Seraphim, Cherubim are close to the throne of God. Thirdly, there are the Thrones. They are the link between our known cosmos and Heaven, and they help relay messages from lower angels to God's throne. Next, the fourth level, are the Dominions, the very ones you asked about, Bina. These angels of leadership give God's commands to angels." Father Fiddle paused for a moment to look around the room to confirm he still held the students' attention.

Bina had quietly opened her notebook as soon as Father had begun his explanation and started making notes as he spoke. By the time Father Fiddle had noted Thrones on the white board, a few of the other more proactive students, including Jacob, had followed Bina's lead so that many were busy writing to keep up with the characteristics of each level of angel. Father Fiddle smiled at his flock's attentiveness and the success of his unplanned lecture.

"The fifth class is the Virtues or otherwise known as the shining ones. They have control over seasons and nature, and they provide courage and valor in times of need. Interestingly, these angels also have been said to have powers of miracles in the human world." At this point, even Jeffrey Johnson had begrudgingly started to take a few notes, sighing at the epic failure of what he had been sure would be a class period without notes.

Father Fiddle was on a roll, and continued as he wrote on the board, "Next, are the Powers angels or simply Powers. They are an angel of war, who fight against evil spirits that would otherwise destroy mankind's thoughts and actions with darkness. The seventh class of angels is the most famous, the Archangels. They are said to be fierce fighters for goodness in the world. They have very close relations between God's heavens and the inhabitants of the earth. This can be seen throughout time when an event of great magnitude was going to happen — they are seen in direct communication with a human or a group; for instance, when Mary was visited by Archangel Gabriel, and he told her that she would miraculously become pregnant with the Son of God, Jesus Christ." Pausing once more to allow students to catch up with their notes and to check on whether he had lost anyone's attention, Father Fiddle glanced about the room, and his eyes met Bina's. Bina smiled, nodded thanks for the information that he was offering, and returned to her notes.

"The eighth class of angels is the Principalities," Father Fiddle continued as he wrote on the board once more, and Jeffrey Johnson sighed audibly. "This group of angels is somewhat unknown, but what we do understand is that a great number of them fell with Lucifer when he was thrown out of Heaven. The final, ninth class is known as simply angels. This group holds the closest relationship with humans. They deliver prayers and messages from us to God, and they can help deliver answered prayers to people through God's benevolence. They also have access to all of the other eight classes of angels, so they are like great messengers as well."

"Is it correct to say that there are these classes of angels in Heaven and in Hell?" asked Bina before Father Fiddle could ask if anyone had questions. Jacob wasn't sure, but he suspected that this entire lecture related somehow to Bina's father's condition.

"Yes, I would say that is correct," Father responded, a bit surprised by the rapid fire question and its significance. "When Lucifer was pushed out of Heaven, he took many angels with him. He is known to be very wise and cunning, and I'm sure that he coerced many angels, from different classes, to go with him. It's believed that after being sent to Hell, Lucifer and his angels wanted to rule over the world, with Lucifer wanting to be lord over all, especially humans."

Mr. Wolfe was becoming more and more curious as to why Bina was so interested in these types of questions, but out of respect he didn't interject. He simply gazed upon Bina as if searching for and reading the answer from her mind or soul.

"Do we know why Lucifer was pushed out of Heaven?" Bina then inquired.

"It's theorized that Lucifer was very envious of God's throne, and he raised up an angelic army to overthrow God's rule," Father paced as he spoke at the front of the classroom, and Jeffrey Johnson sat up a bit more attentively in response to the dramatic subject of armies and war. "After Lucifer and his army had been defeated in a great war, they were kicked out of Heaven and sent to Hell."

The spontaneous lecture ended nearly as quickly as it had begun. After a few awkward moments of quiet, Mr. Wolfe thanked Father Fiddle for the riveting lesson on the classes of angels and reminded the students that there might be a quiz over all of the wonderful information that Father had shared in the lesson. In the remaining minutes of class, a few other students asked Father Fiddle about the new Mass schedules for the year and related items, but Bina couldn't wait to have a minute alone with him. When the bell rang and all of the students had left the room, Jacob followed as Bina approached Father Fiddle.

"Father Fiddle, I was wondering if you would come to St. Theresa's Clinic tonight and meet my mother and me?" asked Bina almost apologetically. "We would like you to visit with my father, who is a patient there."

Father Fiddle clasped his hands together as if he was about to pray, looked concerned, and said, "I see. Your father is ill?"

"Yes, sir. He has been for a while, but recently his condition has changed," Bina said and then paused, searching for the right way to broach the subject of her father's apparent possession. "It's difficult to say, but there seems to be...another talking through him." Bina swallowed her fear and embarrassment in a gulp that everyone could hear and continued, "I think he may be possessed by a demon."

Father Fiddle stood almost frozen for a moment, unsure what to say. Then, he looked at Mr. Wolfe, hoping that Bina's teacher might know whether the girl was serious, joking, or delusional. Mr. Wolfe gave Father a look of confidence in Bina, and Jacob moved a little closer to Bina to offer a friend's defense should any question of her intellect or sincerity be questioned.

Having received confirmation that Bina was sincere, Father looked about to be sure that the four of them were alone and softly responded, "Hmm, this is a serious accusation, Bina, but I can see that you are terribly worried and sincere." Then, a bit more confidently he continued, "I have experience in matters such as these. I will meet you there at 7 p.m. tonight, right after dinner. Would that be all right with you and your mother?"

"Father Fiddle, if you don't mind, I would like to observe this evening?" asked Mr. Wolfe. "It would be an honor."

Father Fiddle puffed his chest out a little and nodded his approval just as Bina nodded and thanked him profusely.

That night, Jacob met Bina and her mother, Rebecca, in the front lobby. Dr. Armstrong greeted them as they entered. "I'm glad you've come," he said worriedly. "Levi has been chanting your names and hasn't eaten or slept since your departure last night."

Rebecca tried to smile in reply. Bina held in the tears she had felt welling up as they approached the clinic, and Jacob gently grasped her arm to remind her that he was by her side to lend his friendship and support.

Moments later, the door opened again as Father Fiddle and Mr. Wolfe entered the clinic. Father Fiddle was carrying a briefcase and looked confident. "Good evening students," he said a bit too energetically. "And, Bina, this must be your mother, is that correct?" He turned toward Rebecca and offered his hand.

"Yes Father. This is my mother, Rebecca Feldman."

Rebecca shook Father Fiddle's hand and held it a moment as she guided him with everyone following a short distance away from Dr. Armstrong and said quietly, "Thank you for coming. As my daughter has already told you, my husband, Levi, has been taken over by some outside force. I'm no expert in this field of demonic possession, but whoever or whatever is in Levi did give its name."

"And what did he call himself?" Father replied, a look of genuine concern crossing his face.

"He said his name is Baal and that he is a Dominion," Rebecca explained. "He also said that he took over possession of my husband and kicked the prior demon out because the other demon was not strong enough." Rebecca tried to keep her nerves in check, and Bina wrapped one arm around her mother's waist. "My husband hasn't spoken and has been in full psychiatric care for six years now, so I guess he was demonically possessed for all of these years. One other thing that Baal said was that Lucifer had personally sent him."

Mr. Wolfe and Jacob looked at each other both knowingly, sharing an expression of deep concern. Jacob again recalled the Rabbi's speech at Heldago about Lucifer sending out more demons for possession of sinful, wicked, or weak humans.

From a few feet away, the doctor cleared his throat in order to gain everyone's attention, turned, and led the group up to Levi's room. He stopped briefly and informed the male nurse on guard that the visitors would be entering. The doctor also told the nurse that he could take a break from his shift.

"Jacob and I will wait outside and watch through the window," Mr. Wolfe stated in a matter of fact tone, looking at Jacob specifically as the door was opened. Rebecca and Bina led Father Fiddle into the room.

Levi was sitting cross-legged on the floor, facing the door, with his hands oddly held palms downward and his eyes closed — praying to Lucifer. As the door began to swing closed, his eyes snapped open suddenly and Rebecca and Bina gasped. Levi's eyes had lost any blue that was left in them from the prior day and had turned dark and cloudy. "I sense you have brought more visitors this time," Baal hissed and then sneered. "Are they more flavorful as I requested?"

"We have brought our friend, Father Fiddle," Rebecca answered after gathering herself from being startled by her husband's appearance.

Father Fiddle stepped out from behind Rebecca and Bina, now holding forth a wooden cross in his hands. "I have heard your name is Baal, servant of Lucifer. I have dealt with your kind before." Father Fiddle hadn't really performed an exorcism before, but he had studied so much on it that his education said otherwise. Additionally, with others watching, he had to show he was worthy of such a task.

Baal laughed. "What is this? You've brought me a priest?" He glared menacingly at Rebecca. "Yes, my name is Baal, priest. What are you going to do, sing me a lullaby? Or better yet a good ol' hymn?" Levi's body began rising off the sterile white hospital linoleum, casting a dim shadow where it had just sat.

Father Fiddle's hand holding the cross began to shake. His sweaty hand gripped the cross firmly to not let it slip. His faith was being tested like never before. "You're not welcome here Baal. I command you in the name of the Father, Son, and the Holy Spirit to go back to where you came from." With his other hand, Father Fiddle began sprinkling holy water onto the demon.

Baal became furious. "You serve a dying God and a religion that is falling with him!" Baal howled and spat on the cross, and it burst into flames.

Father Fiddle instinctively threw the cross into the nearby garbage can because it burnt his hand. "My faith is unyielding. Jesus Christ will reign forever!" His words attempted to reflect strength and courage, but the tremulous wavering of his voice and his body contradicted the words spoken.

Baal raised his hand and let out an ear-piercing screech. Father Fiddle was hurled through the air and smashed into the wall, knocking him out instantly. "You fools! I have grown tired of you and this hopeless body I'm in." Baal quickly spun around in midair, stretched out his legs, settled to the floor, and began to stomp heavily toward Rebecca and Bina, who had backed away from the confrontation between priest and demon when the cross burst into flames. They quickly dodged to get the hospital bed between them and the angered demon. Spittle trickled from the corner of Levi's mouth as it curled into an evil, snarling grin, and a horrifying look of hatred burned within his dark, clouded eyes – a sword appeared suddenly in his right hand. "You must die now," Baal's voice hissed from between Levi's lips, spreading vile spit and a puff of breath into the air. As Baal stalked toward his prey, a chill began to fill the room, and Rebecca and Bina's breath could be seen as short puffs of steam as their breathing quickened in fear.

"Don't take another step!" Jacob shouted as he stormed through the door with Mr. Wolfe closely behind.

Baal stopped just shy of the bed that sheltered his prey and slowly turned his head towards the commotion. "Another visitor? I feel so special today." Baal's evil grin spread further on Levi's face, distorting any human semblance that might have before existed.

Mr. Wolfe calmly and purposefully closed the door behind them and stepped in front of Jacob to be clearly seen. Baal's eyes grew large. He took a step backward, bumping into the corner of the bed, forcing Rebecca and Bina to move toward the head of the bed for enough room between the bed and the wall. For the first time Baal looked concerned. "What are you doing here, friend of Jesus?" he snapped. The chill in the air began to quickly heat.

Rebecca only knew Mr. Wolfe as the religion and history teacher at her daughter's school and didn't know that he was Lazarus from Bible scriptures. Nor did she know of the angelic people known as the Veritas and that Lazarus was their leader. She was curious why Baal was so overly concerned with the old teacher's presence.

"The question is why you are here, Baal. Why has your master sent you to our small town? What is so important here that he would send a Dominion, such as yourself, to us?" Mr. Wolfe asked in a steady voice as he stepped toward Baal fearlessly.

Off to Mr. Wolfe's left, Jacob tried to inch his way closer to where Bina and her mother stood dumbfounded by the confrontation occurring before them. Jacob wrestled with whether he should call forth his sword so that he could protect them from the demon if necessary, but he wasn't sure how many more surprises Bina's mother could handle.

Baal kept back peddling away from Mr. Wolfe until his back hit the wall near the room's window. "I will never tell you anything," he yelled defiantly. Baal suddenly and violently threw his sword at Mr. Wolfe's chest. Mr. Wolfe stepped to the side and grabbed the sword's hilt out of mid-flight. Baal's face grew red in anger. He began hurling curses that appeared as black streams of smoke at his enemy's body, but nothing could make contact. A light emanated from Mr. Wolfe as each curse neared him, forcing the evil to fall to the floor harmless.

"Your evil has no effect on me, for I'm protected by the Holy Spirit of God that dwells inside of me," Mr. Wolfe stated confidently as he stood holding his cane in one hand and Baal's sword in the other.

As the air in the room neared a more normal temperature, Baal looked calm and relaxed for a moment as if he was giving up. He closed his eyes, and Bina and Rebecca hoped that he might be leaving Levi. Baal's hands were somewhat hidden behind him between his back and the wall of the room. Unbeknownst to everyone, his fingernails were growing into long, sharp spikes. Without warning, he jumped into the air and thrust his spiked hands towards Mr. Wolfe's neck. Mr. Wolfe expected such a maneuver and in one swift but graceful move parried the deadly claws with his cane so that he did not harm Baal's human host, turned and tossed Baal's sword to Jacob, dropped his cane, and grabbed his attacker by the neck, throwing the demon's face to the ground. Both Rebecca and Bina gasped audibly, Rebecca in complete awe of Mr. Wolfe's surprising cat-like reflexes and Bina in fear and concern for her father. Conscious of the fact that it was Levi's face that hit the floor, Mr. Wolfe used only enough force to stun Baal, and then he pulled Levi's possessed hands behind his back and put his full weight on them to secure Levi for the moment.

"No matter the path you have chosen, you know deep down that God still loves you," said Mr. Wolfe as he struggled to hold Levi's possessed body down.

Baal turned Levi's head to the side and tried to spit on Mr. Wolfe. "Keep your dreams to yourself," he growled. "He has no place for me, and I none for him. Lucifer is my god now, and when he returns to Earth, he will pay back what God did to us all those years ago by killing God's only Son."

Mr. Wolfe looked with concern at Jacob. "Baal, darkness has clouded your judgment, but I will pray for you all the same." Mr. Wolfe used his knees to keep Levi's arms pinned and placed his hands on the back of Levi's head.

Baal screamed, "NO—I will kill this pathetic body!"

"You will do no such thing!" Mr. Wolfe became angry, forgetting for a moment that he was wrestling with the possessed body of someone dear to Bina, and he grabbed handfuls of Levi's hair with more force, pushing his head harshly into the floor to shut the demon up. Mr. Wolfe began to pray, "Father in Heaven, I pray for your Holy Spirit that dwells inside of me to be released into our friend, Levi. May he push out the Dominion, Baal and send him back to Hell through the power and might of your Son Jesus Christ!"

Baal screamed in agony and anger. "If I go, this human's spirit is coming with me back to Hell!" Baal began violently convulsing Levi's body.

Mr. Wolfe held down the demon with all of his strength. "Levi, I know you can hear me. Hold on, help is on the way!"

Levi's spirit was awakened deep within his body and began to fight with Baal. Levi's body went into a seizure. Bina began to cry from all the commotion, "Daddy, you can do it!" she yelled. Rebecca and Jacob fell to their knees and prayed to God for help. A bright light emanated from Mr. Wolfe's midsection. It moved up his chest, through his arm, and out his hand into Levi's head. The light was the Holy Spirit of God, and it rushed through the darkness within Levi's body straight to his soul where he struggled defiantly against Baal.

"NO—get away from me!" Levi and Baal screamed at the same moment, the one voice sounding like it was split into two distinct voices an octave or two apart.

Levi's body suddenly stopped moving, and there was an eerie silence. He was not breathing. Mr. Wolfe slowly lifted himself off Levi's back, and Bina ran from behind the hospital bed to her father and threw her arms around him. "Daddy, Daddy, no! Don't leave! I love you," she cried.

Rebecca began sobbing uncontrollably as she joined her daughter kneeling at Levi's side. Mr. Wolfe and Jacob stood still, gazing at the sorrowful scene speechless. After the heated struggle between good and evil, the air suddenly felt cold and clammy like a lifeless body.

Suddenly, the light that had been seen moving through Mr. Wolfe into Levi's body shined through Levi's chest and then burst forth out onto the floor. The room immediately started to regain its warmth. The light grew larger until it was in the shape of a man. It was the Holy Spirit. He slowly turned his head, looking at the people staring at him. He paused, curiously looking at Jacob, like he wanted to say something. Then, he stepped toward Mr. Wolfe, nodded his head, and stepped back into Mr. Wolfe's body. All of them, even Jacob, were in shock, as they stared at Mr. Wolfe.

Levi's hand rose and came to rest on his daughter's hair. "Bina, my daughter. Is that you?" asked Levi in a hoarse whisper, fighting to regain consciousness.

"Daddy, yes, it's me!" Bina struggled to help her father sit up. Rebecca quickly joined her in helping Levi into a sitting position.

Just then, Father Fiddle began regaining consciousness and opened his eyes at the same time Levi was opening his. Both of their eyes met for a moment. Levi's eyes were no longer white, cloudy, and lifeless but were their normal, healthy, clear blue.

"Jacob, please get Levi something to eat and drink," Mr. Wolfe instructed. "I am sure he is weak." Mr. Wolfe then approached Father Fiddle to lend him a hand in getting to his feet.

Jacob ran out of the room.

"Where—where am I?" asked Levi. "What happened? Who are all these people?"

Bina and Rebecca hugged Levi so hard he could barely breathe. "You have been in the hospital in a catatonic state for six years, father," Bina explained hurriedly. "And, we only just found out yesterday that your condition was due to… Well, it appears that it was all due to you being possessed by a demon. The first demon was too weak, so a stronger one took control of you and spoke through you in the last couple of days. It was all so frightening, father!"

"A demon?" Levi was struggling to regain his full consciousness and clear his sight. He had not used his eyes in over six years, and Baal's possession had caused a curtain of filmy fog to blanket his eyes. He attempted to focus on his daughter. As the blurry image cleared, Levi noted that she was older and bigger than he had last seen. His eyes filled with tears in response to the memories and sudden recognition of his little girl. "Where have the years gone my daughter? And what of your mother? Where is she?"

"Right here, Levi," said Rebecca, holding her emotions in check as best she could. "I've missed you so..." She hugged him again as the emotions, pain, worry, absence of her husband, and the night's events broke through her defenses in heaves of tears. "I love you!" She cried as she hugged him all the more tightly again.

Jacob rushed back through the door, tried to hand Levi a bottle of apple juice and a plate with a sandwich, but seeing that Levi's hands were full with his daughter and wife, he set the food and drink on the floor next to him. Levi's and Jacob's eyes met as Jacob bent to set the food on the floor. "Hello sir, it's good to have you back," Jacob said with a sheepish smile.

"Thank you," said Levi as Rebecca and Bina released their hugging grips a bit. "And who might you be?"

"Jacob Jerlow, sir. I'm a friend of your daughter." He looked at Bina who was entirely focused on her father.

Levi then looked curiously over at Mr. Wolfe and then at Father Fiddle, who was just standing up, but returned his gaze to his daughter without asking for the identities of the other men in the room. "I heard your voice, Bina, and it woke me from my sleep," he said smiling as he stroked Bina's cheek and then held her chin in his left hand.

Then, Levi looked at each person in the room as he began his story, "There was a man." He shook his head again before continuing. "At least I thought he was a man, but it must have been the demon. He called himself Baal, servant of darkness, and he was so very angry. He was trying to pull me into this black hole nearby that was filled with cries of pain and sorrow. I struggled, but he was too strong. I was almost dragged entirely into the abyss when...I saw another man." Levi looked at Rebecca and Bina as if to confirm that they believed all that he was saying. "This second man shined as bright as the sun. He ordered Baal to let me go, and he did." Levi paused and looked again at Mr. Wolfe as if he might recognize the old man.

"Then, he told Baal to leave and return to Hell, and then, just like that, Baal was thrown into the hole of darkness, and it disappeared," Levi continued, shaking his head either in disbelief or to loosen the cobwebs of years of internal imprisonment. When he stopped shaking his head, Levi focused on his wife Rebecca as he spoke, "The man of light came to me and helped me to my feet. He hugged me, and I felt an extreme weight of burden lifted from my inner being. I was so moved with joy that I fell to my knees and pleaded for God's mercy and forgiveness for my sins. I recalled some of my last thoughts and actions of consciousness in my life and the sinful life I was living, and I begged for forgiveness." Levi's eyes filled with tears, and he sighed heavily at remembering the scene that had occurred.

"Another man came to me at this time. He seemed to fall from above. I can't recall what he looked like, but I will never forget the feeling I felt when he was near. It was a feeling of total joy. He said, 'I am the true light of this world, and with me you will never see darkness. Your faith has brought you to forgiveness. Go, and sin no more.' Then, the two men walked away, and somehow, I was brought here, to you." Levi pulled Rebecca and Bina in closer, hugging them both tightly again.

Mr. Wolfe smiled, turned, and placed his hands firmly on Father Fiddle's shoulders. He wanted to give strength and encouragement to the young priest by making him feel as though he had done God's work. "Thank you for your help today, Father Fiddle," he said. "None of this would have been possible without your steadfast faith and devotion."

Since being knocked out, Father Fiddle didn't know

what had happened during the exorcism, so he attributed Mr. Wolfe's words to his work in helping free Levi. "That demon was tough," he said, grabbing the back of his throbbing head. "I trust Jesus worked his graces through me today?"

"Most definitely," Mr. Wolfe replied. "Praise God!"

After helping Levi to stand and helping him back into his bed, Rebecca and Bina joined Mr. Wolfe in thanking Father Fiddle for his act of courage and faith. Father was a little unsure of what had exactly happened, but he went along with it. "It's not me that should be thanked, but our Father in Heaven."

"Amen!" everyone said in unison.

Rebecca and Bina wished to stay with Levi for a bit longer, so they gave Jacob, Mr. Wolfe, and Father Fiddle hugs goodbye.

"I will see you tomorrow in school, Bina," said Mr. Wolfe.

"Yes, sir, and thank you again," Bina said and then smiled. She returned to stand at her father's left between the bed and the window and held his hand while her mother and father spoke softly; Rebecca brushed Levi's hair to one side the way he used to comb it and bent over to kiss his forehead once more.

As Jacob followed Father Fiddle and Mr. Wolfe out of the room, he turned to look back at his friend and her reunited family. He thought back to how only a year before he had hurt his newfound friend with ignorant words and how he was sure his mistake had threatened to strain their friendship. He thanked God that Rabbi Lazarus had accompanied Father Fiddle to the exorcism and that Levi had been brought back from the brink of Hell to rejoin Rebecca and Bina after not being himself for so long. As if she heard Jacob's internal prayer, Bina looked up from staring lovingly at her mother and father, her gaze met Jacob's, and she smiled warmly. Jacob returned the smile, nodded, and let the door close to allow the Feldman family to rejoice and catch up in private.

# CHAPTER 5

# THE CHRONICLES OF ANGELS

Later that night, Jacob entered Heldago as he normally did, but once inside the walls he went into a restroom and used the Oracle medallion that he wore around his neck to disappear. "Amor Vincit Omnia," he said aloud. *I need to get up to the library in the Udall tower and look for the symbol that Michael said refers to God*, thought Jacob. He paused for a moment to look at his absence in the mirror and think about all that had occurred since he first noticed Michael at his father's funeral the year before. He had discovered he was not simply a teenage boy dealing with everything a boy deals with as they finish middle school, but he was a Verita – a descendant of the offspring of angels and humans. As the empty restroom reflected back at him from the mirror, Jacob looked at the walls through where he should be reflected and remembered the awe of his first visit to Heldago, the gate keepers and other unimagined beings he was introduced to, and the friends he made while attending Verita training. Then, he had sought out the four corners of the Dalet – the angelic doorway – in South America, Alaska, and finally Rome, and now, a year since his father's funeral, he returned to Heldago for only the second time since the extraordinary and nearly deadly events in Rome. He thought of how his Verita friends had come to his and Bina's rescue and the memory caused a sudden surge of guilt that he did not expect. Jacob bit the inside of his lip as the wave of guilt rushed through him, and he recalled the fact that Jacques had lost his hand because he tried to defend Jacob. Jacob had meant to check on Jacques the last time he had been to Heldago when Rabbi Lazarus returned for the first time in decades to address the Veritas about the evil that was rising in the world, but when Jacob spotted Michael, he had forgotten Jacques. Jacob looked at his two hands and promised himself that he would check on Jacques as soon as he could after visiting the library.

Jacob was so focused on his guilt and desire to check on how his friend Jacques was doing that he exited the bathroom just as his classmate, Luke Cartwright, was about to enter. Jacob opened the door quickly, and it nearly smashed into Luke's nose. Jacob nearly yelped out loud at his surprise – the shock reminded him that he had to be careful to not be seen because he was not attending his classes. Luke looked around to the other side and opened his mouth, ready to spill the quickest obscenity that came to mind, when he noticed that there was no one there. He looked from side to side — confused for a moment. Jacob rushed away as quietly as possible. "Stupid old building," Luke mumbled as Jacob got out of earshot. "Must have been a draft."

Jacob continued to the east end of the castle where the Udall tower was located. He stopped at its base and looked upward towards where the library was located. The tower was supported by large white bricks and was cylindrical in shape. Jacob entered the tower and noticed a staircase that lined the inner wall that strategically spun upward. There were a few thousand stairs that brought would-be library patrons to their destination. A saying that started many years ago was the adage that "education does not come easy," and Jacob now knew what people meant. To reach the library was a day's workout, at least.

He patiently started his ascent. Jacob would get excited about what he might find in the library every hundred steps or so, and increase his walk to a run, but when out of breath, would pause shortly, so he would not pass out from a lack of oxygen. After about an hour, he finally reached the entrance to the library. As cautiously as possible, Jacob wiped the sweat from his brow and then his hands on his pants. He focused on opening the door to the library much more carefully and slowly than the restroom door and hoped he would avoid being noticed upon entering.

As he opened the door enough that he could look inside, Jacob noticed a wilderness gnome that he had not met before seated at the head librarian's table. The gnome was so short in stature he was barely able to see over the desk, or his long, fluffy, white beard that lay upon it for that matter. Jacob sighed in relief that the door had opened quietly and not disturbed the gnome, but just as Jacob congratulated himself, the gnome raised his head, looked over his reading glasses curiously at the opened door, and raised an eyebrow in interest. He disappeared, transported himself to the closing door, and reappeared just in time to grab the door before it made contact with its frame. Jacob held his breath and stepped to the side. The gnome raised his nose slightly, thinking he smelled something peculiar. Jacob slowly backpedaled away from the scene in the direction of the endless shelves of tomes, scrolls, and books. He was thankful that angels forged the Oracle medallion because it was apparently a power that gnomes could not penetrate or recognize even though the gnomes Jacob knew had considerable power. Jacob looked back to see if the gnome was still in pursuit, but the gnome had shrugged and returned to his seat behind the large librarian desk.

The library had five levels or floors that encircled the room. The shelves and stairs were made of cedar that gave a welcoming aroma, which may have been the design of the first librarians to cover the smell of age that the books, scrolls, and various tomes gave off. *Bina would go crazy if she saw this place*, Jacob thought as he caught himself from whistling out loud at the immensity of wisdom and information that lay before him. He looked around to be sure he hadn't made any noise that might attract unwanted attention, but at this time, only a few Elder Veritas that Jacob did not recognize were present, seated at random tables throughout the library reading, and none of them nor the gnome librarian seemed the least bit wise to his presence.

*Now, what did Michael mean by a symbol that refers to God,* thought Jacob, staring up at the vast arena of books. *Where do I even start?* At the same moment he thought of the word *start*, Jacob's eyes were drawn to the top level's aisle of the library where the books started alphabetically. There, inscribed on a gold tablet, was the symbol for "alpha." Jacob recalled being taught some of the Greek alphabet in school and how God was referred to as the "alpha" and the "omega," or the "beginning" and the "end." *God is the start. He is the alpha*, he realized quietly and quickly, and he decided it was only smart to start at the beginning, so he would have to get to the top level of the library.

Jacob carefully sneaked up the stairs that led to the top level and the golden tablet, pausing on the stairs that creaked a little under his weight.

The sun was shining through a nearby window, and its rays were reflecting off the plate's gold — making it difficult to look directly at it. However, even from a distance, Jacob could tell by its weathering that the tablet looked to be ancient, perhaps as old as the library itself.

Upon reaching the top floor, Jacob looked at and around the golden tablet for some indication or clue to the secret book Michael mentioned. He glanced at the books on the shelf immediately beneath the tablet, but none of them stood out as anything special – each was as dusty and nondescript as the ones that preceded or followed on the shelf. Jacob focused again on the "alpha tablet" itself. The tablet was fixed to a large vertical cedar beam that started at the library's base and ended at its ceiling. Jacob tried moving the gold plate, but nothing happened. It wouldn't budge. He became flustered and sat at a nearby table, staring at the immoveable object. He then focused on the inscription on the tablet further, which shone plainly in the sun's bright light, and Jacob noticed what looked like a small indentation in the metal just beneath the hand crafted symbol for "alpha". He stood up from his chair and slowly walked over to the tablet, carefully carrying his chair with him. This time, he stepped up on the borrowed chair and got as close as he could to the plate of gold to look at the circular depression. Suddenly, he felt the Oracle lift off his chest a bit, as if it was magnetically attracted to the plate.

*My medallion,* he thought. *The indentation on the tablet looks to be about the same size and shape as my Oracle. Maybe the medallion is a key.* Jacob lifted the fluttering medallion from within his shirt and held it against the indentation on the tablet. Both objects briefly lit up brightly. Jacob became nervous that someone would notice and looked around the room. Luckily, no one was near. Jacob slowly released the medallion, and it remained held in place on the plate. He then carefully used both hands and pulled on the tablet once more, and it lifted effortlessly away from the wooden beam with the medallion remaining in the indentation on the plate. In a carved out recess in the wood behind where the gold plate had been, he saw a book. Jacob excitedly pulled the book from its secret home. With his other hand, he set the tablet back in place and then lifted his medallion from its surface — restoring the original position and appearance of the alpha plate.

Jacob carried the borrowed chair and secret book and returned to the table where he had just sat. After setting the chair down as quietly as he could, Jacob looked around the library once more to be sure no one had heard him before sitting down and eagerly opening the leather-bound treasure he had just found.

The pages were nothing like Jacob had ever seen or felt before. The paper was tough, almost like its leather cover, but lighter than normal. Its smell reminded him of a musty basement. As he turned the pages anxiously, Jacob hoped that English words would start to appear, but they didn't. It was penned in some kind of language that Jacob had never seen before. *I've seen Latin, Hebrew, Greek, and Sumerian writing before, and this is none of those,* Jacob thought frustratedly, as he closed the book with equal frustration. He quickly glanced around once more to be sure no one had heard him close the book. He didn't see or hear anyone climbing the stairs, and he was the only one on the upper level as far as he knew, so he calmed down and set his mind to trying to figure out what to do next.

In times of need, Jacob had begun to grow accustomed to a voice speaking in his head that gave guidance, but for the first time, Jacob called upon the voice softly, "Please, whoever you are, I know you're listening right now — please give me some help here. I think this book is very important."

There was only the appropriate silence of a library around him, and the silence echoed in his mind as Jacob held his breath anticipating a response. All that could be heard was the turning of a page from the librarian or one of the Verita elders downstairs.

Jacob continued to hold his breath until he felt ridiculous and exhaled slowly so that it wouldn't make any noise. The silence was awkward, and Jacob's frustration began to grow again.

Then, the voice came into Jacob's head saying, "It is Angelic writing. If you search yourself, you will understand."

"Thank you," whispered Jacob, catching himself quickly and looking around to be sure no one had heard his whisper in the utter silence of the library. He closed his eyes and meditated. Feeling God's grace, Jacob asked for guidance, praying internally, *Father in Heaven, I pray for your direction, through Christ my Lord, Amen.*

Jacob slowly opened his eyes and looked at the cover of the closed book in his hands. The strange language seemed to transform and become recognizable in Jacob's thoughts. He could read the angelic writing. The cover read, *The Chronicles of Angels* in an elegant cursive style of writing. He opened the book to read. As he started skimming the pages, Jacob noticed immediately that the book seemed to be very similar to the Book of Genesis in the Bible, but it also had some drastic additions that the Bible's authors left out of publication.

Jacob returned to the book's beginning and began to read:

It came to pass that God and His Son had an idea that they wished to share with God's kingdom, so they called a meeting of their lead angels in Heaven. The angels that attended were the two chief Seraphim whose names were Heylel and Gould. Also in attendance were four Cherubim angels, whose names were Lutan, Omal, Varal, and Ella and the last angel that attended was a lower-level Archangel, named Leahcim. Generally, lower angels were not allowed in meetings such as this, but since Leahcim was close friends with the Son of God and was well known for his courage and humility—he was asked to attend.

In the gathering of the angels, Jesus expressed the plan that he and his Father conceived to develop the barren planet of Earth into an extension of their kingdom. God would create land, water, plants, and animals, but, most importantly, He would create humankind in His image to inhabit the planet. All the angels were excited and enthusiastic about the plan, except Heylel. He was the most beautiful and powerful creature God had ever created—and was just boastful enough to let others know it. For some time, God had grown concerned about Heylel's role in Heaven but did not give a second thought to what was to happen.

Heylel had planted the seeds of jealousy in his heart when God's Son was born into Heaven, making Jesus his new favorite, and during this meeting, the seeds began to grow violently. "And we are to let these humans grow and multiply. What if they become stronger than us and take us over, or what if they turn their back on you, God, their creator?" he asked.

"Their destiny is their own," said God. "They will be free to choose."

"And if they don't desire you, and they put themselves above all else, what of mankind then?" asked Heylel.

Then God said, "If they choose the life that we have set forth for them, they will live in harmony with each other, but if they choose their own path, they will most certainly live in darkness and heartache. They will be born with an innate urgency to search for love and goodness, which leads them to me, but their choice and their destiny is that of free will."

Leahcim knelt in respect before the throne of God and said, "I know you, God, are all powerful, but how will you create such a creature that you call mankind? How can you give them life?"

God smiled. "Ah yes, this is the miracle and breath of life that I shall put into the human. However, there must be a connection between our world and theirs in order for them to live. I will create in them a spirit that never dies and will have an eternal destination. I will create a garden that will be home to two trees that will bring harmony between our two worlds. One will be a link between us in the breath of life and the other in the knowledge of good and evil. These two trees will give life and meaning to their world. Without them, the humans would perish."

"Such trees would also give a connection between our two worlds," said Leahcim in a respectful tone of concern. "If the humans learned of this, there could be a future uprising, and they could have a doorway into your kingdom."

Jacob paused for a moment and asked himself, *The trees in the Garden of Eden are a doorway between Heaven and Earth? What if evil got a hold of this?* Jacob regained his focus and continued to read.

"Yes my faithful servant," said God. "I enjoy your fortitude and insight. What you have said is true, but many precautions will be in place that will prevent this from happening."

The meeting ended with Heylel retreating to a nearby secluded forest. He was furious and filled with jealousy. "How could He create such creatures? There is no purpose, but to raise them above us and make us their servants. He and his precious Son, hand and hand, strolling through the garden, creating humans from the dust, what a disgrace to our people. God is unfit to be the ruler any longer. I would be a better ruler than He." At this moment, all love and devotion to his creator left Heylel's body, and he began his strategy to overthrow Heaven. Evil and sin had entered Heaven.

While God and Jesus developed the planet Earth for humankind's inhabitance, Heylel was secretly pulling angels to his side. Heylel was very cunning in his actions and words and won over the hearts of many angels. In this time, Earth years were innumerable, but, in heavenly time, mere days passed.

On the fifth day of creation, God was roaming Earth, creating creatures to live in its waters and its skies, when a great battle erupted in Heaven. Heylel and his angels, who he deceived to follow him, declared war on the angels that kept allegiance to God.

Sword met sword and power met power on that day, and many angels fell to their eternal rest.

The rebel angels wanted nothing more than to kill God's only Son and control Heaven. Soon after the battle spread,

Jesus became trapped in the Holy Palace with his faithful guardian of the throne, the Seraphim Gould, and an angelic castle caretaker.

The outnumbered angels of the castle fought valiantly to save the kingdom and Jesus, but with the rebels' countless numbers, they had fought their way up to Jesus's locked chamber.

Heylel came upon Jesus's room and called for him to open it. He knew that Jesus was too powerful for him to confront openly, so he had a plan. At this time, Jesus didn't know that Heylel was leading the revolt. He thought Heylel was there to help him, so he opened the door to let him in.

"Are you hurt, Jesus?" asked Heylel feigning innocent and genuine concern.

"No, Gould and I are ready to fight to save the kingdom," said Jesus. "How many rebels are there?"

"Their number is great, my Lord." Heylel walked behind Jesus and without warning, struck him in the back of the head with the jeweled pommel of his sword's hilt, knocking Jesus unconscious.

"Heylel, how could you?" Gould yelled, as his sword appeared in his hand and he leaped to Jesus's fallen body. "You are the leader of this treachery?"

"I am, and I will soon be the rightful ruler of our world. I will do away with this mankind nonsense."

Gould stormed after Heylel, and they fought ferociously. Both angels were very evenly matched, but at one point during the clash of steel, Gould's defense faltered briefly, and Heylel cut off one of Gould's wings, making him fall to the floor. Then, Heylel opened the chamber's locked doors and let the remaining rebel angels into the room. Gould and Jesus were surrounded.

At this time, even though Jesus was unconscious, a tear fell from his cheek that turned into a shining ray of light. This light was sent to the "one that should be deemed worthy." It was a piece of Jesus's soul.

Then, the Horn of Truth, the horn that was used by angels to proclaim God's approach, blew loudly from outside the castle. Seven Archangels, led by Leahcim, had fought their way to the castle's doors. Leahcim had blown the Horn of Truth that had suddenly appeared to him. God heard the horn from Earth and rushed toward Heaven. Many of the angels trembled from its sound, but not Heylel. He jabbed his sword toward Jesus's heart, but a faithful angel blocked the mortal thrust, throwing himself upon the blade. The angel that selflessly gave his life was not a soldier, but the humble castle caretaker that had found himself trapped with Gould and Jesus during the siege of the castle. His name was Heldago, and he will forever be remembered as the first to give the greatest gift of all—the giving of one's life to save another's.

At that very moment, the light that had come from the tear of Jesus flew into the chest of Leahcim. He was found worthy to carry such purity.

Although they were greatly outnumbered, Leahcim and the Archangels fought through the mass of deceived angels to get to Jesus. Leahcim showed the power and might of ten angels that day, slaying angels far more powerful than him that stood in his path. With every step forward, he felt a presence of power inside of him grow exponentially.

"And now, you, precious Son of the Almighty will die, and I will be the new light of Heaven," Heylel boastfully growled. "From this day forth I will be Lucifer, the true light." Heylel wanted the name of Lucifer because it meant *to bring light*. Lucifer raised his sword again to strike Jesus down when Leahcim ran through the doorway. Leahcim threw his sword at Lucifer's back. Lucifer spun quickly and blocked the sword with his. Leahcim called for his sword to return to him, as he looked at a badly beaten Jesus and wounded Gould, who were both still lying on the floor.

God sensed what was happening in His beloved world on His return to Heaven, and He chose to do nothing against the revolt because He already had another plan. In His omnipotence and omniscience, He had, and always would have, the eternal plan for Heaven and Earth. A bolt of dark flames came bursting forth from His hands that created a darkness that would be void of His goodness. God named it Hell.

"You... Leahcim," said Lucifer. "You dare challenge me? You are but a peasant angel compared to me." Lucifer's six wings burst forth from either side of his back. He was trying to scare his opponent, but no such maneuvers affected Leahcim. He was filled with righteousness, not fear.

A dark black hole that led to Hell opened on a nearby wall, making both angels stop and take notice. "It looks like God knows what you have done and has set aside a special place for you, Heylel," said Leahcim.

"My name is Lucifer!" he yelled. "For I am the new light! And you, peasant, will never get me through that hole." Lucifer approached Leahcim. "After I am done killing you and Jesus, God will be so weakened by His losses we will block His entrance back into Heaven. Give up now, and I will let you live to be a footstool before my throne."

"Unlike you, I do not betray those whom I love and who love me," said Leahcim. "That black hole is your destination." Leahcim attacked. He felt the being of light that was growing inside of him gain strength with every inch of expended power in his fight. He fought with virtue as his shield and justice his sword. He pushed Lucifer backward with his might.

Lucifer could not believe the strength of the Archangel. Every maneuver and power he hurled at Leahcim was countered with even more power. They stopped for a moment. "How can this be? Who is helping you?" asked Lucifer. "Come, be with me, and we will rule Heaven together. All of the angels and creatures of Heaven will be under our command."

"Do not tempt the Lord, God!" Leahcim shouted as he

hurled all of his power at Lucifer, knocking him into the dark hole of Hell. The opening closed, barring Lucifer from returning. Leahcim rushed to the aid of Jesus and helped him recover. Soon after, God returned to Heaven. His anger and sadness upon seeing the dead angels and destruction of Heaven thundered throughout the heavens and the Earth He had created. Many of Earth's largest and greatest creatures died that day and in the days to come as God's wrath rained from above. God rushed to His wounded angels and to His Son to help them heal.

As that day neared its end, God and His faithful angels gathered all of the fallen angels, who had betrayed their Creator and cast them into Hell with Lucifer. Then, God called all of His angels and creatures to His castle. "On this day and forever more, you, Leahcim, have made yourself into a new creation through your righteousness, strength, and humility. For this display of courage, loyalty, and love for me, your name henceforth shall be ------------."

The author or someone else had drawn a line through the angel's name on the page, making it illegible. Jacob quickly thumbed through the upcoming pages and saw that the angel's name had been deliberately scratched out of all the pages. *Why is this angel's name being hidden?* Jacob thought. He pondered this question briefly, but continued to read:

"Your name shall be told for all eternity for your allegiance and bravery. With your undying love and faithfulness to me and Jesus, you have allowed a divine being to reside in you. He is the Holy Spirit, and he is the light of righteousness. He will be a helper for us and mankind."

In private, ------------ went before God and asked, "Father, this new place that you call Hell, which is separated from us, is there any connection between it and Earth?"

God paused for a moment, looking concerned. "Yes, I'm afraid there is. Because I was halfway between Earth and

Heaven when I created Hell, I had no choice but to create a link between Earth and Hell. It was the only way. Lucifer will undoubtedly have plans to take over the humans' hearts and minds. But, for now, we must have faith that the humans can endure and not submit to his evil. Our powers will still be available to help mankind."

"And what are Lucifer's constraints? Is he free to roam the Earth?"

"At this point, yes, he will be able to freely wander the Earth, just as all angels are able to do so," explained God. "This is just a natural connection that is between their world and ours. However, what concerns me is that Lucifer and his followers will be able to enter the animals and humans that I will have created — trying to change their hearts and minds to evil actions and thoughts that lead to sin. The more followers he can convert to his cause the stronger he will become."

With this, the day ended with righteousness being restored to Heaven.

The following day, which was the sixth day of Earth's creation, God and Jesus journeyed to the planet to create the land animals and the first humans. After creating many kinds of animals, God went to the beautiful garden that He had created by a place called Eden. Here, He had created the tree of knowledge and the tree of life. "With the help of the tree of knowledge and the tree of life, here, in the Garden of Eden, we will create the first humans," said God. Then, the first two humans were shaped from the dust of the ground in the image and shadow of God.

God gave forth a wind from His mouth that blew through the tree of life — entering the human's nostrils. This gave them the breath of life. God made one human a man and the other a woman so that they could marry, have children of their own, and create more humans. He gave them the names Adam and Eve. God walked the humans through the garden and gave them these instructions, "You may eat of any of the plants or animals that I have created but never, never, should you eat of the tree of knowledge or the tree of life." God brought Adam and Eve to the trees, showed them which ones they were, and told them again, "Don't ever eat of their fruit, or you will certainly perish."

That day, God and Jesus left the Earth and returned to Heaven. Later, Lucifer took control of a snake that was in the Garden of Eden and went to Eve. Through his cunning ways, he convinced Eve that eating the fruit from the tree of knowledge was a good, just thing that would only make her stronger and please her Creator. So, she ate the tree's fruit. Upon seeing that the fruit was very delicious, she gave it to her husband, Adam, to eat. So, he ate of the tree as well.

Until this point, Adam and Eve did not know the difference between good and evil — only that of goodness because they were created through purity. However, by their disobedient actions of eating of the fruit of knowledge, they had accepted the knowledge of evil into their lives. The seeds of sin had been placed inside their souls, ready to grow.

God and Jesus felt the presence of evil enter into Adam and Eve. They rushed back to the Garden of Eden. Upon arrival, God asked, "What have you done? Why have you eaten of the tree of knowledge that I told you not to eat of?"

"The snake, he came to me and convinced me to eat of it," said Eve.

"Eve, my wife, gave me the fruit and I ate it," said Adam.

"The snake?" asked Jesus.

"Yes, a snake came to me. He was so convincing in his words. I felt I had no other choice," Eve explained.

Jesus and God looked at each other. They knew that it was Lucifer. He had brought sin into the humans to try to bring them to Hell where he could rule over them. God didn't want to risk any more damage from the humans eating of the fruit that grew on the tree of life, so He expelled them from the Garden of Eden and placed one of His Cherubim angels, named Lutan, with a flaming sword at its entrance to block any intruder. God sent out His will in a command that made all angels, even Lucifer, forget where the garden was located.

God and Jesus went back to Heaven and called a meeting in the Holy Palace for all angels to attend. "Now that sin has entered humans we must have a means of salvation," said God. "The blood that flows through their veins and gives them life is the same blood that flows through the blood of many of the animals that we have created. It will be this blood that needs to be shed, in the name of God and the kingdom of Heaven, that will help them be forgiven of their sins. This act of sacrifice will bring them to goodness and forgiveness. It will lead them back to a path that leads to Heaven after their death."

"I will set aside humans and call them prophets to be my voice to the people. The prophets will teach the humans which animals are to be sacrificed and the procedures they will take to keep the act holy. However, this plan of salvation is not my eternal plan. It is only a temporary fix to a long-term problem because it will take one that is both human and spiritual, and completely without sin, to shed his blood for true sanctification. We must have one that is holy and righteous from Heaven to enter the world of mankind. He will be the light and salvation for all of Earth in human form. Unfortunately, the one that accepts such a path will need to take on the sins of the whole world and be beaten and murdered, all in the name of humankind's salvation. It will be the people's faith in this heavenly servant after his death that will be their salvation for all eternity."

"Through the humans' faith in this man of Heaven, they may be saved from their sins and brought into a spirit of humility and love. This salvation will bring them to life with us, here, in Heaven and not into the darkness of Hell with Lucifer. It has always been my plan for the humans to have free will, and this will never change. Ultimately, it's up to them to pursue their faith and salvation. Their eternity is their choice."

God paused and looked into the eyes of His angels. He then spoke these words, "Who could be worthy in the kingdom of Heaven to take on such a task?"

It didn't take long, and Jesus, the only Son of God, stepped forward and knelt before the Creator. "I will do your will, Father," he said.

God felt a great mix of emotions, from extreme pride to sadness, for He knew the pain and heartache His Son would endure. Tears welled in His eyes as He proclaimed, "My Son has spoken. He will be the salvation of the humans."

Everyone came to their feet and cheered. There had never been such a deafening noise of celebration in Heaven. Angels, hugging and kissing him for his selfless decision, swarmed Jesus, and God smiled.

The sixth day had ended. The next day, the seventh day, which was the end of the week of Creation, brought a time for God and Jesus to rest. God saw this day was good and made it holy for all of Heaven and Earth.

During this day of rest, it came to pass that the humans greatly increased in numbers on Earth, and just as God had said, He created prophets to teach the people the ways in which to sacrifice animals for forgiveness of sin. Also during this time, many angels began roaming the Earth as they had a great interest in humankind. Without God's consent, many angels from Heaven and Hell married humans and had children of their own. As their children grew older, it became apparent that they possessed some of their parents' angelic powers, and they were different from other human children.

During this time, angels from Heaven brought many skills and knowledge to the humans. They helped them to build enormous structures and landmarks. The humans learned how to move heavy objects and cut them with precision. They also learned forms of communication — in speaking and writing.

The heavenly angels' descendants were called Veritas, and the fallen angels' descendants were called Tenebras. Each group of descendants was brought to an angelic realm that was between their homeland and Earth to build a secret sanctuary. The Tenebras called their place of gathering Muerte Palace, and the Veritas, with the help of their fathers and mothers, named their castle after Heldago — the angel that had sacrificed his life for Jesus.

The angels from Heaven were moving so much upon the Earth that they created a doorway called the Dalet. This doorway would help them and their spouses move from place to place on Earth with ease.

Some time passed, and God found out about the marriages between the angels and the humans. He also saw that their children possessed angelic powers, and they could easily rule over other humans. This angered God. He ordered the Dalet to be dismantled and forbid angels from marrying the people of Earth any longer.

He placed a powerful invisible wall between Earth and Hell that would no longer let the fallen angels freely roam the Earth. It would keep their bodies from Earth, but because there was the connection between angelic beings and humans, their spirits could not be blocked completely from entering Earth through its humans. Mankind would still have to battle temptations of evil because Lucifer and his followers could enter the bodies of a sinful man or woman.

At this time, ------------ took the Dalet and concealed its four corners in four distant, secret places on the Earth. It was too powerful to destroy, so he dismantled it, as instructed, and hid it as best as possible. ------------ had been married to a human woman named Maddie for over 20 Earth years, and they had a son named Elli. ------------ loved his wife and son very much and was angry and saddened when told to leave them. However, God was first in the life of ------------, so he obeyed His command and left his Earthly home for Heaven. It came to pass that ------------ missed his wife and son terribly, so he created something that could help them come together. It was a medallion, called the Oracle. In the medallion, he constructed hidden powers that would enable his wife and son to disappear. This helped them to see one another until his wife's eventual death.

It came to pass that humans grew more and more evil — full of selfish actions and evil towards one another and their Creator. God decided that He would start anew with mankind and told his human servant, Noah, to build an ark. Noah was told to put his family and land animals of the world on the ark so that they could be saved from Earth's judgment. The angels got messages to their human children and told them to stay in Muerte Palace and Heldago for safety during this time. God was going to make the rain fall like never before, and all of the Earth would become flooded — killing every human that was not on the ark or in the safety of their respective castle within the angelic realm.

After the flood, the humans repopulated as did the angelic descendants. Many civilizations grew throughout the world, but so did mankind's insatiable appetite for sin.

After many years, it was time for Jesus to fulfill his promise. He went to Earth in human form and did what he said he would do at the beginning of mankind. He suffered, was murdered on a wooden cross, and rose again three days later to speak to the people before his ascension to Heaven. He laid the foundation for God's eternal plan of salvation. Whoever wished to choose the path of salvation then had the option before them. Jesus brought to Earth the "Helper", known as the Holy Spirit, who had come forth inside --------- --- in the time of Lucifer's revolt, to all that would believe in the Son of God. The Holy Spirit was to be on Earth to help all Jesus's believers choose the path of righteousness over sin.

So, I, ------------, have recorded this information in this

book for history to know the true story of the creation of mankind. But be of good spirit because in humankind's future, when all that is to take place on Earth is done, its time of heavenly peace is at hand, and God can stand to see sin in His people no more, Jesus will return to bring Heaven to Earth. Jesus, who brought tenderness, kindness, and love in his first coming, will bring the sword of veracity in his second coming. With the sword, he will bring judgment upon the wicked and nonbeliever, and Lucifer, along with his fallen angels, will no longer have an evil influence over humans, for goodness will be the victor over sin.

You will know man's judgment is near when the son of my descendants fulfills his destiny as the chosen one — the Electus. He will help to once again make goodness the crown of mankind and will help cut through the air of human immorality with the sound of courage. The Lord God's peace, love, and power be with you always.

Written on this, the day of Jesus's ascension back into Heaven.

Here, the *Chronicles of Angels* ended, but Jacob's questions had only just begun to form.

Jacob closed the book and carefully returned it to its secret resting place. He had much to think about. His reading of the book had made him very tired, and the night had passed close to morning for him. Jacob decided it was far too late to seek out Jacques or his other friends, and he stayed invisible while going to the Peddle Room and returned to his house.

## CHAPTER 6

# A VISITOR

The next day Jacob met Bina to walk to school.

"Jacob, I have something I need to talk to you about," Bina started.

"I have something, too," said Jacob. "You go first."

"Well, my mother and I were looking at my father's paperwork and saw that Felix Matthews had checked in to see my father the day before we went there."

"Felix went to see your father? How did he have permission to see him, and why would he want to, for that matter?"

"On the records, it stated that my father had requested to see Felix," Bina explained. "Well, it wasn't really my father, but that demon—but you know what I mean. Anyways, when a patient requests to see someone, family or not, as long as it isn't completely out of the ordinary, the request is granted."

"So, how did the demon, Baal, get word to Felix for him to come and visit?" Jacob asked.

"I'm not sure. There aren't any records of a phone call being made out of my father's room. There's only that record of my father asking the nurse to place Felix's name on the visitation sheet."

"Hmm, I think we're going to have to look into this." Jacob looked puzzled.

The growing sound of children's voices told the two

friends they were nearing their school by this time.

"So, what did you want to tell me?" asked Bina.

"Oh, yeah. You got me thinking about your story—I forgot about mine." Jacob laughed. "Last night, at Heldago, I found the book that Michael had told me about. It was written in angelic writing, and it was called THE CHRONICLES OF ANGELS. I'm not exactly sure how I could read it, but I could. The book was written by an angel named Leahcim… well, that *was* his name anyways."

"What do you mean, *was* his name?" Bina asked.

"God changed his name from Leahcim to something different after he pushed Lucifer from Heaven and into Hell. But, what's strange is that someone purposely scratched out this angel's *new* name from the rest of the book. Someone didn't want anyone to know who he was."

"Okay, that IS strange. So what was the story about?"

As Jacob and Bina walked to their lockers, Jacob finished telling the story that he had read the previous night. While walking to their first-period class, Jacob and Bina saw Felix walking nearby with some football players.

"Hey, Felix," Jacob shouted.

Felix turned, obviously irritated that he had been yelled at, and said, "Well, if it isn't my two best buds. I'll catch up with you guys later." Felix motioned to his teammates.

"Why did you go visit Bina's father in the hospital?" asked Jacob, looking annoyed.

"Hey, it's a free country. At least, right now it is." Felix joked.

"Very funny!" Bina snapped. "So, why'd you really?"

"Believe me. I really didn't enjoy being face to face with your father, Bina, but, I had some things to discuss with Baal. Let's just leave it at that. You're supposed to be such a smart girl, you figure it out." Felix walked away.

"Oh, I will," she replied. Bina raised up the book in her hand and was getting ready to launch it at the back of Felix's head when Jacob reached over and caught her arm in mid-throw.

"We'll figure it out, Bina," Jacob reassured. "It's gonna be okay."

For the rest of the school day, Bina had nothing else on her mind. She was bound and determined to find out what Felix was up to. Even the awkward feeling that she and Jacob felt in the lunchroom didn't affect her. Jacob also noticed that she didn't seem as engaged in any of their afternoon classes as she normally would be, not even Latin. When school had finished, Jacob had to run to keep up as Bina raced to Mr. Wolfe's room.

"Ah, and how are my favorite two students doing this afternoon?" Mr. Wolfe asked.

"Concerned," Bina answered quickly.

"Concerned? And what are you concerned about?" Mr. Wolfe looked a bit worried as he questioned Bina. "Your father is recovering from the possession, is he not?"

"Yes, he seems fine, but –"

"I'm sorry, but wait a moment, Bina," Jacob interrupted. He knew Bina was already getting riled up, and he hoped to calm the situation by starting his story. "Mr. Wolfe, yesterday, I found an old book that was written in angelic writing."

Bina walked frustratedly away toward the back of the classroom, but she started pacing impatiently back and forth behind the first row of desks with her arms crossed on her chest and her right hand holding her chin as she thought. She was upset with Jacob cutting her off so rudely, but she continued to consider why Baal would have Felix visit him. Because she was upset and because she was so focused on figuring out why Felix visited Baal after he had possessed her father, she only half paid attention to Jacob's discussion with Mr. Wolfe.

"Angelic writing? And you could read it?" Mr. Wolfe was intrigued.

"Yes, sir," Jacob continued. "The book told the history of

how Lucifer was pushed out of Heaven when he tried to overthrow God's kingdom, and it also went into detail about the creation of mankind. An angel, who used to be named Leahcim, wrote the book, but God changed the angel's name after he defeated Lucifer. What is really strange though is that someone deliberately scratched Leahcim's new name out of the entire book."

"Someone was or is trying to hide this angel's name then?" Mr. Wolfe leaned upon his cane.

"Yes sir, but that's not what troubled me the most. In this angel's recollection, he stated that before God created man he created the tree of knowledge and the tree of life in the Garden of Eden because they were needed for the creation of humans. However, by creating these two trees, God had created a connection between Earth and Heaven. This angel, formally known as Leahcim, made a special point about how these two trees could be used to allow someone into Heaven, kind of like a gateway."

A look of concern grew upon Mr. Wolfe's face. "I see…and you are worried that Lucifer might try to find the hidden Garden of Eden and use the trees to bring himself and his followers back to Heaven?"

"Yeah, Mr. Wolfe. I believe his first option was to gain control of the Dalet doorway so that he could get back into Heaven, but when that failed, his second plan is now to find the Garden. What I don't understand is why he would wait until now? Why didn't he try doing this a long time ago?"

"That's it!" Bina shouted.

Jacob and Mr. Wolfe were both startled.

"That's why Felix visited my father! Lucifer and the Tenebras must have some kind of plan to find the Garden of Eden because the demon, Baal, had asked to see Felix. I bet Baal was relaying a message about their plan to Felix, and that is why Baal came to our small town."

"Indeed." Mr. Wolfe stroked his long gray goatee once again. "I think you're both correct. Moreover, Jacob, I believe the answer to your question about why Lucifer has waited until now to find the garden is because he has been waiting patiently through the years — to get stronger. As evil thoughts and actions have spread throughout the world over the centuries, and with every soul that he conquers and pulls to Hell, he has grown stronger. Maybe, now, he has reached a confidence in his strength and numbers that he believes if given another chance in Heaven, he will be able to overthrow God's kingdom." The look of concern grew upon Mr. Wolfe's face and his brow furrowed in thought.

"If he gained control of Heaven, Lucifer would also have complete control over Earth. There would be more pain and suffering than could be imagined," Bina's voice trembled as she recalled the horror of her father being possessed by Baal, imagining the world ruled by such hateful demons.

"So what now?" Jacob asked. "Where do we begin?"

"It looks like the race to find the Garden of Eden has begun," said Mr. Wolfe energetically. "We must find it before evil does. All of time and space depends on us. I will go to Heldago right now, call a meeting of our brothers and sisters, and tell them of this news. You two must go to the Dalet. You must figure out how it works so that it may help you find the Garden. Go now! There is no time to waste!"

Jacob and Bina first went to the bushes that were not far from the playground so that they could be sure that no one was following them. Then, once they had reassured themselves that neither Felix nor anyone else was tailing them, Jacob activated his Oracle medallion, grabbed Bina's hand, and they rushed to the secret Hokmah, where they had carefully hidden the Dalet only weeks before after their return from Rome. Mr. Wolfe raced home, locked all of his doors, laid down on his sofa, and left for Heldago.

Upon arriving at the hillside by old man Johnson's farm, Jacob placed his hands on Abel's Stones and opened the door into the secret chamber. Jacob and Bina ran inside and quickly closed the secret door.

Jacob ran over to an old clay jar filled with dirt that was on a nearby shelf and reached into it to retrieve the first hidden Dalet corner. In excitement, he ran over to the Hokmah chest and removed one of its side handles, exposing the second corner. To reach the third Dalet corner, he boosted Bina up on his shoulders to reach its hiding place. It was up high, in one of the earthen walls behind a stone about eight feet up from the floor. Bina grabbed the third corner. Jacob paused for a moment after helping Bina to the floor. "Now, where did I put the fourth corner?" Jacob mumbled to himself. "Oh yeah," he said out loud as he hurried toward a gnarled tree root in the corner of the room.

"Did you say something?" Bina asked as she walked to the table in the middle of the room.

"Yes, but I was just reminding myself where we hid the fourth corner," Jacob replied before grunting as he lifted the tree root growing through the corner of the earthen room. "I've got it," he grunted again as he held the root up and reached into a small cavity just under the part of the root that bent toward the floor.

Jacob rubbed the dirt off the last corner of the Dalet and laid the three corners he held on the table, and Bina set down the one she held as well.

"Great, now what?" Jacob joked while trying to catch his breath. "I don't think that this thing came with an instruction manual."

Bina bent over and looked at the corners more closely. "Jacob, I don't think these markings were here a moment ago. I think they showed up when I placed the fourth corner next to the three you gathered."

"Let me see." Jacob bent over to get a closer look. "It's angelic writing. Huh, that's a change. I am able to read a language that you can't." Jacob chuckled.

Bina rolled her eyes. "Funny. So what's it say?"

"It says girls should always listen to guys because guys are the best." Jacob smiled and nudged Bina's arm.

"OK. Funny. So what's it really say?"

"OK. OK. Let me see here." Jacob struggled to make out the small writing. "It's instructions. It says to place the corners around the wrist and extend your hand out to open the gate. Then, it says to say a known destination to open the pathway."

"So, it's a wristband?" Bina asked. "I was thinking we'd have to set it up like the four corners of a doorway on a wall and then enter it."

"Hmm." Jacob rested his left arm on the table and with Bina's assistance linked the four corners together around his wrist. Each connection point, where the corner touched the next, glowed bright yellow. The corners were letting out a lot of heat as they joined each other. Jacob closed his eyes and bit his lip because it felt as if the Dalet burned his skin. Suddenly, just like that, the heat was gone. Jacob opened his eyes, hoping that his hand was still intact, and saw that the corners had melted together, forming a continuous bracelet around Jacob's wrist.

"There, now that wasn't so hard now was it?" Bina smirked.

"Oh yeah, piece of cake." Jacob turned his hand in different angles looking at the bracelet. "So, I don't see any way to take this thing off."

Bina giggled. "Maybe you can't."

"Oh, great! Now, what have I gotten myself into?" Jacob moaned, genuinely concerned. "How am I supposed to shower with this thing on?"

"Okay, Jacob, that's not important right now. Let's see how this thing works," Bina instructed. "Maybe you can place your hand out, open a gateway to the Garden of Eden, and BANG, there you have it. We won."

"I don't think that it's quite that easy, Bina," Jacob said. "The angelic writing said the place of destination needed to be known, and by the sound of things, we and everyone else on this planet have no clue to the whereabouts of the Garden of Eden."

"So, start with an easy place. Try your house."

Jacob nodded. His hand was visibly shaking as he raised it and thrust it out in front of his body. "My house," he said, nervously, because he wasn't sure what to expect.

Nothing happened.

Bina looked at Jacob and said, "Well, it was made by angels. Maybe you need to speak the angelic language. You can read it, but can you speak it?"

"I don't know. I haven't tried." Jacob closed his eyes for a moment, gained focus, and said, "Numorea", which he sounded out slowly as *NEW-MORE-EE-AH*, which he also somehow felt or knew meant one's house in angelic.

A bright oval shaped light appeared just in front of Jacob's extended arm. The oval glowed with an orange light and was at first no larger than Jacob's fist, but it grew quickly to be about Jacob's and Bina's height. Jacob opened his eyes, but he couldn't make out what was beyond the light due to its intensity. Jacob looked at Bina, and she smiled and shrugged. Jacob grabbed Bina's hand and jumped into the opening, pulling her with him. Both of them had closed their eyes for fear of the unknown, but when their feet touched the ground as if they had only leaped a few feet across the Hokmah, they felt relief. They opened their eyes, and Jacob's house was standing before them.

Jacob looked behind them at the still open gateway and said, "Efor", which meant close. The lighted oval doorway disappeared. Somewhat in shock at what had just transpired, Jacob and Bina walked around the house looking at the yard, just making sure they were not dreaming.

"Oh, hey you two," a woman's voice said from the garden in the backyard. It was Jacob's mom, Sarah. She was somewhat hidden because she was crouched down pulling up weeds. "What are you guys doing?"

"Oh, uh, hi ma...mom," Jacob stuttered. "Not...nothing much. Just exploring."

"You two and your explorations," said Sarah. "I'm sure your dad is looking down on you and is so proud." Sarah smiled proudly at Jacob.

Jacob was still somewhat in shock and didn't have much of anything to say. "Well, okay then. I'll be home soon for dinner." Jacob tugged on Bina's arm to walk away.

"Sounds good. Love you," Sarah responded.

"Love you too, mom." Jacob started with Bina toward her house.

"So, we have a tool to travel with," said Bina. "Where do we begin?"

"I'm not sure yet. We need some guidance," Jacob said as he paused outside Bina's front door. "God will show the way, right?"

"Right," said Bina. "I'll see you tomorrow at school."

Just then, Jacob heard a call in his mind to go to Heldago as soon as possible that night. It was the Veritas' leader, Rabbi Lazarus, instructing all Veritas to attend an important meeting that night. Jacob knew what the meeting would be about.

"I'll see you tomorrow, Bina," said Jacob, waving and then quickly turning to return to his house to get some supper before he would travel to Heldago.

After eating dinner, Jacob told his mom he needed to go to his room to finish homework. Once there, he lay on his bed, closed his eyes, and traveled to Heldago to attend the assembly. Rabbi Lazarus told the Veritas of the need to find the Garden of Eden before the Tenebras and the reasons why. "If anyone has any information or clues to help us get started, please, see me straight away," he requested. "I'm sure Lucifer will have his followers searching the world for clues as well. They have a head start on us. We must act swiftly. Look for God's guidance and may His presence lead you all."

As he left the meeting, Jacob began searching the immense crowd of Veritas for a sign of his classmates or his friend Jacques, but his search was stopped by a familiar voice. "Hey Jacob, how've ya been?" said Shawn.

Jacob turned quickly. "It's really good to see you, Shawn." They hugged.

"Another adventure, eh?" asked Shawn, smiling. "Mystery and suspense be followin' ya more than not."

Jacob laughed. "I guess you're right, Shawn. Only, on this adventure I've no clue where to start."

"Hmm. Well, the Garden of Eden be one of the biggest hidden secrets of the world, hidden from even the angels' memories it was, but ya find that first clue, and the rest be fallin' into place. It'll come to ya. I'll be seein' ya soon. Take care of yerself."

"You too." With another hug, the two friends went their separate ways.

Jacob went to classes with Don, Sarge, and Master Kang that night and was reminded by all three that it was time to proceed to his Clevan testing—to see if he qualified to move from the Bethal class to the Clevan. "With these new turns of events I've not thought about my testing," he said. "But, I understand it's important, so let's do the testing tomorrow." With the plan of action in place with his teachers, Jacob sought out his friend Jacques. Jacob had not seen Jacques at any of his classes, which worried Jacob. He hoped that his friend's lost hand would not keep him from continuing his training as a Verita.

"Hola, Jacob!" Jezebel's voice rang out as Jacob was trying to figure out where to seek out his friend Jacques.

"Hello, Jezebel," Jacob said distractedly.

"What is wrong?" Jezebel's broad grin changed quickly to a look of concern.

"Oh, nothing, really. I was just thinking about trying to track down Jack to see how he is doing, but I didn't see him in classes tonight," Jacob replied with more warmth as they started walking together. "Did you ever see him or get a message to him the other night?"

"Yes, I did," Jezebel said as she intertwined her arm with Jacob's. "I had to send the message through Triple E, though. Jacques hasn't returned to Heldago yet – not since that night in Rome. He's been healing at home, but Sarge told me at Clevan sword training tonight that he had visited Jacques and he should be returning soon to continue his training."

"That's good to hear. I was just starting to worry that the loss of his hand might prevent him from continuing with his training here," Jacob said relieved.

"You're such a good friend," Jezebel replied. She began to pat Jacob's arm reassuringly as her right hand grasped his left, and they walked arm in arm toward the peddle room. "Say, what's this?" Jezebel pulled back the sleeve of Jacob's robe, exposing the Dalet wristband that encircled is left forearm.

"Oh! That?" Jacob hesitated in his surprise. "It's…it was a gift from my friend Bina. It's a wristband…it sort of celebrates our trip to Rome…and…and the start of our freshman year of high school." Jacob's face turned red at the white lie he felt he had to tell to keep the Dalet a secret in order to keep it safe.

Jezebel looked at the Dalet for a moment and then said, "Interesting look it has, no?" Her tone seemed a bit sarcastic to Jacob as she released his hand, waved, and headed toward the chamber that would return her to her home. "Adios, Jacob. I will see you here again soon I hope."

"So long Jezebel!" Jacob shouted, though he doubted Jezebel was still in the peddle room. He got to his chamber, meditated for a moment or two, and returned home.

The next morning, Jacob was eating breakfast and thinking about how glad he was that Jacques would be returning to Heldago soon when his attention turned unexpectedly to the national news that was on the TV. He wasn't normally one to watch the news, but the important bulletin that was flashing on the screen grabbed his attention.

"Thank you for joining us," the reporter started. "In the past several weeks there has been a sharp increase in crime throughout America, and experts can't explain why."

The screen went to a criminal psychologist to give his opinions on the topic. "Since we've begun collecting data over one hundred years ago, we have never seen such a rise in criminal behavior as we have witnessed these past few weeks. With the increase in population, we've naturally seen an increase in violent crimes in the past two decades, but never have we seen such a dramatic increase in such a short amount of time. Some cities have seen rapes, murders, and theft increase by as much as tenfold in this short period." The camera view returned to the news anchor and a new image flashed on to the screen behind him showing a globe of the world with areas marked in red that expanded as the anchor continued the report.

"This is unheard of in *any* population. However, what's even more suspicious is the fact that this increase in crime hasn't just been seen in America, but it has been seen throughout the world."

The television screen began showing pictures and short videos of the crime aftermath in different areas of the world. Then the view returned to the reporter.

"In some cities throughout the world, war has begun to break out with Muslims attacking, and sometimes killing, Christians—blaming them for what they call 'God's condemnation on the unbeliever.' In many densely populated Islamic areas of the world, many are calling for a Jihad against all Christians. Meanwhile, in many larger cities across the world, an immediate growth in the hiring of police to help battle the increase in crime has begun."

A look of concern grew over Jacob's face as the new report changed to a quick check of the international weather. *This increase in crime must be related to Lucifer sending more of his angels to Earth to possess humans,* he thought. *People that aren't living in the plan of Christ are so easily susceptible to demonic possession. We have so many people in our world like this right now. This could get real bad.*

"Wow! What's going on with people nowadays?" exclaimed Sarah, startling Jacob out of his internal reverie. She had been watching the news as well. "You be extra careful walking to and from school, Jacob. This rise in crime might even spread to our small town."

"Yes, mom. I will," Jacob comforted.

# CHAPTER 7

# CHRISTIANITY RETURNS TO HELDAGO

That morning in school, Jacob and his classmates were surprised when their science teacher, Mr. Matthews, was not present because he never missed the chance to be in school and have control over his students. He would rather revel in his complete dictatorship than let someone else do the job for him.

"Now class, my name is Mr. Jones, and I will be your substitute science teacher for a little while because Mr. Matthews has gone on an emergency trip," said the teacher.

Jacob and Bina immediately looked back to Felix's seat. He was gone too. They both looked at each other and knew they were thinking the same thing, *the Matthews family was searching for clues for the Garden of Eden.*

At lunch, Jacob and Bina discussed many of the scrolls and secrets of the Hokmah, hoping that something might come to mind that would help them get started in their search, but nothing stood out as obviously related to the Garden of Eden.

"There have to be clues," said Bina. "Whenever something is created, there is always a trail that is left behind. We just have to find that trail. Tonight, I will go to the library and start looking for signs and evidence."

Jacob thanked Bina and told her of his upcoming test at

Heldago for the Clevan class. Being a caring person, Bina was worried for Jacob but tried not to show it, so she wished him luck in his test.

That night, Jacob and his mom went out to dinner. Afterward, Sarah wanted to share some old memories she had of fishing with her father, so she took Jacob fishing on the Sheyenne River. The night was filled with starving mosquitoes and humidity that could be cut with a knife, but being with one another seemed to drown out any inconvenience. Since the death of Jacob's father, Sarah and Jacob tried to make it a point to show their love for one another, and this was just one of those times.

The disturbing international news they had seen that morning about an increase in violent crime weighed heavily on both of their minds that day because they were concerned for each other's safety, but because Jacob knew the meaning behind the increase in evil, he had a little more on his mind and shoulders.

After their mother-son quality time, as Jacob retired for the night, he approached the gate of Heldago and was about to ask the two guards for entrance when he was surprised when one of the lion-headed gatekeepers asked him a question. This was odd because both Laborc and Raman rarely said a word, and, if they did, it was usually condescending.

"Are you ready for your test today, Jacob Jerlow?" asked Laborc.

"Ahh, yes sir. I believe so," Jacob answered sheepishly.

"A little more confidence," said Raman.

"Yes, sir. I am ready," Jacob restated with more confidence.

"That's better," Laborc said. "By not breaking the Bethal record and putting another above yourself, you have shown great humility. I once thought you wore a mask of fear to cover a prideful spirit, but now I think otherwise."

"You may enter," said Laborc and Raman in unison.

The gate opened to Heldago, and Jacob took a step back because of what he saw. All Veritas were present and were gathered in the courtyard's inner meadow. Upon seeing Jacob, they all cheered loudly. It was a celebration that had brought all of the creatures of Heldago and the Veritas, young and old, to witness Jacob's first test. Word had spread quickly of how Jacob had not wanted to break the Bethal class record that his friend Ramiro Vasquez owned. A Tenebra had killed Ramiro while he tried to save Jacob's life in Rome, and Jacob wanted Ramiro's memory to live on through his record. This spirit of honor and humbleness needed to be celebrated.

Jacob entered the castle and approached the noisy crowd. Many of the people ran to Jacob to pat him on the shoulder saying, "Good luck! We know you can do it!"

Jacob was startled when the wilderness gnome, Yelkie, popped out of the air directly in front of him. "Miss this I could not," said Yelkie. "Pass the test I know you will."

"Hey, show-off," said a voice from behind. Jacob turned around and saw that it was Luke Cartwright, who had yelled with his usual sneer. With him were some of Jacob's other friends, Fred Albas, Jack Leroux, Miguel Cruz, and Jezebel Flores. They all shouted encouragement. Jacob was especially glad to see Jack was there and looking healthy. Jack's and Jacob's eyes locked for a moment, and Jack winked, smiled, and raised his left hand – his only hand after losing his right hand to the Tenebra Rico in Rome – to give Jacob an enthusiastic thumb's up.

Jezebel had recently passed her test to move to the level of Clevan, so hearing her say, "I know you can do it," from the crowd of his friends was a great inspiration to Jacob.

Jacob smiled and tried not to show his growing nerves. The roaring crowd was quickly calmed by Rabbi Lazarus when he said, "Jacob Jerlow, come and enter your first test — the sword."

Jacob was dressed in his long dark brown robe, and his

sword's hilt was tucked in his belt. He heard an Elder
whisper to another upon seeing his sword, "He is but a
Bethal and was already able to call upon his sword."

Rabbi Lazarus called for silence and a prayer. "Almighty
ever-living God, grant that we may always conform our will
to yours and serve your majesty in sincerity of heart. We
pray this through your son, Jesus Christ, our Lord. Amen."
Everyone present echoed the Amen.

The crowd patiently anticipated the first trial. Jacob
grasped the grip of his sword's hilt from his belt and made
the blade appear. Its polished steel shined brightly in the
sun's light. His sword instructor, Sarge, had laid out a series
of tests in the castle's meadow to assess Jacob's accuracy and
skill. After receiving instructions, Jacob cut through the
course with extreme precision and strength. On his last
maneuver, he closed his eyes, to play to the crowd a little,
and successfully beheaded the wooden dummy that hurled
toward him. He had finished the sword trial with no
mistakes, and the crowd's level of cheering matched his
performance. Sarge deliberated for only a moment with Don
and Master Kang and then silenced the crowd saying, "Jacob
Jerlow, you have passed the Bethal Sword test." The crowd
celebrated again.

Next, Master Kang directed Jacob and the mass of
onlookers to the other end of the courtyard's meadow for the
Martial Arts and Body Control test. The test entailed a
balancing exhibition. Jacob would have to balance himself
and cross a fifty-foot long, three-inch wide wooden plank
that Kang had suspended five feet off the ground. While he
proceeded across the beam, Jacob would have to block,
punch, and kick his way through large, heavy balls that
resembled overgrown coconuts, which were suspended
from above by long ropes. Master Kang had selected some
Elders as volunteers to systematically drop the balls toward
Jacob in the challenge. The Elders were standing above in
hidden locations that were covered by straw and leaves so

that Jacob would not know when they would drop the heavy objects.

Jacob took a deep breath and calmed himself for the test.

Because the stranger, Michael, had been around numerous times in the past, Jacob could feel Michael when he was near. Michael had some form of connection with Jacob that Jacob didn't understand. Jacob looked to his right through the crowd and saw Michael watching him. Michael smiled at Jacob's recognition. Jacob smiled in response and then refocused his mind on the task at hand.

After a brief meditation and prayer, Jacob started the test. He quickly went across the balancing beam as the first ball dropped from its rope toward his head. Jacob ducked the ball, while keeping his balance, and moved forward. Two more balls came at him at the same moment from opposite directions. As the balls swung toward Jacob, all of the spectators held their breath in concert. No one cheered so that it would not distract Jacob. Jacob quickly spun and kicked at the balls, making them collide and break into pieces. A unified gasp of relief hissed from the crowd amid the loud crash of the two obstacles, and silence prevailed as Jacob continued along the suspended, narrow beam.

Jacob took another deep breath, shook off the narrow escape, and advanced. He could see the end of the balancing beam not far ahead, but it was no time to get excited. The hidden Elders dropped four balls from above, and Jacob could only see the ones coming from the front, right, and left. He had no idea that one was also swinging behind him at the same instant. Jacob jumped and kicked the front ball, breaking it in half. While still in the air, he punched outwardly with his left and right arms, breaking the balls falling from either side as well. Jacob landed back on the beam and shook slightly to the left and right, almost losing his balance. Again, the entire gathering of onlookers held their collective breath as the fourth ball neared Jacob's head.

With no time to react, he felt the presence of the fourth

ball nearing the back of his head. Because the Elder had thrown the ball and not just let it drop, it was moving faster than the other three. Just as the ball was about to strike his head, Jacob jumped backward, kicking up his right leg in an amazing flip and reverse kick. He struck the ball with such force that it broke free from its rope and flew 20 feet rearward into the crowd — into Luke Cartwright's stomach. Luke caught the ball but fell to his knees in pain. While trying to catch his breath, Luke glared at Jacob and mumbled, "Show-off."

The courtyard erupted in cheers of excitement and relief. Jacob landed on his feet and ran carefully across to the finish. Master Kang deliberated with Sarge and Don for a moment and announced, "Jacob Jerlow, you have successfully passed my test of body control and martial arts."

Don made eye contact with Jacob and gave a somewhat crooked smirk. Jacob knew that Elder Don's smirk meant that the Powers test would be the most difficult for him to pass, and he would have to control any fear or anger that still resided within him in order to use his powers effectively.

Don led the still excited crowd of spectators and Jacob to a large room in the basement area of the castle. The room was rarely used, usually only needed when the weather was uncooperative. Torches hanging sporadically along the wall lit the vast subterranean chamber, but it was by no means bright. In fact, it was quite difficult to see. The large collection of observers stood or knelt wherever they could find room to view the test.

The room was filled with random garbage strewn across the floor. The pieces of trash were of many different sizes and weights — from paper to heavy, old, rusty pieces of metal. The short, obese teacher walked into the center of the room to explain the test.

"Jacob Jerlow, for your Powers test, you will need to

remove all of the clutter from this room using the Valoria power," Don said as he gestured with his arms extended and spinning to indicate all of the garbage throughout the room. "Once you have picked up an object with your powers, it may not touch the floor again." Don smiled a devilish grin as he finished his explanation.

Don then waved his short, pudgy arm towards the center of the room and a large fire erupted from the floor. "I wish for you to throw all of these pieces of trash into the fire to be burned," Don instructed. "You may begin."

Jacob's concentration was grabbed by a man kneeling in prayer in the corner of the room. It was Michael. Moved by this action, Jacob knelt in prayer as well. Seeing Jacob being reverent brought many of the standing crowd to their knees, too. Jacob prayed, "All knowing Father in Heaven, bring Your grace and mercy upon me, Your servant, through Jesus Christ I pray, Amen."

Jacob rose to his feet. He had to fight back a tear when he saw that many of the Veritas remained kneeling in prayer. The Holy Spirit was moving through Heldago once again, and the Veritas' faith was renewed. Jacob turned his head to take in everything that was around the room. The light given off from the fire blazing in the center of the room was intense, almost as much as the heat it delivered, but oddly, the magical fire didn't produce any smoke. *I'm just supposed to move these objects into the fire?* Jacob thought. *I've got a feeling that there's going to be more to it than that*, he concluded. Jacob concentrated on the paper that was gathered in the corner to his left and said, "Valoria." The paper began floating to the fire. A large flame suddenly burst forth from the fire, one of the test's attempts to distract Jacob, nearly striking him in the face. Many of the onlookers were thrown back by the heat of the burst of flames, but Jacob was steady as a rock and sent the paper into the fire.

Jacob continued to move the trash into the fire, piece by piece, and with every diversion the flames threw at him, he grew more confident that he could succeed. Finally, there was one piece of trash left to throw into the fire. It was an old, metal cabinet. It was the heaviest piece, and would be the most challenging. Jacob would have to maintain complete concentration in his levitating power, or it would certainly fall to the floor.

Jacob focused on the cabinet and said, "Valoria." The cabinet lifted slowly from the floor and moved toward the fire. It was massive, and Jacob was using all of his mental strength and concentration to raise, suspend, and move it.

Jacob's friend, Jezebel, broke away from her view of Jacob for a moment and looked at Don. The teacher had somewhat of a sinister look on his face. *What do you have up your sleeve,* she thought. *Is your test not difficult enough already?*

Don raised his hand slightly from his leg, trying not to give notice of his plan, and casted a power towards the flames. From within the raging fire, the figure of a man grew. Sparks flew from the flames, and the fiery human figure approached Jacob. "Hey Jacob," said the familiar voice. "Did you miss me? I killed your father, and now I'm back to finish off his son." It was the voice and form of Vladimir, the Tenebra that had murdered Jacob's father.

Jacob struggled to maintain his concentration. "You're not real," he shouted. "Shawn killed you. You're dead!"

Many of the Elders in the room were thinking the same thing. "This test is far beyond the level of a Bethal. What has come over Don for him to test Jacob like this?"

"Oh, I'm real," hissed Vladimir with the menacing hiss and sparks of flame. "I'm standing right in front of you. Come on, now's your chance for revenge."

Jacob concentrated on the heavy cabinet as hard as he could. It was almost to the fire.

Vladimir stepped closer to Jacob, so others could not hear what he said. He whispered, "Your father was nothing. He was so easy to kill. And now, I'm going to kill your mother next."

Jacob tried to hold back the anger, but he couldn't. A great light burst forth from inside of him, outshining the blazing fire in the center of the room and temporarily blinding many who looked on in anticipation. All of his energy went into the cabinet. The piece of furniture was hurled into the fire with such force that the flames were thrown towards Don. Don was so surprised by the action he froze. He was about to be burned to a crisp when Rabbi Lazarus stepped in front of him and put out his hands to shield him. The flames parted to the right and left of Lazarus and Don with no one being hurt.

The subterranean chamber echoed with the sound of the cabinet being consumed by the flames, and, then, as the flames died down with the echoes, the silence became nearly unbearable. Jacob could only hear his heart throbbing in his ears as his anger subsided with the flames and echoes of the cabinet's destruction. The silence reached the point of awkwardness when Jezebel's voice suddenly rang out from the crowd, "Bueno Jacob!"

Suddenly the entire crowd cheered Jacob's name and everyone in the room rushed Jacob to congratulate him. There was a huge celebration. Don sat back in his chair, swallowed some of the black soot that covered his face and mouth, and sighed in relief. The crowd made Jacob quickly forget about the anger that he just felt. After regaining his composure, Don convened with Sarge and Master Kang. "Jacob Jerlow, congratulations, you have passed my test and the level of Bethal," he mumbled.

The Veritas and other creatures of Heldago roared loudly in cheers once more. Shawn grabbed another Elder, and they lifted Jacob upon their shoulders. The crowd moved together with Jacob at its lead back up to the meadow area of Heldago's courtyard and Maribel the Pixie stopped and greeted them. "My friends and I have made a grand dinner for your celebration," she shouted. "Go to the eating hall."

So, the Veritas took their celebration to the eating hall. While dining, whoever wasn't congratulating Jacob was quietly talking about the tough trial that was given by Don. Ever since their Rabbi had stated there was a traitor among the Veritas, small things, such as the overly difficult test, would raise the question, "Is he the traitor?" With this, rumors began to spread rapidly that Don was working for the Tenebras because he was so harsh on Jacob during the Powers test.

Toward the end of the meal, Jacob noticed Michael standing in the corner of the room. Jacob begged the pardon of those who were still congratulating him, walked over to where Michael stood, and asked, "Am I the only one that can see you?"

"For now, yes," said Michael. "In time, this will change. I guess congratulations are in order. Your actions and success are to be commended."

"Thank you," said Jacob. "But I guess I did let my anger get the best of me in the end. I need to release all of that evil."

Michael looked Jacob steadfastly in the eyes. "Jacob, hear me on this when I say that not all anger is evil. Anger can be used for good purposes when controlled with love as its captain. Far too many Christians in the world have become too passive either because they fear that God will punish them or that they will bring a bad name to Christianity if they get angry. This is simply not the case. God will be more disappointed when a Christian stands idly by while evil becomes too commonplace." Michael paused and searched Jacob's eyes as if he could read whether Jacob understood.

"The nonbeliever is winning the war in the world, and Christians are helping their cause by not being passionate for God's righteousness. Complacency can be very dangerous. Even the Son of God, Jesus, showed anger many times, but he did so in the name of goodness and justice and never in a manner to degrade or depreciate the sanctity of life. So, yes, please, get angry sometimes," Michael said as he grasped Jacob's shoulders. "But remember to do it with the sword of love and for God's glory—never your own."

"I understand," said Jacob.

Rabbi Lazarus was drawn away from his conversation with Sarge regarding Jacob's amazing test when he noticed Jacob standing alone near the corner of the room. He saw that Jacob appeared to be talking to someone, but Lazarus didn't see anyone else present, so he became very concerned.

"I found the book that you told me about," Jacob continued. "It was in angelic writing, but I was able to read it."

"I knew you would find it. You're a smart young man," Michael said as he released Jacob's shoulders and stood erect, smiling. "As for the angelic writing, it's in your spirit to know this writing because that's in your history. So, did you learn something?"

"Yes sir," said Jacob. "I learned that an angel named Leahcim had his name changed, and whatever name he was given was scratched out of the book."

"Hmm. His name was taken out of the book, you say?" Michael's right eyebrow arched in curiosity. "Is that all you got out of the book?"

"Not quite," Jacob replied. "I learned that Lucifer could have a pathway to Heaven if he's able to find the Garden of Eden."

"The Spirit of God has revealed this to you. And now, you and your people will need to find the Garden of Eden before Lucifer and his evil followers?" asked Michael.

"Yes sir, but we haven't a clue where to start. People have been looking for the Garden of Eden since mankind was cast out of the garden." Jacob could hardly contain his frustration.

"I'm sure something will surface," said Michael. "Keep

your faith. I must go for now. Again, congratulations on your victory today."

Just as he was saying goodbye, Jacob was startled from behind by Rabbi Lazarus. "Hello, Jacob, were you speaking to someone?"

"Oh! Hi, Rabbi," Jacob said as he spun around to face Lazarus. "Yes, I was speaking to Michael." Jacob gestured back toward where Michael had just been standing.

"Michael? Really?" Lazarus looked quickly around the area. "He was here again? I couldn't see anyone."

"Yeah, that's what he said," Jacob glanced around as he explained. "He said I was the only one that could see him."

"And everything is okay, Jacob?" Lazarus's concern was obvious in his facial expression.

"Yes, sir."

After Jacob and Rabbi discussed some plans for finding clues about the Garden of Eden, the celebration came to a close with many of the Veritas, including Jacob, returning home.

# CHAPTER 8

# THE WILDERNESS

The next day, Bina was relieved to see Jacob had gotten
through his Bethal test and had returned safely and
uninjured. Jacob and Bina sat at lunch together as usual, but
it was especially important so that they could discuss
anything new that Bina had learned during her research the
night before. Bina was also anxious to hear all about Jacob's
Bethal test, so they sat where they could talk without being
overheard.

"I found many theories about where the Garden of Eden
might be located," Bina began. "But I'll start with the facts.
In the book of Genesis, Moses described the Garden as being
located in a place where four rivers meet." Bina pulled out
the Bible and read from Genesis 2:10-14, "'A river watering
the garden flowed from Eden; from there it was separated
into four headwaters. The name of the first is the Pishon; it
winds through the entire land of Havilah, where there is
gold. (The gold of that land is good; aromatic resin and onyx
are also there.) The name of the second river is the Gihon; it
winds through the entire land of Cush. The name of the
third river is the Tigris; it runs along the east side of Ashur.
And the fourth river is the Euphrates.'" Bina paused to check
Jacob's attention and understanding.

Bina closed the Bible and continued, "The Euphrates and
Tigris rivers still exist today, but the Pishon and Gihon rivers
are just dry river beds. What's more troubling is that many

scholars believe that this area of the world could have been changed so drastically by the great flood that these rivers wouldn't have their same shape or direction. Many Garden seekers have searched this area of the world countless times, but never turned up any clues to its existence." Bina stopped seemingly frustrated.

"My dad once said that all treasures leave a trail, either by man or by nature," said Jacob reassuringly. "Someone or something has left a trail for us to follow. It's just a matter of picking up the scent."

"Have you found anything?" asked Bina.

"Nothing yet, but I have great news. I passed my Bethal tests last night." Jacob said with a grin.

"That's so cool. Congratulations!" Bina hugged Jacob, bringing attention and subsequent gossip from some of the other students in the noisy lunchroom. On the first day of classes, rumors had started at the high school that Jacob and Bina were *an item*, and this hug just reinforced the idea. The two friends were oblivious to the rumors, and their focus on finding the Garden of Eden only made the attention and whispers of other students even less important. They finished their lunch and decided to continue with their research into the garden's whereabouts using whatever resources they could find.

The following weeks seemed to fly in what seemed like just hours to Jacob and Bina. They both searched through the Hokmah and experts' research into the areas of Biblical artifacts. Jacob found himself many nights in Heldago's library, searching through very old, dusty books, but everything came back to the same conclusion — God had hidden the Garden of Eden, and there seemed to be no chance that anybody would ever find it.

During these weeks, training also continued for Jacob at Heldago. Jacob and Jezebel were the first in their Bethal class to move to Clevan, but their success was a great inspiration to their other classmates. This motivation pushed Jack, Fred, and Luke to test for the level of Clevan not long after Jacob passed the test. Jacob originally had concerns about Jack's ability to pass the sword test, but discovered that Jack was almost as skilled with his left hand as he had been with his right, and Sarge had designed a special prosthesis for Jack to wear over the stump of his right arm. The prosthesis was a simple protective dome of some silvery metal that had a ten or twelve-inch long sharpened dirk protruding from its center. Sarge had also taken Jack under his wing and spent extra time working with Jack to improve his left handed use of the sword while using the dirk as a means of defending against unexpected strikes that made it through his weak left handed defense. Jack quickly learned to use both his sword and his new prosthesis in concert to parry blows and deliver his own unexpected counters using the dirk. Fred and Jack passed the test on their first attempt, but, being a little slower learner, Luke took the test three times before finally passing. Some of the Elders jokingly commented that Sarge, Don, and Master Kang felt bad for Luke and helped him along to the next level with an easier test.

The class of the Clevan level for the western hemisphere was almost empty. Other than Jacob and his recently graduated friends, there was only one student, and her name was Emily Helmsworth. Emily was from Jamaica. She had dark skin, caring eyes, and long black hair that was always in dreadlocks. Most students liked Emily because of her contagious sense of humor.

Also during this time, under Rabbi's direction, the religion classes were reestablished at Heldago and were to be taught by the castle's priest, Father Santiago. Jacob enjoyed the religion classes because spending time learning of God had grown nearest to his heart. In addition, with the achievement of reaching the level of Clevan, Jacob and his friends had two new classes with two new teachers. The first new class was fine arts, taught by Shir, who Jacob had met the summer before. The second new class was history of the

Veritas, taught by a teacher that Jacob only knew in passing. Her name was Olga Hanson, and her strong Norwegian accent told everyone she spoke with that she was from Norway. She wore reading glasses perched on her long slender nose, and she wore her hair in a tightly wound bun atop her head.

When Rabbi Lazarus introduced Jacob to Olga, he told Jacob, "Olga is the only one in the world that I know of that knows more about history than I do, and that is saying quite a lot, considering she is half my age."

The new Clevan students eagerly attended each of their classes to learn the powers, sword skills, martial arts that were more difficult than the Bethal level. They had each faced the Tenebras and knew that they must master their skills and increase their understanding in order to defend against and defeat the rising threat in the world. Each night classes began with religion class with Father Santiago, followed by powers class with Don, Verita history with Olga, sword with Sarge, fine arts with Shir, and finishing with martial arts with Kang. It was a grueling schedule, but Lazarus and the Elder teachers made sure to separate the more difficult and physically demanding classes with the more spiritual or cerebral classes. Soon, the students found their rhythm and they found that they enjoyed the rigor and regularity of the schedule.

Over these few weeks, Jacob also became obsessed with watching the news every evening during dinner. He was startled to see the growth of crime in the world every night. The peace that had been shown for hundreds of years amongst tribes and religious factions in the world was being broken, and small wars were spreading like a sick cancer. Sin and evil were taking a foothold amongst humanity like never before, and Jacob knew that the cause of the mayhem was Lucifer's angels possessing people. Lucifer's servants were in search of clues to the Garden of Eden, just as Jacob and the Veritas were, but the Tenebras couldn't help but create mischief along the way — it was in their nature.

One night while watching the news, Jacob saw something a little different. The news anchor came on and said, "With the massive increase in crime in our nation over the past month, Americans have been searching for answers, and some have worried that some do-gooder-rebels may rise up and take their cause into their own hands. Well, this may just be the case, as a gang, who was on America's Most Wanted List for many murders and rapes, was found with their limbs cut off and their torsos nailed to crosses along a major city street in New York City early this morning." The screen behind the anchor showed quick images of a busy street with police barricading off pedestrians from getting too close to the gruesome scene. Jacob was glad that the victims' bodies had been covered with sheets in the video, but the bloodstained sheets did little to hide the horror of the scene or the crosses.

"Each of the victims had a sign hung around their neck that read, 'Let this be a warning to evil. Judgment is upon you!'" The screen behind the anchor flashed as one of the signs was shown being held by a detective against a white background. Jacob thought it looked like the sign had been painted by the perpetrators dipping their fingers in the victims' blood and crudely smearing the letters on the grungy cardboard. "Some are calling these do-gooders saints while others are touting them as religious fanatics. I guess we shall see soon enough if this is a one-time event or just the beginning of a war on terror."

*Who could've done this to these criminals,* thought Jacob. *Veritas fight for good in the world, but none of us would ever do something like this.*

That night, Jacob arrived a little later than normal. He had given himself some time to get homework done and to actually sleep a little before lying down, meditating, and focusing on Heldago. Jacob suddenly stood in the open grass field before Heldago, his bare toes grasping at the cool green grass in preparation to run to his third period of Verita history, but he stopped before he could even leave the starting gate when he saw a boy walking towards him. The boy looked to be a little younger than Jacob, and because he was wearing his pajamas, Jacob knew straight away that this was the boy's first night in Heldago.

"Is this your first night?" Jacob asked as he squatted down to be eye-to-eye with the younger boy.

"Yes sir," said the boy, bashfully. "H-h-how did you know that?" He stuttered.

Jacob giggled. "Not too long ago, I was standing in your same position, in pajamas, staring at this massive castle for the first time. What's your name?"

"My name?" The boy was still in shock. "Uhh, my name is Henry. Henry Beckham"

"Well, ok, Henry Beckham," said Jacob as he held out a hand. "It's very nice to meet you. My name is Jacob Jerlow." Henry took Jacob's hand in his and tried to grip it as tightly as he could while shaking hands. "Don't be frightened," Jacob continued as he smiled warmly, stood up, grabbed Henry's shoulder, and turned him toward the gate. "We're all friends here. Come, I'll show you how to get into Heldago."

From the castle gates, the guards, Laborc and Raman looked on and were impressed by Jacob's kindness in how he welcomed the new boy. Laborc went inside the gates and retrieved Heldago's caretaker, Triple E, so that the new student could enter and receive his first tour.

"This here is Triple E, Henry," said Jacob, introducing the two. The three walked through the gates and noticed Sarge practicing his Camtra skills on a wooden post. Sarge was very intimidating with his war scars and muscles erupting from his robe. Seeing this master of the sword from this vantage point made Jacob recall the first time he had met Sarge and the feelings of terror he had. Jacob looked over to Henry and saw his face turning paler by the second.

He bent over and whispered, "That there is Sarge. He's a great warrior and a good friend. Don't let his looks intimidate you. Listen and do as you're told, and you will grow to love him like a father." Henry regained some of his color and cracked his first smile.

"Thank you, Jacob," said Triple E. "Now, Henry, is it?"

"Yes sir," said Henry with a little more confidence.

"Come, follow me, and I will show you the majesty of that which we call Heldago," Triple E said grandly as he proceeded to walk just a few steps ahead of the bewildered boy. They had gotten only a few paces away when Henry turned and looked back over his shoulder and waved to Jacob. Jacob smiled and waved back as Henry turned to sprint a few paces to catch up to Triple E who was gesturing toward the white castle, likely offering some historical tidbit about Heldago's beginnings.

After Henry and Triple E had disappeared into the school, Jacob went to his third period of Verita history with Olga. When he entered the room, he saw that he was the first student to arrive. Olga was at her desk, doing what she was usually doing—reading a book related to history.

"Ahh, Jacob Jerlow," said Olga. "And how are we this fine evening?"

"Just fine, Olga. And you?"

"Never better. So tell me, how is your hunt for the Garden of Eden going? I'm most intrigued by your search."

"Well, unfortunately, not so well. When God hides something, He does an excellent job of it," Jacob said smiling, but also a bit frustrated with the dead ends he and Bina had run into in their research.

"I wish that I could be of more help to you, but any trace of its whereabouts is not in any known literature," said Olga. She paused for a moment to think as she closed the book she had been reading. "But there is one that may know something."

Jacob's eyes grew big. "Really! Who?"

"The oldest living creature on this planet. The horsorian named Lamech. That ol' fellow is thousands of years old. He doesn't speak much, but maybe he will have some answers."

Jacob recalled the first day he entered Heldago and saw the six-legged, horse-like creature that Olga was referring to. Triple E had pointed him out. Jacob had not seen the creature since. "I saw this horsorian once before. Where can I find him?"

"He was taken from Earth and brought to Heldago many years ago," Olga started as she rose from the chair behind her desk and turned to look out the window. "He has made his home in the western wilderness outside the castle's gates." She pointed out the window toward an immense forest that Jacob had never entered before. "He's a reserved creature that likes his privacy."

"That's a start." Jacob ran out of the room, stopping just outside the door and turning back to face Olga. "Thank you," he said sincerely before turning to continue running toward the gates of Heldago.

"I thought you may be leaving," Olga said more to herself than to Jacob. *I hope he doesn't spook easily,* thought Olga as she sat back down and reopened her book.

Jacob was running down the hall when he nearly ran over Jezebel, who was coming around the corner.

"Where you going in such a hurry?" asked Jezebel.

"I'm going to find the horsorian." Jacob was trying to leave, but didn't want to be rude.

"The horsorian? You mean Lamech? What do you want with him?"

"I want to see if he has any clues for me about the Garden of Eden," Jacob explained.

"Well, ok then, I'm coming with you."

Jacob was in no mood to argue. He was excited to see if Lamech had any leads for him. He also did not want to linger too long and have more of his classmates join them in skipping class. The two Clevans left the castle gates and stood in front of Laborc and Raman, staring toward the outreaches of the forest.

"I see you are looking into the western wilderness," said Raman. "Looking there can mean only one thing. You must be searching for Lamech."

"Yes sir," said Jacob. "You haven't seen him, have you?

"No, not in some time. He seldom comes around anymore. But, words of advice in your search, keep to the right in the trees," Raman said sternly.

"If you follow the same direction in which the trees lean," Laborc seemed to pick up Raman's thought and speech with the same caution in his voice. "You will find a grove of apple trees. Apples are Lamech's favorite meal. Take him some of this fruit, and he'll be friendlier. But, beware of the rodents that live in that area of the forest. It's because of those creatures that Lamech rarely travels there." Both Raman and Laborc nodded in unison as the gates opened, allowing the two Verita students to leave the protected grounds of Heldago.

"Thank you," said Jacob as he and Jezebel passed through the gates.

Jacob and Jezebel started walking down the stairs as the gates closed behind them, Jezebel said, "Those two are never that friendly to me."

"Yeah, I can believe that. It's only as of late that they've started acknowledging my existence," Jacob explained as he shrugged his shoulders.

The two friends walked across the meadow towards the trees. As they neared the forest, they began to realize just how thick the trees were. It was difficult to see five feet into the darkness of the wilderness. Jezebel drew a little closer to Jacob, almost grabbing his hand while they entered the trees. The forest was so thick that half of the sun's light was blocked from entering. The quiet stillness was somewhat eerie, but the smell of moss covered in fresh dew had a calming effect that helped to ease any anxiety.

"Look, Jezebel, you can see that the trees are leaning to the right," Jacob stated, "just as Laborc had said."

Jezebel nodded. Again, she considered grabbing Jacob's hand, but her thoughts overruled her emotions, and she pulled her hand back to her side, content to walk as close to Jacob as the tree trunks and undergrowth permitted.

They struggled through the thick brush and tall grass while using the leaning trees as their compass. Jezebel hadn't received her sword yet, so Jacob would occasionally take his sword out from his belt and cut through the denser thicket so that they could maneuver more freely. They had traveled for some time when they came to an apparent clearing. This area of the forest was more open and brighter because the sun's light was able to easily penetrate the few branches that created the leafy dome overhead. The air was filled with the fragrance of sweet fruit.

"There! There are the apple trees," Jezebel pointed excitedly in her relief to be free of the dark, thick wood behind them.

Jacob and Jezebel swiftly grabbed apples from the trees and began filling their pockets. They stopped suddenly when they heard a loud SNAP behind them. A fallen branch had broken.

"What was that?" whispered Jezebel.

"Uhh, I don't know," whispered Jacob in reply.

The two young Veritas slowly turned to see what had caused the disturbance and saw a rat. However, it was not just any rat; it was an enormous king rat that had ruled this part of the forest for millennia. It stood up on its rear legs and dwarfed Jacob and Jezebel. Its height was more than eight feet, and its yellowed teeth stuck out of its mouth, making it all the more frightening.

"When Raman said to watch out for the rodents, I was picturing little rats that nip at your ankles, not ones that could bite my head off," Jacob said, trying to lighten the situation.

Jacob drew his sword and moved in front of Jezebel as she took a step backward.

"Easy fella. We mean you no harm," Jacob said as he tried to reassure the creature of their intent.

"Harm? I do not fear that you will hurt me," the king rat said and then laughed a loud wheezing and squeaky laugh.

Jacob and Jezebel looked at each other. *It can talk*, they both thought.

"You do not have permission to take my apples, humans," he said. "Moreover, you are trespassing on my land."

"We're sorry for taking your apples," said Jezebel as she peered fearfully over Jacob's shoulder. "We didn't know that they were yours. We wanted to take them to the horsorian, Lamech."

"I've been trying to keep that cranky old goat out of here for centuries," said the king rat. "He's been stealing from me for far too long, so your thievery for the horsorian only makes this situation sweeter. Speaking of sweet, I have not had human flesh in years." The rat's beady black eyes glared intently at Jacob and Jezebel as its greyish, pink tongue quickly licked over the large protruding yellow teeth.

"Uhh, can't we talk about this...," Jacob stuttered as he stepped back slowly, trying to keep between the rat and Jezebel without running over her.

The king rat jumped at Jacob and Jezebel, trying to sink his teeth and claws into his uninvited dinner. Jacob lunged his sword at the beast's heart, but its sharp claws threw the blade to the side. During the attack, one of its claws came down upon Jezebel's shoulder — cutting it deeply as she instinctually screamed due to the pain. Blood began drenching her robe.

The two friends got up and ran, but the king rat was too fast. With one swipe of his paw, the rodent knocked the two Veritas off their feet, Jacob's sword flying into the heavy undergrowth to his right. Jezebel fell soundlessly on her back and didn't move and Jacob feared the worst. He quickly rolled toward her lifeless body and on to his back, called forth a fireball, and threw it at the beast. The king rat, acting as if he had seen such a maneuver before, snapped his arm to the side and caught the fire ball midair. "You try to use your silly powers on me?" he growled. He spat on the fire ball—extinguishing it. The king rat's powers were greater than Jacob had ever imagined.

The beast leaped again, this time landing on both Jacob and Jezebel, pressing down on the two captives with his huge forepaws. The sharp claws of the king rat's forepaws easily penetrated the Veritas' robes and began to dig into their flesh. They were pinned to the ground. The lack of any sound from Jezebel as the rat's weight and claws only worsened the wound on her shoulder confirmed for Jacob that she must have at least passed out in shock. As he struggled and fought to stand up, his medallion fell out from underneath his robe. The king rat rose up a bit, releasing some of the pressure of his weight, and stared at the necklace. "Where did you get the Oracle?" the king rat asked in a high pitched surprised squeak.

Jacob stopped struggling a bit. "It was given to me by my father."

The king rat bent down again, placing both forepaws on Jacob, ignoring Jezebel altogether, and pressed down even harder on Jacob's chest as his snout came within an inch or two of Jacob's face. "So, your father is a thief?" The king rat's warm, sour breath rushed over Jacob's face as its teeth moved frightfully with its words.

"No, no, it's been in my family for years." Jacob struggled to breathe, not only due to the rat's weight but also due to the stench of its breath.

The king rat pulled his paws off of Jacob and Jezebel and sat back on his rear. He paused to think for a moment. Jacob looked over at Jezebel who had groaned as the creature had shifted its weight from her body. Jacob was relieved that she had only been unconscious, but he was puzzled by the creature's actions. *Why's the king rat concerned about the Oracle*, he thought.

"My name is Juba, and because of a debt that I and my kind owe from long ago, you are free to leave," he said as he rose completely and moved away a pace or two from Jacob and Jezebel, turning to face them again. "You may also take my apples as a gift of gratitude." Juba gestured toward the tree and then pointed over Jacob and Jezebel toward a rocky outcropping opposite of the way they had entered the clearing with the apple tree. "To find the horsorian, you must follow the flow of the creek that's just on the other side of that ravine."

Jacob slowly sat up and then got to his feet and quickly checked on Jezebel who was shaking her head to clear the cobwebs and holding her injured shoulder tenderly. Jacob gave Jezebel a look as if to ask if she was okay and she nodded. He helped her to her feet and then they both turned cautiously to face the king rat again. They were both somewhat confused by the turn of events but didn't want to stick around to ask questions.

"Thank you, Juba," they said in concert as they gathered up the apples they had dropped during the brief attack. They then backed away from the king rat, not allowing their eyes to stray away from him too much, in fear that he might change his mind as quickly as he had just done. Once they had reached the rocky boundary between the clearing and the ravine, they turned and followed the direction that the king rat had pointed, and, just as he had said, after crossing the nearby ravine, they saw a creek. At the top of the hilly, rocky outcropping of the opposite side of the ravine, Jacob looked back at Juba, who was still watching them and saw the king rat bow in thanks.

# CHAPTER 9

# THE HORSORIAN

Before following the creek and reentering the forest that crowded the creek's banks, Jacob and Jezebel knelt at the water's edge so that Jacob could help Jezebel clean and temporarily bandage her wounded shoulder. Jacob ripped the t-shirt he wore beneath his robe into a strip of cloth and dipped it into the creek's cool water and dabbed at the wound. Jezebel winced at the touch of the cool cloth, but her training and time at Heldago wouldn't allow her to pull away or cry out. Jacob was impressed with Jezebel's warrior spirit and control. He wasn't sure he could grit his teeth and take the pain he knew she must be feeling, but he continued to clean and bandage the wound quickly so that it was over quickly. He tied the bandage in place with another strip off of his t-shirt, and they each drank a bit of water before following the creek in the direction that Juba had pointed.

After walking for some time, Jacob and Jezebel came upon a clearing next to the water that had a shelter. The makeshift home was constructed with trees and rocks as its walls and roof and hardened sap as its mortar. A circular stone structure that resembled a chimney protruded from one of the roof's corners. It was emitting a dark sweet smoke that reminded Jacob of his mom's apple pie.

Jacob approached the structure and looked for a door. With no door handle visible, Jacob's best guess was a large piece of tree bark covered with spiders feasting on trapped insects. He knocked on the rough wood. "Hello, Lamech, are you home?" asked Jacob loudly.

Something was heard hitting the floor. Lamech was startled and had dropped a pan. "Juba, is that you?" he asked. "I haven't been stealing your apples again if that's what you're after." Lamech was obviously irritated. In fact, Lamech had stolen some apples just that morning. He hurriedly tried to hide the freshly baked apple pie under some sheets and frantically started waving a pillow back and forth trying to make the smell escape through the window.

"Lamech, it's not Juba, it's Jacob Jerlow and Jezebel Flores from Heldago," Jacob explained.

"Oh," Lamech paused. "Well, what do you want?"

"Just to ask you a few questions," said Jezebel.

"Go away! I'm busy!" he snapped.

"We brought you some of your favorite apples," said Jacob. There was silence. Jacob saw Lamech peek through a crack in the wall.

"Let me see."

Jacob and Jezebel reached into their pockets and held out the apples that they had picked about thirty minutes before. "They're fresh," said Jezebel.

A sniffing sound came from inside the home. Lamech was smelling the gift that was held in the humans' hands. The door slowly opened. "Come," he ordered.

Jacob and Jezebel entered the shelter. Lamech slowly peeked his head out the entrance, looked around to check for danger, and cautiously closed the door behind the two visitors. He looked at the apples that were being set upon his table and said, "So, Veritas, have you brought a bribe for information?" Lamech stepped into the light that was shining through the window to show himself. He resembled a horse with the same body, hair, and head shape, but that's where the similarities ended. The creature had six legs, but at the end of each leg was not a hoof, but a hand, which looked more like a gorilla's than a human's. He could walk on all six hands or just two. He had a head on the front of his body and one on the rear that made it confusing to onlookers as to which direction he was going—forward or backward. When he spoke, one head would start a sentence, and the other head would interrupt from time to time to finish the sentence. Jacob discovered that talking to a two-headed creature could be very difficult and unsettling.

"Yes sir," said Jacob as he tried to decide which head to look at as he spoke. "We've heard that you are very wise."

"Wise?" Lamech snapped. "I don't think I'm wise, but I'm old. Older than most of the dirt that you walk on every day I would gather."

"No, not really. How old are you really?" asked Jezebel.

"Have you heard of Noah and the big boat that he built?" asked Lamech.

"Yeah, everybody has," said Jezebel.

"Well, let's just say, I saw him build that boat. I was on that thing when the floods came, but my wife died during the adventure and left me alone in the world. So, I've been the last horsorian since then." Lamech stopped talking and stared into his firepit. He grabbed a nearby sword and poked the fire to revive it. "Sometimes, I think that God has forgotten about me. Maybe He left me here to rot away with the living—"

"Maybe He has a purpose for you that you aren't aware of yet," said Jacob.

"Ha-ha," Lamech chuckled. "Maybe."

Jacob looked at the swords that were standing in the corner of the room, leaning precariously and haphazardly against the wood. They were covered in dust and spider webs. "I see you have some swords. Are you a swordsman?"

"Used to be," Lamech explained. "But that was a long time ago." He grabbed a sword and poked the fire again. "These," he waved the sword in his hand, "are just good for stoking my fire now. Come, I know you two didn't come all the way over here to chat about my old memories. What is it that you want?"

"Have you heard of the Garden of Eden?" asked Jacob.

"Yes, silly children, I've heard of the Garden of Eden," he said, rudely. "But, if you're wondering if I know where it is, you've made a wasted trip. It's hidden and for good reason."

"We understand that it's hidden," said Jacob. "But there must be clues to find it. Every object or place in time leaves a trail that can be followed."

"Hmm, did you just make that up?"

"No, sir. It's something my dad taught me."

"Well, it's true. Your father must be a smart man."

"My dad died earlier this year in the spring," said Jacob. "But he taught me a great deal."

Lamech looked as if he cared for a moment. "I'm sorry for your loss." Then, in a flash, his empathy was gone. "At least he wasn't the last of your kind, like me," he said with a snort. "Why do you want to find the Garden?"

"We've learned that Lucifer is trying to find it to use the Tree of Knowledge and the Tree of Life to gain access to Heaven," Jacob said. "With his numbers and increased power, he is going to try and overthrow Heaven and rule Earth forever."

"I see," said Lamech. He stopped to think for a moment and then finally turned away from his fire to fully face his two uninvited guests for the first time since they had entered his abode. Both of Lamech's heads looked from Jezebel to Jacob and stared intently at Jacob. "Rumor has it that you have the Dalet in your possession. Is this true?"

"Yes sir," said Jacob.

Lamech paused again in thought. He moved both of his heads closer together, making each of his sets of eyes stare into the others. He seemed to be having a conversation with himself. "Is this boy worthy of such a task?" The head to Jacob's and Jezebel's left asked the one to their right. "Are we to trust him?" Asked the head to the right. "Let's look inside his heart," they said in unison. Lamech turned his heads towards Jacob's. "Come closer, Jacob Jerlow."

Jacob slowly stepped forward and closer to the strange animal.

"Closer," said Lamech. "If we wanted to hurt you, we would've already done so."

Jacob inched closer and nervously grabbed the outstretched hands of the horsorian. Lamech's eyes stared intensely into Jacob's. He was looking at Jacob's inner being—into his very soul. A moment later, Lamech let go of Jacob's hands, and each head glanced at the other. "I see a challenging past in your family's history," he said. "I also see an even more challenging future... I have traveled throughout the world in my years and have seen many strange things." Lamech reared up to stand on just two of his hands, grasped the middle pair and rested them on his belly, and scratched his chin with the pair closest to the head that rose before Jacob.

*He has seen many strange things? That is the pot calling the kettle black,* Jacob thought to himself and smiled.

Lamech continued, ignoring the smile he saw on Jacob's face. "There was once a secret sect of your Verita family that swore an oath to keep the Garden of Eden in hiding, for they feared that Lucifer would one day try to find it and gain its power." Jacob flashed a look of curiosity at Jezebel at this astounding news. He had never heard nor read anything about a secret sect of Veritas in his research to find the Garden of Eden, and judging by Jezebel's equally surprised look and shrug of shoulders, Jacob assumed few had ever heard of the sect.

Lamech turned back to the now dying fire, grabbed the sword he had used to stoke the fire once more, and rattled it among the embers and ashes as another set of hands grabbed two logs from beside the fireplace. He continued, "I would wager that because of their great secrecy that even Rabbi Lazarus doesn't know of such people." It was as if

Lamech were answering Jacob's internal question. "They hid themselves from all history and let only a few into their family. They took every precaution to hide themselves and their knowledge from the world." Lamech paused again to throw the two logs on to the embers he was stirring at the same time with the old sword. The pause dragged on as if he was considering whether he should continue with the story of the secret sect that protects the Garden of Eden. The head that did face Jacob and Jezebel seemed to be searching Jacob's soul. Lamech's large brown eyes gazed at him intently during the pause, and Jacob thought a look of sadness passed quickly over the eyes just as Lamech turned and returned to all six of his legs so that both heads could face his guests.

"However, they also knew of the prophecies that someday the Electus would come, and he would need to find the Garden. With this foreknowledge, they left clues spread throughout the world as to the whereabouts of the Garden." Lamech announced the existence of clues to the hidden Garden of Eden very matter-of-factly, as if it came as no big surprise to him, but Jacob and Jezebel were quite surprised.

"Well, that's great," said Jezebel. "How can we find them – this secret sect of Veritas?"

"They're all gone except one, and he gave me very specific instructions to ONLY send those that I deemed worthy." Lamech grabbed some of the apples that they had brought to him and began cutting them up for a snack.

"Well, am I worthy?" Jacob asked, worried that he might have finally found someone with a clue to the Garden of Eden only to have the clue snatched away because he was unworthy. He was after all only a freshman in high school in the human world, and he had only just recently passed to the Clevan level of training at Heldago. There were others likely more qualified and more worthy than he was in the grand scheme of things.

Lamech stopped cutting the apples for a moment and said, "You are, Jacob Jerlow, you are worthy, but are you without fear?"

Jacob looked at Lamech curiously. "As God is my salvation, I am without fear," he said, confidently.

"Hmm. Indeed. Very well then. The man you seek is Galaman Kalfas. He lives in Angul in the state of Odisha. This is in India. You will find him in the poorest area of town. There, he helps needy children that are starving physically and spiritually." Lamech bit into a crisp slice of apple.

"Thank you, Lamech," said Jacob and Jezebel respectfully but excitedly as they approached the tree bark door of Lamech's home.

"God be with you," said Lamech.

Jacob and Jezebel paused at the door, and Jacob turned and said, "And with you." He noticed that Lamech's two heads were watching him intently, the light of the rekindled fire shining off their large sad brown eyes. "Thank you again, Lamech," Jacob said as he waved. As he turned to follow Jezebel into the wilderness, Jacob noticed the two heads had begun to talk quietly between themselves.

Jacob caught up to Jezebel, and they left Lamech's home, following the creek back to the ravine and Juba's clearing. They did their best to follow the path they had taken into the forest and returned to Heldago much more easily than they had found their way to Lamech. Neither was certain how long they had been away, but they decided to speak with their history instructor, Olga Hanson. Jacob and Jezebel were surprised to find that Olga was just finishing her history lesson with the other Clevans when they arrived. Apparently, the round trip journey to Lamech had only taken one class period.

"Any leads, Jacob?" Olga asked distractedly, and then she gasped when she noticed Jezebel's wound and bloody robe.

Jacob's classmates were just exiting, but, when they heard Olga's question and gasp, they stopped to listen. Jack and Fred sat Jezebel down so that they could take a closer look at her shoulder.

"Yes. Lamech gave us a name and location of a person that can help us," answered Jacob. "But Olga, I was wondering about something. What do we know of the Electus?"

"The Electus, you say?" Olga's right eyebrow rose. "I haven't taught about the Electus in some years now." She stepped up onto a ladder and began searching a bookshelf that was built into the wall near her desk.

"Shouldn't we take Jezebel to the infirmary to have her wound looked at?" Jack asked with the weight of concern of someone who understood the dangers of being wounded.

"No, I want to hear this," Jezebel said sternly as she pulled the shoulder of her torn and bloody robe back up over the makeshift bandage. She noticed the pained look of concern on Jack's face and patted his left hand and took his right arm in hers, saying reassuringly, "I'm okay Jack, truly I am. It's only a scratch from a rat." She smiled warmly at Jack, and that seemed to calm some of his concern as they both looked back to see what Olga was seeking on the bookshelf.

It took her a few moments, but she soon pulled a book out of its place. "Ahh, here it is." Olga held the book up for all to see the result of her search as she gingerly stepped back down the ladder. She sat at her desk, opened the book, licked her forefinger, and began to leaf through the pages.

All the Clevans were intrigued now, so they all sat down at a table near Olga's desk where she had papers, books, and grading spread out. They all peered intently at the book she had found and hoped they were close enough to not miss anything about the legendary Electus.

Olga continued paging through the book and skimming the pages. "OK—this is what I was looking for. It says here that the Verita prophet, Jeremiah, prophesied of the coming of a Verita Electus in 2520 BC. He said the Electus would be born of pure angelic bloodlines, meaning that he will be the only one to survive history that has both mother and father angelic bloodlines that are traceable to the first marriage between an angel and a human. In addition to that, the Electus's angelic ancestor is not just any angel, but this angel will be a great warrior from Heaven." Olga looked up from the book and was pleasantly surprised to see that she had all of her students' attention. She quickly looked back down at the opened book to find her place so that she would not lose anyone's attention.

"Jeremiah also said that the Electus will help bring purity and goodness back to a fallen world, and he will blow the Horn of Truth on Earth. This sound will mark the end of evil's reign and the beginning of a permanent imprisonment for Lucifer," she continued as she used her finger to keep her place in the book. "Jeremiah goes on further and foretells that the Electus will come out of a nation that was born on the footsteps of God's righteous one. This righteous one he spoke of we now know is God's Son, Jesus Christ."

"When will this happen?" Fred Albas interrupted in his hasty curiosity. "Did Jeremiah say anything about that?"

Olga searched a bit more in the book, flipping pages back and forth as she skimmed over the text. "Nothing is said specifically about when the Electus will come, only that he will come during a time when the *world sees evil as good and good is seen as evil*." Olga closed the book and looked at her students' attentive and expectant faces. "With this description, I guess, if we were to look at what is happening on Earth today with Christians being persecuted for their righteous beliefs, and people that are openly sinning looked upon as someone to aspire to, it's a safe guess that the time is near."

The reality of the rising evil in the world and its meaning settled heavily in the hearts of the Clevan students.

Each of them had seen the news from around the world, and they all knew and understood the implications of the wars and crimes against Christians and sinners alike. All of the students paused at the horrible truth that the world was dying around them and that they might be part of the last stand against the rising tide of evil.

"What about this Horn of Truth; what else do you know of it?" asked Jacob, interrupting the heavy silence that had fallen over the room as each of his classmates and Olga thought about the meaning of what she had told them about the Electus. He remembered reading about the horn in the "Chronicles of Angels" that he found in the library. It was the horn that Leahcim had blown before he entered God's castle on the day of Lucifer's rebellion.

"It's said that the Horn of Truth was made by God and presents itself in a battle to one that is found righteous and full of courage and strength," Olga explained, eager to move on from the thoughts she had about the evil in the world. "When blown, the Horn of Truth is rumored to bring its enemies to their knees. It has been in battles throughout the universe."

"Olga, let me get this straight," Luke Cartwright interrupted. "Are you telling us that there are other beings in the universe other than us? So, there are aliens out there?"

"I wouldn't call them aliens, Luke, but yes, there are billions of galaxies with millions of planets in those galaxies in the universe, and there are other beings that exist. God's angels have seen times of peace and times of war with many of these creatures."

Luke rolled his eyes at this notion, but Jacob understood what Olga was saying. He had read in the "Chronicles of Angels" how the Horn of Truth had been used in other battles.

At the end of their conversation, Jacob and his friends continued with the few classes they had left that night, but all of them were distracted by what they had heard in Olga's classroom. Jacob found that he was especially distracted by all that he had learned from Lamech and Olga concerning the Electus, the Horn of Truth, and the last survivor of the secret sect of Veritas – Galaman Kalfas – who held a clue to find the Garden of Eden. The rest of the night passed in a foggy blur for Jacob, and he was quite surprised when Jezebel grabbed his elbow outside of the Peddle Room.

"Gracias, Jacob, for an interesting night and for patching me up," she said in her heavy Mexican accent.

"How is your shoulder?" Jacob asked in genuine concern.

"Bueno," Jezebel smiled and then winced as she showed Jacob that she had changed robes and had gotten a better bandage from the infirmary. "You didn't even notice that I left sword skills class to go to the infirmary to get it properly bandaged."

"I'm sorry, Jezebel," Jacob said a bit embarrassed at his seemingly lack of concern. "All of this information about a secret sect of Veritas, the confirmation of an actual Electus, and the possibility that we might find the Garden of Eden before the Tenebras has distracted me a bit."

"A bit?" Jezebel said and then giggled as she intertwined her arm into Jacob's and started walking into the Peddle Room. "It is okay Jacob. I understand. After last summer, I know you feel somehow responsible for all of this, but remember you are only one person. Don't take it all on your shoulders yourself, or your wounds will be much worse than mine." Jezebel smiled warmly as she released Jacob's arm and caressed his cheek with her right hand before turning and walking toward her portal home.

"You're right, Jezebel. You could…" Jacob stammered a bit before Jezebel could get to her portal's station. "I could…I could use some help with all of this. Do you want to go with me to India to find Galaman Kalfas?"

"Sí! Of course I will go with you," Jezebel ran back to where Jacob stood in the doorway of the Peddle Room.

"When do you intend on going?"

"As soon as possible," Jacob said as he blushed a bit due to how close Jezebel stood in front of him. "I will contact you, and I promise you can go with."

Jezebel stood on her tiptoes and hugged Jacob warmly. They stood awkwardly for a moment and then Jezebel released her hold on Jacob, turned, and ran to her station. "Adios, mi amigo," she called out as she disappeared into the rows of portal stations.

Jacob distractedly walked to his personal portal station in the Peddle Room and returned home still thinking about everything he had learned and all of the questions that had arisen from what he had learned that night.

# CHAPTER 10

# ANGUL, INDIA

The next day after school, Jacob and Bina walked home with a plan to ultimately get to the Hokmah cave. On the way, Jacob filled Bina in on everything that he had experienced and learned the night before. As they walked and talked, Bina pointed out the beauty of the fall colors of October as the Maple, Oak, Elm and other trees' leaves had changed in the passing weeks into the warm reds, oranges, and yellows. In the chilly fall afternoon the two friends took a few moments to enjoy the colors while kicking through small piles of less colorful leaves along the sidewalk. The days were growing shorter, and it was nearly dusk when they arrived at their homes. They stopped at each of their homes to get their sleeping bags, extra clothes, and tents, explaining to their parents that they wanted to camp out at their special place near the river one last time before the temperatures got to be too cold. Jacob's mother was a bit concerned about her teenage boy being out in the woods with everything that was going on in the world, but he convinced her that if she let him take her cell phone with him that they would be only a call away if anything happened. He knew he couldn't tell her his real plans because she would forbid him from going, and he needed to pursue the clue Lamech had given him as quickly as possible.

After some convincing and a bit of a chilly walk under the protective invisibility of the Oracle medallion, they stepped into the Hokmah cave, and Bina asked, "So, we're really going to do this? We're going to use the Dalet and go to India? Tonight?"

"Yeah, I know. Crazy isn't it?" Jacob paused a moment. "But, Bina, I did promise Jezebel that she could come with as well. I hope that isn't a problem."

Bina recalled the last time she had met Jezebel and the jealousy that she seemed to have where Bina's friendship with Jacob was concerned. Of course, Jacob didn't notice the jealousy because he was clueless about such things. "Of course, no problem," Bina said as genuinely as she could while wondering about Jezebel's intentions with her friend.

"Ok. Great. I'll be back in a few minutes. Jezebel is waiting for me at Heldago right now." Jacob unrolled his sleeping bag on the earthen floor of the Hokmah. "Could you maybe start a fire in the fire pit so that this place isn't so cold?" Jacob asked as he prepared to leave. "Jezebel is from Mexico, so the North Dakota autumn chill might be a bit of shock for her." Jacob sat down on the comfortable sleeping bag, concentrated on Heldago, and soon disappeared from Bina's sight. Bina stood for a moment surprised. She had always assumed that when someone traveled to Heldago they did so in a sort of spirit or duplicate form of body. She thought about what would happen if any of the parents of Veritas students would sneak quietly into the bedrooms of their children to check on them at night only to find them gone, but she shrugged the passing thought off as she gathered some small kindling to start a fire in the fire pit.

In Heldago, Jacob quickly went to the Peddle Room where Jezebel was waiting and took her back to his home through his station. When they arrived at Jacob's house, Jezebel didn't even have time to see Jacob's room before Jacob grabbed her hand, held out his left arm where he wore the Dalet, and he and his Verita classmate stepped through the magical portal and into the Hokmah cave.

They suddenly stepped out of the portal behind Bina,

who was just starting a fire, startling her.

"Oh, Jacob, you didn't tell me your *friend* would be here," Jezebel said, sarcastically. Jezebel gave Jacob a sharp look and then looked again at Bina and smiled a weak smile.

"Hmm, I could've sworn I did." Jacob grinned innocently and shrugged as he moved to the table to grab his backpack. "Oh well, are you girls ready to travel to India?"

"Jacob, we will have to wait for a little while before we use the Dalet," Bina said suddenly, looking at Jezebel with a brief look of contempt and then looking at Jacob with a look that told him she knew something he didn't.

"Why wait?" He asked.

"Well, we will be traveling to Angul, India, right?" Bina said in a slightly condescending tone.

Jacob looked at Jezebel, and they both nodded.

"Angul, India is approximately 10.5 hours ahead of us, so if we leave now... What is it, about 4:30 p.m.?" Bina looked at both Jacob and Jezebel for confirmation, which she got when Jacob took out his mother's cell phone and looked at the time on the default screen.

"It's 4:38," Jacob said as he held out the phone for Bina to see.

"Well, if it is 4:38 here in Hickson, it is approximately eight minutes after 3 a.m. in Angul, so if we use the Dalet, we will arrive in Angul while everyone is fast asleep," Bina finished her explanation and smiled triumphantly, pleased to show off her intellect in front of Jezebel.

"Okay, Bina," Jacob said a bit dejectedly due to the delay in his plans. "Let's go over everything Jezebel and I learned from Lamech in the meantime, and let's make a plan for how we will track down this Galaman Kalfas once we get to Angul."

"I brought some cocoa and granola bars," Bina said excitedly. "I can heat some water on the fire and we can have a snack while we plan. I'm a bit hungry since we haven't eaten since lunch." Bina started digging through her backpack.

Jacob smiled at Jezebel, who hadn't said much since her arrival at the cave. She was looking around in wonder at all of the things that Jacob's father had collected and hidden in the small underground chamber. "This is the Hokmah cave, Jezebel. Welcome to our secret hiding place."

Jezebel turned from the table where the Hokmah was sitting to smile weakly at Jacob as she rubbed her arms and shivered slightly. "It's am...amazing," she said as she shivered.

"Are you cold Jezebel?" Bina asked with genuine concern as she noticed the all too thin sweatshirt that Jezebel was wearing as her only protection against the autumn air. "Come get a bit closer to the fire to warm yourself," Bina invited as she pulled a nearby chair closer to the fire and tried to guide Jezebel to the warmth by her shoulders.

Jezebel winced and pulled away from Bina's friendly attempt to help her to the chair, because Bina's hand had accidentally grabbed her wounded shoulder.

"Oh, I am so sorry!" Bina exclaimed. "Jacob told me you were injured, but I had forgotten. Please, sit down you two and tell me about your adventure last night. The water should be hot enough for cocoa soon. Have you had cocoa before, Jezebel?"

Jezebel shook her head as she rubbed her hands together near the fire. "It's some kind of heated chocolate drink, isn't it?" She asked as the fire started to warm her up.

Bina, being the caring girl she was, mixed the cocoa for everyone and handed each of them a cup and a granola bar as Jacob and Jezebel took turns telling the tale of the brief fight with the king rat Juba and the conversation they had with the six-legged horsorian, Lamech. It wasn't long before the cocoa and the fire had warmed the trio, and after Bina showed sincere concern for Jezebel when Jacob told about how she had been wounded, the three young adventurers seemed like lifelong friends as they planned what they would do upon arriving in Angul, India.

The few hours that they had decided to wait and plan before leaving passed quickly, and everyone jumped when the alarm that Jacob had set on his mother's cell phone went off suddenly. Everyone laughed at being startled by the alarm, and they gathered up the cups from the cocoa, put out the fire in the pit, and prepared to leave.

"Is everyone ready?" Jacob asked after they had cleaned up the cave and gathered their backpacks.

The girls nodded. Jacob grabbed Bina's hand and instructed her to grab Jezebel's. He looked at the Dalet that was around his wrist, stuck his arm out before them, and said, "Angul, India."

The bright doorway appeared before them, and they entered cautiously. It was as easy as stepping through a doorway of a house, but they were about to travel thousands of miles in a split second, so they weren't sure what side effects they should expect. Suddenly, they were in a destitute area of an unfamiliar town, assailed by a horrible stench that nearly made them retch. Because of a lack of hygiene and public restrooms, the smell of feces and decomposing trash permeated the air. The piles of garbage, which in some areas were as tall as Jacob and his friends, formed walls along the streets. The makeshift cardboard houses of the homeless people littered the alleys and sidewalks, offering the poor their only shelter from the hot sun and harsh environment. The three young travelers had never seen such poverty, but by the looks of the people's ethnicity and the sounds of some nearby conversations, they knew they had made it to India.

It was early morning, but it was much warmer than Hickson, so the three young friends quickly removed and stowed away their coats and sweatshirt in their backpacks. The sun was just rising, and some of the homeless sleeping in the streets were just waking. Those homeless who had woke up stared at the three foreigners and wondered about their intentions. The three travelers began walking the streets, trying to figure out where they should begin their search. None of them had anticipated the maze-like streets, alleys, and temporary shelters, so the plans they had made to find a starting point was useless, but an elderly man, disfigured by the effects of leprosy, suddenly stopped them as they walked aimlessly along. He was hunched over, and his hands were curled inward in a painful looking arthritis or result of his disease. His clothes were stained and torn, and, because of the wear and frailty of the fabric, the material strained to cover his body. "Do you have anything to eat?" asked the man in broken British English.

Jacob and Jezebel searched their pockets but found nothing. Bina reached into Jacob's backpack and pulled out a granola bar and gave it to the man. "Here you are," she said. "We are travelers to your nation and are looking for a man that has been described to us as a helper of the poor."

The man began ravenously devouring the bar, seemingly ignoring Bina's question. Obviously, manners and couth were unheard of in his situation and environment, and judging by his inhalation of the gifted food, he hadn't eaten in days. He paused for a moment, swallowed, licked the bits of granola from his lips, and asked, "What is this man's name?"

"Galaman Kalfas," said Jacob.

The homeless man finished eating the snack bar, wiped his face with what was left of his shirt, and said, "Follow me." After walking through some very narrow side streets, the man brought the three into an even narrower alley that ended at an old, gnarled, wooden door to a small brick building. The man pulled a key from his pocket and opened the door. "Come in," he said.

Jacob and his friends looked around cautiously because they didn't know this stranger who guided them. They also felt that they had no other choice but to see if this homeless man had a clue for them in their search for Galaman Kalfas.

Upon entering the room, the stranger locked the door behind them. "Why are you looking for Galaman?" he asked.

"We wish to speak to him about a private matter," said Jacob. "Is he here?"

"He is, but he wishes to know why you have traveled so far to see him? What you say to me, you say to him." The diseased, old man gazed at the three young travelers expectantly.

"Please sir," said Bina. "We mean him no harm. We only need some information that he holds. It's very important."

The man walked closer to the three and stopped in front of Jacob. His smell was overbearing, but Jacob kept his manners. "What's your name, young man?" he asked.

"Jacob Jerlow, sir. Why?"

"Hmm. Jacob Jerlow, you say. Funny name isn't it?" he commented and laughed hoarsely.

"Sir?" Jacob frowned. "Will you show us to Galaman or not?"

"Yes, yes, I will go and fetch him." The stranger walked behind a wall and immediately came back into sight. He hobbled back in front of the three.

"You didn't even talk to anyone," said Jezebel. "Why are you playing games with us? Where is he?"

"I'm the man you seek. I am Galaman. I saw you walking in the streets. You looked lost and confused, so I approached to see if you needed help. Then, you showed great kindness to me by offering me food. Most others would have turned the other cheek and walked away. I have vowed a life of poverty, even to the point of contracting leprosy, so to be sought out intrigues me. You said my name, and this made me all the more curious. Now that you know who I am, what is it that you want of me?"

"Lamech, the horsorian, sent us to you," said Jacob.

Galaman's eyes opened a little wider. "He did, did he?"

"Yes, and we know that you hold a clue to help us find

the Garden of Eden," Jacob explained. "Lucifer's numbers have greatly increased, and he's also trying to find it."

"I have foreseen this day." Galaman slowly paced the room. "I'm the last of our sect. It was prophesied that I would be the one that would meet one of tremendous heart, who is worthy to seek out the Garden of Eden. We've been protecting hidden clues that lead to the garden for thousands of years. Its powers are not of this world and must not be trifled with. We've not told anyone our secrets to protect mankind from what they might do. Man is weak in the face of temptation."

"We understand the dangers, but we also understand what may happen if we do nothing," said Jacob.

Galaman stared at Jacob intently. He limped over to a dilapidated wooden table, which by its appearance had not been touched in years. "Come here, Jacob Jerlow."

Jacob walked to the table with Bina and Jezebel close behind.

Galaman took two deep breaths in that were followed by forceful exhalations. He was blowing some of the dust away that had made a comfy home on the cedar planks of the tabletop. "We've performed this test on only a select few men who have lived righteous lives. I don't know you or the life you have lived, but, because Lamech saw something inside you, I will give you the test."

Galaman blew toward the table again, revealing a plate of gold, similar to the gold plate with the Alpha symbol on it in the library, but this one had some inscriptions on it. Jacob and his friends looked at the plate. "What is written on this plate from long ago?" asked Galaman.

Bina and Jezebel couldn't read the writings as it looked like a bunch of incoherently yet beautifully scribbled lines, but Jacob could because it was angelic writing. He bent over a little closer to read the writing aloud. "It says, 'Purity of the heart is the first step in righteousness.'"

Galaman didn't show any emotion. Instead, he grabbed

a box that was at his feet and dumped its contents on the table. There were dozens of children's toys. They were all very old, many of which were carved out of stone or wood. "If you were to choose one of these toys, which one would it be?" he asked.

Jezebel and Bina both whispered to Jacob their favorites on the table, but Jacob didn't agree. As soon as the toys had appeared, his focus came upon a small stone carving of a bear. He knew he had never seen or held the toy before, yet he felt as if it were his. "I would choose the bear." Jacob said as he grabbed the figurine to admire it.

Again, Galaman showed no emotion and didn't say if Jacob's actions were correct or not. He returned the toys to their box, and reached for a tray of seven goblets that rested on a shelf behind him. He placed the goblets on the table and asked, "If you were thirsty which would you drink from?"

Jacob grabbed each goblet and inspected them to see if he felt any connection to one in particular. When he picked up the last cup, Jacob felt the hair on the back of his neck stand on end when he saw an inscription carved on its side that read, LEAHCIM. *That is the name of the angel that threw Lucifer out of Heaven. His name was changed but the new name had been scribbled out in the "Chronicles of Angels" that I read,* thought Jacob.

Jacob tried to cover up the surprised look on his face as he answered. "I would drink from this cup," said Jacob. "This cup that says Leahcim on it."

Without giving notice, Galaman grabbed Jacob's hand and cut his palm with a knife that Jacob had not noticed before the attack. Everything then seemed to occur at once. Through his training, Jacob instinctively blocked Galaman's attack, causing Galaman to drop the knife a moment too late. Bina gave a short shriek and jumped backward nearly knocking Jezebel over just as Galaman had attacked, and Jacob found himself holding his bleeding palm, trying to stem the flow of blood. Bina's backward jump had sent her sprawling on the floor, looking up in fear.

In the commotion, Jezebel felt she needed to protect Jacob. She didn't have her sword before, but in this moment of need, she called for it, and it appeared in a flash through the air. Her previously empty and open hand was now filled with cold steel. With confidence, she pointed it at Galaman's neck. "What are you doing?" she commanded.

Galaman seemed to care not that the sharp blade was inches from his throat. He forced the goblet into Jacob's cut hand. "Take the cup and read it," he said, ignoring the obvious threat from Jezebel.

Jacob was still in shock from his hand being sliced, but he pulled the goblet from his bloody hand and looked at its side. Bina and Jezebel carefully slid to Jacob's side to get a glance, but Jezebel kept her sword pointed at Galaman. Jacob's blood covered the engraved name of Leahcim. Then, the letters suddenly began to glow and slowly rearrange themselves into a new word – Leahcim was now spelled in reverse and became MICHAEL.

"Michael?" Jacob whispered as he read the changed name. *Were Leahcim and the stranger, Michael, who has visited me on several occasions, the same person,* Jacob thought to himself in wonder.

"What does all of this prove?" asked Bina from behind Jezebel's protective stance still unsure of Galaman's intent.

Galaman smiled. "After thousands of years of waiting and searching our job is complete. You, Jacob Jerlow, have fulfilled the prophecies."

As Jacob, Bina, and Jezebel looked at him, Galaman seemed to be withering away. His skin was drying, and his eyes were turning a dull, lifeless black. He was dying. "Father in Heaven, Your servant has done Your will. Into Your hands, I give myself."

"Wait! Wait! Don't go!" Jacob exclaimed as he raced to Galaman's disintegrating form. "I don't understand. What's happening?"

"You have passed the tests, Jacob," whispered Galaman weakly. "You've been the only one to ever do so. You have chosen all of the items that have been kept throughout the years from your angelic forefather's house. In the first test, you fulfilled the prophecy of being able to read angelic writing from a plate that hung on his wall. In the second, you chose the childhood toy of your angelic ancestor's first human child. In the third, you chose the goblet of your angelic forefather that was left with his human wife. In the final test, your blood reversed the name of Leahcim and spelled Michael, the very name that was given to him by God." Galaman's body stumbled into Jacob's arms.

"Only your blood could have done this. It's the blood that flows through your veins that is the same as Michael's. You are the descendant of the Archangel Michael. The angel credited with forcing Lucifer out of Heaven because of his betrayal. All of your fathers and mothers in history since Michael have been of angelic bloodlines. Jacob — you — are — the Electus!" Galaman's voice faltered as his weakening body forced him to a kneeling position.

"What? Me? That can't be!" said Jacob.

"Accept your destiny, Jacob." Galaman coughed as he became weaker. "My time is almost done here, so I must tell you one more thing... Each of my brothers and sisters throughout the years who've sworn to protect the Garden of Eden has left a clue to help the Electus find the garden when the time was right. Each clue will bring you to the next, until finally you arrive at the garden itself. The clue that I must give you will help start you on your journey. You must find the garden before evil does. The Earth and heavens above are depending on you."

Galaman fell out of Jacob's trembling arms completely to the floor and began gasping for air. Jacob knelt at his side and leaned in to better hear Galaman's raspy whisper. "Go to the Newport Tower in what is now Rhode Island, in the United States, and you will find a stone that is different than all others. It will start you on your path." With those last words, Galaman died, and his body turned to dust before the disbelieving eyes of the three young people.

A great wind came crashing upon the building, blew open the door, and swirled through the small room, lifting Galaman's ashes and carrying them in a small whirlwind back out the door. A sudden, eerie chill in the air sent shivers down the teenagers' bodies.

"Can we get out of here now?" asked Jezebel. "This place is creeping me out!"

Jacob quickly stuffed the toy bear, goblet, and plate in his backpack. "Jezebel, give me your word that you will not speak of this Electus thing to anyone," Jacob instructed. "I don't want anyone acting differently towards me." Jezebel agreed with a nod, and Jacob started to lead his friends out into the alley. He paused at the door and shook his head in disbelief at the reality he was faced with by Galaman's announcement that he was Michael's descendant – the prophesied Electus.

"Wow...so THE Archangel Michael is my great, great, great, great, great, great, great, great..." Jacob paused to breathe, think, calculate, and ask Bina, "Wait...how many 'greats' do I have to list to trace this lineage anyway?"

Bina shrugged and responded, "Why don't you just refer to him as grandfather? It will mean the same thing."

"Sí, Jacob. In my culture we refer to our respected elders as *abuelo*, which is also the word we use for grandparent," Jezebel added.

"Yeah," Jacob replied a little wearily after thinking about how he should refer to Michael. The thought of saying hello with the long list of additional *greats* before grandfather made his head spin. "You're both probably right. Besides, it's not like I could confuse Michael with Granddad Jensen." Jacob shot a knowing look at Bina, and they both chuckled as they fondly recalled Jacob's peculiar recluse of a maternal grandfather who they both met and stayed with in Alaska.

The same loveable old man who had helped them retrieve the third corner of the Dalet.

Bina started to explain why they were chuckling to Jezebel, and Jacob lovingly recalled his grandfather as Bina described his love of road kill, seclusion, and fishing. The sudden recollection of Granddad Jensen eased his mind as he held out his left hand to open the Dalet doorway when he heard screams bursting forth from somewhere very nearby. Jacob ran towards the sound and hid behind the corner of the building that formed the left side of the very narrow alley leading to Galaman's doorway. Jezebel and Bina followed closely and quickly behind him, Jezebel still holding her recently claimed Verita sword at the ready and Jacob calling forth his. They peeked in the direction of the horrific screams and saw a young woman surrounded by a group of men. The men were ripping at her clothes and laughing in their debauchery.

"Let's get those losers," said Jezebel whispered angrily, grasping her newly summoned sword and starting to walk from their hiding place.

Jacob saw someone coming down the street. He grabbed Jezebel's shirt and pulled her back out of sight around the corner from where he and Bina watched. "Wait a second," he ordered.

A tall, attractive woman came into the light in front of the men and commanded loudly, "Let this young lady go!" She wore a robe similar to the Veritas, but Jacob had never seen or met her before in Heldago.

One of the men began to tease the lady. "Whoa! Guys, it must be our lucky day! We've got two ladies to enjoy." The man approached the woman and slowly grabbed her long hair to smell it.

Two of the men separated from the group and reached to grab the woman from behind. In one swift motion, she reached into her robe, pulled out a sword, and cut both of the men's hands off. The men fell to their knees, next to their dismembered hands, screaming in agony as they began to bleed out from their wounds.

The rest of the men surrounded the woman. They had knives and steel pipes. "Kill her!" yelled one of the men. They attacked. The woman showed she was a great fighter and threw back each man one by one with ease. She seemed to be toying with the men, cutting off limbs and causing as much pain as possible, before finally killing all of the men by beheading them. The woman walked over to the young lady that had been attacked and helped her to her feet. She whispered something to the injured woman and then walked away.

"Who was that?" asked Bina in horror at what she had just witnessed. "Is she a Verita?"

"None that I've ever seen," said Jezebel.

"I've never seen her before either," said Jacob. "But I'm gonna find out."

The three returned to the Hokmah cave using the Dalet. They said their quick goodbyes, and Jacob congratulated Jezebel on being able to summon her sword. She hugged him briefly, said she would see him at training soon, and then she focused a moment and returned to Heldago to use her station in the Peddle Room to get home. Jacob used the Dalet to travel first with Bina to her home and then from there to his own bedroom. As Jacob laid down to get some well-earned sleep, he wondered if he or Jezebel would be in trouble for being late to training at Heldago that night, but he convinced himself that what he had learned from Galaman would be important enough to excuse their tardiness, and he very much looked forward to talking with his Elders at Heldago.

****

At this time, in Heaven, many of the orders of angels had gathered to watch Jacob take the tests and fulfill his calling as the Electus. They stood before a large pool of water outside the Holy Palace. This body of water was known as the Pool of Siloam, and it was a window for all of Heaven's inhabitants into the human world.

A powerful warrior angel in the order of Dominions, named Zoman, stood in front of Archangel Aaron, Archangel Gabriel, and Archangel Samuel. The Dominion towered over the Archangels in size, and his very shadow darkened the area around them. "The boy has begun his destiny," he said in a deep voice. "Does Michael still follow him?"

"We believe so," said Archangel Samuel. "Michael is still in hiding most of the time."

"It was prophesied that his son would someday help bring goodness back to Earth," said Archangel Aaron. "Michael has disconnected himself from Heaven as much as possible since God separated him from his human wife. He has wandered the Earth watching over his son's descendants, waiting for this day to come – the day that his descendant would become the Electus."

"Before there can be goodness, there will be death," said Zoman. "War is inevitable. God has foreseen it since the fall of man. Our armies stand readied…"

# CHAPTER 11

# DAVID AND GOLIATH

That night at Heldago, Jacob ran into Shawn near the front gates. "Hey, Jacob me boy, how've ya been?"

"Good, Shawn. Today we found a clue to get us started in our search for the Garden of Eden."

"That be great news. I've been tryin' to help goodness in the world wherever I can. Evil has been a spreadin' everywhere. It be like a cancer. But, ya know I've always got yer back first," said Shawn. The two friends made their way to the chapel for Jacob's first period, which was religion class with Father Santiago Rivera. "I'm gonna sit in religion class with ya today. I be needin' some food fer me soul."

Jacob was the last to enter class as all of his other Clevan classmates were already present, including Jezebel, who Jacob realized must not have gone home after leaving the Hokmah cave. He quietly made his way toward the pew where Jezebel sat. Jezebel looked at him knowingly as he genuflected and sat next to her. Shawn had remained near the back of the chapel and had taken a seat in one of the last couple of pews near the chapel's entrance.

Father Santiago stood at the front of the chapel by a lectern and bowed to pray. "Father in Heaven, please give us Your wisdom, power, and might so that we may give Your name and kingdom glory forever more, Amen." He opened the Bible and read from 1 Samuel 17:1-58...

"'Now the Philistines gathered their forces for war and assembled at Sokoh in Judah. They pitched camp at Ephes Dammim, between Socoh and Azekah. ²Saul and the Israelites assembled and camped in the Valley of Elah and drew up their battle line to meet the Philistines. ³The Philistines occupied one hill and the Israelites another, with the valley between them.

⁴A champion named Goliath, who was from Gath, came out of the Philistine camp. He was over 9 feet tall. ⁵He had a bronze helmet on his head and wore a coat of scale armor of bronze weighing 125 pounds; ⁶on his legs he wore bronze greaves, and a bronze javelin was slung on his back. ⁷His spear shaft was like a weaver's rod, and its iron point weighed 15 pounds. His shield bearer went ahead of him.

⁸Goliath stood and shouted to the ranks of Israel, 'Why do you come out and line up for battle? Am I not a Philistine, and are you not the servants of Saul? Choose a man and have him come down to me. ⁹If he is able to fight and kill me, we will become your subjects; but if I overcome him and kill him, you will become our subjects and serve us.' ¹⁰Then the Philistine said, 'This day I defy the armies of Israel! Give me a man and let us fight each other.' ¹¹On hearing the Philistine's words, Saul and all the Israelites were dismayed and terrified...'" Father paused and scanned his students' faces for recognition of the tale he had begun reading. Satisfied by the looks of acknowledgement and engagement of his students, Father Santiago looked back down at the opened bible to find his place.

Father Santiago continued in his reading about how the small Hebrew boy named David conquered all his fears, with God's strength, and faced Goliath with just a sling and a stone. Even the powerful army of Israel wouldn't face the giant, but with David's great faith he fought and killed the massive warrior. Father Santiago closed his Bible and said, "You have undoubtedly heard this story before. But, what does it mean to you?"

"To me, it means overcoming adversity," said Fred Albas. "No matter how giant the challenge may seem, when a person trusts wholeheartedly in God, he or she can accomplish great things."

"Exactly, Fred," said Father Santiago. "David looked at this giant man named Goliath from a different perspective than the army of Israel. With his strong faith in the Lord, David saw just a man in front of him, who was mocking God, not some unbeatable giant. So, when we look at problems, or seemingly insurmountable situations with faith-filled eyes, we see as God sees. When we see as God sees, we know that God will fight with us and for us. In this way, we are to be courageous when evil temptations try to pull us away from God's laws and plans, because we know that God's laws are not hateful or judgmental but are for the good of mankind." Father paused again in thought.

"Why do you think David declined Saul's armor?" Father Santiago continued. "Was it only because it was heavy and cumbersome? I don't think so. I believe he was showing something far greater. He was showing that his true armor — was God. It was the Lord that would protect him, not some piece of metal. So, my Verita brothers and sisters, I'm not telling you this so that you will go into battle with no sword or plan of action but to amplify the importance of your faith in your creator because it's through Him and Him alone, that you and this world have salvation."

"It's rumored that we have a traitor in Heldago," said Jack Leroux, rather unambiguously. "If this is true, has this Verita fallen victim to the Tenebras' mind control because he or she doesn't have strong enough faith in God?"

Many of the Veritas were still rumoring who could be the traitor that had given information to the Tenebras. Since Jacob's Powers test, Don had risen to the top of the gossip, and Jack's question caused some whispering among the students that echoed more loudly than any expected in the large chapel.

"If there is a Verita that is giving information over to the Tenebras, I don't think that we could say unequivocally that he or she is without faith in God," Father Santiago answered, his voice carrying over the momentary disruption that Jack's question had stirred up. "I, for one, don't believe that someone can lose their faith. They may misplace it because of fear, anger, or sin, but it is still deep inside of them. It doesn't take a faithless person to be overcome by evil. Sometimes, a person can be taken over by evil, such as the Tenebras' mind tricks, because they turn away from righteous acts and replace them with sin." Father could tell that he had regained control over the class and that they were once again fully attentive to what he had to say.

"In the Bible, Jesus Christ often taught us about sin. He said our life's actions and choices will rule its outcomes. This means that if you live a life dominated by goodness and faith then the fruits of your life will be a unity with God that gives strength and courage. However, if you live a life controlled by sin then your unity with God weakens, leaving you susceptible to Tenebras and Lucifer's other followers. Even the most faith-filled people will sin. What separates them from evildoers is their connection with God and their humbleness to repent when they sin."

"So, why doesn't God just round up all of the people that don't believe in Him and His rules and throw them into Hell with Lucifer?" Luke Cartwright asked loudly.

"God gives everyone a chance," said Father Santiago. "In many situations, He offers hundreds and hundreds of chances, but He lays before mankind choices to make throughout their life. Accept Him or accept the world. It's mankind's decision—no one else can make it for them. Even in as much as some would like you to think that the world and all of its evil has made them sin, it's undoubtedly the individual's duty to take responsibility for their own actions." Father stepped out from behind the lectern and smiled as he continued, "But… God doesn't give up on people. You've probably known someone yourself that has lived a sinful, faithless life for years, and then one day –" Father Santiago snapped his fingers suddenly with a dramatic flourish. "– they change. They choose God and pray for forgiveness."

Father Santiago opened his Bible again and read from Matthew 13:24-30.

"24 Jesus told them another parable: 'The kingdom of heaven is like a man who sowed good seed in his field. 25 But while everyone was sleeping, his enemy came and sowed weeds among the wheat, and went away. 26 When the wheat sprouted and formed heads, then the weeds also appeared.

27 The owner's servants came to him and said, 'Sir, didn't you sow good seed in your field? Where then did the weeds come from?'

28 'An enemy did this,' he replied.

The servants asked him, 'Do you want us to go and pull them up?'

29 'No,' he answered, 'because while you are pulling the weeds, you may uproot the wheat with them. 30 Let both grow together until the harvest. At that time I will tell the harvesters: First collect the weeds and tie them in bundles to be burned; then gather the wheat and bring it into my barn.'" Father paused as he turned the page of the bible.

Then Father Santiago read from Matthew 13: 36-43 that explained the parable.

"36 Then he left the crowd and went into the house. His disciples came to him and said, 'Explain to us the parable of the weeds in the field.'

37 He answered, 'The one who sowed the good seed is the Son of Man. 38 The field is the world, and the good seed stands for the people of the kingdom. The weeds are the people of the evil one, 39 and the enemy who sows them is the devil. The harvest is the end of the age, and the

harvesters are angels.

[40]As the weeds are pulled up and burned in the fire, so it will be at the end of the age. [41] The Son of Man will send out his angels, and they will weed out of his kingdom everything that causes sin and all who do evil. [42] They will throw them into the blazing furnace, where there will be weeping and gnashing of teeth. [43] Then the righteous will shine like the sun in the kingdom of their Father. Whoever has ears, let them hear.'" Father Santiago gently closed the bible again.

"You see, God wants nothing but the best for you and me because he loves His sons and daughters," said Father Santiago. "We must do our best to live a life without sin, but when we do sin, we must accept our mistake and ask for God's forgiveness through the saving graces of His Son Jesus Christ. But—it's up to us to choose His plan."

The Spirit of God was again moving through the walls of Heldago, and the students could feel His presence. After religion class, Jacob and his classmates left for their powers class with Don.

# CHAPTER 12

# THE NEPHILIM

The powers class was much the same as it had been during their Bethal level training, but there was an awkwardness in the air. Most of the students remained quiet and attentive, and they did as they were instructed by Don, but after Don's treatment of Jacob at his Bethal test, many of the students felt uneasy around Don, so they weren't as talkative or inquisitive as they had been before as they learned about the next level of powers that they would learn as Clevans. In fact, few students spoke with Don except to respond to his directions with a simple "yes," "no," or "yes, sir." Don had avoided Jacob since his test, and Jacob was all too eager to help Don out, even though he was curious why Don had tried so hard to distract him during the test.

Olga Hanson was eagerly awaiting the Clevan students when they entered her room. She had a lesson plan covering the history surrounding the building of Heldago castle, but it was to be quickly interrupted by Jacob and his friends. "So, during the days of angelic inhabitance of earth...," she started.

"Olga, I'm sorry to interrupt, but I have some questions, and I think that they would be beneficial for our class," said Jacob.

"Uhh, okay, Jacob, what's your question?" Olga was caught off guard.

"Who is torturing and killing many criminals throughout the world?" asked Jacob. "Why do I feel that we Veritas have some connection with these people?"

Olga paused. She went behind her desk, picked up a pair of reading glasses, and opened a drawer. She pulled out a Bible. "The Bible gives many hints into the past where angels and humans lived together on Earth. It doesn't come right out and say this, but in several passages the concept is given to a reader that not only reads with their eyes, but with their spirit as well. For instance, in 2 Peter 2:4, Peter wrote of the angels that married humans when he said, 'the angels who sinned.' Again we see proof in Jude 6 when the author speaks of our history on Earth when writing of angels, 'who did not keep their proper positions of authority but abandoned their own home.'"

"But you may not be so familiar with the passages in Genesis and Numbers. Many people read quickly over these sections, but they hold great history." Olga flipped through the pages of her Bible and read the passages from Genesis 6:1-4. "When human beings began to increase in number on the earth and daughters were born to them, 2 the sons of God saw that the daughters of humans were beautiful, and they married any of them they chose. 3 Then the Lord said, "My Spirit will not contend with humans forever, for they are mortal."

4 The Nephilim were on the earth in those days — and also afterward — when the sons of God went to the daughters of humans and had children by them. They were the heroes of old, men of renown."

Olga quickly flipped the pages of her Bible to Numbers 13:31-33 and read again. "31 But the men who had gone up with him said, 'We can't attack those people; they are stronger than we are.' 32And they spread among the Israelites a bad report about the land they had explored. They said, 'The land we explored devours those living in it. All the people we saw there are of great size. 33 We saw the

Nephilim there. We seemed like grasshoppers in our own eyes, and we looked the same to them.'"

Olga closed her Bible and stepped toward the students as she removed her reading classes. "These Nephilim spoken of in the Old Testament still live today. They get their name from a verb series in Hebrew that means 'to fall.' And they received this name because of their fall away from the Verita people. The Nephilim are giant people with extraordinary strength. They are the offspring of great warrior angels from Heaven. Some stand eight feet tall and are covered in hair. Throughout the years, humans have spotted them in their hiding around the world and have labeled them Big Foot, Sasquatch, Yeti, Yeren, and others. They are our brothers and sisters in heredity, but they hold many values that are different than our own." Olga looked at her students and though they had changed her intended lesson, she was pleased to see how receptive they were to the impromptu lesson brought on by Jacob's question.

Olga continued, "This is why they separated from us at the beginning. It's their opinion that those who are evil should suffer and pay for their sins. Veritas, on the other hand, have a different approach to evil — with righteousness and forgiveness as their compass."

"So these Bigfoot are actually angelic born?" Luke barked out in his less than convinced tone.

"Luke, they aren't really Bigfoot." Olga rolled her eyes. "That's just one of the names that have been given them by mankind that doesn't know who or what they truly are. Their real names are the Nephilim, and they really don't have a home, so they hide in mountains and wildernesses."

"Olga, I think Jezebel and I saw one of these Nephilim recently and she was beautiful," said Jacob. "She was a great fighter, but definitely not big and hairy."

"Really?" Olga asked in a rather surprised tone. "Well, there are legends that the Nephilim can change their appearances into more of a human looking form for brief periods of time. Maybe this is the case in your own encounter with one." She looked intently first at Jacob and then at Jezebel.

"That's why they've been spotted so few times because they can transform into a human appearance, but why are they out in the open now?" asked Jezebel. "Why would they be waging war against evildoers now?"

"Throughout history the Nephilim have risen together to fight evil on many occasions," said Olga as she turned and walked around to stand on the other side of her desk. "Yes, they may do it in a cruel manner, but their overall goal of stopping the spread of sin and evil runs through to their very bones. Their angelic grandfathers were, after all, great warriors in Heaven. It seems to be that they've seen the great rise in Lucifer's followers throughout the world and have waged their own war in fighting it. One of their biggest assets is their ability to communicate with one another through mental telepathy. One Nephilim can speak to another on the other side of the world without speaking a word."

"So, you think it's the Nephilim that are fighting and killing evil doers?" asked Jacob.

"I do," replied Olga.

With that last question, the class ended. As the students left the room, Rabbi Lazarus stopped Jacob just outside of the doorway. "You've had success in your search, I hope?" he asked.

"Rabbi! Yes, I have. I found the first clue that'll lead me on my journey to find the garden. It's in…"

A great temptation immediately came over Lazarus to gain control of the Garden of Eden and all of its powers. He knew it was evil trying to insert thoughts of greed and power into his soul. Lazarus was a holy man, but just because he stood for righteousness, it didn't exempt him from being tempted by the evil one. His body was flesh, and as such, it was weak to sinful desires—just as all humans. He closed his eyes for a moment and overcame the temptation.

Lazarus held up a hand to cut Jacob off mid-sentence. "No, Jacob," he interrupted. "I don't want to know. Not now anyway." Lazarus saw the mixed look of surprised pain and eagerness in Jacob's face, and smiled to reassure his pupil as he continued, "When the time is right, maybe, but not now. Just know that I and your people are here for you — to our very last breath. I will pray for you."

Jacob understood his leader's request. He hugged Lazarus and left to practice his sword skills with Sarge. Jacob was gaining skills of the sword at an extremely high rate. In sparring bouts of sword skills with his Elder, Sarge, he was pushing the limits of his teacher's capabilities. Even Sarge was shocked at the growing power of his young student.

After their class with Sarge, the Clevans were eager to have the chance to calm down and enjoy fine arts with Shir, and then finish the night practicing their martial arts with Kang. Once training at Heldago had ended, Jacob was excited to return to his bed and rest before having to get up for human school. It had been a long day.

The following day, Jacob and Bina were in music class with Mrs. Rubis when their conversation about their after school travels was quickly broken when the flash of a fast moving object flying in their direction caught their attention. Jacob snapped his head to the side and dodged the music book that skimmed the top hairs of his head. But, the flying pages of notes had gotten his and Bina's attention. "I don't hear you warming up," Mrs. Rubis shouted. "I hear a lot of mumbo jumbo about after school activities, but no music." Mrs. Rubis couldn't see very well, even with the help of her bottle-bottom lensed glasses, but she could hear like a bat, and she could use her heightened hearing to pick out a target just like a bat could use sonar to hunt insects.

"I'm sorry," said Bina and Jacob in unison. Bina began warming up her voice, and Jacob tuned his trumpet.

At the end of the music lesson, Mrs. Rubis excused the students but stopped Jacob and Bina as they exited. They thought they were in for a tongue-lashing but instead were complimented. "So, are my two star pupils going to try out for the homecoming dance band that we're putting together?"

Jacob and Bina looked at each other confused. With all of the distractions outside of school, they had completely forgotten about the auditions.

"Yes, we will, Mrs. Rubis," Bina replied. "When were they again?"

"Uhh, tomorrow?" she said, surprised.

"Of course, tomorrow, we'll be there," said Bina. She grabbed Jacob's hand and pulled him from the room.

After lunch, Jacob and Bina had 15 minutes to spare, so they went to the school's library to do some research on the structure known as the Newport Tower. In India, Galaman had told them to start their journey to find the Garden of Eden at this Rhode Island site. Upon some investigation on the internet, Jacob and Bina learned that the Newport Tower had many stories revolving around how and when it was made. Some archeologists dated it to around 1650 and others around 1325, but even more debate surrounded the purpose of the structure. The cylindrical stone structure, which was supported by 8 large columns, was 28 feet high and 24 feet wide. Its center was empty but appeared to serve some purpose.

With so much discussion by historians over the purpose of the structure, nothing was apparent or came across as striking to Jacob and Bina. Even with the numerous pictures of the tower on the internet, there was no way that they would find the stone that held the clue they needed on such a large structure in a photograph. They decided they would have to go inspect it, personally.

After school, Jacob and Bina met in a grove of thick trees near the playground to hide themselves from entering the

Dalet. Jacob held Bina's hand and called out the town of Newport in Rhode Island. The doorway opened, and they wearily entered. The whole jumping through a hole in space and landing thousands of miles away was somewhat unnerving to them both—even after performing the feat a few times now.

They immediately saw that they were in Newport as the town's welcome sign was just before them. Adjacent to the city sign and the street signs for the intersecting streets of American Cup Avenue and Farewell Street was another sign that read, "Newport Tower ¼ mile ahead." The trees' leaves were beautifully adorned with yellow and red colors, and the smell of burnt leaves wafted through the air from a nearby yard. They walked down the street until they found another sign pointing toward the tower down Touro Street. Jacob and Bina discussed what they would do for the auditions for the Homecoming band as they walked in the chilly fall air. Bina thought she would try out for the female lead, and Jacob, naturally, said he would try out with his trumpet, if there was a trumpet needed. As they turned down Mill Street, following yet another direction marker pointing the way to the Newport Tower, the tower came into sight at the end of Mill Street. It seemed much larger than they had imagined from the photographs on the internet. There was only one man in the area of the tower when they finally arrived, and he sat on a nearby park bench. He was an elderly man with his hat tilted down to block the setting sun's rays from his eyes so that he could catch a nap.

"Well, now what?" asked Bina.

"I guess we look for a stone that gives us a clue," replied Jacob.

The tower was surrounded by a protective fence to shield it from the hands of many tourists, so Jacob and Bina followed the fence to be away from sight of the old man should he awake. At the far side of the tower, they hopped the fence and started their examination of the tower. Bina began searching the stones that were towards the bottom while Jacob used his levitation power to rise a little higher. He was very careful not to let anyone see him floating in the air by checking the area frequently for any passersby. They had checked the stone tower for about an hour, and the sun was just setting when Bina was startled from behind by the older man from the park bench. "What ya looking for?" he asked.

"Uhh—a stone, sir," Bina replied.

Jacob was up high on the other side of the tower, so he didn't see the man approach, but the chilly autumn air carried the voices to where he was, so he released his power and clung to the cold rocks.

"A stone you say?" the old man laughed. "Well, I think you found a whole bunch of them." The man gestured with his right hand toward the tower, which was built of tons of field rocks.

"Yes, sir. It's a special stone." Bina bit her tongue, wondering if she had said too much.

"I see," said the man as he nodded and looked at her suspiciously. "There have been stories told of this tower for generations. My family has lived in this area for over 200 years and has drawn its own theories. From it being an old grain mill to being an old lighthouse, they've been guessing for years. With no real record of it being built and no literature to support its reasons for being here, we've all been baffled for years, but I enjoy coming here every evening and dreaming of its purpose."

"And what do you think its purpose is?" asked Bina genuinely curious.

Jacob was still struggling to keep his grip on the stones with his tired hands and find niches for his feet while listening to the conversation below. He gritted his teeth and hoped Bina would find a way to get the old man to move along.

The man looked up towards the top of the tower. "Me?

I'm not sure, but I do know one thing; this tower was made for something extraordinary. It wasn't any old mill or light tower. I believe it's much more than that. I know it sounds strange, but I think it has more of a divine purpose, like it was built to give us a message."

"I don't think that's strange at all," said Bina. "In fact, I think you're probably right."

"You do? Well, that's a first. Everyone else thinks I'm crazy. Now then, about this stone — you have obviously been led here to look for a stone that has significance?"

"Yes, sir."

"Well, I'll let you in on another theory of mine." The man motioned for Bina to follow him and enter the center area of the tower. "You see that channel cut into the wall of the second story?" He pointed up toward an area about twenty-five feet from the ground. "It appears to have been designed to hold a slab of stone, a picture, or a tablet of some kind. I believe that when the missing piece is present in that channel that it will reflect light from the moon and reveal its hidden secrets."

"That seems like a great idea, but may I ask why you have come to such a theory?"

"I have been here, standing in the middle of this tower on the night of winter's solstice on many occasions. There is a brief moment when the reflection of the moon comes through that upper window directly opposite and shines directly onto that channel cut into the wall. Whoever built this tower had a secret that they wanted to be revealed at a specific time, but to only the person that holds the object that goes in the channel up there."

"The winter's solstice is the shortest day of the year," said Bina. "If I'm correct, it should fall on December 21st this year."

"That's right," said the man. "You're a smart girl. What's your name?"

"Bina, sir."

"Bina, huh?" he said. "And, by the accent, I would guess that you're from Israel?"

"That's right," Bina said, astounded at the accuracy of the old man's guess.

"Yep, spent a little time there after the war, I did. My name's Hubert. Hubert Winston."

"It's nice to meet you, Hubert," said Bina. "I tell you what. If my friend and I find anything out about something that goes inside that channel in the wall, we'll let you know."

"Friend? I thought I saw you with a young man earlier. Where did he get to?" Hubert looked around the immediate area, squinting as he looked into the dusky darkness around the tower.

"He went to look for…" Bina paused, a bit unsure what excuse to give.

"Ah, heh," Hubert chuckled. "I see. He must be at the *facilities* by the information center. Well, Bina, I'd be much obliged if ya did let me know what ya find." Hubert reached into his pocket and pulled out a card with his phone number on it. "Here, take this and give me a jingle if ya find anything out." Hubert placed his hand on one of the cold stone pillars of the tower as if to say goodbye and walked away.

Jacob peeked around the edge of the tower once Hubert was out of sight, used his levitation power, and lowered himself to the ground.

"Did you hear all of that?" asked Bina.

"Hear all of it? You bet I did," said Jacob as he rubbed circulation back into his aching hands. "He seemed like a nice guy."

"Yeah. I hope you didn't mind that I told him that we would call him. He and his family have been waiting for years to find out the meaning of this tower."

"I don't think we have anything to worry about with him." Jacob stared up at the channel in the stone that Bina and Hubert had been talking about. Then, it came to him. "No, could it be?" he asked aloud as he struggled to remove his backpack.

"What?" asked Bina.

Jacob opened his backpack and pulled out the gold plate that he had received from Galaman, in India. "This plate of gold looks like it's a perfect fit to be placed inside that channel up there," Jacob said as he held up the tablet and glanced from the tablet to the channel.

"You're right!" Bina shrieked excitedly. "Maybe it will reflect the moon's light and show us the hidden clue, just like Hubert said."

Jacob closed his backpack, said "Valoria," and rose to the channel. Once he had steadied himself, he slid the tablet into the channel. It was a perfect fit. Jacob's eyes grew large in anticipation. He returned to the ground and grabbed a flashlight from his backpack. "I think it's dark enough now. I'll shine this light through the window that is across from the tablet and see if it shows us anything."

Jacob stepped outside the tower and flew up to the window. He turned the flashlight on and directed its light at the tablet. "Do you see anything?" he asked.

Bina moved from side to side, but the light that was reflecting off of the gold tablet was not shining to anything in particular. "No, Jacob. I don't see any clue."

Jacob turned off the flashlight, put it in his pocket, returned to the other side of the wall, and grabbed the tablet. He flew up a little higher and held the tablet so that it would capture the moon's light. The tablet's gold began to reflect the moonlight in various directions. Jacob tried lowering himself to get at the same angle as the window would shine onto the tablet if it were resting in the channel, but it didn't work. "The tablet definitely reflects the moonlight in a different way than the flashlight," he said. Jacob lowered himself back to Bina's side.

"It seems our only choice is to return here on December

21st so that the moon will be at the correct angle to shine through the window and onto the tablet," Bina said.

"I'm afraid you're right, Bina," Jacob agreed as he repacked the plate of gold in his backpack. "Let's just hope and pray that Lucifer and his followers don't find a way to the Garden of Eden before then."

Jacob and Bina packed up the rest of their belongings after a quick snack, checked for any possible witnesses, and returned to the Hokmah cave outside of Hickson through the Dalet. From there, they left for home.

That night at Heldago, Jacob updated Jezebel on what he and Bina had discovered at the Newport Tower. Jezebel seemed a bit upset that Jacob had not thought to invite her along on the trip to the tower, but the excitement of the next possible clue and the night of training smoothed over any ruffled feathers Jezebel might have originally felt. The two Verita friends talked quietly when they could about the plans for the trip back to the tower at the winter's solstice. Jacob was not comfortable sharing any of the clues yet with anyone other than Jezebel, and he reminded her not to say anything to anyone about Galaman's proclamation that he was the prophesied Electus.

# CHAPTER 13

# HOMECOMING

After the next day of school had ended, Jacob and Bina went to Mrs. Rubis's music room to audition for the band she was putting together for the upcoming homecoming dance. There were many students standing in line to audition for the performance, but one stood out as peculiar. Exiting the audition room just as Jacob and Bina arrived was Felix Matthews. He had just returned from his family's so-called emergency trip that afternoon.

"Oh hey, how are my favorite classmates?" asked Felix sarcastically as he was passing by.

"Wait, just a minute." Bina stopped Felix. "You're not in music class. Why are you auditioning for the band?"

Felix turned and approached the two friends. "I don't need to be in your stupid music class to be the best singer in the school, and I am the best singer in this school. Besides, the band needs a male and female singer. Who knows? Maybe it will be me and you, side by side, hand in hand — singing to the crowd." Felix was trying to upset Jacob, and he had done just that.

"The only reason that you're trying to get this gig is to make me mad." Jacob gritted his teeth.

"Maybe. Well, yes, and no. You see that senior girl right over there?" Felix pointed a bit too obviously at a redheaded girl in the hallway. "Her name is Lynn, but that's not what matters. What matters is that she digs singers." Felix grinned widely as he stared at the redhead. Lynn was a very pretty girl that was constantly hounded by guys in the school to go out with her.

"Nice!" said Bina. "So you want to sing in the band to make Jacob and me mad and to try to impress a girl?"

"Yep. That about sums it up." Felix grinned evilly, turned around, and walked away.

Bina raised her book to throw it at the back of Felix's head, but was stopped, once again, by Jacob. "You're next, Bina," he said.

"I know I'm next. I'm next in line to smack Felix in the back of the head," Bina snapped angrily.

"No, you're next in line to audition," Jacob smiled.

Bina calmed herself as best she could and started to warm-up her voice for the tryout. Jacob began his warm-up as well on his trumpet but had to stop himself from laughing every few moments, as Bina would throw condescending words towards Felix in her warmup song.

Soon, Mrs. Rubis stuck her head out of the door. Because of her poor sight, she couldn't see that Bina was standing five feet in front of her. "Bina. Bina Feldman, you're next," she yelled.

"I'm right here, Mrs. Rubis," said Bina, waving her hand in front of her teacher.

"Oh, there you are my dear. I didn't see you standing there," Mrs. Rubis gushed as she rushed Bina into the audition room. "Come. Come in. I'm excited to hear your audition."

Bina auditioned. She did a marvelous performance. Jacob followed her audition and also did a great job.

After tryouts, to get their minds off of things, Jacob and Bina both thought it was a great idea to go fishing. The temperatures were getting cooler, and they hadn't fished in a while, so they were excited to 'rip some lips.' After a quick stop at Bina's house to ask permission, Jacob and Bina left for Jacob's house to grab some fishing rods and worms.

Being her normally caring-self, Jacob's mom led the teenagers into her kitchen and sat them down at the kitchen table for a quick peanut butter and jelly sandwich upon their arrival. "So, you two are going fishing, huh?"

"Yes, mom," Jacob replied. "We just need to get away for a few hours and catch some catfish."

"Well, don't be out too late. Seeing all of this craziness going on in the world on TV has me worrying about you." She looked lovingly at Jacob, smoothed out his hair, and went back to bustling about the kitchen, stopping for a moment to peer out the window. "Especially, when it's dark outside." Sarah turned and wiped a streak of peanut butter off of Jacob's cheek with a towel and went back to cleaning up the small mess made while making the sandwiches. "I don't know how you talked me into letting you camp out there by yourselves the other night."

Jacob blushed. "We'll be careful, mom." Jacob tried to cover-up his mom's babying him, but Bina giggled. Jacob kissed his mom on the cheek and was off to grab the rods and tackle boxes.

Bina was close behind. "Thank you for the sandwich, Mrs. Jerlow," she said as they slipped out of the closing door.

Jacob and Bina dug up a jar of worms from the garden in the back yard and were off for some fishing. Soon, they reached the secluded Sheyenne River. The trees' leaves in the surrounding area were still surrendering their summer green for the yellow, orange, and red colors of fall. Unlike most teenagers, Jacob and Bina took enjoyment in natural beauty and loved to be surrounded by such things. They were very alike in that they didn't find technology in the form of games and social media as their first choices of entertainment. They were much happier being in the woods with a fishing rod in hand.

They entered through a trail that they had entrenched by

walking upon it so often over summer break. It was a cool evening with a light breeze, which was nice because it was helping to keep the mosquitos at bay. Jacob spotted their favorite fishing spot and raced over to the river's edge. He trudged through some grass that had overgrown the area to find their favorite two, rod holders. They were four-foot long sticks with a 'Y' shape at their ends that held their rods up nicely. He stuck the two pieces of wood into the soft soil, next to the water, and they began to thread worms onto their hooks.

Jacob and Bina smiled at each other as they cast their hooks into the water. It wasn't long and they were reeling in one catfish after another. The fishing was so good they ran out of worms quickly and decided to lean back on the grass to watch the sun setting through the trees. Jacob saw branches moving on the opposite side of the river, but he couldn't see what had disturbed them. He sat up to take a closer look. Then, from that same area, came a loud snap of metal clashing with metal. A very loud bellow immediately followed the metallic crash. The howl didn't sound like a human's, but more like a bear's roar.

By this time, Bina was also looking off towards the disturbance. Off to the far right of the inhuman yell, they suddenly heard men shouting and talking. One voice said, "This way. I think it went this way." The men seemed to be following something.

"I think there's something hurt over there, Bina," said Jacob. "Let's go see."

Jacob led Bina down the river a ways where he knew the river was shallow and not too wide. He took Bina by the hand and began to wade across. The water came up to their chests, but the bottom was filled with sticky mud that made their crossing even more challenging. Upon reaching the other side of the river, they rushed to where they had heard the yell. As they came through the trees, they saw a hairy animal curled up on the ground. At first, they could not see what kind of an animal it was because of the way it was lying, but it was whimpering in pain. It had a peculiar smell that both Jacob and Bina noticed immediately.

"What is it?" asked Bina.

"I'm not sure," replied Jacob. "There aren't supposed to be any bears around here."

They kept their distance because they didn't know if the animal was dangerous, but they had heard the old adage about a wounded animal, so, for the moment, they were better safe than sorry. They simply stared at the creature, wondering what it could be. The sounds of the men talking and their bustling through the trees could be heard off in the distance.

Then, the creature started to raise its head to show itself to Jacob and Bina. It was human looking, but because it was covered in hair, it looked more like an ape. However, its eyes were significantly larger than a human's or an ape's.

"No. It can't be. Is that a Big Foot?" asked Bina in disbelief.

Jacob remembered Olga's recent lesson and said, "No. I believe it's a Nephilim." He cautiously approached the creature and noticed that its foot was caught in a huge metal trap. The trap was anchored to a large tree with a thick, heavy, logging chain. There was blood everywhere. "It's okay. We're here to help you. Do you understand?" Jacob said as he knelt next to the creature.

The Nephilim, breathing heavily from fighting the pain and stress of the situation, weakly nodded its head, confirming that it understood. The Nephilim continued to remain as motionless as possible because each movement made the injury and pain worse.

Bina rushed over to Jacob's side, and they both carefully pushed and pulled with all of their strength to release the trap.

They could hear the sounds of the pursuing men growing closer. "This way! The trap I set is this way," one of them shouted. They were Big Foot hunters, and they had chased this Nephilim right into their trap.

The trap was too strong; Jacob and Bina couldn't open it. Jacob drew the hilt of his sword from his belt and made the blade appear. He closed his eyes for a moment and concentrated. His sword's blade became so hot that it glowed bright white. Jacob opened his eyes and held the blade steadily against the hinge point of the trap, careful to not touch the leg of the Nephilim or seriously singe its hair. In just a few seconds, the metal began melting away. The trap came snapping open, releasing its grip on the trapped creature. The Nephilim let out a loud growl in agony and grabbed for its injured leg.

Jacob could hear the approaching hunters had stopped when they heard the Nephilim's growl. "We're almost there!" yelled one of them. Their pace quickened through the thick brush. Jacob turned toward the noise and could see one of the men's shirts through the trees. "Quickly! Bina, help the Nephilim to his feet!" Jacob and Bina grabbed the creature's arms and helped it stand.

Jacob stuck out his left hand with the Dalet and opened the doorway to the first place that came to his mind – the Hokmah cave. The angelic portal opened. "Help him through!" Jacob ordered as he stepped quickly into the portal.

Just as the three were stepping into the doorway, one of the hunters broke through the branches and saw them. "Stop!" he yelled. The man ran towards the opening, trying to grab his prize. Jacob looked back after entering the doorway and saw the man was about to grab them. He shouted, "Efor!" quickly closing the portal behind them. The man leaped towards the closing brightly lit oval, but it had just closed, and the hunter fell to the ground face first into a patch of poison ivy.

The two other hunters that were with the man came rushing through the trees and stumbled upon their friend.

"Are you okay?" asked one of the large burly men. "What did you see?" They helped their friend to his feet as they looked around for the creature.

The man that had fallen in the poison ivy strained to see as his eyes were beginning to swell. He grabbed a water bottle from his friend and began dousing his face to relieve the itching. He walked over to the trap and lifted it to find the melted metal was still scalding hot. "Ouch! Dag nab it!" he yelled and dropped the smoldering trap. "There were two kids. They helped the Big Foot escape through some kind of portal."

The man's two friends looked at each other and grinned. "OK. OK. We can see the blood here on the ground. You had something in your trap. Are you sure it wasn't a dog?"

"I know what I saw!" yelled the hunter. "I don't care if you two nitwits don't believe me. I got a good look at those two kids, and I'll find them. They'll lead me right to that Big Foot. You'll see."

Meanwhile, at the Hokmah cave, Jacob and Bina were helping the Nephilim to a seat. "I'm a she, not a he," the Nephilim growled as it sat down.

"What? What did you say?" Jacob asked, almost surprised to hear the creature speak.

"Back in the trees, you called me a *him*," the Nephilim explained. "As you can plainly see, I am no *him*, I am a SHE!" The Nephilim growled again as she gingerly reached for her injured ankle.

Jacob and Bina looked at each other, curiously. The Nephilim didn't have any clothes on, nor did she have any obvious characteristics that would lead one to her gender. Bina was polite though. "We're sorry we called you a *him*," she said. "We've never met one of your people before."

The Nephilim giggled but grimaced in pain from the wound on her leg. Jacob took off his hoodie and tightly wrapped it around the wound. "Thank you so much for saving me," said the Nephilim. "My name is Laura. What's yours?"

"My name is Bina, and this is Jacob," Bina explained. "We're happy that we could help you. Do you live in those woods near the Sheyenne River?"

"No," said Laura. "I've been traveling for days now. I'm lost. I'm sure my parents are terribly worried about me. Those men that were chasing me — why were they trying to hurt me?"

"There are some people that have been trying to find your kind for years," said Bina. "They think they can make a bunch of money if they capture you. They call your people Big Foot."

Laura winced in pain as she laughed. "Big Foot? That's a funny name, but, I guess it's fair."

"Fair?" asked Jacob.

"Yeah, it's fair because we call your people the Calvo, which means the hairless ones."

They all laughed.

"What is this place that you have taken me?" asked Laura, looking around at the interior of the Hokmah cave.

"This is a secret place that has been hidden by my father," Jacob explained. "Laura, I've heard that your people can change shapes to look like a human and blend in. Is this true?" he asked as he finished binding her wound with the makeshift bandage.

"Yes, it's true, but for only an hour or two and then the ability fades. Additionally, it takes so much energy to perform and maintain the mental ability that we usually need to sleep afterward. Some of my people have died trying to keep themselves in the illusion of the human form for too long."

"Why didn't you use the ability to turn yourself into an appearance like ours when those men were chasing you?" asked Bina.

"I've not learned yet how to perform the spell. I'm only ten years old."

Jacob and Bina were surprised at Laura's age because even while sitting down she was almost as tall as they were. This made them think how huge the Nephilim adults must be.

"So, Laura, is it also true that your people can communicate without talking?" asked Jacob.

"Hmm, you sure know a lot about us, Jacob, but yes, that's true. Unfortunately, again, I'm still young, and I haven't mastered this form of speaking. Right now, my parents are probably trying to talk to me in that way, but I just can't hear them yet. They are probably so worried." Laura began to cry.

Bina wrapped her arms around Laura for comfort. "Where should we take her so that she can recover?" she asked Jacob.

"I think Mr. Wolfe's house is the safest bet," said Jacob. "Come, Laura, we'll take you to our friend's house. He'll help you get better and will help you find your parents."

Laura wiped a tear from her cheek and smiled. Jacob and Bina helped her to her feet. Jacob opened the Dalet to Mr. Wolfe's house for safe passage. "What is this doorway?" asked Laura.

"That's kind of a long story. I'll fill you in when there's time. Let's go."

It was getting terribly dark outside, but Jacob and Bina wanted to protect Laura's identity by all means. Upon arriving at Mr. Wolfe's house, Bina hid behind some bushes with Laura while Jacob knocked on the door.

"Jacob, how are you?" Mr. Wolfe answered the door.

"Oh, me? I'm fine," Jacob cut right to the chase. "Ya know those stories that have been told of the Nephilim at Heldago?"

"Sure, yes. Why?" asked Mr. Wolfe.

Jacob looked over at the bushes that hid Bina and Laura. "Well, we have a new friend. Her name is Laura."

Bina nudged Laura to stick her head up to be seen. Mr.

Wolfe saw the hairy creature's head and large eyes poke out from the bush and quickly went to his couch to grab a blanket that was draped over it. "Here, put this over her and bring her inside."

As instructed, Jacob wrapped the blanket over Laura and led her into the house. Mr. Wolfe noticed that Laura was limping badly, and by the look on her face, she was in a lot of pain. "Here, lay her on the couch." Mr. Wolfe closed all of the blinds on his windows and placed some towels under Laura's leg to elevate it. "Jacob, go fill up a bag with ice from my freezer."

"A large trap had snapped down on her leg," said Bina. "We found her in the trees by the Sheyenne River."

Mr. Wolfe didn't know Laura's age, but by her eyes he knew that she was young. "Now, Laura, is it?" asked Mr. Wolfe "I'm going to remove this jacket from your leg and foot. It may hurt some, but I need you to be strong. Don't yell and alert anyone to your presence here. Okay?"

Laura nodded.

Mr. Wolfe slowly removed the hoodie that Jacob used as a bandage to reveal the wound. He inspected the wound intently. "You are a very strong girl. It seems that the trap hasn't broken any of your bones, but you are still bleeding, so I will need to get that stopped. Tell me, Laura, what's your favorite memory?"

"My favorite memory?" she asked surprised. Laura thought for a moment. "I guess, right now, it would be the last time I saw my mother and father," Laura replied longingly.

Mr. Wolfe was trying to get Laura to think about other things while he was going to cauterize the wound to stop the bleeding. "Oh, that sounds wonderful. Would you tell us about that?" Mr. Wolfe was sending an extreme amount of power to his fingers making them very hot. He slowly and gently rested them on the bleeding flesh to stop the bleeding.

Laura was in a lot of pain, but recalling her parents was

taking her mind off the situation. "I love my parents more than anything in the world. But… but sometimes my parents are too protective of me. Last week, I wanted to go on an adventure with some of the older kids in our village, but my parents wouldn't allow it. They said I was still too young. I was humiliated in front of the older kids. They treated me like I was a baby."

Laura's hands were grasping the sides of the couch that she was lying on and the wood and metal could be heard being crushed in her grip as she became upset. She and all Nephilim were very strong. Earlier, she could have ripped the trap to shreds that had ensnared her, but she was scared and her emotions had gotten the best of her.

Mr. Wolfe was just about done sealing up the wound. "We all get upset sometimes. It's part of growing up. Heck, look at me; I'm old and I'm still growing up."

Laura smiled. "Yeah, I guess you're right, but I was mad and not thinking straight, so I ran away."

Mr. Wolfe finished cauterizing the wound, and the bleeding stopped. Jacob handed the bag of ice over so that Mr. Wolfe could place it on the injury. "This ice will help keep the swelling down. You'll be safe here. I won't let anything happen to you. Why don't you get some rest now, and tomorrow we'll see about finding your parents."

Laura was exhausted from her adventure and gladly accepted the offer. She had been on the run for days and finally felt safe again.

Mr. Wolfe instructed Jacob and Bina to go home and return to his house the next morning since it would be Saturday.

# CHAPTER 14

# MOM AND DAD

That night at Heldago, Jacob went through his classes and, at times, found himself biting his lips so that he didn't tell anyone about the Nephilim that he had found. Just like anyone that finds something new and exciting wants to share with their friends, Jacob wanted to tell his friends about Laura, but he felt it would be safer not to talk about her yet.

After some breakfast the following day, Jacob and Bina rushed back to Mr. Wolfe's house to see Laura. Upon arrival, they found Laura sitting at the kitchen table with four plates of pancakes, sausage, and eggs in front of her. The house's interior was giving off a peculiar musky smell that was emanating from the Nephilim. Jacob and Bina had noticed the smell around the Nephilim the prior day, but it was even more recognizable now that Laura had spent the night in closed quarters.

"I had to make a quick run to the grocery store this morning because Laura had already eaten everything in my fridge," Mr. Wolfe whispered and smiled. "She is very hungry."

Jacob and Bina walked a little closer to the busily eating Nephilim. Laura raised her head for just enough time to crack a smile and then was back to devouring the food. Jacob turned to Mr. Wolfe and asked, "How are we going to get Laura's parents here?"

"Ahh, yes, I sent for Shawn this morning," Mr. Wolfe said. "He has a gift with reading thoughts, and I believe that he'll be able to help make contact with them."

Just then, there came a knock at the door.

"That must be him now," said Mr. Wolfe. He walked to the door, started to open it, but was surprised to see Mr. Matthews and his son, Felix standing there, so he stopped short of opening the door more than enough to stick his head out. "Uhh, Mr. Matthews, to what do I owe this visit?" Mr. Wolfe said a little more loudly than would be expected in a normal greeting.

Jacob and Bina overheard Mr. Wolfe greet Mr. Matthews and tried to signal to Laura to stop eating and be quiet, but Laura's hunger apparently outweighed her better judgment, and she continued to wolf down her breakfast. Jacob motioned to Bina for her to try to get Laura to quiet down, and he went to the corner between the kitchen and the door where Mr. Wolfe stood talking with Mr. Matthews.

Mr. Matthews was trying to peek into the house as he responded to Mr. Wolfe's greeting. "Felix said he heard some strange animal sounds coming from your house last night. Is everything okay?" Mr. Matthews was just being nosy. He didn't actually care if everything was safe; he just wanted to fulfill his curiosity.

Mr. Wolfe stepped through the doorway and closed the door behind him. "Why Jonas, I haven't the foggiest idea what you're talking about. Animal sounds you say? I knew I was a loud sleeper at times, but this is just getting out of hand." He smiled.

"Don't play coy with me, Lazarus!" Jonas gritted his teeth. "I know you're hiding something. We saw Jacob and his little girlfriend enter your house just a few moments ago."

Mr. Wolfe bit his tongue to keep from chuckling. The

sight of the short, plump, fat man before him getting irritable was amusing. "Nothing to worry about here. Just spending some time with two of my students."

"You won't think things are so funny when the Master unleashes all of his power!" Felix shouted.

Mr. Wolfe raised an eyebrow.

"Now Felix, our time here is done. Save it for another day," instructed his father. "We'll see you at school on Monday, Mr. Wolfe." Jonas gave a crooked smirk before turning and guiding Felix toward the street.

"Indeed. Have a nice weekend," Mr. Wolfe shouted toward the father and son, but he kept a wary eye on them as they left.

As Felix and his father were walking away, they nearly ran over an approaching person accompanied by what looked like a child. Both adult and child had Verita robes on with the hoods over their heads, pulled down in the front to conceal their faces, so neither Felix or his father recognized them. They were so flustered by Mr. Wolfe's casual dismissal that they didn't fully realize they were being passed by two people in Verita robes. The hooded man looked back at Felix and Jonas, and when they were out of sight, he pulled his hood down. It was Shawn.

"Little early fer visitors, aye Rabbi?" asked Shawn, jokingly.

"That it is Shawn. That it is. Please, come in. Thank you for coming on such short notice."

Shawn, followed by the shorter person, entered the house and took his robe off. "It's OK. Don't ya be scared. Ye can be takin' yer robe off now."

The shorter hooded person with Shawn was the wilderness gnome, Yelkie. With his ability to transport to different locations instantly, he had picked up Shawn in Ireland that morning and brought him to North Dakota. Yelkie slowly removed his robe and began looking for Jacob, who was still in the kitchen. Yelkie was very fond of Jacob and couldn't wait to see his young friend again.

Shawn was covered in dirt and had bloodstains covering his shirt. He looked as if he hadn't had a bath in weeks. "We've been in many a battle as of late, Rabbi," he said. "Evil be massin' their forces throughout the world. Everywhere we be a turnin' there be good people bein' hurt." Shawn began walking toward the kitchen. "I haven't eaten in two days. Could I get something to –" Shawn stopped in his tracks. As he rounded the corner, Shawn saw Laura at the kitchen table still eating ravenously.

Mr. Wolfe was closely behind. "Shawn? Oh, sorry about that. I was going to try to warn you before you saw, well, you know." Mr. Wolfe squeezed pass the still stunned Shawn and entered the kitchen. "Shawn, meet Laura, the Nephilim. Laura, this is our friend, Shawn."

Laura was finally slowing down in her eating. She was almost full – almost. She raised her head from her plate and said, "It's nice to meet you. Are you going to help get my parents?"

"I'll... I'll be doin' what I can." Shawn was somewhat startled at the sight of the Nephilim. He had heard stories of them, but like most people, he thought they were a fairytale.

Laura smiled. She cocked her head to the side for a moment, as if to think, and suddenly let out a floor-shaking burp that was so loud it made the next-door neighbor's dogs start barking.

Yelkie walked around the corner to check on the noise. "Oh, hi Laura. Good have you been?" he said casually, as he looked around to see if he could locate Jacob.

"Yelkie!" yelled Laura. With more speed and dexterity than her size seemed capable of, Laura was up from her breakfast at the table and ran over to Yelkie. Her massive body shook the walls with each falling footstep. A picture on the wall came crashing to the floor. Laura grabbed Yelkie like he was a Barbie doll and flung him into the air.

"Arrgh!" Yelkie groaned.

"Have you seen my parents?" asked Laura, who was cradling Yelkie like a baby.

"Seen them, I have not. Not in a long time." Yelkie responded while trying not to let his rather embarrassing position get the best of him.

Jacob and the others looked at Yelkie in bewilderment. "You two know each other?" asked Jacob.

"Oh, Jacob, there you are." Yelkie smiled. "Know each other, we do. The Nephilim are friends to the Wilderness gnomes. Live with them, many of us do."

"Yelkie, you've never told me that," said Mr. Wolfe.

"Oh, Rabbi Lazarus, I know, but ask you have not," Yelkie pleaded as he tried to sit up or get into a more respectable position in Laura's large arms.

Mr. Wolfe started to say something, but nothing came out. The truth was that no one had ever asked the gnomes about the Nephilim. It just wasn't something to bring up in a conversation. "Well, Yelkie, do you know where Laura's parents are?"

Laura set Yelkie back on the kitchen floor and eyed what little food remained on the kitchen table. "Oh no. King Enoch and Queen Robin have been moving so much, know where they are, I do not." Yelkie said as he straightened his clothing.

"Wait. Yelkie, you said King and Queen?" asked Jacob. "Well, that means that…" Jacob looked back over to the kitchen table where Laura had returned to her seat to finish all of the remaining food. "Laura, you're the princess of your people?"

Laura raised her head, smiled, and nodded.

"Hmm, news to me." Mr. Wolfe chuckled. "Well then, Shawn, do you think you can help Laura connect with her parents?"

"I'll do me best, Rabbi." Shawn walked closer to Laura. She was just finishing the last of the remaining food. "Laura, Shawn be my name. I be here to help ya." Shawn eased a little closer to the massive Nephilim.

Jacob looked down at Laura's injured leg and noticed it was completely healed. The Nephilim are not only extremely strong, but they recover very quickly as well.

"I'm gonna take a little step into yer mind and see if I can be a helpin' ye talk to yer parents," Shawn comforted. "Is that okay with ya?"

Laura was a little scared but nodded as she set the fork down and turned to face Shawn.

Shawn closed his eyes and connected his mind with Laura's. He had an incredible gift of seeing into another's thoughts. When in her mind, he found a lot of fear. Laura had been running scared for days, and thoughts of being killed had clouded her head. Shawn fought through the fear and found a connection in her mind that he had never experienced before. It was like a bright, sun-filled room with endless boundaries.

The room in Laura's mind didn't let Shawn in easily. He had to focus intensely. After a few moments, a passage opened for Shawn to enter, and there he was face to face with Laura's parents. Their faces looked much like Laura's with hair covering most of their skin, and they had large piercing eyes. "Who are you?" asked King Enoch, forcefully. "And how are you in my daughter's thoughts?"

"I be enterin' her mind at her request," said Shawn. "I be here to help her talk to ya."

"Is she okay? Is my daughter all right?" asked Queen Robin.

"She be safe – scared, but safe."

By the tremble in their voices, Shawn could tell the King and Queen had been very worried. They had been calling to Laura through Nephilim telepathy since she went missing, hoping by chance she would be able to hear their call. A tear of happiness trickled down Queen Robin's cheek.

King Enoch fought back his emotions, trying to maintain a masculine, royal, and stoic posture. "Where is she now?

We will come right away."

"She be at me friend's house in Hickson, North Dakota. I arrived here this mornin' with the wilderness gnome, Yelkie, and –"

"Yelkie?" asked King Enoch. "I know this gnome. His brother is with me right now. We will be there shortly. Thank you!"

Shawn nodded and exited Laura's mind.

"I could hear you talking to my parents," said Laura. "I heard they are coming to get me. Did they look mad?" King Enoch had an awful temper, and Laura was nervous about what her father was going to do when he arrived.

"No, not mad, young one. They be worried fer ya," Shawn replied in the comforting tone that Jacob had heard himself before.

Gnomes had a gift of being able to follow the path of another gnome when they traveled to another location. During their flight through space, they leave a trace that other gnomes can sense. This ability to track one another is why King Enoch said that the gnome that was with him could find where Yelkie had traveled to that morning.

Just then, everyone heard a knock at the door. Mr. Wolfe opened it to see a gnome disguised in a robe, and behind him, a very tall man with dark skin stood menacingly. Behind this huge man stood another man and a woman, who looked like American Indians and who stood even taller than the man in front of them. The three larger individuals were obviously Nephilim, who had transformed themselves into human form.

"My name is Yagmur," said the gnome as he bowed at the waist and then gestured toward the large humans who stood behind him. "I am a servant to his majesty the King of the Nephilim and his wife, the Queen.

"My name is Lazarus. Please come in. You are all most welcome," Mr. Wolfe said as he opened the door fully and gestured toward the interior of his house.

Yagmur entered the house with the three massive Nephilim following closely behind. The Nephilim adults had to duck to get beneath the top of the doorway, and they could only enter one at a time due to their girth. The pungent odor that the Nephilim emitted as they entered quickly caught each of the onlookers' attention.

"This is Moab, guard to the throne." Yagmur introduced the intimidating dark colored skin man. "And this is..."

"Yagmur, we can stop with the formal introductions," said the woman. "I am Queen Robin and this is my husband, King Enoch. Where is our daughter?"

Lazarus turned his head towards the kitchen. Laura gingerly peeked her head around the corner to see her parents. "Mother," she said hesitantly.

Queen Robin cried when she saw her daughter. "Come here, child. It's okay, we're not mad at you. Right, Enoch?"

Enoch's eyes held anger and disappointment that his daughter had run off, but his heart said otherwise. "Laura, we're not mad at you. Please, come here."

Laura ran to her father's outstretched hands. With each footstep that fell, the sound of dishes in the cupboard could be heard clanging against one another. "I'm so sorry I ran away, father," she cried.

"It's okay, Princess. You're safe now. You're safe." King Enoch said as he lovingly hugged his daughter. His bodyguard, Moab, discreetly nudged the king, gesturing for Enoch to look at Laura's ankle. It had a large scar on it where the trap had closed down on her. "What happened to you? Are you in pain? Has a Calvo done this to you?"

"I'm all right, papa," said Laura. "These two young humans saved my life," Laura nodded toward Jacob and Bina as she continued. "I was being chased by hunters, and I stepped into a trap. If it weren't for them, I could've been killed. This is Jacob and Bina, and I don't think they like it when we call them Calvos. They like to be called people."

"Is this true, children?" asked Queen Robin as she

turned her attention to Jacob and Bina. "You saved our baby's life?"

"It was the least we could do," Bina answered. "I'm sure she would have done the same for us if we were in her situation." She smiled warmly at Laura and Queen Robin took her turn to hug her daughter tightly.

Jacob and Bina were standing side by side unsure whether they should bow or curtsy when King Enoch stepped forward and threw an arm around each of them, squeezing them together. He lifted them up as if they were toys while giving them a hug that was so tight and the musky odor emanating from him was so strong both were certain they would suffocate. "Thank you," the King said loudly. "The Nephilim are forever in your debt, but I don't think it's by chance that our paths should meet."

"Neither do I, King Enoch," said Jacob trying to breathe in the king's bear hug. "It's too coincidental that my friends and I were talking about the Nephilim just a few days ago."

"You were talking about us? What do you mean?" asked the King as he set Jacob and Bina down, knelt, and looked inquisitively at Jacob. "Why would you be talking about us?" He paused for a moment and looked around. "Wait a minute. In all of the emotion of our reunion with our daughter, I forgot to ask you." He pointed at Shawn. "How do you have the power to go into someone's mind? And, how do you know Yelkie?"

Lazarus stepped forward. "We're going to be straight forward with you. We're not going to hide anything. We are Veritas. Well, all of us except the young girl, Bina. She is our friend."

The King and the Queen were shocked. "Why didn't you tell us, Yelkie?" asked the Queen. "Why didn't you tell us you knew the Verita people?"

"Uhh, ask you did not, my Queen." Yelkie poked his head out from behind Jacob. He had hidden himself behind everyone and seemed to be avoiding the visitors. Moreover, he was avoiding his brother, Yagmur.

Yelkie had not seen the Nephilim or his brother in five years. The last time he had been with them was a horrible night for him and his family.

Yelkie, his brother, and his parents lived in a small hut near the King and Queen's home, deep in a secluded Canadian forest at that time. They enjoyed the hospitality of the King, Queen, and their people, but a group of goblins, who love to eat gnomes, had picked up on their scent. Although gnomes are extremely powerful, their powers are mysteriously weakened when confronted by goblins.

Yelkie's family had been warned by a group of Nephilim that had traveled through their area the week before that they had seen a pack of goblins hunting in the night not too far from the King and Queen's home. Yelkie's parents decided to have each member of their family take turns during the night on watch to keep the entire family safe. During Yelkie's watch, he fell asleep, and the pack of goblins attacked his home without anyone being warned. During the horrible first moments of the attack, Yelkie had awakened at his post as goblins crashed through the front door of the small home. Yagmur and Yelkie's parents were taken by surprise, and everyone scattered. Yagmur fought valiantly before fleeing into the forest to seek aid from the Nephilim. Yelkie had stayed under cover in the trees where he was supposed to have kept watch, and he heard the screams of his parents as they were killed by the goblins in the attack.

Yelkie couldn't tolerate the sadness, pain, disappointment, and accusation in his brother's eyes when they had returned to what little remained of the small house. Their parents' bodies were nowhere to be seen as Yelkie and Yagmur searched in vain for anything that could be salvaged of their former lives. Guilt and grief overwhelmed Yelkie, and that very night he left his home and returned to the Verita people, whom he had known for some time. That was the last time he had seen his brother – five years ago.

Because the goblins knew where the Nephilim King and Queen lived, everyone in their tribe was forced to move to a different location. Yelkie's mistake caused pain for many that night.

Yagmur was still very upset with Yelkie and did everything in his power to not even look in his direction.

"All the stories we've passed down through the centuries had fallen into what we thought were fairytales," said the King. "They became stories that we've told our children at night about times when the Nephilim fought side by side with the Veritas on the battlefield against the Tenebras."

"We have ourselves told stories of the Nephilim," said Lazarus. "Much has been lost over time."

"Our people fight for good, still to this day, but mankind sets traps for us and hunts us like we are some kind of wild animal," Queen Robin said bitterly as she put her arm around Laura.

"People don't understand you," said Jacob. "Humans fear what they don't understand."

"No matter!" exclaimed the King. "We have kept ourselves hidden from Calvos for this long, and we will continue to do the same. But, we'll not stand idly by while evil spreads across the lands. Even from our hiding places in the mountains and the trees, we have watched and witnessed the growth of evil and sin in the world. What spreads in the world around us will reach our doorstep. We will put an end to it all!"

"We are in the same battle you are," said Lazarus. "We have men and women around the world fighting for God's kingdom." Lazarus knew that the Nephilim were brutally slaying evildoers around the world, but he was trying not to be confrontational. "By all means necessary, we must first try to use goodness as our shield and purity as our sword. Violence should only be used as the last resort."

King Enoch laughed. "God? You speak of God? Are you

that blinded that you can't see that God has forgotten about Earth? He has moved on. He's seen what mankind has become. He's done with them. Lucifer is massing his forces, and you speak of peace. Surely, your leader doesn't speak like this."

"Excuse me, your highness," Shawn interrupted. "I be beggin' yer pardon, but ya be speakin' to our leader. This here be Rabbi Lazarus."

"Huh, figures. Pathetic! I see why my people left the Veritas long ago. You and your people are weak!" King Enoch turned to Jacob and said, "I will not forget your kindness young Verita. As I said, I am in your debt, but my stomach has turned, and it is time for us to leave. Take us home now, Yagmur."

The four Nephilim grabbed each other's hands and touched Yagmur, and in a flash, they were gone.

# CHAPTER 15

# A REUNION

That same day, on the other side of the globe, the Archangel Michael was searching for clues to find the Garden of Eden in a remote area of Iraq. The area he was in was a barren desert that hadn't seen rain in months. He had been searching this region for hundreds of years without any luck. He had a hunch that something was hidden in this area of the world that would help him uncover the pathway to the garden, but he had found nothing of consequence in centuries.

Michael was walking through a steep mountainside that he had yet to search. The ledge was narrow, and its surface was slick with sand and shale. Through his struggles, Michael came upon an opening on the side of the mountain. Above the opening, there was a carving. It was extremely weathered and difficult to read, but one angelic word he could understand meant serpent.

Michael had been on his own for so many years, wandering the Earth; fear was something that never entered his mind. He stepped boldly into the passage. It was dark inside, but for every few steps he took, there was a small hole above that went through the mountaintop and towards the sky, allowing some daylight to enter the tunnel. Someone or something had purposefully cut through the mountainside to let air and light into the cave.

Michael was all the more curious. He kept moving forward through the cave. Up ahead, he could hear what sounded like a light wind blowing through a tunnel. He stepped around the rock wall towards the sound and stopped dead in his tracks. He didn't move a muscle. Lying in front of Michael was a massive serpent that seemed to be sleeping. As he examined the serpent from a safe distance, Michael noted not only the unusually large size of the creature, but he also noticed that along its sides it had peculiar nubs where it had apparently once had eight legs. The wind that Michael had heard was the beast breathing. It had massive, razor sharp teeth, with four much larger fangs erupting from the corners of its mouth. Although the dirt and dust covered the serpent's skin, it looked to be shiny, like gold. Each time it inhaled and exhaled, its expandable frill of skin would move in and out from around its neck — resembling the hood that flaps open on a Cobra snake when threatened.

Michael squatted and stepped closer to the creature, carefully avoiding the loose rock and shale on the floor of the cave. Looking even closer at the beast, Michael saw an iron tablet that looked to be broken in half, lying under the serpent's chest, just beneath the blackened and shriveled remains of the front two of the eight legs. Though the danger was obvious, Michael had to see what the tablet was. *Could it be a clue to the Garden of Eden,* he thought. He slowly pulled his sword from his belt and started crawling closer to investigate.

When Michael was about ten feet away, the serpent's nose wrinkled and it made a sniffing noise as its forked tongue whipped out of its mouth to taste the air. It had smelled him. Michael tried to make himself disappear, as angels can do, but there was some hidden power in the cave that wouldn't allow him to use his ability. The serpent opened its eyes and wrapped its tail quickly around the confused Michael—making him drop his sword. He was captured. The beast's head rose up, its midsection remaining firmly planted on the ground, and it shook itself vigorously to remove all of the dirt from its body. It easily coiled itself twice, brought its tail to its face, and glared at its prisoner. "Michael! I knew you'd find me eventually!" it said.

Michael recognized the voice immediately. "Lucifer?" he asked in surprise.

The beast that now held Michael was the serpent from the Book of Genesis in the Bible. Lucifer had created and inhabited it after God formed Adam and Eve. Through the serpent, Lucifer had disguised himself so that he could tempt Eve into eating from the Tree of the Knowledge of Good and Evil in the Garden of Eden – the same tree that God had forbidden them to eat from. By tricking Eve to eat the fruit from the forbidden tree, Lucifer helped sin enter mankind. He had started the flow of evil and sin into the world that could not be erased. By doing this, Lucifer knew he would be able to gain power and mass forces of darkness as the centuries passed.

After He had forced everyone, including the serpent, out of the Garden of Eden, God placed a veil over the minds of all that had entered or seen the Garden so that they couldn't remember where it was located. Some centuries after this, and after Lucifer had massed enough human followers to control, Lucifer had his serpent's cave created so that his beast could safely sleep until the time was right.

The serpent and Lucifer were forever to be connected, so Lucifer could enter and leave the creature as he wished, just as he could with any evil animal or human.

"Yes? You can still recognize my voice?" asked Lucifer.

"That's something that I would never want to forget," said Michael. "Nor would I let myself forget."

Lucifer laughed. "After all of this time, you're still angry with me. Isn't it I who should be angry with you? It's you who sent me here. After all, look at me! Think about where I live. Think about how I have to live. I have to inhabit something or someone just to bring myself to this filthy planet. I don't know what's worse, being on this planet made by God, or being in the entrapment of Hell."

Lucifer wrapped another coil around the archangel's body and squeezed his tail with all his might to break Michael's body.

"I know, brother," Michael said as he struggled to breathe. "There hasn't been a day…that has gone by…that I haven't felt sorry…for what happened that day…in the Royal Palace. Why…why did it have to…come to pass, as it did that day?" Michael had not communicated for years with anyone in Heaven, but he saw the danger he was in, so he sent out a secret message in his mind to one of his closest Archangels. He wasn't sure if the cave's magic would block the signal sent to his brother, but he had to try.

"God didn't love me anymore!" Lucifer shouted through the serpent, his voice echoing in the chamber as it shook dust from the ceiling. "All He wanted was His precious Son and His pathetic humans!" Lucifer hissed with hatred, but he did not want to kill his brother just yet. He calmed himself to learn the things he had long wanted to know. "What has troubled me for all of these years is how your strength grew the day that you threw me out of Heaven. How could an Archangel overpower someone as powerful as me?"

Michael was still struggling to breathe. The serpent's tail gripped him more tightly and coiled tighter with every breath he took. "It was love," he gasped.

"Love? Love you say? Love for what? How could love make you stronger?" Lucifer loosened his grip on Michael so that he could answer. Lucifer was curious. He had loved himself and things of the world for so long. It was all he knew of love.

"Love is the strongest thing seen or unseen in the universe," said Michael after taking a moment to breathe deeply. "All true strength comes from love. Why does a pregnant mother place her baby, who she has never known, above her own life? Because of love. Why does a father discipline his son, even when deep down it breaks his heart? Because of love. It was love that brought the Holy Spirit inside of me that fateful day. It was, and still is, Him inside of me that gives me strength. He is pure love."

Lucifer was confused by what Michael was saying, but he understood the concept of the Holy Spirit because his armies had fought against him since Jesus Christ had come to Earth, 2,000 years before. "You speak of nonsense. There is only one kind of love, and that love is the kind that takes care of yourself. Survival of the fittest." Lucifer started crushing Michael with his tail again.

As Michael struggled to breathe again, he recalled why he had entered the cave in the first place, so he strained and focused to see the broken piece of iron that remained pinned under the serpent's withered foremost pair of legs, but he couldn't make out what it was. It had to be very important. Why would it be guarded by Lucifer's pet if it weren't important?

Lucifer saw that Michael was struggling to see what was under his ribs just where his neck rose from the cave's floor and said, "I know you want so much to know what it is that I have beneath me. I can smell your hunger to know it. I have guarded this last piece to the puzzle since being exiled from the Garden of Eden, and it will be the last thing that you'll ever see."

The serpent's hood of skin flashed open around its neck like an umbrella as it opened its mouth wide. It lowered its tail to toss Michael into its mouth. Just then, from around the last turn in the passageway to the chamber jumped Michael's brother, the Archangel Gabriel. He had been waiting for the most opportune moment. Gabriel forced his blade down upon the tip of the serpent's tail, cutting it off. Michael fell to his back.

Lucifer screamed in agony. He was dazed and confused.

Michael rolled twice and grabbed his sword but was too weak to battle with the serpent. Gabriel threw his arm around Michael and rushed him out of the cave. They could hear the beast approaching quickly from behind. Once outside, Gabriel regained his angelic powers, and he transported himself and Michael to his home in Heaven.

Gabriel laid his brother on a bed. Michael had been weakened by not just the tail of the serpent alone but also by the evil he had been in contact with, which had drained the strength from him. Lucifer's evil had a way of draining love and spirit from his victims. With every breath he took in Heaven, Michael regained strength. The air in his homeland was healing to an angel.

Michael opened his eyes to see his childhood home. It was the house that his brother, Gabriel, and he grew up in many years ago. Memories of his parents began running through his mind. They had given their lives in the battle against Lucifer and his angels that dreadful day.

Michael's father, Orion, was a humble archangel who served the Lord God in humility for centuries as keeper of God's Holy Scriptures. Michael's mother, Adalane, was also very humble. She worked in the kitchen and dining halls of the Royal Castle, making meals for God, Jesus, and the angels of the throne. Lucifer killed Orion and Adalane while they fought to protect the Royal Palace during the war between angels.

A tear fell from Michael's cheek as he recalled the last time he had dinner with his parents. He stared at the dining room table that they had sat at during that meal. He remembered seeing how much his father and mother loved one another, and through their words and actions, they had molded Michael into who he was today – someone who stood for virtue, morality, and dignity.

"Are you regaining your strength, brother?" asked Gabriel.

"I am, Gabriel." Michael wiped the tear from his cheek, trying not to let his little brother see. "Thank you for coming to my aid. You saved my life."

"It's what I'm here for." Gabriel smiled. "I was so happy to hear your voice when you called me. It has been too long."

"I'm truly sorry for that. I didn't mean for anyone to get hurt by my absence. I've missed you and my homeland greatly."

Just then, there was a knock at the door. Gabriel opened the door and knelt in reverence. "Please rise, son of Orion," a man's voice said.

Michael lifted his head to see who it was. Jesus, the Son of God, entered the house and approached. Michael struggled to bring himself to his knee to kneel in respect. Jesus grabbed him and helped him back into his bed. "Rest, Michael," said Jesus.

"He had been caught by Lucifer's serpent," said Gabriel. "He called for me, and I rushed to his aid."

Jesus nodded. "It's been a long time dear friend," he whispered. "I, and your people, have missed you. But, understand, no one holds any anger towards you for leaving. No one. Not even my Father. We only hold love and esteem for you."

Michael cried in response to the love and forgiveness shown by what Jesus told him. "I am sorry for turning my back on those that love me. Please forgive me."

"You are forgiven, Michael," said Jesus. "God knows your heart."

Jesus and Michael were very close friends. This friendship was sometimes looked down upon by higher angels because of the archangels' place in Heaven's society, but there were many similar characteristics in the two that made them enjoy one another's company. Jesus was not one to ever treat someone different because of their place or role.

Jesus knew Michael's heart, and it was because of his

heart, and loyalty to God, that Jesus's tear had been made into the Holy Spirit inside of Michael the day of Lucifer's revolt. It was, and is, the Holy Spirit that gives strength to Michael.

"Have you seen what is happening on Earth?" asked Michael. "Religions that claim to know God have infiltrated the minds and spirits of millions of humans. They kill each other in the name of our Father, but they don't know Him at all. In addition to that, there are people that have no faith in God at all. They think He is just a made-up fairytale. The only thing they believe in is themselves…"

"Michael," Jesus interrupted. "There are also millions of people that do know our plan of salvation. Those, that do love God and the One He sent to them. It is these that I hold faith in. It is through these that mankind still has hope. We can do nothing for those that don't wish to know God or His Son. We have sent prophets. We have sent signs. I have visited them and taught them. If they don't wish to accept our salvation, it is their choice. It is by free will that they make decisions, and it is by free will that they seal their own destiny to Hell or to Heaven." Jesus stopped to look deeply into his friend's eyes.

"We cannot cry for those that have chosen their own path. They laid every brick in their road to darkness." Jesus grasped Michael's shoulders strongly and lovingly and smiled as he continued, "However, we can celebrate in those that have chosen the path that leads to us."

Michael sighed. Hearing Jesus's voice again was very comforting and reassuring.

Jesus thought for a moment. He walked to the window and looked out at the waterfall that rushed picturesquely on the horizon. "The Horn of Truth that you blew the day of Lucifer's revolt, Michael. Have you seen it since then?"

"After the day had ended, when I awoke from sleep, it was gone," said Michael. "The only other time that I have seen it since was when it presented itself to God's servant,

Joshua, when he was at the walls of Jericho. When he blew the horn, the walls of Jericho fell to the ground. That was a great victory against evil."

"I remember that day," Jesus said as he continued to gaze at the beauty that was Heaven. "Now, the Horn awaits another cause. It will reveal itself to someone found with a pure heart at a time of great need. We shall see when and where it will arise again." Jesus paused and then turned to face Michael. "I feel the time is near."

"Lucifer has gained great strength in power." Michael struggled to stand. "He has amassed vast numbers in Hell and on Earth."

"My Father has foreseen this," said Jesus as he held his hands up to stop Michael from exerting himself too soon after his ordeal. "His prophets have warned humans since the beginning to avoid fear, sin, and Lucifer's temptations — to accept God's love and laws. Those who have chosen an alternate path will meet their end, accordingly. The first time I went to Earth was in humbleness and gentleness so that a plan of salvation could be set in place. My words were my sword, used to cut to the humans' souls and teach them the truth." He crossed the room and helped Michael sit back down on the bed before continuing.

"The second time I go to Earth will be in judgment. Heaven's armies and I will come in might and power like never seen before. The sun will be blocked from the humans' sight by Heaven's numbers falling from the sky. On that day, I will not bring the sword of salvation, but the sword of judgment." Jesus placed his hand on the hilt of the sword that rested in its scabbard, which was secured to his belt. "Those who have chosen darkness and sin will be cut down."

He didn't want to hurt humans because he loved them dearly, but he also knew that those that hadn't chosen a path of righteousness and salvation couldn't come to Heaven because Heaven was pure goodness and holiness. Jesus knew deep down that the humans had been warned repeatedly. If they had chosen a path away from God, then they had chosen the path of death and torment in Hell. It was no one's fault but their own.

"When will this day be?" asked Michael, a tinge of strength and eagerness in his voice. "Why don't we go today?" Michael's energy level increased as he grew excited for battle.

"Only God knows the day and the hour," Jesus explained as he patted Michael's shoulder to calm him and show his appreciation for Michael's valor. "His omnipotent plan is the only plan."

"Jesus, you know Lucifer and his followers are searching for the Garden of Eden, right?" Michael asked with concern.

"Yes. I have had this discussion with my Father. We remember the day we created the Garden, and how you warned us of the two Trees' capability to transport Lucifer back to Heaven. Whatever steps that can be taken to secure the Garden's whereabouts have been taken. However, if he and his army somehow are able to get back into Heaven our armies stand ready to defend our land."

Jesus could sense that Michael was thinking about his descendant, Jacob. "The boy looks so very much like your son."

"I know. I think the same. I visit my wife and son once a month in the human spirit kingdom. I pray one day we may be reunited."

"We shall see God's plan, soon enough," Jesus said in a comforting tone as he patted Michael's shoulder again.

Michael was thinking that because he was in Heaven now, Jesus would not allow him to return to Earth. He was saddened about not being able to help Jacob.

"As for now…" Jesus started. "You are free to return to Earth. This time, with my and my Father's blessing."

Michael rose quickly and hugged Jesus. "Thank you. Thank you. I will help to glorify your name and kingdom."

"I know you will, Michael." Jesus placed his hands on Michael's shoulders and looked him in the eyes. "Just remember, your descendant can only fulfill who he needs to become through adversity. It is through trials that he will grow in faith and strength. Even in as much as a parent loves his child, sometimes, not helping them and letting them struggle through a situation is the most beneficial." Jesus held Michael's face in his hands lovingly as their eyes met.

"I understand," Michael said as he sat back down on the bed heavily.

Before leaving, Jesus instructed Gabriel to let Michael rest before returning him to Earth.

# CHAPTER 16

# THE DANCE

That week at St. Charles High School, Jacob, Bina, and Felix joined the other members of the high school band each day after school to practice for the upcoming Homecoming dance. During practice, Felix was being Felix and took every opportunity to play jokes on others in the band. Jacob made Bina promise that she would not throw her music book at Felix's head each day, even when he was at his worst. Because they were the lead vocalists, Bina and Felix had to work side by side in practice. Jacob would act as the mediator when the two became confrontational.

During lunch each day, Jacob and Bina would place bets on who was going to ask whom to the dance that Saturday. They would giggle as nervous boys and girls would stare at their victims and search for the most opportune moment to dive in for the kill. However, Jacob and Bina could feel nothing but pity at the numerous shutdowns that were thrown at many of the eager askers.

Because everyone in the high school thought Jacob and Bina were an item, no one bothered asking either one of them to the dance. Ironically, Jacob and Bina didn't have any thoughts of the dance as being what it was — a dance. All they pictured of the event was a musical performance. Nothing about holding someone of the opposite gender closely while swaying in rhythm to the music had ever entered his or her thoughts.

The week passed by quickly. On Friday night, in Heldago, Jacob was casually talking with some of his Clevan classmates about the Homecoming dance. He had just finished religion class with Father Santiago and was talking about playing his trumpet when Luke Cartwright asked, "So who's your date?" Luke's general demeanor and personality lacked tact.

"My date?" Jacob looked puzzled. "I don't have a date; I'm playing in the band. What would I need a date for?"

"Is the band going to play for the whole dance?" asked Luke.

"Well, no. We play for the first half of the dance, and then, a DJ will play music for the second half."

"So what are you going to do during the second half? Play paddy cake?" Luke laughed. "You need yourself a date, my friend. You do know how to dance, right?"

"Umm, well, I…" Jacob stuttered.

"Your answer is very reassuring!" Luke joked. "Maybe you should just head home after playing in the band."

Jacob had never danced before, let alone been to a dance before. He became very nervous as the other students left the room – everyone, except Jezebel. "Jacob, I could show you how to dance. If you'd like?" asked Jezebel.

It was no secret that Jezebel had a crush on Jacob. Everyone could see it, except Jacob, of course. He was clueless when it came to girls. Jacob still had somewhat of a deer in the headlights look about him, so Jezebel asked, "Did you hear me, Jacob?"

"Uhh, yeah," said Jacob. "Do you think you could give me some pointers?"

"Definitely!" Jezebel led Jacob to Shir's music studio. She pulled out an old vinyl record – just one of many that Shir had stacked on a shelf and placed it on the record player. The music started, and Jezebel approached Jacob, who was standing a little too stiffly, nervous about what was to come next.

He didn't know which was more sweaty, his forehead, his armpits, or his hands. Jacob tried to work up enough saliva in his mouth to swallow, but his tongue stuck to the roof of his mouth. "Aokr, les dofis…" Jacob mumbled.

"Que? I'm sorry, what was that you said?" Jezebel looked puzzled.

Jacob struggled to find some inkling of spit to wet his mouth and remove the tongue that had found refuge on its roof. "Okay. Let's do this," he repeated, somewhat confidently.

Jezebel guided Jacob's hands to her waist, and she put her hands on his shoulders. Jacob began to see a mixture of white and black spots before his eyes. He thought he was going to pass out. Jezebel gave instructions on how to keep time to the music, swaying back and forth. All the while, Jacob was thinking about fishing so that he didn't fall over from a lack of blood flow to his brain.

After three songs, Jacob was relieved when he was able to separate from the closeness of a slow dance song when Jezebel put on some music that was upbeat. "Just let your body go naturally. Feel the music." Jezebel instructed while dancing.

Jacob decided to let loose a little. *This is easy enough,* he thought. *I can do this.* Jacob danced. Well, if you want to call it that. At least, he thought, he was dancing. Others probably would have labeled it an epileptic seizure, which would have been quickly followed up by a call for help to 911, while others may have skipped the formalities and just thrown him to the ground to perform CPR.

Jezebel had to giggle, but Jacob didn't hear. He was too focused on throwing his body into convulsions. She slowed Jacob down by grabbing his hand. "Sometimes, in dancing, less is more, Jacob," she instructed. "Just small motions with your arms and feet like this are more appropriate."

Jacob began mimicking Jezebel with a more slow and

controlled approach. He was dancing, and it felt great. They began laughing and really enjoying one another's company. Jacob was grateful for his friend.

Meanwhile, at Bina's house, she was doing the same thing that all of the other high school girls were doing at this time – trying on clothes. It is a well-known phenomenon that somewhere around 14 years of age people of the female gender grow a group of neurons in their brain that blocks out all visual awareness when they step into their closet. It's called, 'I don't have anything to wear syndrome,' and Bina had just contracted the malady.

She had tried on seven different outfits, and nothing was right. She wasn't consciously thinking about it, but somewhere deep inside in her female brain was a yearning to be seen as beautiful, which is something all women want. It wasn't just a desire to be viewed as beautiful on the outside, but the inside as well. Bina was no different. She was becoming a woman, so finding the perfect outfit was something that helped to fill this calling. It wasn't as if she was consciously trying to impress someone; she just felt the urge to look dazzling.

Bina heard a knock at her door. It was her mother. "I have something for you," Rebecca said through the closed door.

"Come in," Bina whined.

Rebecca held up a beautiful long black dress as she entered. "If you like this, you can have it," she said. "I was your size when I wore this last. It was the dress I wore on your father's and my first date. It was part of the first stepping stone in my wonderful life, and maybe now it could be yours." Bina's mother beamed a smile and then her face twisted into a look of sheer horror at the mess of clothes strewn about her daughter's room.

A tear fell from Bina's eye. "I love it. Let me try it on." Bina grabbed the dress and stepped into her closet. A moment later, she stepped out bright-eyed and gleaming from every pore. The dress fit perfectly. She spun around in front of the full length mirror on the closet door and jumped into the air.

The door opened, and her dad stuck his head through the small opening. He stared at his daughter in disbelief. She had grown up. "You look as beautiful as your mother did when she wore that dress," said Levi. He smiled sadly yet proudly.

Bina ran to her father and jumped into his arms. "I'm so happy that you are here, father."

"I am too, princess. There isn't anywhere else in the world that I would rather be." Levi was still regaining his strength from his demon possession and hadn't returned to work yet, but he was enjoying every chance he had to spend time with his wife and daughter.

Jacob and Bina did their best to get some sleep that night. Both of them were very excited for their first dance. They met late that Saturday afternoon to go watch the Homecoming football game. They had never been to a football game before, so it was a new experience to see the players on the field and the fans that filled the stands.

Felix was a wide receiver on the football team and was playing very well. However, Jacob was the only one at the game that could tell that Felix was cheating. He was using his powers to make the occasionally poorly thrown ball come to his hands for a big play. Felix would also make the would-be tackler trip just before he was about to tackle him. He did these things just often enough so that no one would catch on, so he could still look like a superstar.

After a big win by their high school, Jacob and Bina went home and changed into their formal clothes. Jacob's mom took about 100 pictures after he was all dressed up. She was so proud. Jacob and Sarah stepped into their rusty old car to drive to the dance. Sarah tried turning the key, and nothing. It wouldn't start. Jacob looked at his watch.

"You'd better just walk, sweetheart," said Sarah. "But

please be careful. It's getting dark out."

"Nothing to worry about, mom" Jacob reassured. "I'll be fine." Jacob grabbed his trumpet case and started rushing towards the school. He didn't know it, but he was being watched. When Jacob came around the row of bushes at the end of the block, he was jumped by three large men. One of the men shoved a towel in Jacob's mouth so that he couldn't yell for help. It all happened so quickly that Jacob did not have time to react.

The men pulled Jacob into a nearby shed. Jacob could now see their faces, and he recognized one of them as the man who nearly caught them as they helped Laura escape the trap a week before. He realized that these were the men chasing the Nephilim princess, Laura. "I've been looking for you! Now, where did you put that Big Foot that I trapped? You stole it!" the man Jacob recognized yelled as he pointed his finger in Jacob's face.

One of the men that was helping said, "Hank, this better work out. I ain't goin' to no jail for no kidnapping."

"Hush you!" shouted Hank, who was the man that Jacob had seen in the woods the week before. "I told you already. This is the boy that took that Big Foot. I'm sure of it. I saw him jump through a hole in the air with it."

Hank's friends didn't really believe him, but they were playing along with what seemed like a charade, hoping that he would come to his senses after he got a chance to talk to the boy he was accusing.

"Now, where is it? Where's my Big Foot?" Hank put a knife to Jacob's throat. "I'm gonna take this here towel out of your mouth, and if you so much as yell one syllable, I'm gonna cut your throat. You hear?"

Jacob nodded.

"I don't know what you're talking about, sir," Jacob stuttered after Hank removed the towel from his mouth.

Hank slapped Jacob across the cheek. "Don't you lie to me, boy! I saw you with your girlfriend and how you stole my Big Foot. Where did ya put it?"

Jacob was seeing stars from the slap across his face and tried to regain focus.

"Go easy, man. He's just a boy," said one of the men.

"You shut up!" Hank shouted. "Now, how'd ya like it if we took a little visit over to your mom's house? See if we could slap some answers out of her?"

Jacob's blood began to boil. His mother had been threatened. He couldn't control it. His skin and eyes began to glow red-hot. The two men that were holding him had to let go because Jacob's skin was burning their hands. "Let's get outta here," said the two men, running out the door of the shed.

"Get back here you two buffoons!" Hank ordered. "It's just simple backyard magic tricks. Ain't it boy?" Hank stepped a little closer to Jacob's face.

Jacob put his chin down and closed his eyes. The fire inside of him was growing like a spark in a dried up forest. Jacob didn't have his sword with him as he usually did, or he would have already cut Hank's head off. Jacob opened his eyes. For the first time, the man became frightened as he saw the growing darkness in Jacob's eyes. They were as black as the darkest night.

"What are you?" Hank asked. He began to shake as Jacob's eyes pierced through the core of his soul. "I didn't really mean what I said. I was just..."

Fire shot from Jacob's hands and landed directly on Hank's chest, making him fly back into the wall. He gasped for air. Jacob began to speak, but his voice was much deeper and sinister. "If I see you again, you will die!"

Hank struggled to lift himself off the floor and ran out of the shed as fast as his weakened legs would carry him.

A few moments later Jacob, regained consciousness, but he was dazed and confused. He couldn't remember anything after being pulled into the shed by the three men and recognizing one of them. Shaking his head back and forth, he tried to focus. Jacob looked at his watch. "The dance is about to start," he screeched.

At the high school gym, Bina was warming up with other members of the band. She had just taken a drink of water and was practicing her first song when she felt something in her throat. Her voice began to crack, and then all of the sudden, it dropped very low. So low, she could sing bass in a men's vocal choir. Bina became very nervous. Thankfully, no one had heard the odd change as she warmed up, but someone had done something to her water that changed her voice into a man's.

*I can't sing like this,* she thought. She ran to one of the changing rooms and locked herself in.

A few minutes later, Jacob arrived. He began frantically searching for Bina. One of the stagehands saw that he was looking for her and pointed to the room he had seen her enter.

Jacob knocked on the locked door, "Bina, are you in there? Our first song is about to start." He heard some mumbling on the other side. "Are you okay? Open the door."

The door unlocked. Jacob entered. He saw Bina sitting on the floor, crying. "What's the matter? Why aren't you coming out for the start of the dance?" Jacob asked in a panic.

Bina didn't answer. She continued to cry into a towel and shook her head violently in response to Jacob's quick interrogation.

"Why aren't you talking?" Jacob asked, getting more worried by the moment. First he got to the dance nearly too late, and now his best friend seemed to be suffering from some kind of extreme episode of stage fright. He knelt down and touched Bina's shoulder and asked again, "Are you okay, Bina? Why aren't you talking?"

Bina looked at Jacob and said, "Because my voice... It sounds like this."

Jacob was thrown back for a moment in surprise and stood up as he recoiled from the voice that was not the voice of his friend. "What the...Bina? What happened to your voice?"

"I don't know. A few minutes ago, I just went from soprano to bass. I can't go out there like this," Bina whimpered in her new deep, Johnny Cash sounding bass. "The school will laugh at me until I graduate in four years."

"It's gonna be all right," Jacob said in an attempt to comfort her. "I'll be right back."

Jacob returned a few moments later with Mr. Wolfe, who was helping to chaperone the dance. "Okay. Now, what seems to be the problem here?" Mr. Wolfe asked.

"My voice is the problem!" Bina snapped in a voice that was even deeper than moments before when she had spoken with Jacob.

Mr. Wolfe's eyes grew large. "I see. Let me have a look inside your mouth."

Bina opened her mouth and Mr. Wolfe saw that the back of her throat was blackened. "Have you recently had anything to drink?"

Bina handed the bottle of water that she had been sipping from over to Mr. Wolfe. He smelled it. "Just as I thought. Someone has put a curse on your water. Jacob, grab me a fresh bottle."

Jacob grabbed a bottle and quickly returned. Mr. Wolfe held the opened bottle in his hands and began citing a prayer, while breathing the words onto the water. "Here, drink this quickly, before the curse becomes permanent."

"Permanent!" Bina shouted, her eyes growing as large as dinner plates. She grabbed the bottle from Mr. Wolfe and drank the entire bottle in one breath. "Is my voice back?" Her question came out crystal clear, in her own voice, answering her own question.

"Hmm. I'll give you one guess who could have possibly changed your water," challenged Jacob.

"Felix. Felix Matthews. I'm gonna kill him!" Bina ground her teeth together, sprang to her feet, and began to run out the door.

Jacob grabbed her arm. "Bina, wait. I have a better plan." Jacob quickly gave his idea to Mr. Wolfe and Bina.

Jacob and Bina ran out to the stage where the rest of the band was waiting. "Nice of you to show up. Everything okay?" asked Felix as a sneer spread across his face.

"Oh, just fine," Bina answered. "Just wanted to make sure my face and hair were just perfect for our big debut." She smiled and flipped her hair playfully.

Felix was shocked. He had expected Bina's voice to be changing by now.

They started into their routine and playing for the dance. With each song that passed by Felix grew angrier. *Why isn't the curse working?* he wondered. His thoughts were quickly interrupted when he noticed that the senior girl, Lynn, who he had joined the band for, was staring at him. Now, he was all about impressing her.

Halfway through the performance, they finished their first set and took a break in songs so that the band could get a drink and use the restroom.

Felix rushed over to the table that held bottles of water, and grabbed one that had his name on it. He saw Bina's water bottle on the table. *She hasn't drunk it yet,* he thought. "Hey guys, there's free water over here with our names on them," he yelled out to everyone and pointed.

The band grabbed their water bottles with their names on them, including Felix, and they began taking a drink. Felix saw Bina tilt her head back for a drink and chuckled, as he took a drink from his bottle.

"Something funny?" asked Bina.

"Oh no, nothing at all," Felix smirked.

After the break, the band went back to their performance. Felix was so excited to hear Bina sing, he could barely keep it a secret. "Hey, pay special attention to this next song," he shouted to a group of his friends.

They started playing the popular rock song with Felix and Bina on lead vocals and Jacob in the background on his trumpet. Felix would occasionally glance over at Bina, waiting for her voice to drop, but he directed his confident stare mostly at the one he wished to impress, Lynn. Halfway into his solo part of the song, Felix's voice rose so high that it made many of the dancers throw their hands over their ears. He sounded like an emasculated Mickey Mouse.

Jacob and Bina had asked Mr. Wolfe to put the opposite effect on Felix's water. Felix was in shock but kept singing. With each chorus line, he thought his voice would go back to normal, but it didn't. He sounded like a boy struggling through the worst puberty induced change of voice imaginable. Felix didn't know what to do. If he stopped singing, he would be a coward, but if he kept singing, he would be humiliated by his voice. He decided just to keep singing.

By this time, all of the dancers had stopped dancing and were staring at Felix. His voice was so high and squeaky that everyone in the room could do nothing but point fingers and giggle. Bina and Jacob almost felt sorry for him – almost!

The song came to an end, and Felix's cold, pale face was emotionless. He stared hopelessly at the crowd, who were now doing the same. Felix slowly moved his stare downward at Lynn. She couldn't hold it in any longer. Lynn broke the awkward silence in the room with an outburst of laughter. Soon, everyone joined her – everyone, except Felix! In his embarrassment, he screeched something in the microphone that sounded like, "I seem to be having some issues with my voice. I need to go now," and he rushed off the stage.

"Well then… I hope that he'll be okay," said Bina into the microphone. "We have a couple more songs for you, and then we'll be switching the music over to the DJ."

Jacob and the band finished playing and then cleared the

stage. He was nervous. Who would he ask for his first dance? Bina thought for certain it would be her. After all, Jacob and Bina spent almost every waking moment together. Why wouldn't they share this special moment together? They walked down to the dance floor and stood awkwardly next to the juice bowl. Fidgeting with his drink while the song played was all that Jacob could do. He was thinking about who to ask to dance, all the while, with Bina standing right next to him — waiting for a gesture or invitation.

Bina had enough of Jacob's non-committal attitude. She was about to take control of the situation and ask him to dance, when she noticed Jacob staring toward the entrance. "Who's that?" he asked. Bina snapped her head toward the entrance in interest. "Is that... Jezebel?"

It was her. She was dressed in a long beautiful white dress. Jezebel looked amazing. Many in the room took notice and stared. Bina wasn't one to normally become jealous, but she couldn't help it. Some kind of weird female gene inside of her was taking over.

Jezebel walked toward the two. "Hola, Jacob. I hope you don't mind that I came to your dance," she said. "I asked Rabbi Lazarus if it would be okay, and I had a gnome drop me off down the street. I'm not imposing, I hope."

Bina was just about to answer the question, but Jacob beat her to it. "Of course not, Jezebel. You are most welcome," he stuttered. Even Jacob was shocked at how nice Jezebel looked. The DJ's first song had just ended, and a slow song had just started. Jacob's hands were dripping in anticipation. "Would you... Would you like to dance?"

"I would love to," Jezebel said, confidently.

Jacob quickly and nonchalantly wiped his hands on his pants and grabbed Jezebel's hand. He nervously led her onto the dance floor. They started dancing just as they had practiced. "Thank you for coming," said Jacob. "It means a lot."

"It's my pleasure. I didn't want to miss your first

dance." Jezebel held Jacob tightly around his neck.

Bina didn't know if she was going to cry or scream. She was hurt.

Many in the room who had noticed Jacob was dancing with the beautiful stranger were asking, "I thought Jacob and Bina were a couple?" A boy named Justin Reardon, who was a tenth grader, caught on quickly. He approached Bina and asked, "I thought you and ..."

"NO. We aren't!" Bina answered before Justin finished asking. "So, are you?"

"Am I what?" asked Justin nervously after Bina's first response.

"Are you going to ask me to dance, or what?"

"Yes, of course." He blushed. "Would you like to dance?"

Bina grabbed the boy's hand and dragged him onto the dance floor, in plain sight of Jacob, of course. She pulled Justin in as close as possible and began to dance. As usual, Jacob was clueless. He was so anxious all he could think about was Jezebel and trying to dance well.

The next three songs went by with the couples dancing and having fun, until Bina attracted Jacob's attention when she started laughing. Jacob hadn't noticed Bina after their band had finished playing for the first part of the dance — until then. He began staring at Bina in her long black silk dress. He noticed how strikingly beautiful she was. It had taken seeing her dancing and enjoying another's company for him to realize it. Now, he couldn't keep his eyes off her.

After the second time Jacob stepped on Jezebel's toes, she got the hint. Jacob was distracted by Bina. She grabbed Jacob's hand and asked, "Would you like to go for a walk?"

"Uhh... yah... sure," Jacob mumbled.

Jezebel and Jacob walked out of the room with Jacob carefully looking back over his shoulder at Bina. She was doing her best not to look concerned. Bina knew Jacob was looking but decided it best not to make eye contact. It had worked. Jacob was the jealous one now.

Jezebel and Jacob went for a walk and talked about many things. Jezebel was trying to gain a closer relationship with Jacob, asking him questions and doing her best to increase Jacob's curiosity, but all Jacob could think about was Bina. "Does she like that boy?" he asked, randomly.

"Que? I mean what? Does who like who? What did you ask me, Jacob?" asked Jezebel.

"Uhh... nothing, never mind. It's nothing," Jacob said as he tried to shake off his thoughts of Bina and focus on Jezebel. "What were you saying?"

Jezebel had gotten the hint. Jacob was embarrassed but didn't know what to say. She and Jacob walked back to the school and said goodbye for the night.

Jacob sat on the steps to the school looking up at the star-filled sky. Bina, who was concerned as to what Jacob and Jezebel were doing, kindly dismissed herself from her dance partner so that she could go outside. She peeked her head out the school's door and saw Jacob seated on the stairs. She tried to pull her head back inside before Jacob would notice but wasn't successful.

"I'm sorry I didn't tell you," said Jacob.

"Tell me what?" asked Bina as she hesitantly stepped out to join him on the steps.

"How nice you look tonight. You look very pretty."

Bina blushed. "Thank you, Jacob. That means a lot, coming from you." She sat down next to Jacob, leaned back, and stared into the sky. Just being next to one another brought both of them happiness, and all of the night's issues and jealousies disappeared into the night's sky.

# CHAPTER 17

# ANOTHER GRANDFATHER

After the dance was over, Jacob walked Bina home. While walking to his house, Jacob saw the silhouette of a man sitting underneath a tree. Jacob cautiously walked past the man while not making eye contact.

"You think you can embarrass me in front of the whole school and get away with it?" the shadow said angrily.

Jacob recognized the voice; it was Felix Matthews. His high squeaky voice was back to normal. "And it was okay for you to do it to Bina?" asked Jacob equally angry at the tone in Felix's accusation. All of the night's events, his temporary encounter with the Bigfoot hunters, the threat against his mother, and his guilt over how he had overlooked Bina at the dance flooded into his mind, turning his gut with the bile of anger.

"I don't care about your girlfriend!" Felix shouted as he stepped confidently into the light of the street lamp, his hands clenching into fists. "You're going to pay for what you did tonight." Just as Felix's face became recognizable in the glow of the street lamp, five of Felix's Clevan classmates also appeared from their hiding places amid the shadows on either side of the street and surrounded Jacob.

"Not man enough to face me on your own?" asked Jacob with as much confidence as he could muster as he glanced nervously from one Clevan to the next. Though he tried to mentally prepare himself for whatever might happen next, his primary concern for the safety of his mother or Bina flooded his mind, confusing him and his Heldago training. The Clevan test had been just him against dummies, inanimate obstacles, and Don's flames…he didn't have to add the safety of a friend or loved one to his strategies for success.

Felix laughed. "Famous last words, you filthy Verita!" The boys grabbed Jacob and held his arms before he could clear his mind and think of a plan for escape. Felix began viciously punching and kicking his enemy. Within the first few solid strikes, Jacob lost the strength to stand any longer, but the boys held him upright so that Felix could keep hitting him. Jacob's pain and agony showed not only on his battered face but also on his shirt, which was covered in blood. He tried to focus, but as Jacob tried to see clearly through the blood that flowed into his eyes from the cuts and abrasions on his brow, Felix threw his elbow directly into Jacob's forehead, knocking him unconscious. The boys holding Jacob let him fall to the ground.

Felix's sword flashed into his hand, and he raised it for the final stroke as he bent down to grab Jacob by his hair to lift his head from the pavement. His friend, Diablo, stopped him by grabbing his right wrist and asked, "Didn't Prince Muammar command that no Tenebra kill Jacob Jerlow?"

"We will tell the Prince that Jacob died in an accident," Felix spat back at Diablo, yanking his wrist free and holding the point of the sword at his friend's neck. "We'll cover it up. No one disrespects me like he did tonight and gets away with it." Felix angrily shook Jacob's limp head by the fistful of hair he held tightly as his spoke.

Felix turned his attention back to his unconscious victim, and raised his sword to remove Jacob's head. A sudden flash of black robes blindsided Felix from behind, and he was thrown to the street. Felix was furious. He sprang up from the cold pavement, turned, and raised his sword to strike his unknown attacker. The mysterious man threw out his hand from the long sleeve of his robe — throwing a curse at all of the boys at the same time. In the blink of an eye, before any of the young Clevan Tenebras could react to the sudden and unexpected attack on their friend, Felix, or defend themselves, black smoke shot forth from the man's fingers forming tendrils that snaked out to each of the boys and wrapped around their throats, strangling them in its evil. They all fell to their knees, choking and gasping for breath as their fingers tried futilely to pry the tendrils from their necks. The thickest tendril of the curse – nearly as thick as a man's upper arm – stretched and curled forth from the shadowy man's palm, wrapping itself around Felix's entire body and throat like an anaconda, constricting Felix so that he laid on the street unable to struggle at all as the curse squeezed all oxygen from his lungs. The man in robes held his hand and the curse as the young Clevans fell to the street, rolling and writhing as they struggled to breathe. The boys' faces turned from red to a ghastly purple, and one by one their struggles weakened and ceased. Just when all of the boys faded into unconsciousness from a lack of air and blood flow, their bodies lying limp and motionless on the frosty pavement – just as all of them were about to die, the dull grey curtain of death falling before their terrified open eyes, the man closed and raised his hand. As the man stood erect and crossed his arms before him, the black smoke of the curse dispersed and fell harmlessly to the street, creating a frosty film on the pavement and releasing the boys so that they could breathe again.

Felix and his friends gasped painfully and hurriedly to fill their lungs, their exhalations forming small clouds of fog in the chilly autumn night air. Each of them slowly struggled to their feet and stood in defensive poses – Felix taking longer than the others to shake off the effects of the curse. All of the Clevan Tenebras stood or crouched and looked at the man angrily and fearfully as they rubbed at their throats where the deadly fingers of the curse had choked off air and blood. The imposing figure of a man wore a dark robe with a hood over his head. Before any of the young Tenebras could take offensive action, the man pulled his hood down to reveal himself to them. It was Prince Muammar.

"Prince!" the boys said in unison. They fell to their knees again in subservience. Felix, still consumed by his anger and hurt pride, ground his teeth in anger and was the last to kneel before their Tenebra leader.

"We didn't know it was you!" Felix's friends all said in unison, as he growled a similar phrase through his teeth, his jaw still clenched tightly in anger.

"Silence! You fools!" Prince Muammar shouted. He stepped slowly toward the boys. "I think I made myself perfectly clear in my directions that Jacob Jerlow was not to be harmed. Did I not?"

"Yes sir," the boys all replied in unison once again.

"Then, why has the Master come to me this evening and told me of your heresy?" Muammar asked, hissing each "s" in his seething anger as he stopped to stand immediately in front of Felix Matthews.

"It's my fault, Prince," said Felix, realizing too late the mistake of his hurt pride and anger. "I take full responsibility."

Prince Muammar raised his hand and struck Felix with all of his might, knocking him once more to the cold ground. "You idiot! If your grandfather weren't a dear friend of mine, I would kill you as surely as I stand before you now." He paused to think and turned his back on Felix, who was still prone on the street. "I think the leader of this dissent should be taught a lesson," their prince continued as he took a few steps away from Felix. "…but not by me, rather…by his peers."

Prince Muammar turned to face all of the boys and pointed at each of them. "You others," Prince Muammar said slowly and deliberately. "You are to beat Felix until I say stop, or he dies…whichever comes first."

The boys paused for a moment, looking at their friend Felix. Prince Muammar grew angrier. "Beat him down now, or I will beat you ALL down."

The boys immediately moved to encircle Felix, any concern for him disappearing as quickly as the fog of their breath in the chilly October night's air. Felix had just begun to stand and glanced angrily at each of his friends, daring them to strike him, as he took up a defensive posture holding his sword firmly in his right hand. Prince Muammar then pointed his long, bony finger sternly at Felix – its yellowing fingernail stretching well beyond the fingertip like the claw or talon of a bird of prey "And, Felix, if you raise so much as a finger against these faithful Tenebras, I will surely kill you," Muammar instructed.

The fire of anger, pain, and fear slowly faded from Felix's eyes, and he dropped his sword, the metallic clang echoed into the pitch black beyond the dim light of the street lamp. The Tenebra boys didn't want to hurt their friend, but they desired to not be killed by their leader even more. Slowly at first, Diablo punching first, they each attacked Felix. He did his best to show he was strong by taking the punches and kicks, but soon he fell to the ground. He only covered himself instinctively as his friends continued to kick him. As Felix laid on the cold pavement, trying desperately to not cry out in pain, only his hatred for Jacob Jerlow burning and blazing deep within kept him from losing consciousness. He grunted as each blow landed, and his body curled into a fetal position instinctually. Suddenly, the nauseating sound of the cartilage of his nose breaking crackled through his already throbbing head, and the iron taste of fresh blood ran down the back of his throat. Before he could bring his arms up around his head, Felix felt a stab of excruciating pain as one of his friend's boot strikes caught and tore his left ear. The concussion of the kick resounded through Felix's head, sending multicolored sparks and spots across his tightly closed eyelids. Felix felt unconsciousness falling over his senses, and he wondered if this was just the beginning of the torment he would suffer at his master's hands once he died. His friends didn't stop, even though their legs burned with exhaustion. Their choice was to keep kicking the now unflinching body of their friend or find themselves lying next to him in the pooling blood — blood was everywhere.

"Stop!" commanded Prince Muammar loudly.

He stepped forward, pushing through two of the young Tenebras who were panting from their efforts. Prince Muammar lifted Felix's chin, shook the boy's bruised and bloodied head to bring him back from the brink of unconsciousness. When he was convinced that there was a flicker of recognition in Felix's swollen eyes, Muammar growled through his clenched teeth, "If you EVER disobey or make me look like a fool to the Master again, I will personally rip your still beating heart out of your chest and stuff it down your throat."

The Prince forcibly and unfeelingly threw Felix's head to the ground and ordered the boys to help Jacob to his house while Felix was left to fend for himself. The boys carefully carried Jacob the half-block to his house. Jacob was beginning to regain consciousness, so the boys quickly laid him down on the doorstep, rang the doorbell, and ran away, disappearing into the darkness of the late night.

Jacob's mother opened the door to see her son beaten, bloodied, and nearly unconscious. His face was swollen and almost unrecognizable. "Jacob, my son, what's happened to you?" she cried. Sarah quickly helped Jacob into the house, looking over her shoulder into the front yard terrified that his attacker would leap from the small bushes on either side of the front walkway to finish what they had started.

After laying Jacob down on the couch, Sarah ran back to the front door to be sure that she had locked it securely against the horrible, evil world she no longer recognized.

Then, she ran into the kitchen to get a dishtowel wetted with cold water. All through this she was moaning and mumbling to herself in her worry over her son.

As she began to gently wipe the blood from Jacob's face, he regained full consciousness and reached up gently to grab his mom's hand. "I'm going to be okay, mom," said Jacob, reassuringly, though somewhat weakly. "Some men jumped me, but I'm going to be fine. Don't worry." Jacob winced as the cold dishtowel, no longer the bleached white but a deep crimson from his blood, rubbed a cut above his right eye. Though the pain of his head and body cried out for the loving touch of his mom, Jacob focused on trying to explain with a lie to protect his mother.

Sarah was crying and shaking as she let her son take the blood soaked rag from her limp hand to wipe his own face. She jumped up from next to the couch and reached for the phone that was laying on the coffee table. "I'm going to call the police!"

"NO! Mom, please don't!" Jacob shouted weakly as he reached out for her arm. "Trust me…I'm fine," Jacob pleaded, unsure whether he really was okay but certain that he did not want the police involved.

Sarah grabbed the washcloth from her son's other hand and looked at him for a moment to decide whether she should believe him. She shook her head sadly and patted Jacob lovingly on his head, tried to straighten his hair as a mother has a tendency to do, and gently caressed his swollen cheek before turning to go to the kitchen to rinse the bloodied cloth and grab some ice from the freezer. She returned and sat on the edge of the couch next to her badly beaten son, and helped Jacob clean up. She was scared for her son but trusted him when he said to not call the police. As she handed him a fresh washcloth wrapped around ice cubes to hold against his swollen brow, Jacob further calmed her by telling her about his night at his first dance. Even though Jacob was badly bruised and one of his eyes was nearly swollen shut, she could see a spark in his eye, which made her all the more curious and eager to hear about his adventure-filled night. Jacob needed his rest so badly after his conversation with his mother he did not go to Heldago. As he fell to sleep, Jacob worried about not going to training, but he was also thankful he didn't have to explain his cut and bruised face to Jezebel and his other Clevan classmates.

After church the next day, Jacob saw the Archangel Michael standing outside under a tree some distance from the entryway. After taking what seemed like forever reassuring his mom that he was safe, Jacob went outside to talk with his friend and recently realized ancestor. He hadn't seen Michael since his trip to India, so he was excited to see him. Now that Jacob knew that he was related to Michael, things felt a little different as he approached.

"So, should I call you grandpa or grandfather?" Jacob joked once he was close enough to Michael that he could speak without being overheard by other attendees of church.

"I think Michael is fine," he smiled. "Sorry, I couldn't explain that I am your ancestor when we first met. Some things are better discovered on your own. The steps along the path of life build strength and faith. With each step forward, you become who you are meant to be."

"Yes sir," Jacob replied, suddenly blushing as he became aware of Michael's look of concern as he seemed to be examining Jacob's battered face.

"Your face is swollen, been in some trouble recently?" Michael asked.

"Oh, this? It's nothing. I was jumped last night by some Tenebra boys that I know," Jacob replied sheepishly.

"And how'd you get out of that?" asked Michael, his look changed from concern to genuine curiosity.

"Not exactly sure," said Jacob a bit worried. "I was knocked out. They could've killed me, but I don't know who or what saved me. When I came around, my mom was helping me into our house to the couch."

"Interesting," Michael paused and seemed to look over Jacob's shoulder at nothing at all. "I have a feeling that both the Veritas and the Tenebras want you safe for their own reasons."

"And…what of this *Electus* thing? What am I supposed to do?" asked Jacob.

Michael returned from his momentary thoughts and returned his gaze solidly upon Jacob. "It's been prophesied for millennia that my future descendant would become the Electus and would help to bring goodness back to Earth," Michael said with a tone that implied he was reminiscing as he spoke. Then, he put his hands on Jacob's shoulders and looked deeply into Jacob's eyes. "However, trying to decipher who, what, or how the Electus is defined is completely up to you, Jacob. It's your free will and the choices that you make that will explain who you are to be. No one else can make the choices for you. You are Jacob Jerlow; no one else is." Michael smiled and after a moment released Jacob's shoulders.

"I understand what you're saying. I just don't understand what I'm supposed to do differently." Jacob sighed. The idea of being the Electus, and the responsibility, destiny, and everything associated with the prophesied designation overwhelmed Jacob. He kicked at a small pile of browning leaves at his feet in frustration.

"Nothing. You are to do nothing, differently," Michael instructed. "What will be, will be. What will come to pass, will pass. Follow your heart with God as your compass, and you cannot fail," Michael said as he took hold of Jacob's shoulders once more. "Be wary of what your mind asks that is contrary to God's laws because one can only serve one master. Either you serve God and His goodness, or you serve evil. This simple choice has always been the truth, and forever will be." Michael again released Jacob's shoulders once he was convinced that Jacob understood.

Jacob could tell by Michael's tone and posture that he

was preparing to leave. "Have you been the one who talks inside of my head?" asked Jacob quickly before Michael could disappear on him again.

"Talks inside your head? What do you mean?" Michael asked, genuinely curious again.

"Yeah, sometimes, when I'm really in need of something, someone talks to me inside my head. I'm the only one that can hear him. I figured that it was you."

Michael looked puzzled. "Hmm. No, that isn't me. Maybe, your conscience speaks a little louder than most."

Jacob was a bit surprised but shrugged his shoulders. He knew that the voice that he had regularly heard in his head wasn't just his mind or conscience, but since Michael didn't know what he was referring to, he dismissed it to ask about something that mattered more at the moment. "Are you going to help me find the Garden of Eden?"

"I will do what I can, where and when I can, but the journey belongs to you. It's your destiny. Be with God." Michael smiled warmly, checked to see if anyone was watching, and disappeared.

Later that day, after he had shared lunch with his mother and convinced her yet again to let him go off by himself, Jacob visited Bina. Bina felt pain just looking at Jacob's bruises and swollen lip and eyebrow, and she was angry at what had happened to her friend, but Jacob's reassurance that everything was okay calmed her down to some degree. They changed the topic and took their minds off everything that had occurred the previous night at the Homecoming dance by talking about their search for the Garden of Eden. They discussed their pending return to the Newport Tower in a couple of months on the night of the winter solstice. Jacob and Bina also discussed Lucifer and his servants' plans and the status of their hunt for the garden. They were worried that as they sat idly by, waiting for the winter solstice to find their next clue, Lucifer was inching closer and closer to the Garden of Eden.

They discussed their fears of what was happening in the world around them and what they were witnessing on TV and the internet. Much of the world was moving further into darkness and evil. With the loss of faith, an increase in numbers adhering to illegitimate religions and sin were spreading like wildfires around the globe, Lucifer had been winning the battle between good and evil for decades. Now, Lucifer's power grew even more; with Lucifer's angels taking over Godless people at an alarming rate, the wickedness, immorality, murder, and fear that they were helping to spread were nothing out of the ordinary to humans across the globe. So many had become immune to the sight of evil that they couldn't see the corruption and fall of the world that was happening before their very eyes.

Many Veritas were doing their best in trying to save as many as they could from the spread of such evil and murder. There were battles that were starting around the globe, and the angelic descendants were helping where they could, but trying to stay hidden while helping humans was proving to be more and more difficult. Meanwhile, the Tenebras and possessed humans were getting more fearless about their secret identity as each day passed, and as their numbers grew, Lucifer's strength and power expanded exponentially.

Even though the prior night was quite awkward, Jacob and Bina enjoyed each other's company that Sunday afternoon and quickly forgot about the stressful Homecoming dance environment or the night's events.

That night at Heldago, Jacob was shocked to see how many Veritas were injured from fighting in the raging battle between good and evil. The injured were mostly Elders, but there were some Moldan students in the mix as well. Some Veritas had already died in battle, causing their numbers to shrink while the number and forces of darkness grew stronger in the spread of evil.

The younger Veritas, such as Jacob and his friends, were

not asked to join the fight yet. Rabbi Lazarus had made the decision that their place was at Heldago, learning Verita ways instead of fighting.

Jacob saw Shawn on a gurney near the infirmary's door where the injured were being treated. Shawn was covered in dirt and dried blood, and he looked as though he hadn't bathed in weeks. The look in his eyes sent a shiver down Jacob's back. Shawn's eyes were darkened with pain and death from the field of battle. An elder was bandaging his arm that had been cut severely.

Shawn tried unsuccessfully to lift himself up to the elbow of his uninjured arm in response to Jacob's presence. "Hey, I be awful sorry I haven't been around fer ya," Shawn said more weakly than Jacob had heard him speak before. "I be a missin' ya lad, and from the looks of ya face, ye be missin' me, too." Shawn chuckled and smiled to try to ease the worry he saw in Jacob's eyes. Shawn's entire body shook with the effort of getting up on one elbow.

"Please don't try and get up. You look good, Shawn," Jacob smiled even though he was concerned for Shawn's condition. "And, yes, I've missed you too."

Shawn gave up trying to raise himself up and laid back down on the gurney as he asked, "What be happenin' to yer face?" Shawn was equally concerned for the young man he had protected over the previous summer.

"You look worse than I do, and you're worried about me?" Jacob joked to alleviate the obvious tension of the situation. "I'm the least of your worries."

"Oh no, Jacob. That not be true. You be at the top of me list. If I…"

"Shawn, it's okay," Jacob interrupted and held his hands up as a signal for Shawn to stop trying to get up. "I just got into a fight with Felix. I'm all right. Please, relax and get some rest." Jacob hugged Shawn gently around his neck so that he didn't disturb the recent bandage. "We'll talk after you're feeling better."

Before Jacob had taken three steps away from his injured friend, Shawn had fallen into a deep sleep brought on by days without rest, his injury, and the medicinal herbs the healers were using on their patients. Jacob looked off into the meadow and saw someone kneeling in prayer. He was curious who it was, so he approached the man. As he got closer, Jacob could tell by the bald head that it was Sarge. He, too, looked beaten and worn down. Sarge's sleeveless shirt was stained with enemy blood, and his arms had recent wounds and scars to match the old ones.

"Jacob, how've you been?" Sarge opened his eyes as he broke from his meditation upon hearing approaching footsteps. "By the looks of your face, you've seen some battles yourself."

"Yes, sir," Jacob answered. "Nothing like you've seen, I'm sure."

Sarge was silent as he stood up and faced his student. Even Jacob could see the emotion and pain building in his teacher's eyes. "War is hell, and hell is alive and well on Earth," Sarge said after a few moments. The disgust, anger, and worry Sarge was feeling permeated every syllable "We knew that mankind was growing further away from God, but I believe that even Rabbi Lazarus is surprised at how many have actually turned to evil. The demons that possess the wicked are powerful, and their numbers are great. With both the Tenebras and the possessed fighting against us, we are greatly outnumbered." Sarge shook his head in disbelief and frustration.

"But, we have something that neither of them has," Jacob said proudly. "God."

Sarge smiled weakly at his student's youthful exuberance and faith. "That we do, Jacob. That we do, but what we must pray for is His help from Heaven."

"God has not and will not forget about us," Jacob said confidently.

"What God needs to do is to stop watching us get

slaughtered and send us reinforcements!" Sarge snapped angrily. By the look on Jacob's face, Sarge knew that he had frightened his young student. "I'm sorry, Jacob. Lack of sleep, injuries, and our losses have made me less than myself."

"I understand," Jacob said gently. "Please, get some rest and know that I will pray for you and our brothers and sisters who are fighting to defeat evil," Jacob said as he left Sarge to recuperate and return to his meditation and prayer. He didn't see, but Sarge looked on in admiration as Jacob walked away.

Jacob left the meadow area and walked to powers class with Don. Jacob still felt awkward around his instructor, ever since Don had gone overboard in Jacob's powers test for the Clevan level. There were still rumors flying around Heldago that Don may be the traitor that had been giving information over to the Tenebras. Some were wary when speaking around him because they were afraid that he might pass along information to the enemy. This distrust was also growing more apparent in battle because no other Verita wanted to be teamed up with Don to fight against the growing evil in the world.

Don began class but was interrupted momentarily by Jezebel coming in a little late. She quickly glanced over at Jacob and took her seat. She was feeling a little uncomfortable, and Jacob could sense it.

This class, like all of the Clevan-level classes, was much more advanced than the Bethel level because the powers they learned demanded more concentration and strength. As they went through some of the in-class testing, Don could sense that Jacob and Jezebel were not quite themselves and were not focused. "I may be old, but I'm not stupid," he said in his strong British tongue. "Jezebel and Jacob, if you don't mind, would you two step outside and discuss whatever it is that you need to resolve?"

"Oh, but sir, we are..." Jezebel started.

"No, no, no, I don't want to hear any of it. Out you go," Don instructed as he pointed at the door.

Jacob and Jezebel walked outside the room and began walking down the hall — both of them searching for what to say.

"I'm sorry…" they both started at the same time. The tension was broken, and they started laughing as their nerves calmed.

"I really don't want our friendship to be changed," Jacob tried to explain. "Who knows what the future may hold, but for now, I really like being your friend."

"I agree. I don't want anything to weaken or destroy our friendship either," said Jezebel. "Last night was fun, and I really enjoyed seeing your school and your classmates."

By the end of their walk, powers class had ended, and the other Clevans were exiting the classroom.

"Everything okay now?" asked Don.

"Yes sir," they both said.

Jacob nodded his head at Don in thanks and wondered whether his powers instructor was indeed the traitor that everyone else thought he was.

The students left and went to history class with Olga. On the way, the others were curious about Jacob and Jezebel being excused from powers class, but no one wanted to pry. No one except the less than tactful boy from New Jersey that is.

"So, you two having a lover's spat, or what?" asked Luke Cartwright. His normal sneer stretched across his acne filled face and laughed as if what he had said was the funniest thing in the world.

Jacob rolled his eyes, but not Jezebel. She was irritated. "First off, we are not lovers. Second, it's none of your business. And, lastly, and I know this is a very difficult concept for you to understand, Luke, but you need to know when to keep your mouth shut!"

The other classmates bit their tongues and an awkward

silence fell among the close group of classmates. Luke looked a bit ashamed and did not say anything at first because he feared Jezebel's skills. After the tension faded, the group began to walk again down the hall toward Olga's classroom.

"Jeesh! I guess love is not bliss," Luke whispered a bit too loudly to Jack and then snickered.

Before Luke could say another word, he found himself face down on the white stone hallway floor with a knee in his neck. Jezebel was exceptional at martial arts and just proved it once more. "I think I made myself clear," Jezebel said, the muscles of her clenched jaw fully flexed and protruding within her cheeks. "You need to know when to shut up!" She pushed her knee even harder into Luke's neck—cutting off the circulation to his head.

Luke was about to pass out, but he mustered enough strength to say, "Sorry! Pareo, pareo!" He wisely used the word that was like crying *uncle* in the Certatim competition.

Jezebel removed her knee and helped Luke to his feet. "Come on. We're going to be late for class."

Olga started her class, but, as usual, was interrupted by questions. The students felt very comfortable with her and knew that they would never get the cold shoulder when they had questions.

Jacob raised his hand. "Olga, why is it that Hell's angels can possess humans, but Heaven's angels can't?"

"Angels were placed under restrictions when they were banished into Hell," explained Olga. "But, because in the beginning God formed a connection between all of His creations, the bond between angels and humans can never be broken. So, with the restrictions, angels in Hell aren't able to freely roam the Earth without taking a host to carry them. However, what's unnerving is that all of the angel's powers can come through the host. Angels in Heaven are not under such restrictions, so they may come to Earth as they wish, especially when they are carrying out the will of God."

"Can angels in Hell possess anyone on Earth?" asked Jezebel.

"No, they can enter only those that don't have the Holy Spirit living inside them." Olga pulled her pointy glasses from her face. "Those that have not taken Jesus Christ as their savior and master don't have the gift of the Holy Spirit, which makes them susceptible to possession."

"There are some in the world that say Christianity is full of hatred and bigotry," said Fred. "Because we say some things are a sin that others say is just normal."

"God made very clear laws and rules that have been sent to us through His prophets and His Son. The laws that point out what qualifies as a sin are clear. God has been very straight to the point in telling us that His rules are not to be broken at any time. Sin is sin. It hasn't changed; only people have changed. Rules are for the benefit of humanity. Who knows what's better for us than God? No one. Does a father show he loves his son by letting him steal without any word, action, consequence, or punishment? I should hope not. He shows love by telling his son what he has done is wrong and disciplines him to help him learn the lesson. No rules, or rules without consequences, which is worse?"

"Why are there so many religions in the world?" asked Luke. "I mean, why is Christianity right, but others are wrong?"

Olga grinned. She relished when students thought outside the lines. "This question has been asked since the beginning, but I feel that it comes down to one thing—free will. There are always other options in life. This road will take you here, yet this path will take you there. When someone truly finds their connection with God, they will be led to Christianity. It's God's only plan of salvation from a life that would be separated from Him."

"So, if Lucifer, his angels, or dah Tenebras get to dah Garden of Eden, they can unlock Lucifer and his angels from their imprisonment?" asked the Jamaican girl, Emily

Helmsworth.

"That's correct," Olga answered quickly. "If they gained the power of the Garden of Eden, they could not only free themselves to come to Earth, but they would also have a doorway into Heaven. They would certainly try and overthrow God's kingdom again."

The young Clevans were nervous about what Olga said to them, but they also appreciated her honesty.

After Verita history had ended, the students were told that due to the recent battles against evil and battle fatigue they would not have sword skills with Sarge, so they went to an earlier than normal fine arts class with Shir. Fine arts class was a nice break away from the stress of speaking or thinking about war and the evil that was seen every day in the world, but everyone worried about Sarge. Though he was a tough teacher and expected a great deal from his swords skills students, the Clevan class knew that he was not someone to be feared but respected. They had all grown fond of Sarge, and they hoped he would return to teach them again soon.

# CHAPTER 18

# A PROPHET FROM GOD

The following days passed with Jacob and Bina's fascination with the international news growing more with each day. They found themselves watching the news every night just to see what war had broken out between which countries, or what world leader had been murdered. Chaos was spreading faster than could be imagined. None of the large, super-power countries, like the United States, had stepped into any of the wars yet, but the rise of crime in even the super-powers continued to escalate at an alarming rate.

The wars that had begun were mainly between smaller Middle Eastern countries, but Israel had managed to stay out of any major conflicts thus far.

Every other day, or so, a news flash would come on the TV about "the gang of rogue religious zealots" that were killing criminals. Jacob and Bina knew that these reports actually referred to the Nephilim, but they had kept their true identity a secret from the world. More troubling though was that as the days passed, the news began taking its concentration off the criminals and the wars, and focusing on the so-called rogue vigilantes. The news was becoming increasingly biased against the Nephilim, and making the criminals look like the victims. Governments and police agencies offered rewards for the capture of the so-called religious vigilante criminals, dead or alive.

Lucifer was again winning the battle that he had been waging for years—that of taking people's attention off true evil and refocusing it on something else. Since the beginning of mankind, confusion between what is truly right and wrong has been the cornerstone of Lucifer's evil plans.

One night, while watching the national news, Jacob noticed a quick piece that came on, showing a man in Jerusalem, Israel that was beginning to get national and international attention because of a miracle he had performed. He had made a woman, who had been blind since birth, see again. He claimed to be a prophet from God, sent to help bring people to repentance of their sins.

The news piece on the prophet was small and presented in such a way as to make the viewer think the man was crazy, but it definitely grabbed the attention and curiosity of Jacob and Bina.

The next night, Jacob and Bina's interest in the prophet they had seen on TV made them decide to visit him in Jerusalem, and the Dalet would make quick work of that. They decided that they should travel to Israel that very night because it was a Wednesday, which would mean that they would arrive in Jerusalem an entire day before Sabbath, which would increase the odds that they would get to see the prophet. Bina reminded Jacob that they would have to leave at about 12 a.m. because of the eight-hour time difference, so they made the plan that Jacob would use the Dalet first to travel to Bina's bedroom and they would use it to travel to Jerusalem from there.

It was morning in Jerusalem when they arrived. Bina knew the area very well and was quick to lead the way. "The picture they showed of the prophet had him standing next to the Wailing Wall, which is the old wall that surrounded the second great Jewish temple," she said as she started off at a quick walk.

Jacob had been to Jerusalem before with his father, but

he didn't know it nearly as well as his Israeli-born friend. As they neared their destination, there were many visitors already pushing their way into the courtyard that leads to the Wailing Wall. The wall was not only a regular visiting site for Jewish priests and Jewish citizens of Israel, but it was also a tourist attraction for people from around the world. The 62-foot wall with its massive supporting boulders was impressive, even to those that lived nearby. The Wailing Wall had been a site for Jewish prayer and pilgrimage for centuries. It is considered one of the holiest places on Earth for the Jewish people.

The surrounding area was loud with people talking, but one voice stood out clearly. A man was shouting at the top of his lungs. Jacob and Bina pushed their way through the crowd toward the man's voice. When they broke through the people, Jacob and Bina clearly saw the prophet that they had seen on the news. He was yelling out scriptures and calling people to repent their sins. He had long hair that was pulled back into a ponytail, which was matched in length by his white beard. His robe was made of wool, and it covered all of his body, except his hands and head. A leather strap was tied around his waist to hold his garment in place.

"That's the man!" Jacob yelled to be heard by Bina above the noise of the crowd.

"Repent! For the kingdom of Heaven is at hand!" the prophet shouted. "You, you who have pushed away the Holy One! Repent! For your father's sins are your sins, and your sins will be your children's sins! You who have been waiting for centuries for your salvation; you have been blind because of your selfishness! The Holy Son of God has come in all His glory, but you turned him away like a lamb sent to the slaughter. And still, to this day, you search the heavens looking for a sign, waiting for the Messiah, but your pride has blinded you so that you can't see that He has already come. Repent! Now! Before it's too late!"

The prophet was speaking specifically to the Jewish

people. He was telling them to repent of their sins and accept Jesus Christ as the Messiah. The Jews did not believe that Jesus was God's Son, known as the Messiah, and they were still waiting for their prophesied Messiah to come.

An elderly Jewish priest, who was known as a Bible scholar in the area, approached the prophet. The scholar wore the traditional long black jacket, black pants, and his head was covered with a white prayer shawl known as a tallit. The man's name was Noam. "Who are you to tell the chosen people of God who we are or are not?" Noam asked.

"You are correct in calling the Jews the chosen people of God, but don't assume that your heredity brings you salvation!" replied the prophet.

Many of the Jews screamed at the prophet. "Heresy!" they yelled. "Throw him in prison!"

Noam was calm and didn't overreact. "You speak as though you have authority?"

"I have only what is given from above," said the prophet.

"And, God has sent you to us?" asked Noam. He was trying to set up and discredit the alleged prophet. However, he also showed interest in what the prophet had to say.

"God knows." The prophet looked to the sky.

"God hasn't sent the Jewish people a prophet since Haggai, Zechariah, and Malachi over 2,500 years ago," Noam explained. By now, the crowd was gathering more congested around the prophet at the base of the wall. They had settled down some and were listening more closely. "And, now, you are here to tell us that we are to believe you? After 2,500 years, just like that, God has sent us a prophet to speak to us?"

"The sins of the Jewish people have been great, but forgiveness is at hand. Repent of your sins and accept my Son, so says the Lord. Rebuild my Temple that you have desecrated. Heal my people." The prophet stretched his hands toward the Temple Mount—where the Jewish Temple once stood.

Noam was growing all the more curious who the man was but wasn't convinced that a prophet from God had finally been delivered to the people of Israel. "Who are you? What is your name?" Noam asked.

"I came in spirit within another, before the Son of Man, preaching and making way His kingdom," explained the prophet. "But most of you denied me, and He who sent me."

The Jews that were there didn't know what the man was referring to, but the few Christians that were present did. He was referring to Luke 1:17 where it says, "And he will go on before the Lord, in the spirit and power of Elijah, to turn the hearts of the parents to their children and the disobedient to the wisdom of the righteous — to make ready a people prepared for the Lord." This scripture refers to John the Baptist. The prophet who called for repentance and readied those Jews who were willing to accept God's teaching of Jesus Christ. John the Baptist spoke and lived through the spirit of the Old Testament prophet, Elijah. Jesus also talked about John being Elijah in Matthew 11: 13-14, "For all the Prophets and the Law prophesied until John. And if you are willing to accept it, he is the Elijah who was to come."

Many of the Jews, 2,000 years ago and still to this day, didn't believe that Jesus was the prophesied Messiah because they hadn't seen Elijah come yet. They were waiting to see Elijah, literally, because of the prophecy in Malachi 4:5, "See, I will send the prophet Elijah to you before that great and dreadful day of the Lord comes." Because they hadn't seen Elijah come to them yet, then Jesus couldn't be the great, long-awaited Messiah. What they didn't understand was that Elijah had come, not in body, but in spirit — through John the Baptist.

"We denied you? When did we know you?" asked Noam. "I've never seen you before."

"I came before the Lord to make his way straight, calling upon Israel to repent and to be baptized, but most of your fathers' hearts were hardened and didn't listen to God. I'm here a second and last time to bring the same message of salvation before the judgment." He was saying the same things that he had spoken some 2,000 years before, but again, the Jews knew the prophecy and were looking for Elijah.

"You still haven't given us your name" Noam challenged.

"I am Elijah, and I do what the Father asks of me."

A loud conversation erupted in the crowd. A younger priest approached Noam and whispered something to him.

"Shh, please quiet down so that I may speak with this man," Noam ordered. "You are the same Elijah from our scriptures? You are the Elijah from 2,800 years ago?

"I am."

Many onlookers began laughing, but not Noam. He took such words seriously but still didn't believe. "Surely, you can give us a sign so that we may believe?"

"Blessed are they who believe with their spirit, not with their eyes!" said Elijah. "I don't wish for any acknowledgment or praise, for I am but a servant of the Lord God."

There was a young priest named Sigmund, who had been watching Elijah since he had appeared a few days earlier. Sigmund was a zealot of the Jewish faith and a firm believer in the extremists' anti-Christian philosophy. He had grown outraged with this blasphemer, who called himself Elijah. Darkness and sin had clouded the young priest's judgment, and he had seen enough. Sigmund approached Elijah from just behind his left side and pulled a stone from his pocket to throw at the prophet's head. His face was flushed with rage as he drew his arm back.

Elijah sensed what was happening and turned to the man to speak. "You are not to raise your hand against God!" As he spoke, each word became fire shooting from his mouth, engulfing the young priest in flames.

All the witnesses present were in shock at what they had just seen. *Who is this man?* they thought.

****

Standing nearly a mile away from the Wailing Wall is a Muslim shrine called the Dome of the Rock. It sits on a location known as the Temple Mount. The building's large golden dome is easily seen from miles around. Muslims built the Dome of the Rock atop the mount believed to be the exact site of the first and second Jewish temples. The first temple, constructed by Solomon around 964 B.C., was destroyed by the Babylonians in 587 B.C. The second temple was finished by Herod the Great around 10 B.C., but it was destroyed by the Romans in 70 A.D.

In the center of the Dome of the Rock is a massive stone in the ground that is the spot where Abraham took his son, Isaac, to be sacrificed — but ended up not doing so because he was stopped by an angel of the Lord. This stone was also in the Holy of Holies in both of the Jewish temples. In the first temple, the Holy of Holies held the Ark of the Covenant, which held the Ten Commandments tablets that were brought down from Mount Sinai by Moses after he spoke with God. The Ark went missing after the first temple was destroyed by the Babylonians and has been searched for ever since.

The Holy of Holies was the most secret and sacred sanctuary in the inner part of the temple. It was separated from the temple by a large curtain. Only once a year, the high priest would enter into the Holy of Holies to place blood from a sacrificial animal onto the lid portion of the Ark of the Covenant called the mercy seat. The blood was poured there for the forgiveness of Israel's sins. Only the high priest was allowed to enter this section of the temple, and if anyone else entered, they would die instantly. The Holy of Holies was a place for God and was extremely holy. Jews are not allowed to enter the Dome of the Rock even now that it has been opened to non-Muslims because rabbis have deemed that entry to the area of the Holy of Holies remains a violation of Jewish law.

The curtain that divided the Holy of Holies from the temple represented the division between man and God because all men, except the high priest once a year, were not allowed into God's most holy house. When Jesus died, it is written, that the curtain that hung at the Holy of Holies' entrance was torn in two by God from top to bottom. This was a sign from God that through Jesus Christ, man would no longer be separated from God's grace. Through man's faith in God's Son they would be united with God and would not be separated from Him by sin or any curtain.

Well after the second Jewish temple was gone, the Muslims built the Dome of the Rock as a shrine in 691 A.D. They built the shrine around the large stone in the earth because it was considered to be a holy site to their faith. First, Muslims also site it as a holy place because it marks the place that Abraham showed his faith in God by offering his son, Isaac, as a sacrifice. Secondly, it is holy for Muslims because the stone marked the location that the Muslims believed their prophet, Muhammad, ascended into Heaven.

It is primarily due to the fact that all three Abrahamic religions of the world – Judaism, Islam, and Christianity – see the Temple Mount and the Foundation Stone specifically as a holy site that there has been controversy over the dome-shaped shrine ever since its construction.

People of the Jewish faith and some Christians today believe that the third great temple must be built where the Dome of the Rock stands today – the same location where the first two temples stood – but if they destroy the Dome of the Rock to build their temple, they would be destroying the third most holy site in the religion of Islam. Such an act would undoubtedly start World War III, so the people of Israel have waited patiently. They have waited for centuries for a sign and a way for their third temple to be built where the dome now sits. The people of Israel also believe that if the third temple is built it will usher in the arrival of their Savior — the Messiah, the Son of God.

Christians also believe that the third temple must be built, but they believe this because it will be a sign that Jesus Christ, the Messiah will be return to Earth to destroy evil and sin. This will be His second coming, and He will judge the believer and the unbeliever. He will cast the sinful unbeliever into Hell and grant the believer passage to Heaven.

****

The young priest lit on fire by Elijah began running towards the Dome of the Rock. Some of his friends followed him, trying to extinguish the flames, but the flames would not go out. Sigmund kept running. Onlookers were amazed that he was able to keep running for so long while being on fire. They didn't know that the fire wasn't hot and didn't burn him; it only scared him terribly. People moved in from all directions to get a better view of the quickly moving ball of fire.

Elijah knelt in prayer. "Father in Heaven. Let your people be witness to your might. Let them know of your salvation. Let the mysteries of old be revealed."

Sigmund reached the Dome of the Rock and began to circle the building. He didn't know why he was running around the building. It was as if something or someone was telling him to do so. People inside were ordered to evacuate and the area was cleared by police. Armed Muslim security men pointed their guns at the priest and threatened to shoot. Upon completing his third time around the building, he stopped at the steps that led to the entrance of the dome and fell prostrate. He begged for forgiveness to God for his sins, and the fire left him as quickly as it had come upon him.

There was an eerie silence. Jacob, Bina, and many others climbed up onto higher ground to better see the Dome of the Rock. The ground began to violently shake in an earthquake. The Dome of the Rock building began shedding its outer walls like a snake sheds its skin. Tiles and columns began falling. The building was tumbling apart, but amazingly none of the building fell inward onto the holy stone in the earth. All of the shrine disintegrated, falling apart away from the stone outwardly.

In a matter of minutes, the over 1,000-year-old building was shaken into mere rubble. When the dust cleared, all of the building was on the ground, but not one piece had fallen onto the holy rock that rested for so many years at the center of the dome.

Muslims fell to their knees and cried at the site of their shrine. Jews were still in shock. Not one person said a word.

The Earth violently shook again. Windows of buildings were heard shattering. The sounds of young children crying in fear filled the air. Approaching sirens from emergency vehicles grew louder. An ear shattering thunder came from the large stone embedded in the earth.

The earthquake suddenly stopped and gave birth to silence. People began walking up to the massive pile of debris that encircled the stone. Many were very curious about the sound that had emanated from the rock and wanted a closer look, so they began climbing over the rubble, ignoring the prohibition of the Chief Rabbinate of Israel against any religious Jew from entering the area of the Dome of the Rock. The prohibition existed because of the prohibition of non-priests approaching the holy of holies, which had been placed at that exact spot when Solomon's Temple of Jerusalem had been built. One of the young priests that had chased after his burning friend saw a large hole in the ground near the rock. His name was Uri. "Look! Look there! There's a hole in the ground!" he yelled in Hebrew.

Some other younger priests climbed down the debris toward the hole. They followed Uri into the hole and emerged a few moments later carrying a large golden box with statues of angels on its top. It was the lost Ark of the

Covenant that held the Ten Commandments and other relics. The large box had been buried in a stone cave by priests before the Babylonian invasion. It had been kept safe for over 2,000 years.

The priests were yelling praises to God as soldiers, police, news agencies, and emergency responders were just arriving at the Temple Mount. The priests carried the Ark of the Covenant out of the debris while singing praises to God. By now, there were hundreds of people looking on. The people of Israel fell to their knees in praise.

The military was blocking off Muslims, who were starting to riot in the area. The Muslims thought Israel had blown up their shrine. Chaos was quickly spreading.

Jacob, Bina, and many others were following Elijah up the hill toward the Temple Mount. Elijah walked up to the Ark of the Covenant and yelled, "See the hand of God!" He pulled open the chest and pulled two large stone tablets out that had the Ten Commandments etched in them. "Oh, you wicked and faithless people! Oh, you who need to see to believe. Where is your faith now? You put to death the only begotten Son of God and celebrated in your sin. Accept Jesus Christ as your Messiah and repent for the sins of your grandfathers and for your own!"

It wasn't long, and the news was casting the events over live television and the internet. Millions of Jews around the world were seeing what had taken place. Most of them fell to their knees and cried out to God for forgiveness. They cried for mercy in rejecting Jesus Christ as the Messiah. The Jewish and Christian faiths were becoming one.

The news was also spreading through the world to the Muslim population. Muslim leaders were calling it high treason and demanding a holy war, known as Jihad. They believed that Israel had destroyed their holy shrine, and the Muslims were sure that the Jews would further desecrate the site by building their third temple.

Mobs of Israelis began filing onto the Temple Mount to

catch a glimpse of the Ark of the Covenant. In the masses of people, Elijah slipped past many of them. Jacob and Bina saw him leaving and followed. When they had reached a secluded garden area, they were startled when Elijah stopped to greet them. "You two young ones are curious?" he asked.

"Yes sir," they said. "Sorry for following you."

Elijah stared at Jacob. He seemed to be reading his soul while listening to God's guidance. His intense gaze turned quickly from that of curiosity to concern. "Ah Jacob, God has seen your future," Elijah said. "Since the beginning of man, only Jesus's temptations during His forty days in the wilderness will compare to what you will see."

Jacob's eyes opened a little wider. "I wish to serve God. I hope I'm worthy."

Elijah grinned. "Fear has conquered even the most faithful. You will need strength, my boy. Where you receive the strength will lay along the path before you."

"I know I've got a lot of trials in my future," said Jacob. "I can sense it. I recently learned that the Archangel Michael is my grandfather. Will his blood give me the strength I will need to fight the evil and the fear in my future?"

"The blood of Michael is strong, courageous, and faithful," Elijah explained. "But it's not his blood that will bring judgment."

Jacob and Bina were confused. *What does Elijah mean?* Jacob wondered.

"Will the third temple be built on the Temple Mount?" asked Bina

"It will be done. God's house on Earth must be rebuilt to bring about the end of evil and prepare the way for righteousness."

"The Muslim countries will try and invade and destroy Israel now that their shrine has been destroyed," said Bina.

"God has protected the people of Israel from far greater threats." Elijah turned and began to walk away. "I must go for now." He stopped just a couple of steps away, and it seemed as if he wished to say more but was instructed not to. "I will pray for you both to the Lord God. Peace be with you," he said as he continued into the streets of Jerusalem.

Departing with questions unanswered was not how they wanted to leave, but Jacob used the Dalet and brought Bina home.

CHAPTER 19

# HALLOWEEN

The next few days after Jacob and Bina's return from Jerusalem were uneventful for them, but the problems in the world continued to worsen. The tensions were especially worrisome in the Middle East since the astounding fall of the Muslim shrine that they had witnessed. It wasn't long after the trip to Jerusalem that Jacob was reminded that Hickson also had some tension, though it was not nearly as political or volatile as the unrest in Israel. Ever since the night of the Homecoming dance, Felix and Jacob had kept their distance from one another at school, but if looks could kill, both Jacob and Bina would have been dead before they had ever settled back into the day-to-day normality of high school. Meanwhile, the seasons had not changed their courses or timing, and the colors of fall took over completely, and Halloween decorations appeared in classrooms, on front porches, in windows, and storefronts.

Felix had been suspiciously distant and quiet in the few weeks since Homecoming. Jacob and Bina had their concerns about why he wasn't his normal, spiteful self, but they didn't want to push the issue. The week after Homecoming, Felix had been absent from school, and Jacob and Bina had suspected that he was on another special "emergency trip," seeking clues to the whereabouts of the Garden of Eden, but when he had returned to school, it was obvious that he had been in some kind of accident because he was still healing. It was hard for Felix to hide the fact that his nose had been broken because he still wore a strip of adhesive that assisted in keeping his nasal passages open so that he could breath. He also had a curious injury where his left ear looked like its top had been bitten off. A few days after his initial return, the story reached Jacob and Bina that Mr. Matthews had given Felix a ski trip that had ended badly when Felix allegedly had been trapped in an avalanche that carried him down the mountain at incredible speeds, smashing him against trees along the way before depositing him roughly on some rocks at the base of the mountain. Each time Felix told the story it got to be more and more of an adventure, and he became braver and more courageous as he faced nature's wrath like some kind of action hero and braved a whole night with a broken nose and torn ear while he waited for the rescue teams to arrive and find him barely alive. Neither Jacob nor Bina believed the tall tale, but neither of them could come up with a better explanation for Felix's injuries, so they let the matter drop.

The day before Halloween, Jacob and Felix were among other boys getting ready for phy. ed. class in the locker room and most of the boys were excitedly chatting about the rumor that their teacher, Mr. Colby, had set up an obstacle course for his students. Again, the look that Felix gave Jacob sent chills down Jacob's spine. He hadn't forgotten what Felix and his friends had done to him after the Homecoming dance, but with everything else that had happened since that night, Jacob had forgiven and forgotten. Felix apparently had not. Jacob sighed in relief as Felix left the locker room, and after the rest of the other boys had left, Jacob focused on the Dalet that stood out on his wrist like a large wart on the end of a witch's nose. He and the other Clevans had been learning a power that allowed them to turn inanimate objects invisible to any but the most scrutinizing examinations. After focusing for a moment or two, Jacob opened his eyes and was relieved that the oddly shaped wrist band that served as an angelic doorway had faded and blended in to the backdrop of his arm. He had told anyone who had seen the Dalet that it was a special gift from Bina from their trip to Rome, but old, Mr. 4x4 had told Jacob early in the year that such a wristband could be dangerous during phy. ed., and he forbade Jacob from wearing it to class, so Jacob had to come up with a way to hide the Dalet when he was in gym.

Among many of the students at St. Charles, the phy. ed. Teacher, Mr. Colby, had the nickname, "Mr. 4x4" because he was about 4-foot tall and 4-foot wide but packed with muscle. He spoke like a drill instructor, so students did what he asked in a timely manner out of fear of being squashed like a grape.

The ninth grade students entered the gymnasium that afternoon and saw that it had been staged from corner to corner with an intense obstacle course. Mr. Colby walked the students around the area while explaining how to conquer each obstacle through the course. "We're going to test your mental and physical strength today!" he barked. "I'm going to pair you up with someone of equal abilities so that you can race one on one. The boy and girl with the best times for the day get a secret prize."

Mr. Colby began sorting through the students as diplomatically as possible not to hurt any student's feelings. He came to Jacob, who had gotten much stronger and confident since the prior year, but Mr. Colby still had in his mind that Jacob was an underachiever. He pulled Gregory Fellows over to Jacob and paired them up. Gregory was a nervous boy, who stuttered and was as thin as a rail.

Jacob whispered to Mr. Colby, "No disrespect to Gregory, but I need someone to race against that will push me hard. Why don't you pair me with Felix Matthews?"

Mr. Colby snapped his head towards Jacob in surprise.

"Really? You want to race against the best athlete in your grade? Maybe the best athlete in the school?"

"Yes, sir," Jacob replied confidently and respectfully.

"I like it. I like it a lot!" Mr. Colby smiled. "Felix. Felix Matthews, come over here. You're now paired up with Jacob Jerlow," He ordered.

Felix strutted casually over to Jacob. Felix's face was finally back to normal from the beating he had sustained by order of Prince Muammar. "Really? You requested to race me? You really are pathetic, you know that?"

Jacob smiled.

After all of the other paired racers had completed the obstacle course, it was Jacob and Felix's turn. They stepped up to the starting line. Jacob stared intently forward, focusing on the course and each of its phases of obstacles. Felix glared in Jacob's direction. He was furious that someone would challenge him in front of the other students. Jacob ignored his intimidation.

Jacob knew that he was going to have to use his powers, secretly, to compete because, without any doubt, Felix would be using his.

"Athletes, to your mark. Get set! Go!" Mr. Colby started his stopwatch.

Jacob and Felix ran over the hurdles and through the tunnel. They were neck and neck at the beginning, but Felix was faster and began pulling away. Felix dived and weaved through the obstructions with ease, but to the surprise of many, Jacob was closely behind. Felix reached the final obstacle first. It was a climbing rope that went to the ceiling of the gymnasium. Mr. Colby had attached a bell to the top of each rope that the climber needed to ring to signal Mr. Colby to stop his timer. Felix wrapped the rope around his foot and began climbing. Closely behind, Jacob reached the rope, leaped up, and grabbed it. With great confidence, Jacob let his feet dangle and started his ascent using upper body strength only. The class was cheering and yelling encouragement at the climbers, Jacob in particular.

Felix looked down when he heard the cheers and saw Jacob closing in quickly. Frustrated and frightened by the possibility of another humiliation as his memory of the Homecoming dance flooded his mind, Felix used the Valoria levitation spell to help him rise faster, but he used it subtly so that it wouldn't be overly obvious. Though the students cheering at the perimeter of the safety mats below couldn't tell that Felix had done anything out of the ordinary, Jacob could sense what Felix had done, but he decided not to use his power. Instead, he became all the more determined. Jacob clenched his jaw, put all of his strength into his grip on the rope, and focused on getting one hand over the other as quickly as he could. In a few seconds, the two boys were tied and only two feet away from the bells at the top of their ropes. Jacob gave one final large pull with his arms, grabbed the bell a second before Felix, and gave it a ring. The gymnasium echoed with the loud cheers of the entire class as Jacob and Felix slid down the ropes. Even Mr. Colby got into the commotion.

"A new school record!" Mr. Colby yelled more in surprise than praise. "Jacob, you broke the school record for the obstacle course!" Once Jacob was safely on the large mat beneath the rope, he watched in shock as 4x4 held out his hand to shake Jacob's. After the brief congratulations, Mr. Colby held Jacob's hand high in the air once more declaring him the winner, and the class erupted again in hoots of praise. Mr. Colby announced that the special prize for the winners was a gift bag that contained a brand new combination lock for their gym locker, a coupon for a free pizza at the popular pizzeria in town, and two tickets to the haunted house and haunted corn maze for Halloween night.

Felix was furious inside, but outwardly, he shrugged his shoulders as if it meant nothing.

Jacob relished the moment. He had never won something at his school before. By the end of the school day, students from every grade were congratulating Jacob on his performance. He was instantly popular.

On the walk home, Jacob asked Bina to come over to review for a Math test. "You're not going to become a snob now that you're popular, right?" Bina joked.

"Nah, but it was fun beating Felix in front of the whole class," said Jacob.

After studying Math for an hour, Jacob and Bina turned on the TV and grabbed a snack. A news flash rolled across the screen, and the regularly scheduled program was being switched over to a live newscast. The headlines that ran across the bottom of the screen read that there was a mob of angry protesters at an abortion facility in Indianapolis, Indiana.

"Lisa Magnuson here, on location at Indianapolis's largest abortion facility where a sizable mob of abortion supporters and opponents have turned away from just a war of words to physical aggression and confrontation," said the Reporter. "Many pro-choice supporters are calling the anti-abortionists *fanatics,* and the pro-choice rioters are blaming the anti-abortion protesters for the violence because they have been hindering the mothers' rights to choose. There has been no explanation for the reason that both sides had more people on hand today, but witnesses have told us that shortly after heated exchanges between the two massive groups, pushing and shoving started. It's impossible to estimate the numbers involved from our aerial videos, but it is obvious from the tension that is growing that the crowd is on the verge of an all-out riot. The city's police force, which has been spread thin battling to keep up with rising crime, is just entering the scene now."

The camera panned across the mob of people. "Wait! Who was that?" shouted Jacob.

"Who? Where?" asked Bina.

Jacob grabbed the remote, rewound the TiVo DVR, and paused it. He walked closer to the TV screen and pointed at a woman in the crowd. "That is the same lady that we saw in India," he said. "She was that Nephilim woman that protected the girl from those thugs. And, look over here in the other corner." Jacob moved his finger across the screen. "You see this woman? Does she look familiar?"

"She's a Tenebra," Bina gasped. "I saw her at the Certatim. "Her name is Li Ting, isn't it?"

"Exactly. I have a feeling that something major is going to happen here," Jacob said. "Halloween is tomorrow, and that is normally a night for trouble. Imagine what it will be like with the world the way it is now, not to mention when there are Tenebras and Nephilim present. We'd better go to this abortion facility in Indianapolis tomorrow night," Jacob said pointedly as Bina nodded in agreement.

After dinner the next day, Jacob and Bina traveled with the help of the Dalet to the site that they had seen on TV the previous day. It was dark outside and the street lights were eerily dim. The crowds that were present in the newscast the previous evening were nowhere to be seen. A thumping sound was coming from behind the abortion facility, so Jacob and Bina moved cautiously to investigate. They peeked around the corner of the building. It was the Nephilim. Because it was Halloween and most people were in costumes, the Nephilim were not afraid of presenting themselves to the world in their natural hairy appearance.

Most of the Nephilim were standing around five bodies on the ground that were covered in blood. The thumping sound that Jacob and Bina had heard was one of the Nephilim pounding a wooden cross into a hole in the ground. By the sounds of the Nephilim's conversation, a battle had just ended, and they were getting ready to hang their enemy's bodies on the crosses being erected.

Jacob and Bina smelled a pungent odor that suddenly became stronger. Then they could hear the breath of someone standing behind them. They slowly and carefully turned around to see the eight-foot tall Nephilim royal bodyguard, Moab, intensely watching their every move.

Moab recognized Jacob from Lazarus's house; otherwise, he would have already ripped them apart. "Come to join the party have you?" he growled.

Jacob and Bina were in shock at what they were seeing. Moab grabbed their arms and pulled them towards the other Nephilim. "Your majesty, we have visitors," Moab announced loudly.

King Enoch turned towards them. His expression of anger shifted into a smile when he saw that it was Jacob. "Jacob Jerlow? You are a young man full of surprises," said the king.

Jacob looked at the dead on the ground. There were two doctors, two nurses, and one decapitated woman that he thought was the Tenebra, Li Ting. "What's happened here?" he asked tentatively.

"We've brought justice unto these that kill the helpless," King Enoch explained in a matter-of-fact tone. He was speaking of the doctors and nurses that worked at the abortion facility. "I wish our numbers were greater so that we could do this across all the land," Enoch explained. "Then, this Tenebra showed up and tried to stop us, and by the looks of her, she wasn't too successful." The other Nephilim chuckled.

"You have killed helpless and unarmed humans," Jacob said emphatically.

The King's demeanor quickly turned to anger. "Don't speak to me about the helpless and unarmed, boy! If I shoved your face into that trash can behind this house of murder and deceit, your sympathy for those you call helpless would quickly change. If you saw the arms, legs, and bodies of the truly helpless, the babies thrown out like trash, would you think the same? Stripped apart, limb from limb – disemboweled! – all in the name of convenience and personal *choice*." The King was spitting with each word that forcefully came from his mouth. "So, don't tell me about the helpless. Who is more helpless than a newborn child, who cannot be heard inside her mother's womb?" Enoch paused, the anger and sorrow creating an odd mixture of tones in his voice as he shook his head in disgust.

King Enoch glared at Jacob and Bina as he continued with the tone that befits a king, "The world has been slipping into darkness for years. Marriage has been turned into a political motivation, instead of the holy obligation sent from God. The world has become a place where good is seen as evil, and evil is seen as good; where speaking the truth is defined as hatred and bigotry." Enoch's tone and demeanor grew angrier and lost its kingly deportment as he continued. "No! We will not be deceived. We've seen this coming for years. Mankind has brought this upon themselves, and now, Lucifer is having his way!"

"I believe that killing the unborn person is wrong," Jacob said timidly, trying to choose his words and tone wisely. "But, killing helpless adults doesn't make it right."

"Well, while you and the rest of this nation stand around and let evil such as this spread and fester, we are going to do something about it," Enoch said with obvious contempt. "Obviously, doing nothing is doing just that. Nothing! So we will take matters into our own hands. We've been silent and hidden for far too long. It's time for the Nephilim people to show themselves and kill all evil!"

"You cannot play God," Jacob replied, his own frustration beginning to resound in what he said. "You're not the judge, jury, and executioner. Yes, help those in need, but what you are doing goes against God's plan."

"God's plan?" yelled King Enoch. "You speak to me of God's plan? Where is God? Have you seen what's happening in the world? God has left Earth. He has left it for the dogs. We must fight for what is good, and if that means killing whomever is evil, then so be it."

"But..." Jacob started. The sound of an empty bottle rolling across the pavement and bouncing off the clinic's wall interrupted the debate. The Nephilim had dropped their guard. They looked around and saw that a group of Tenebras had surrounded them during Jacob and Enoch's argument.

King Enoch pulled his sword out and growled.

The gnome, Yagmur, who is the King's means of travel rushed away as two goblins began flying after him. Goblins love to eat gnomes. In fact, it's their most prized meal. Unfortunately, for gnomes, their powers are almost useless against goblins. Yagmur would have to use his quickness and wits to escape.

The presence of Rico Estrada quickly grabbed Jacob's attention. Rico was the Tenebra that had killed Jacob's friend, Ramiro Vasquez in Italy. "Hi, Jacob. Miss me?" Rico said sarcastically. Rico and the other Tenebras knew not to kill Jacob because of Prince Muammar's orders and recent punishment of Felix Matthews, but that didn't mean that Rico couldn't hurt him. Besides, Rico earnestly believed that the order might be disputable, and he might avoid the Prince's wrath if he killed Jacob while defending himself.

There was no time to pray for calm, and Jacob's anger, which had begun to seethe during his frustrating argument with King Enoch, began growing and spreading within him like a raging forest fire, his recent doubt burning away the withered self-control and confidence like drought dried kindling. He quickly assessed the situation – they were extremely outnumbered, and their outlook seemed grim. Jacob glared at Rico and then moved his gaze from one Tenebra to the next as they stood encircling him and the Nephilim. He recognized all of the Tenebras because he had seen them either at the Certatim or in Italy at the battle between Tenebras and Veritas in the catacombs the previous summer.

During the pause after the Tenebras had revealed themselves, the Nephilim had picked up or drawn their weapons. Some Nephilim, like King Enoch, like to use a sword for battle, while others prefer a large wooden club that is studded with broken glass or steel spikes. They growled and snarled at the Tenebras as they held their weapons at the ready.

"You killed our sister today," Rico shouted. "Now, you're all going to die, starting with…you!" Rico unexpectedly pointed his drawn sword at Bina.

Jacob had nearly forgotten Bina was even there, but Rico's threat caused Jacob's anger to blaze throughout his body. His skin glowed with his power, and even King Enoch took notice of the power radiating from Jacob.

In the shadows, a man stood watching and waiting. The man was possessed by Lucifer. This one man's body had been used by Lucifer since the beginning of mankind. He had lived for centuries, serving his master. Lucifer would come and go as he pleased from the man's body.

The ruler of Hell needed to see something this night, personally. He was patiently waiting and had been for years, but waiting for what? No one knew, except Lucifer.

Bina visibly shook with fear. She could not tear her eyes from the cold steel blade that glimmered in the dim light, which Rico held steadily pointing at her. She reached for Jacob's arm but nearly burnt her hand when it came close to Jacob.

The Tenebras attacked the Nephilim ferociously. Steel met steel as their swords clashed with sparks and loud metallic clangs that resounded in the small enclosed area behind the abortion clinic. Flashes of light from the powers that the combatants directed at one another lit up the dimly lit back alley. Astoundingly, rather than spring into action, Rico very calmly and confidently approached Jacob. He wasn't going to let Jacob's odd glow intimidate him. He flourished his sword dramatically and took up a sword fighting posture.

Jacob looked at the blade, and it brought back memories of his battle with Rico at the Certatim and the night Rico had viciously bitten Jacob's friend Ramiro's neck under St. Peter's Square and drained his life force and blood. Jacob then noticed that Rico's intense glare settled on Bina, who stood just behind and to his right. Jacob drew his sword from his belt and made the blade appear. "You won't put one finger on her," he said defiantly, his body's glow intensifying as his doubt, fear, and anger rekindled the blaze within and throughout his entire being at the thought of Bina ending up as his friend Ramiro had in Italy.

"Ooh, such anger," Rico jeered as he turned his focus from Bina to Jacob. "Are you sure you're not a Tenebra?"

Jacob lunged and swung his sword as hard as he could at his enemy without any warning. Rico easily parried the stroke with his own blade, but the power behind Jacob's strike was so strong it threw Rico backward. Jacob could somehow sense Ramiro's blood running through Rico's body. Rico had taken Ramiro's powers from him when he bit his neck that night under the Vatican, making him that much more powerful.

"I'm going to kill you!" Jacob yelled in fiery fury. He rushed Rico, once again slamming his sword down against Rico's.

Rico was very skilled with the sword. In fact, no one had ever beaten him in practice or in battle, but with every defensive maneuver he tried, Jacob overpowered him. For the first time in battle, Rico started to feel fear and doubt. A blinding blast of light came from Jacob's hand and hit Rico directly in the chest. Rico flew backward once more, landing painfully on his back. He was extremely weakened. The energy that had burst from Jacob was so intense that it emanated from his entire body in waves that struck combatants several feet away and made some of the Tenebras and Nephilim stop fighting to look in his direction.

Jacob's skin still glowed brightly, but he didn't look like himself anymore. His face had changed, and his eyes looked dark and empty. Jacob's consciousness had been taken over by something else. He callously approached Rico with his sword held at the ready. Rico had not recovered from being thrown backwards and was lying on the concrete near the dumpster, trying to come to his senses. Jacob paused for a moment and looked back over his shoulder at Bina, whom he desperately wished to protect.

Bina was already frightened by what was transpiring, but the look in Jacob's vacant eyes made her absolutely terrified. She wanted to call out to him, to bring him to his senses, but the words stuck in her throat under the evil, dead look in his eyes – as if he didn't even recognize her as he glared in her direction before turning back toward Rico.

Rico had come to his senses in time to see with horror Jacob's approach. "Don't kill me!" Rico pleaded at the top of his lungs as he tried to scramble backward away from his approaching doom. The look in Jacob's eyes stopped him in his attempts to flee. "Don't kill me!" For the first time in his life, Rico was frozen with fear. He was so terrified that he was unable to even raise or hold his sword weakly before him in a final attempt to defend himself.

"You have shown no mercy, so none will be shown to you," Jacob snarled in a raspy unrecognizable voice. Jacob drew his sword back and in one unfailing swipe beheaded Rico.

Even the Nephilim were surprised at Jacob's ruthless disdain.

The Tenebras scattered in the sudden turn of events. No one among their ranks had ever defeated Rico Estrada, and they had never seen a Verita kill a downed opponent with such disregard for honor. They were strong when they created fear in others but weak when fear entered their own hearts and minds.

Lucifer stepped out from the shadows and showed himself to Jacob and the Nephilim. A colder dark chill filled the already frosty Halloween's night air. No one knew for certain who he was but presumed he was another Tenebra looking for a fight. Jacob readied himself for battle and took up a defiantly offensive posture over the headless body of Rico as if to dare the newcomer to attack. Lucifer smiled evilly and then vanished back into the shadows of the trees.

The glow of energy faded from Jacob's skin, his face lost its emotionless expression, and life replaced the dark emptiness of his eyes as he returned to normal. "What happened?" he asked, shaking his head as if waking from a dream. "Why is everyone staring at me?" He couldn't remember killing Rico. Jacob looked down at Rico's decapitated body lying at his feet and the fresh, oozing blood on his blade. He became frightened. "What have I done?" he asked, his voice shaking in fear and confusion.

"First time killing someone?" asked King Enoch as he approached to congratulate the young Verita warrior.

"I killed him?" asked Jacob, shocked.

"Yes, and nicely done I may add." Moab grinned.

Bina could see that Jacob had returned to himself and was confused and scared. "It's going to be okay, Jacob," she said quietly as she tentatively reached for his arm. "I'll tell you about it later. Let's go home."

Jacob and Bina began to walk to a place that was more out of sight so that they could use the Dalet when the king stopped them. "Hey, Jacob, when you're ready to come over to our side, let me know," he said, smiling broadly, which was an unsettling look that neither Jacob nor Bina had seen on the King's face before. "Today, you took the first step in the right direction."

Jacob paused and stumbled in his confusion, but Bina pulled him away.

When they got home that night, many of the trick-or-treaters were just finishing their expeditions for free candy. Bina explained to Jacob what had happened during his battle with Rico to the best of her ability. She described the horrifying transformation that overcame him, but she did not fully express her suspicions about what had really happened to him. He was comforted by his friend's voice, but Jacob was frightened by what he didn't understand.

"The night of the dance I was confronted by those three guys that were chasing Laura, and the same thing happened," Jacob explained. "I couldn't remember a thing. It's like something inside of me took over."

"I'm sure it will all become clear soon," Bina comforted as well as she could. "Just keep praying, and God will give you strength." Unfortunately, it was difficult for Bina to fully reassure her best friend when she could not completely reassure herself against her fearful suspicions.

The two friends said goodbye for the night and went home for some much-needed sleep.

The following day at school, Jacob and Bina were stopped by Mr. Wolfe in the hallway. "Come with me," he said. Mr. Wolfe pulled the teenagers into a nearby office and locked the door behind him. "Where were you two last night?" he said as he turned to face them.

Bina looked at Jacob for confirmation and direction about what they would say.

"It's an easy question," said Mr. Wolfe more sternly than they were accustomed to hearing.

"We were in Indianapolis at an abortion facility," said Jacob.

"I thought so," said Mr. Wolfe. He pulled a newspaper out and showed the front page. It had the picture of one of the Nephilim hanging a body onto a wooden cross. In the background, Jacob and Bina could be faintly seen talking to King Enoch. It was difficult to see them, but Mr. Wolfe had picked them out. A passerby had taken the picture and turned it into the newspaper. At first, the witness had thought it was some people pulling a prank, because it was Halloween, but when he saw the dead bodies hanging from the crosses the next day, he knew it was no prank and immediately reported what he had seen and photographed.

The newspaper article demonized the Nephilim for

murdering thousands across the United States. Even though the Nephilim were killing murderers, criminals, evildoers, and the worst of the worst, the newspapers depicted them as being uncontrollable savages that needed to be stopped. There was undoubtedly going to be a nationwide manhunt because a bounty had been set up in many states for as much as $50,000 for just one of the "beasts" to be turned into authorities — dead or alive.

"What were you two doing there?" Mr. Wolfe asked. He was clearly and openly upset.

"We thought we might be able to help," Bina explained weakly. "So we…"

"You thought you could help?" Mr. Wolfe interrupted. "What could you have possibly thought you could've helped with?"

"On the news, we saw a Tenebra and a Nephilim, both of them we recognized," Jacob said as he came to the aid of his friend. "So…Well, we went there to see if we could stop something bad from happening." Jacob felt ashamed under the abnormally intense look of disappointment he saw on his Rabbi's face.

"You can't just go flying around the Earth whenever you want, especially unmonitored." Mr. Wolfe said tersely. He was obviously bothered, but he wasn't about to share whether it was simply Jacob and Bina's irresponsibility causing his concern or something else.

"Sorry," said the friends quietly. Their shame and heartfelt guilt rang true in their voices.

"It's a miracle you both got out unscathed," continued Mr. Wolfe a bit exasperated. "But that's not what's bothering me the most. I sensed a great surge in the presence of evil the night of the dance, and I felt that same feeling again last night." Mr. Wolfe looked sternly first at Bina and then settled his stare on Jacob. "Is there anything that you wish to share with me that may shed some light on these feelings that I've had?"

Jacob and Bina hesitated. Their silence spoke many words as far as Mr. Wolfe was concerned. They were both frightened by what Mr. Wolfe would think of Jacob. "Nothing comes to mind," said Jacob, rather unconfidently.

"Very well," said Mr. Wolfe. It looked like he had more to say, but he kept whatever it was to himself. "Off to class then," he instructed.

For the rest of the day, Bina couldn't get Mr. Wolfe's words out of her head. She really wanted to tell their teacher and friend about Jacob's seemingly troubled and hidden dark side, but she couldn't bring herself to betray Jacob.

# CHAPTER 20

# RETURN TO NEWPORT

Throughout the month of November, Jacob grew more and more troubled inside. It seemed as if something was rising inside of him that he had no control over. It was like a thistle seed had been secretly planted in a field of abundant crops, and it was uncontrollably spreading while devouring the life from the harvest. He tried prayer, but it didn't help. *Has God forgotten me?* he thought. In his daily life, his conscious mind would try and choose actions that were good and righteous, but his subconscious was telling his body to do otherwise. His patience had been lost. His once growing spirituality and faith in God was suddenly stagnant. His love for others was diminishing. More than ever, he felt lost and abandoned by God, and the shortest day of the year, the winter's solstice, and the clue to the Garden of Eden it might divulge were approaching quickly. Jacob feared whether he would have the courage, faith, or guidance to find the clue or to follow wherever it might lead to next. He even began to question whether he was indeed the Electus. *How could the prophesied Electus be abandoned by God? How can I be the Electus if I was capable of killing Rico Estrada without being aware that I was doing it?* These doubts, fears, and worries began to envelope and smother Jacob's confidence, purpose, and faith just as the frost and first snows blanketed and shrouded the recently beautiful North Dakota plains, turning everything into a dull, lifeless, and dreary grey landscape.

Normally, Jacob looked forward to the holidays, but his mood and the fact that it would be the first holiday season without his father soured everything to do with the approaching Thanksgiving. He put on a brave face for his mother because he knew she, too, suffered the renewed memory of her departed husband and the depressing thought of celebrating the holidays without him around. Jacob came home after school during the first snow storm to find his mother sitting in the living room crying over a large storage bin of holiday decorations. He sat down next to her and wrapped his arm around her to offer comfort, but as he sat staring at the decorations he felt nothing. It was as if the cold outside had numbed him to the very marrow of his bones. As his mother cried into her handkerchief, Jacob tried to bring a tear to his eyes, but nothing happened. Deep within where his memories of his father and the sorrow at losing his dad normally resided, Jacob found only a hollow emptiness. He chastised himself for not feeling something…anything…even just compassion for his hurting mother, but the more he tried to make himself feel guilty for the apathy that he felt, the ever glowing embers of anger found fuel to begin to burn brightly again.

"Oh, Jacob…The holidays represent joy, but here we sit feeling self-pity," his mother said as she wiped her red swollen eyes and looked warmly and pitifully at her son. "And I should be comforting you, but here you are trying to console me. Your father would be so proud of the young man you are growing up to be…look at you, holding in your tears to be strong for the both of us. It's okay, Jacob, if you want to cry."

Jacob smiled weakly, and rather than say what was on his mind, he reached out and hugged his mother tightly. "We'll be okay, mom. Dad would want us to celebrate the holidays joyfully and reminisce openly about the happier holidays we had with him rather than cry because we miss him." His words rang untrue in his own ears, and he hoped his mother was not as perceptive as he was about the truth of his words' tone.

"You're right, dear. You are so right," she said as they stopped hugging and she looked again at the bin of holiday decorations. "You go upstairs and get ready for supper, and I will put these off to the side until we get the tree on Thanksgiving. Then, we'll have eggnog and sing carols that your father loved while we decorate the whole house. How does that sound?" She smiled warmly as she pulled off his stocking cap and tousled his hair playfully and lovingly.

"Okay mom. Sounds good," Jacob said as he started upstairs to his room. When he got to the door to his bedroom, Jacob could hear his mom softly humming "Joy to the World" as she set the bin of decorations somewhere off to the side in the living room. For a moment, Jacob felt an undefinable warmth at his core, and for the first time since Halloween, he smiled a genuine smile as he entered his room to get ready for supper.

Sarah invited Bina's family over to Thanksgiving dinner, and whether it was the holiday spirit or the love that permeated the house like the smell of his mom's marshmallow, brown sugar yams, Jacob felt like himself again that one day out of all of November. The brief break from the doom and gloom that had grown within him since Halloween was bitter sweet because as soon as he and Bina returned to school after the holiday break, the momentary taste of being his old self made him even more frustrated as the uncertainty, fear, guilt, and anger quelled the good feelings.

One night a week or so after Thanksgiving at Heldago, while Jacob attended powers class with Don and was working on a technique of mind control and moving objects, Don approached him. Although Jacob and his classmates didn't talk about it, Don still had a stigma attached to him in the minds of his students that he could be the traitor who had been leaking information to the Tenebras.

"I know what you and the others think of me," Don whispered. "I can sense it."

Jacob acted as though he didn't know what Don was talking about. "What? What do you mean?" he said without even looking directly at Don.

"You think I am the traitor," whispered Don. "Well, I'm not, you know. I would never do such a thing. I just wanted you to hear it from me."

"Thank you, Don," Jacob replied casually under his breath.

"And Jacob, I know what you're going through right now." Don placed his hand on Jacob's shoulder. "I've seen that as well. We all go through times of trials and tribulations, but never forget that there is a God that loves you far greater than such things. During our adversity, we think only of the present and how the problem affects us in the now. We can't see into the future and understand God's plans. It's only through trust and faith in God that you will understand the end to your story."

Jacob had never heard Don talk about spiritual things before, so it came as somewhat of a shock to hear him give uplifting advice. He didn't completely understand what Don was speaking about, but he appreciated his concern. Jacob nodded his head and continued his powers exercise.

After class, the other Clevans approached Jacob.

"We want to come to the tower with you in a couple of weeks on the day of the winter's solstice to watch your back," said Jezebel. "You don't need to show us anything secretive; we are just worried about you and want to help."

"Well… I'm not sure." Jacob was hesitant as he recalled how he had forgotten at first that Bina was with him in the heat of the moment the night that the Tenebras attacked them and the Nephilim.

"The older Veritas are spread too thin right now," said Fred. "We are tired of just sitting around. We want to be a part of helping the cause."

"Yah, we've already asked de gnome, Yelkie, an' he said he'd take us to dah site," Emily pointed out as she joined the conversation.

Jacob thought for a moment. "Okay…all right. It wouldn't hurt for me to have some backup. Meet me and Bina at the Newport Tower in Newport, Rhode Island at 11:30 pm local time. Just give me your word that you won't look at whatever I find," Jacob paused as he noticed the looks on his friends' faces. "It's not that I don't trust you; it's just that it's my responsibility to keep what has been entrusted with me a secret."

Relieved that their friend did not distrust them, the Clevans all agreed to Jacob's terms, even Luke, which was a sign of how much it meant to each of them. They were excited to finally help and contribute in the battle against evil that was spreading throughout the world. They might not be allowed to fight among the ranks of the Elder or Moldan level Veritas, but they could do their part by offering their friend some companionship and security as he sought out the next clue to finding the Garden of Eden.

Jacob's mood seemed to rub off on quite a few people as the Christmas break quickly approached, especially his fellow freshman classmates, including Bina, but it wasn't that his dreariness was infectious; it was the first semester finals that any of the freshman had ever taken, and their importance weighed heavily on everyone. Though the energy level rose with each day that brought the students closer to Christmas, the excitement normally felt with the approaching holidays was tempered by worry and weariness as students studied for the exams. Again, Jacob felt neither excitement for Christmas, nor did he feel worried about his first set of semester finals. The only time he seemed to feel anything beyond a grey numbness occurred when he thought about the winter's solstice and getting back on the trail of the Garden of Eden. He convinced himself that he'd get back to himself once he felt like he was doing something to find the next clue to the mystery.

Bina noticed how distracted and depressed Jacob had been acting since Halloween, and she did everything she could think of to bring him out of his doldrums. She continued to hope that her suspicions about what she witnessed that night that Jacob killed Rico Estrada were unfounded, but she did not go to Mr. Wolfe to tell him her fears. She decided she would simply keep a close eye on Jacob and be there for him as his friend in any way that she could. Bina recognized how different Jacob acted whenever they discussed the quickly approaching winter's solstice, so she found any excuse she could to bring it up as often as she could – even during their *cram session* for finals. Ultimately, the week of finals actually passed like a blur and most everyone did well. Jacob couldn't recall actually taking finals, but on the last day of school before break his name appeared near the top of the academic list in the main hall near the Principal's office. He and Bina had both been selected as freshman of the first semester, which meant that over the break the Principal and custodians would put their pictures up with the male and female students from each grade that had been selected as students of the semester. Bina proudly congratulated her best friend, and Jacob did his best to energetically congratulate her.

The next few days – the first of the Christmas-Semester break – passed quickly with everyone who would be involved with the visit to Newport Tower being eager to see what the winter's solstice would disclose. On December 21st, Jacob and Bina made their excuses to their parents that they wanted to ice skate at the local rink, but they met once more at the Hokmah cave, shared some cocoa as they waited anxiously for the appointed time of 10:30 pm to leave. Jacob's Clevan friends all knew that they should arrive at the tower at about 11:30 pm Newport time to give them time to prepare for the 11:49 pm winter's solstice and the clue that the moonlight would divulge. Jacob and Bina talked about their plans to get the golden plate into the channel, and they prayed that the night sky would be clear before packing up their backpacks and using the Dalet to travel inconspicuously to the Newport Tower at precisely 10:15 p.m. Hickson time.

When they finally arrived at the tower after walking a few blocks, they checked their cell phones and were glad to find that it was just about 11:30 p.m. As they entered the small park where the tower rose above the snow covered sidewalks, they were met by the old man whom Bina had talked to the last time they were in Rhode Island. "Remember me?" he asked. "Hubert Winston is my name."

"Yes sir," Bina replied a little surprised.

"I thought you may be coming back here on the winter's solstice, so I waited until just after 11 to walk down and wait to see if I was right," said Hubert. "Did you find something that might go into that channel in the tower?"

Jacob was reluctant to say anything to the man that might expose their purpose at the Tower, but Bina was comfortable with him, so it eased his concerns. *If Bina trusts him, he must be all right. She's a good judge of character,* Jacob thought. "We have a metallic plate that…our research indicates should be placed in the channel just before the solstice," Jacob said as he patted his backpack.

"Yes, and according to the National Weather Service the official solstice occurs at 11:49 p.m.," Bina told Hubert, who checked his watch.

"Well then, that's in just 20 minutes or so…" Hubert said with a note of excitement in his voice. "What do you say we get this show rolling?"

A moment later, Jezebel, Jack, Fred, Luke, and Emily showed up with Yelkie and the Pixie, Maribel within the cover of some bushes about a block away from the Newport Tower. Even though Maribel was only the size of Yelkie's head, their affection for one another had grown into a dating relationship ever since their trip to Italy. The group walked in view of Hubert, who was talking to Bina. "Whoa! Where did all of you children come from?" Hubert exclaimed after being startled by their sudden appearance.

"We're friends of Bina and Jacob," said Jezebel. She looked over at Bina and was happy to see her smile back. The awkwardness of what transpired at the Homecoming dance had weighed heavily on her mind. "We just arrived…by bus…and it looks like we're just in time."

"I see," said Hubert. "Well, the more, the merrier, I always say." He looked down at Jack's arm that was missing its hand and swallowed deeply. He quickly glanced over at Yelkie and thought his long beard looked peculiar, but thought he was merely a dwarf man. Maribel had hidden herself out of sight in Yelkie's shirt pocket. Yelkie was content in showing himself in public, but the thought of a human seeing a less than one-foot tall flying pixie was something Maribel wanted to try and avoid.

"Seems like a nice old guy," Luke whispered to Fred.

Fred nodded in agreement.

"You do what you got to do, and we'll keep a watch out for you," Jezebel whispered to Jacob, hoping that their purpose at the tower would not be overly obvious to the old man whom she had never met.

"Thanks," Jacob whispered in reply. "I've got a bad feeling that something is going to happen."

Jezebel and the others spread out and circled the tower.

Jacob, Bina, and Hubert walked closer to the 28-foot tall tower. They paused and stared at the eight columns that made a cylinder shape out to about 24 feet in width. "Oh, crud!" Jacob mumbled. "How are we going to get up to the channel in the wall? I can't just float up there in front of this man," he whispered to Bina.

As Jacob and Bina looked hopelessly up the interior wall toward the channel where Jacob would have to insert the gold tablet so that it would reflect the moonlight, Hubert looked on as well. Jacob racked his brain for some sort of diversion that would distract Hubert long enough to allow him to use his Valoria power to levitate up to the channel. Jacob walked over to the wall just below the channel and felt the rocks that jutted out, remembering painfully how difficult it had been to hold on to the wall without the Valoria power the last time they had been at the tower. It would be even more difficult and uncomfortable now that they were frost covered and frozen by the wintery air.

"I brought a ladder just in case you didn't have one," said Hubert suddenly as Jacob looked about to try to climb up using only his hands and feet. The old man walked over to the other side of the tower and grabbed the ladder. "I don't think you want to climb the wall while trying to hold on to that plate you got there," Hubert said, smiling as he returned with the extending ladder.

"Thank you, Hubert!" Bina said and smiled warmly.

Jacob was relieved and felt even more at ease with the elderly gentleman. He grabbed the ladder from Hubert and set it up near the channel in the wall. By the looks of the moon's light, it was going to take a little while before it would shine through the window in the wall and onto the channel in the wall, so he had time to get the plate in place.

Jacob grabbed the golden tablet that he had received from Galaman in India out of his backpack, climbed the ladder, and placed it in the channel that was carved into the stones.

Hubert was curious what exactly the tablet was and kept trying to look closer to see what was inscribed upon it. "What is that tablet?" he asked. "Where did you get it?"

"Well, let's just say that it's been in my family for a long, long time," Jacob said and grinned knowingly at Bina. "When the moon's light shines on it through that window, the legend says we should get a reflection that reveals the true secrets of this tower."

"Tonight, all of your family's questions will be answered," said Bina to Hubert. "We can't tell you exactly what may be revealed, but I think the tower's true purpose will be shown to you tonight."

Hubert's wrinkled and weathered face cracked a gentle smile.

As the moon rose toward the solstice point, its light finally started to shine through the lower part of the window opening on the tower wall and onto the opposite wall just above where the channel held the gold tablet. The circle of light was slowly creeping its way towards the channel that held the tablet as the minutes passed.

Jacob, Bina, and Hubert waited patiently, watching the moon's light approach the tablet. Their hands were sweaty and their breathing quickened in anticipation, little puffs of freezing breath rising through the open tower into the moonlit sky. They had waited a long time for this moment, none more so than Hubert, who looked like a child waiting to see if Santa Claus would land on his roof at any moment.

Moments later, the moon's light started to reflect upon the golden tablet, and the tablet reflected the light in four different directions, but it wasn't clear where the rays of reflected moonlight were pointing to just yet. The light needed to be perfectly centered on the tablet.

"It appears we will be looking for four stones," Bina said when she saw how the moonlight was separating into four different reflected beams. "When it is exactly on the middle of the tablet, I think the reflected moonlight will point to four distinct stones in the wall of the tower," Bina continued to explain. "We'll have to make note of where the stones are before the moonlight continues on its natural course and off of the tablet."

No one was more excited than Hubert. Stories and legends of the tower's purpose had flowed through his community and family for years, and finally, before his very eyes, he was going to see fables and rumors turn into fact.

Jezebel and the others keeping watch could sense the tension mounting and readied themselves for any surprises.

The moonlight finally settled upon the center of the tablet, and the four reflections of light coming from the tablet pointed to four separate stones among the myriad of fieldstones that were at opposite points of the circular interior wall of the tower. There seemed to be an order of the light reflections, as one ray went to one stone, and the second to the next, and so on.

"Quickly, before the light moves away, stand and keep track of the stones that the light is pointing to!" Jacob shouted. "Hubert you keep an eye on that one, Bina, you take that one there, and I'll watch these two that are closer to each other."

Hubert's stone was down by his knees, and Jacob's two were near his eye level, but Bina's was up about eight feet off the ground. She quickly grabbed the ladder and set it up next to the stone. Just as she regained sight of her assigned stone in the moon's light, the moon continued its vertical climb along the outer wall of the tower, drifted above the window opposite of the channel, moved off the tablet, and then, as quickly as the reflections from the tablet had shined on four stones on the tower's interior, the reflections were gone.

"Everyone has their stone?" asked Jacob.

"I've got mine," said Hubert, grunting as he squatted to put his finger on the stone.

"I've got mine, as well," said Bina, stretching a little to put her finger on her stone as she stood precariously on the ladder.

"Okay, great," Jacob sighed. "Now, look at them closely for any clue that might be on the stone."

Jacob pulled a piece of gum from his pocket, chewed it up, and stuck it to one of his two stones to mark it while he examined the other one. Bina and Hubert, who both had wisely brought flashlights, got as close to their respective stones as they could to look for any markings. The stones were badly weathered and stained with mildew, moss, and remnants of the timeworn white plaster that had once covered the walls, and all of that was covered under a fine layer of December frost.

"I see something here," Bina pointed after breathing on her stone to melt away the crystalline film of frost. "It's three letters, A-S-P."

Hubert rubbed some of the moss from his brick with his fingers and said, "Mine looks to have a C-H-R."

Jacob looked more closely at the first of his two stones and saw the letters E and U. He went over to his other stone that had the gum stuck to it, pulled the now frozen gum off, and revealed that it had the letters A-T-E-S. Jacob grabbed a piece of paper and a pen from his backpack and wrote all of the letters down— ASP, CHR, EU and ATES. "When the light first reflected off of the tablet, it landed on one rock first, which one was it?" asked Jacob.

"I believe it was mine, Jacob," Bina answered.

Jacob wrote the letters ASP below his others letters and left a space after them. "Okay, got it. Which one was next?"

"I think it was one of yours. The one that you didn't stick your gum to," said Hubert.

"I think you're right, Hubert," said Jacob. He wrote down the letters EU and left another space after them. "Okay, and if I remember right, the third stone that was lit up was Hubert's. Does that sound right?"

"Yes," said Bina as she climbed down the ladder to join Jacob.

Jacob wrote the letters CHR and then followed them with the final letters, which were ATES. Jacob had written, ASP EU CHR ATES.

"Does it spell something? What's it say?" Hubert asked excitedly as he joined his two young friends near the center of the tower.

Jacob was cautious. Up to this point he was fine with Hubert being around, but now he was careful. He looked at the letters and tried to decipher their meaning. *It's angelic*, he thought. *Asp, means Oak, like an Oak tree. The other letters are actually one word, Euchrates. That means Island. This spells Oak Island,* Jacob continued to think to himself.

"Did you figure it out, Jacob?" asked Bina as she peered at his notes on the paper.

"I did; I think I know what the letters spell!" Jacob shouted.

Jezebel and the other's standing watch heard Jacob and grew excited at the news.

"Well, what is it? What does it mean?" asked Hubert, who was growing somewhat irritated that he didn't know the answer to years of imagined purposes of the tower.

"I'm sorry, Hubert," said Bina. "But we can't share with you what the letters mean. This is a secret that only Jacob can know. We wanted to share with you the meaning behind the tower, but I'm afraid that's all that we can share. At least you know that it was built to help someone discover these four stones." Bina was genuinely sorry that they couldn't share more with the kindly old man and her voice waivered a bit during her apologetic explanation.

Hubert stood silent and dejected for a moment, his sad aged eyes showing obvious frustration and pain at such an empty ending to what he had hoped would be an answer to all of the mythology about the tower. Then, he turned without further comment and began to walk away toward his nearby home. Jezebel, Jack, Fred, Luke, Emily, and Yelkie with Maribel still hidden away came into the tower to congratulate Jacob on finding and deciphering the next clue.

"Did you get your clue?" asked Luke as he rubbed his hands together and blew on them to warm them.

"I did," Jacob replied. "I don't know quite what it means yet, but I have what we need to move forward." He moved the ladder as he spoke so that he could retrieve the golden tablet from the channel above.

"An' the night was quiet," said Emily in her Jamaican accent. "No worries, an' dat's always a good ting!"

# CHAPTER 21

# ANGEL OF DARKNESS

During their exuberant conversation about their success, everyone had lost track of Hubert, who had started to walk away somewhat despondently at not knowing anything more than he did when the night began. Bina had looked on as Hubert first left. She still felt terrible about being unable to tell him everything that had led them to the tower and the meaning of the moonlight reflecting on the four stones, but Jacob had warned her about how important it was to keep whatever they discovered a secret, even from her newfound elderly friend. After watching Hubert start on his way home, Bina's attention returned to the congratulatory discussion among Jacob's friends as he returned the golden plate to his backpack.

Then, just as Hubert reached the sidewalk to return home, he spun on his heels and returned toward the group, approaching from behind as they congratulated one another on their success. He startled Emily when he stepped up from behind her. His eyes were darkened, and his face was pale. Jacob turned at Emily's gasp of surprise and looked at Hubert. Jacob had seen the kind of look on Hubert before when Baal had possessed Bina's father. The old man's hands began to shake as he struggled to speak, and he turned to face Bina. "I... I'm sorry, Bina," he stuttered. "You were so kind to me. My mother always tried to convince me to accept Jesus Christ as savior, but I never listened. I was always too proud. I tried to stop him, but he… but he was too… too strong." Hubert struggled to speak further.

Hubert was possessed by a powerful demon angel named Baldur. His voice instantly changed over to a deep and sinister growl as he grabbed Emily by the throat and pulled her in close. "Enough, of this!" he hissed. "Tell me what the stones said. Where is the next clue that will lead to the Garden of Eden?"

The Veritas quickly drew their swords and took up a defensive posture. Yelkie casually nudged and backed Bina to the center of the group for her own protection, and Maribel flew from Yelkie's pocket to get a better vantage point above the upcoming confrontation.

"Do nah tell 'em anyting!" Emily shouted in a choked voice.

"I'll never tell you," Jacob declared defiantly. "You might as well go crawl back into the hole that you came from."

Jacob and the others didn't know it, but the demon, Baldur, was a great angel of darkness. Being one of the Powers angels, Baldur had been created specifically for war and battle. Moreover, Baldur just happened to be one of the strongest Powers ever created by God. He had fallen under the influence of Lucifer's lies and deceit, and he had turned to the side of darkness during the time of Lucifer's revolt against God. Ever since then, Baldur had been helping to start wars on Earth by taking over evil leaders' thoughts and actions. Wherever he could kill goodness, Baldur would be found. Lucifer had sent him into Hubert to get the clue from Jacob.

Baldur bellowed in anger. As the demon's outcry echoed in the tower, a hot yellow smoke erupted from every pore on Hubert's skin. Hubert's voice shrieked through the demon's howl one last time in agony as his skin melted from his bones and fell to the ground. Baldur still held Emily, forcing her to clench her teeth as the heat radiating from the demon angel burned her. All that had been the human, Hubert, burned and fell away, revealing Baldur in all of his horrific splendor. Darkness and evil had grossly disfigured Baldur since his fall from Heaven. Dark, stringy, long hair covered his badly burned face, and his body reeked of decaying flesh. His teeth protruded through holes that had been bitten through his lips and mouth during the pain and agony he had endured in Hell. His skin was as dark as a moonless December night sky. If it weren't for the whites of his eyes and the yellowing white enamel of his protruding teeth, he would've been nearly impossible to see as the solstice moon disappeared behind some clouds.

Lucifer's forces had grown so much stronger with the wickedness spreading and multiplying that some of his more powerful dark angels were now strong enough to live on Earth after killing their host body. What had never before been witnessed since the beginning of humankind was becoming a reality before the eyes of the group of teenagers and their gnome and pixie friends – a fallen angel stood before them.

Baldur pulled his sword from the belt that girded his tunic and dirty loin cloth and held the blade to Emily's throat. "I'm only going to say this once," he growled angrily. "Tell me the clue, or she dies."

Jacob was suddenly confused. He didn't know what to do. A month filled with doubt, fear, and a loss of faith addled his soul, heart, and brain. He could feel uncontrollable anger and frustration growing inside of him, consuming and overtaking him. Jacob felt so conflicted that he hadn't even drawn his sword or called forth its blade.

"Do nah tell 'em anyting," Emily screeched. "I would rather die wit a clear conscious, knowin' tat I served God."

Baldur smiled, baring his yellowed demonic teeth. "What's it gonna be? The clue, or her life?"

All of the Veritas stood motionless, not knowing how to

react. Yelkie stepped up in front of the intimidating demon and boldly announced, "Do not be afraid, Emily. Hurt you this demon will not."

Baldur laughed at the site of the small gnome. "And what are you going to do? You are but a child that has grown a beard. Go away before I step on you like a roach." Baldur wasn't familiar with wilderness gnomes and didn't know the powers they possessed. His overwhelming size in comparison to the small creature filled him with overconfidence.

Yelkie held out his hand and with a determined look grabbed the demon's arm with his powers. Baldur felt his arm that held his sword begin to be pulled from Emily's neck. Even more irritated than before, Baldur pushed back with all of his strength, trying to dig his blade into Emily's throat. The blade barely grazed her skin during the tug-of-war making a trickle of blood appear, and at the sight of Emily's blood, Yelkie concentrated even harder with his power to move Baldur's arm away.

Once the blade was far enough from Emily's neck, she noticed that Baldur had dropped his concentration on her for a moment. She threw her arm back and broke free from the demon. Yelkie kept control of Baldur's arm and began to swing the blade toward the demon. The angel of Hell grew furious. "Enough!" he roared in frustration. An intense heat and darkness shot forth from him, knocking everyone to their backs. "Enough games! Tell me the clue now!" Baldur's wings that had been hidden behind him expanded out to his sides to show his might. His once white, beautiful wings were now stained dark with blood and ash.

Jacob felt the anger and fear inside of him continue to grow out of control. Somewhat disorientated from his internal battle, he was motionless while his friends attacked the demon. The young Veritas attacked from all sides, but each one was thrown back with ease. Maribel dived from above and shot powerful bursts of energy at the demon, but

Baldur swatted at her and connected with one of his wild swings, knocking Maribel through the air into the snow covered hedges that lined the park. Yelkie blinked out from in front of the massive demon to reappear at the hedge where Maribel laid unconscious. Baldur saw his chance and stepped closer to Jacob, who remained dazed by the struggle within his mind, heart, and soul. Baldur reached out with both clawed hands to grab Jacob, but Jack leaped between the demon and his friend, swung his sword at the demon's arms and prepared to thrust his dirk into the hell spawn's gut. Jack's sword made contact with one of Baldur's arms, splitting the metal bracer that covered his forearm in two. The demon spun and swung his arm back as hard as he could, hitting Jack directly between the eyes. Jack's body fell limply to the ground, his sword rattling and skidding away from his open hand. Her last defender felled by the demon, Bina retreated quickly to Jezebel's side and hid behind one of the tower's massive columns.

The sight of Jack's unconscious body falling heavily to the ground yanked Jacob from his internal struggle. Jacob stared at his fallen friend, convinced that Jack's heroism to protect him once again had finally cost Jack his life. First his hand in Italy and now his life – it was more than Jacob could take.

Baldur looked sinisterly at the distracted Verita and snarled, "You give up, boy?"

Jacob tried to calm himself, but he couldn't stop the uncontrollable fire that burned inside of his soul. A great light shot from his eyes that hit Baldur's chest. The demon screamed in pain as he was thrown back on his heels. Jacob's face showed ferocity that had never been shown by a human before. He stood from his kneeling position, finally drew his sword's hilt from his belt, and called forth its blade. His blade looked different. It wasn't its normal shiny steel. Instead, it glowed black and purple. Jezebel, who was closest to Jacob, standing behind him and just in front of the now hiding Bina, could feel the heat that was emanating from her friend and his sword, and it frightened her into stepping back a pace. Jacob was not the boy she thought she had loved just two months before.

Jacob flexed and aggressively approached Baldur, swinging his sword ferociously at Baldur's neck while screaming a war cry that made all of the Veritas shiver. The demon parried the blow with his sword, and when the two swords clashed, they sent out large yellow sparks that lit up the darkened tower. The earth shook from the clash of their powers.

Baldur's eyes grew large at the power the boy wielded. Jacob attacked with his sword and threw his powers at the demon, knocking him back until he fell through the ladder that still leaned against the interior wall of the tower, crushing it. Baldur continued to fall and landed painfully on his rear. The demon was obviously shocked and confused. He jumped to the air and flew away into the night sky.

"Come back you coward!" Jacob screamed as he raised his sword in defiance and challenge.

Jacob's friends rushed to help Jack. He was unconscious and lying deathly still on the ground. Jacob was still not himself and staring up into the night sky — searching for his enemy, totally disregarding his fallen comrade and friend.

"Jack, can you hear me?" Jezebel shouted as she held Jack up to a sitting position, his head lolling to the side. "Jack, wake up!" Jezebel pleaded and then began to cry.

Yelkie came to Jack's side and held his hand above his head. He began chanting an old gnome prayer for the power of healing. "Great are his wounds," said Yelkie. "Leaving his body his spirit is. Immediate help he needs."

Bina ran over to Jacob. "We need to get help for Jack," she said with urgency. She stopped directly behind Jacob. He was mumbling angelic language towards the night sky. Her friend's unresponsiveness terrified her. "Jacob, can you hear me? Jacob?"

Jacob stopped talking in angelic and shook his head. He turned to face Bina, and when he opened his eyes, she noticed that his eyes had lost their darkness. He shook his head back and forth to regain his wherewithal.

"What...what happened? What's going on?" he asked.

"It's Jack. He's hurt bad!"

Jacob regained his composure and ran over to his friend who lay lifeless on the ground. He opened the Dalet doorway to Heldago and picked Jack up and cradled him in his arms. "I'm taking him to Rabbi Lazarus. He'll know what to do."

Bina grabbed Jacob's arm and said, "I'm coming with."

"Yelkie, you get everyone else home safely." Jacob commanded briskly as he stepped into the doorway with Jack and Bina.

They stepped from the Dalet's doorway at the doorsteps of Heldago. Jacob saw Laborc and Raman at the gates and yelled, "Get help! A demon has hurt Jacques!"

Laborc saw Jack's lifeless body and immediately disappeared to retrieve Triple E. The massive doors of the sanctuary flew open with Triple E grabbing Jack from Jacob's arms. "Come, let's get him to the infirmary," said Triple E. "I've already sent word to Rabbi Lazarus and Olga."

In the infirmary, Olga was rushing to prepare some medicinal plants to be burnt. "Lay him here on the table," she ordered. "The smoke from these herbs will help him."

"What's wrong with him?" asked Jacob, fearfully. "Is it his head?"

Olga placed her hands over Jack's head and used her powers to feel and search his wounds. She was gifted with such things. "It's not just a head wound," she whispered. "The demon transferred a part of his darkness into Jack's head. It's killing him."

Just then, Rabbi Lazarus came rushing into the room and knelt by Jack's side. He placed one hand on Jack's head and the other on his heart and began to pray. A moment later, Lazarus's head and shoulders fell in sadness. "His spirit has left his body," he said. "There's nothing more that can be done."

"No! You're not right," said Jacob. "Check again. He cannot be gone!" he shouted angrily.

"He gave his life in honor and love," said Lazarus. "He's in the presence of God Almighty."

"No! This can't be! You can save him. Jesus saved you, so you can save him."

"Jacob, that's not how things work," Lazarus said softly as he attempted to console his young student. "I prayed for Jack to be healed, but if it's not the Father's will to heal and to answer my prayer, then we must accept His omniscient decision."

Jacob grew angry and his eyes began to darken, surprising Lazarus.

"No!" Jacob shouted again. "This isn't supposed to happen... but he... he saved my life!"

"There is no greater gift than to give one's life for another," said Lazarus. "It's the most precious gift of love anyone could ever give."

Jezebel and the others entered the room, saw Jack's lifeless body and the gloomy looks on the others' faces, and knew what had happened. Jezebel, who was closest to Jack, ran to his side and began to sob uncontrollably.

"You. You are supposed to be all powerful," Jacob pointed at Lazarus. "You should've been able to save him! This is all your fault!" Jacob's eyes grew more lifeless and dark with each statement. "Why have you brought me into this? I hate you! I hate you!"

Bina reached for Jacob's arm and tried to comfort him, but he wasn't having any of it. Anger and fear were taking a foothold in Jacob's heart, and he was pushing it directly at Lazarus. Jacob furiously yanked his arm away from Bina, nearly throwing her forcibly into the wall, and stormed out of the room.

"It's okay, Bina," said Lazarus as he helped her to her feet. "Let him go. He is upset and needs time."

Bina could see in Lazarus's face that his feelings had been hurt, but he was trying not to let it show. "When he gets infuriated or frightened, something inside of him takes over," she said. "I hate to ask such a thing, but he's not possessed, is he? Please, tell me he is not possessed," Bina's voice cracked in fear and sorrow, and a tear rolled down her cheek.

"No, he's not possessed," Lazarus explained reassuringly as a look of puzzlement passed over his face. "I would sense that immediately. I think there is something else at play here." Lazarus turned and consoled the young Veritas that were mourning next to Jack's body. He knelt next to the valiant young man's body and began to pray. Soon, everyone in the room knelt and joined their Rabbi in prayer for the soul of their departed student, classmate, and friend.

Jacob ran down the hallway and up to one of the higher corridors that overlooks one of the mountains outside the castle gates. He began to calm down and regain his composure. He took a deep breath in and stared out into the hills. The smell of flowers and the tall meadow grass from below was soothing to Jacob's spirit. *What's happening to me,* he thought as a sense of dread filled him. *Some evil is growing inside of me.*

"Jacob," a familiar voice called from behind. It was Shawn. He had been sleeping near the infirmary, and the commotion of Jacob's arrival with the mortally wounded Jack had awakened him. "Ya be okay? I be hearin' what happened."

Shawn's voice struck an emotional cord. Jacob struggled to hold back tears. "I'm…I'm gonna be all right."

"Death be always difficult to handle." Shawn placed his hand on Jacob's shoulder. "Ya be reassured knowin' that yer friend didn't go dyin' fer nothing. Ya celebrate his life. He be in a place where there be no sadness or pain. Don't cha ever be forgettin' that."

"I know. I know," Jacob replied and then hit the stone wall with his closed fist. "So much death and evil around me. It's tearing away at my very soul. I don't know how much more I can bear, Shawn."

"Ye can bear as much as yer heart be lettin' ya," Shawn comforted. "Close yer heart and ye be shuttin' out love. Shut out love and ye be shuttin' out the One who is love. Shut out love, and ya be openin' the gates fer evil to enter yer soul."

"I miss having you around, Shawn," Jacob replied as he turned to face his friend and protector. "You always know the right things to say. You would make a great Rabbi someday."

Shawn chuckled. "I don' be knowin' 'bout bein' Rabbi, but I know I be a missin' ya too. I be overhearin' ya yellin' at Rabbi Lazarus. How ya be feelin' 'bout that now that ya've settled down some?"

"Terrible. I feel terrible. I put all my fear and anger into words and directed them at Lazarus. I said things that I didn't even mean." Jacob hugged Shawn. "Thank you. You've got a way of making me feel better. I'm going to run back down and apologize to Lazarus."

"I'll be a seein' ya soon, brother. Just remember, love be always stronger than anger and fear. But how ya be controlin' it be yer compass."

"Thank you." Jacob ran down the stairs and back to the infirmary. When he entered the room, only Bina and Jezebel remained. The others had taken Jack's body to be prepared for burial. "Where is Lazarus? I need to apologize."

Jezebel was still crying and wasn't able to answer.

"Someone came in here in a rush and whispered something to him," said Bina. "Then he rushed out of here with the man."

Jacob was troubled that he wasn't able to apologize to

his friend.

After comforting Jezebel, Jacob took Bina by the hand and took her home through the Dalet. At Bina's house, after he had apologized for flinging her into the wall during his temper tantrum, Jacob told Bina about the clue that he had figured out. "The stones at the tower point to a place called Oak Island. Have you ever heard of that place?"

"I've read about it somewhere," said Bina. "But I'll need to do some more research on it tonight."

"Awesome! Thank you," Jacob said with more energy than Bina had seen in him since Halloween. Then, he suddenly grabbed and hugged Bina tightly and whispered softly into her ear, "Thank you for always being there for me."

Bina blushed and walked into her house. She was still concerned about Jacob's fear and anger, but she didn't want to let it show.

CHAPTER 22

# THE BLOODLINES

When he got home, Jacob's arrival awoke his mother, who had fallen asleep awaiting his arrival from his night of skating with Bina. He could tell that she was upset with how late it was – it was after all nearly midnight, but she didn't lecture him. Instead, she told him to sit at the dining room table and she brought him a bowl of soup. He talked with his mom for a while over the warm bowl of soup, which he found he wanted much more than he thought he would. Hearing her voice was comforting and reassuring to him, but in the back of his mind, Jacob couldn't shake thoughts of fear and doubt. *What if I can't find the Garden of Eden before Lucifer does,* he thought as his mother told a story of a skate date she had with his father. *What if I get killed or taken? Who would finish my quest? What would mom do without me? She already lost dad. She couldn't make it if she lost me, too. Or, what if the Tenebras took her hostage…used her as leverage against me… or just hurt her outright? I couldn't bear it if something happened to her like what has happened to Ramiro and Jacques. I wouldn't be able to control myself. Maybe I should tell her my secret. Maybe I should tell her that I'm a Verita so that she can at least be somewhat prepared of what may come.*

"Mom… There's something that I've been meaning to tell you…" Jacob stuttered as he swirled the spoon in the bowl of soup.

"Oh yeah, what's that?" asked Sarah, surprised by her son's interruption.

Hesitation and uncertainty got the best of Jacob. He couldn't tell her. *She'll never believe me,* he thought. Jacob raised his head up from his bowl of soup. "I... I just wanted to say, I love you."

"And I love you, sweetheart," Sarah lovingly. "Is everything okay?" His mom reached over and stroked his hair out of his eyes and looked at him full of concern.

"Yeah, everything is all right," Jacob replied weakly and shrugged. "I just haven't slept well lately."

"Well, why don't you head on up to bed and I'll clean up here."

Jacob gave his mom a kiss and went to his bedroom. He lay in bed for what seemed like hours, trying to fall asleep. The thoughts running through his mind were just the stimulant necessary to keep him from proper rest. He was utterly confused why he didn't have control of his emotions. He felt like he had a close relationship with God, so he was frustrated with why fear was drowning his thoughts and actions. He needed some answers, and he felt moved to visit the one person he felt that could give him such things — the prophet Elijah in Jerusalem.

Jacob jumped out of bed; stuffed a few supplies in his backpack; checked the alarm clock, which read 2 a.m., and prepared to enter the Dalet. When he stepped out of the doorway, there was a man walking by that stopped and started yelling at Jacob in Hebrew. The man appeared troubled at seeing a boy stepping out in front of him from the thin air. Jacob smiled and acted as though he didn't know what the man was talking about. Others nearby glanced quickly in the direction of the loud man, but shrugged it off as crazy talk.

It was mid-morning in Jerusalem and the area was bustling with tourists, shop keepers, and the normal mid-morning traffic. Jacob looked around to gain his headings and started walking toward the Wailing Wall and the site where he had last seen Elijah. When he got to the site, he was shocked to see how far Israel had come on constructing the new Temple in just a couple of months. All of the rubble of the destroyed Muslim shrine had been taken away from where it had fallen, and the foundation was nearly completed for the new Temple. Secretly, Jewish priests had already made plans for the new Temple. They were waiting and praying for the day to come when they could build their newest Temple on the holy site. So, when the spot became available to start the construction, they acted without hesitation.

Jacob could hear shouts of anger coming from a nearby fenced off area where Muslim people were yelling at the Israelis. The Israelis had done an effective job of fencing off the area, securing it with soldiers, and keeping the construction workers free from harm.

Thousands of Muslims had gathered to condemn the Jews' actions of building the new Temple, but, because no one could explain the earthquake that had destroyed the Dome of the Rock, it was labeled a natural disaster. The land technically belonged to Israel, and most of the countries of the world supported Israel in building their temple, so the destruction of the Dome of the Rock by natural forces opened the way for Israel to rebuild the Jewish temple.

Ever since the night that the Dome of the Rock had been destroyed, many Muslim countries had been threatening war against Israel, but the small country of Jewish people was used to such talk over the centuries.

Jacob stopped a young Jew that was walking by and asked, "Have you seen the prophet Elijah? Do you know where I can find him?"

The man barely understood English and struggled to speak. "In morning, Elijah prays… Gethsemane."

"Oh, the Garden of Gethsemane?" Jacob confirmed.

"Yes." The man nodded and pointed to a nearby stand

that had maps of the area.

"Thank you!" Jacob grabbed one of tourist maps, opened it, and got his bearings on the direction he should take. He started for the Mount of Olives, which could be seen in the distance, because the Garden of Gethsemane was at its base.

Jacob had been taught about the Garden of Gethsemane in his religion classes. It was made famous because it was the place that Jesus prayed to God for His strength and courage the night before his crucifixion. It was also the place where one of Jesus's disciples, Judas Iscariot, led soldiers to arrest him.

After walking for some time, Jacob arrived at the garden. He had never seen it before and was immediately drawn in by its simplistic beauty. The aroma of fresh flowers and palms filled the air. A pleasant change from December in Hickson, North Dakota. With very little grass and short, sparse bushes, the main landscape of the garden was decorated primarily by Olive trees. Jacob's attention went directly to the trees and their massive gnarled tree trunks. He remembered hearing from Mr. Wolfe that some of the trees in the garden were dated at over 900 years old.

Jacob walked down the paths of stone, mesmerized by the beautiful trees. Being in such a holy place gave clarity to Jacob's thoughts. He came to the other side of the largest Olive tree and noticed a man kneeling in prayer. Jacob walked a little closer to get a better look without disturbing the man's praying. It was Elijah.

"I felt your presence, Jacob Jerlow of the Veritas," Elijah said.

"Yes… sir," Jacob stuttered. "I – I've come for guidance."

"You seek guidance from a man?"

"I seek God's guidance," Jacob answered.

Elijah smiled. "The truth, you have spoken." He opened his eyes and looked at the massive tree that he was kneeling under. "Just as this tree holds great history and meaning, so does your spirit."

Jacob looked at the prophet, confused.

"This tree is the offspring of one that gave cover to and supported our Lord on the night of his betrayal." Elijah rubbed the tree's bark lovingly with his hand, feeling its rough skin. "There was not a dry eye in Heaven that night."

Jacob knew now that Elijah was telling him that the tree they were looking at was the descendant of the tree that was present when Jesus came to pray on the night of his arrest. "How am I like this tree?" he asked.

"You have strong roots, and your ancestors hold impressive meaning in history, do they not?"

"Oh, you are talking about my great, great, great... you are referring to my grandfather, the Archangel Michael," Jacob answered. "What does he have to do with this thing that is inside of me that I can't control?"

"The Archangel Michael is a great and loyal warrior," said Elijah. "There has been no other Angel that has shown more courage, but it isn't his blood that causes your pain."

"What? I don't understand. Whose blood is it then?"

Elijah began to open his mouth but immediately shut it, as if someone told him not to speak. "This question must be answered in time. I'm not the one to tell you such things."

"What kind of an answer is that?" Jacob was becoming annoyed. He could feel evil welling up inside of him. "So, I came all this way here for nothing."

Elijah rose to his feet and a blinding light came from his hands. "The Lord God has spoken and is not to be trifled with," Elijah shouted. He thrust his hands onto Jacob's chest. Jacob fell to the ground and immediately felt all fear and evil leave his body. A tear fell from his eye as he felt closer than ever to God.

"What did you do to me?" asked Jacob as he sat up. "I feel better, like a heavy burden has been lifted."

"I have done nothing," Elijah explained. "It is God that has given you forgiveness. He has searched your heart and found your faith in His Son, Jesus Christ. However, what lies in your blood and spirit will be awakened again. It can only be forever defeated with the ultimate act of love. Now, go and find that which you were born to uncover."

Jacob bowed in respect to the prophet and turned to leave the garden.

"And, Jacob Jerlow of the Veritas, never forget to keep the one that forgives first and foremost in your heart and mind," Elijah called out as he knelt again to continue his prayers.

Jacob continued down the walk path that he had followed into the garden, contemplating the words of the prophet Elijah and the feeling of peace welling within him, flushing out the evil, fear, and anger he had felt before Elijah had laid his hands upon him. He was very curious about who his other relative could be that Elijah had elusively referred to, but Jacob had felt such a load off of his spirit that his thoughts drifted quickly back to the next clue that he needed to uncover — Oak Island.

The next day, Jacob called Bina and arranged to use his prize from his obstacle course win over Felix to treat her to a pizza for lunch. Jacob and Bina usually had lunch together at school, and just like those lunches, this treat served the more important role of giving them the chance to discuss everything that had occurred at the Newport Tower and the clue the moonlit stones had revealed. They chose a secluded table at the back of the pizzeria where they were pretty sure they would have some privacy and reviewed what they knew. Bina had stayed up most of the night before reading about Oak Island. She began to go into detail about its history and legend.

Oak Island is located off the shores of Nova Scotia, Canada. It had been made famous by a teenage boy named Daniel McGinnis in 1795 when he discovered a circular depression in the ground about 13 feet in diameter on the island. Daniel noticed that a block and tackle lift system had been left above the peculiar hole. Sightings of pirates in the area and rumors of buried fortune were popular topics of discussions among many of the locals in that day, so when Daniel saw the site, the first thing that came to his mind was buried pirate treasure. He grabbed two friends and started digging.

As they dug, they found imprints from pick axes in the walls of the hole, and its circumference began to narrow to seven feet. When they reached a depth of ten feet, they were excited to find a deliberate platform of logs that formed a barrier to block anyone from going down any further. The boys removed the layer of timber and found nothing but more dirt. They continued digging, only to discover another barrier of logs down another ten feet. The boys removed that platform and dug further, only to find, yet again, more dirt, and no hidden treasure.

The boys gave up their digging, but word spread of the hole and the imagined buried wealth that it might hold. In 1803, a new crew began working on the pit, removing dirt from the hole. When the crew reached 30 feet, they too hit a platform of timber, and they discovered and removed more platforms every ten feet as they dug. It appeared obvious to everyone involved that someone had gone through much trouble to hide something below.

At the depth of 60 feet, the wooden platform they came upon was different than all of the previous platforms. The platform was waterproofed with a sappy substance and coconut fibers. Seeing the coconut fibers was very odd because coconuts weren't grown or seen within thousands of miles of Oak Island. More rumors began to flow about mysterious people from another land burying treasure beneath the logs. The treasure hunters pushed on.

When the crews reached 90 feet, they uncovered a square cut stone with strange writing and symbols carved on it. Experts were called in to try and translate the writing, but no one could. They continued to dig and at 98 feet hit another platform of logs. Before finishing up for the day, one of the workers broke through the platform's sappy waterproof barrier that bound the wood together to peek through. He saw no buried treasure under the logs, so the team dismissed for the day to rest.

When they returned the following day, the workers were astonished to see that their 100-foot deep hole had filled almost completely to the top with water. The men tried to remove the water, but the water would fill back up just as quickly as it was removed. Whoever had dug the pit had gone through great measures to set a trap. Unknowingly, the man that had opened the barrier at 98 feet had opened a sealed vacuum tunnel that led from the pit to the ocean. So when the men removed the water from the hole it would immediately fill back up again. The men knew that the ocean was linked to the water in the pit because the water in the hole was salty and would rise and lower with the ocean's tide. Unable to conquer the waters that fed the pit, the crew eventually ran out of funding and had to abandon the project.

The pit remained buried in water for the next 40 years until the next group of treasure hunters arrived. By dumping red dye into the pit's water they found out that the hole was being supplied by the ocean from several points around the island. There was a labyrinth of tunnels that were supplying the pit with water so no matter how they pumped the water out the pit would just fill back up again. The crew tried to block the tunnels, dig holes adjacent to the pit to find a back way, and bore down with mining equipment, but nothing could solve the water flooding issue.

Throughout the years, many more crews came in and tried what they thought was the new great idea that would solve the riddle, but no one could. The pit was named the Money Pit of Oak Island, because of the vast amounts of money that had been expended to retrieve its treasures. Still to this day, no one has been able to solve the flooding puzzle to find what is at the bottom of the pit. Rumors and speculation still flow like the water in the pit amongst the surrounding communities of Oak Island and all that venture to the site.

"Brilliant, Bina," said Jacob. "So I guess all arrows are pointing to our next clue being at the bottom of this Money Pit."

"That's right," said Bina.

"And what of this mysterious stone that they uncovered with strange symbols on it. Does anyone know where it is?"

"Unfortunately, no, Jacob. It seems to have vanished. Fortunately, I believe not all is lost. Last night, after I had finished reading about Oak Island, I was thinking about the stone that they removed from the pit and then it came to me. I remembered seeing a piece of weathered paper in your Hokmah chest that had strange symbols on it." Jacob was astounded at Bina's ability to remember such things. He had looked through the Hokmah and its cave, but he doubted he could recall with certainty anything specific, except those few items that brought memories of his father.

Bina continued as Jacob started to lose himself in thought, "When I saw the paper I remember thinking that it looked as if someone had placed it over a hard surface and colored in the paper with charcoal to imprint the symbols upon it – a stone rubbing as it is commonly referred to by those who do it as a hobby. I think that your father may have uncovered this rubbing of the missing stone some time ago and placed it in your Hokmah for safe keeping. It's got to be what we're looking for," Bina finished excitedly. She was especially happy to see that Jacob's mood had changed and he seemed engaged in the hunt for the next clue to find the Garden of Eden.

"Maybe it has angelic writing on it and I can read it," said Jacob.

"Exactly!"

Jacob and Bina planned to meet after supper that night

and walk to the Hokmah. Excitement grew in their thoughts as the rest of the day passed.

# CHAPTER 23

# THE FUNERAL

After supper, Jacob and Bina convinced their parents to give them permission to go to their special place by the Sheyenne River before rushing to the Hokmah. At the secret location, Jacob placed his hands on Abel's Stone and opened the door to the cave. Bina ran inside and pulled out the paper that she had mentioned at lunch. It was very brittle, stained, and worn, but the charcoal was still effectively showing the symbols and characters that someone had rubbed from the original stone. There was no clear indication that the original stone was the one found by workers at the Money Pit of Oak Island, but Jacob and Bina hoped that whatever was written would confirm that it was indeed the same stone.

"Do you know what it says?" asked Bina.

Jacob looked at the paper closely. "I understand what many of these letters mean in the angelic writing, but they seem to be scrambled. Like it's a puzzle."

Bina's eyes lit up. "A puzzle?" She loved a cognitive challenge. "Tell me what you know, and I'll help."

Still to this day, Jacob didn't know how he knew the angelic language and writing. It just came to him naturally. "Well, in the angelic alphabet there are 32 letters and symbols." Jacob grabbed a piece of paper and began to write down the alphabet in order. As he wrote, he described further. "You see here, when the tail drops down like this, it represents the masculine or male, and when it curls upward like this, the character represents the feminine or female."

Bina grabbed the weathered paper and the one that Jacob wrote on and held them side by side. She sat down on an old wooden stool that nearly cracked and fell apart when she put her weight on it; which at this point, Bina was so enthralled in the puzzle she wouldn't have broken her concentrated gaze on the two papers if she had fallen to the floor.

Jacob looked over her shoulder and tried to decode the riddle as well. Bina grabbed a pencil and began to scribble notes on the paper that Jacob had written the angelic alphabet on.

"It's definitely a puzzle," said Bina. "I have read about these types of riddles before, where the person hides clues inside the phrases. You see here, there are the same letters used in order as each word was written. The first letter written is then used as the second letter in the second word. The second letter in the first word is used as the second in the third word, and so on. If I write these letters down in the order of progression, maybe you can decipher what it says."

Jacob was listening, but honestly, he was merely pretending to understand what it was that Bina had just said. Understanding puzzles was easy for Bina, but explaining them was something altogether different. Bina continued writing the letters down in the order that made sense to her. With each set of letters written, words began to surface. Jacob was beginning to understand what she was writing. "There, I think that's it," said Bina. "What's it say?"

Bina gave the paper over to Jacob so that he could look at it more closely. "It says, 'Greed blinds you. It's through His salvation that you find entry.'" Jacob read aloud. "What's that mean?"

"Hmm, I'm not sure yet," said Bina. "I think we're going to have to see this Oak Island for ourselves, and maybe the clue will make more sense."

Jacob and Bina began walking home, all the while, talking about the trip that they would make to the Canadian island at some point over the upcoming Christmas weekend.

That night at Heldago, Jacob arrived and found everyone gathering in the inner meadow of Heldago for Jack's funeral. The sadness that filled the air seeped into Jacob to the depths of his very soul. He saw Jezebel and his other classmates hugging and crying. Jacob could do nothing but gaze upon Jack's casket. He felt a growing guilt inside of him. "Yet another Verita has died saving me," he thought. "I will not let you die in vain, Jack."

Jacob needed comfort. He needed to find his friend, Rabbi Lazarus, and tell him how sorry he was for how he spoke to him recently. Jacob searched for Lazarus through the crowds, but couldn't find him anywhere. He asked a few Veritas that he knew, but no one had seen the Rabbi either. "What could be so important that our Rabbi couldn't attend Jack's funeral?" he thought.

A group of Elders that had volunteered as pallbearers lifted Jack's casket by its long beautifully carved handles and began leading the procession of Veritas toward the rear of the meadow. A procession of the attending Veritas in the order of Elders, Moldans, Clevans, and finally Bethals followed the pallbearers.

Jacob stepped into the procession next to Jezebel as she passed. Jacob's presence helped to console Jezebel, and she struggled to smile. Losing Jack had been extremely difficult on Jezebel. Through prayer and talking to friends, she was doing the best she could.

After walking for some time, the procession came to a point where the meadow began to take a downward slope. Jacob had never walked this far to the back of the castle walls, so he was surprised to see the walls come together into an iron gate. It was an exit.

Seeing the look of surprise and wonder on Jacob's face, Jezebel whispered, "This gate is only used for funerals."

Raman was waiting at the gateway. The large man bowed at the gate, touching his forehead to where the swinging halves of the gateway met and passed his powers through the cold steel. A loud sound of metal rubbing upon stone could be heard as the gate was unlocked. He pushed the heavy gates open and bowed again as the casket passed by him.

The pallbearers led the somber procession along a path that led into the trees. It curved back and forth, as it ascended the mountainside.

The smell of pine needles and tree sap permeated the air. The aroma sent Jacob back to some of his expeditions with his father in mountains elsewhere in the world. Thoughts of the loss of Jacob's dad, Ramiro, and now Jack, cut deep to his heart. Tears began to fill his eyes.

The Elders started to sing an ancient chant that had many angelic words in it. The song had been sung for thousands of years at Veritas' funerals, but much of the translation had been lost. However, Jacob could understand what the words meant. The song spoke of the undying love that God has for all of His creations, and even though many may fall away, His love for them will never die.

When they reached the top of the mountain, they arrived at a clearing where an underwater spring began and continued its flow over the cliff into a beautiful waterfall. Jacob looked back at the castle and noticed how small it looked. From this vantage, he was struck by its white stones and beauty.

Coming up the hill behind the last Bethals, Jacob saw the horsorian, Lamech, slowly making his way towards him. Lamech reached his forehands out and placed them on Jacob's chest. "I've felt your trouble, Jacob," he said. "I've prayed fervently for you. Always know, no matter what may happen, that we're all supporting you. Many of us know the trials and frustrations that you face each day, but don't mistake our silence for anything but love. It's only through love that you will conquer what's inside your heart."

Jacob hadn't heard Lamech speak with such empathy before. He was used to more of a crass and harsh demeanor from the old creature.

The Elders placed the casket in the mouth of the creek and lined up on each side. They pulled their swords from their belts and raised them above the casket. The rest of the Veritas joined the Elders and began lining each side of the creek until they had filled both sides all the way to the cliff. With their swords raised high, they brought them together toward the Verita opposite them, forming a metal archway over the narrow creek. The swords reflected the sun's light down upon the water and made the creek glow a beautiful yellow and blue.

The spring water coming up from the ground began to increase in volume as it lifted the casket and made it float towards the cliff. The Elders continued their chant in celebration for the new life that Jack was to experience. The casket slowly floated by Jacob's feet. "Goodbye, my friend, for now," whispered Jacob.

Jack's casket came to the edge of the huge drop-off and fell out of sight. The Elders went silent as if they were waiting for something. In a flash of lightning, which was almost invisible to the eye because of his speed, an angel flew down from the heavens and grabbed Jack. Just as quickly as he had appeared, the angel disappeared into the sky holding Jack around his chest. Jacob and the other younger Veritas that had never witnessed this before were in awe.

"There be no greater act than to be givin' one's life fer another," said Shawn from behind. Jacob turned around and hugged his friend. "God wouldn't be a lettin' Jack's body be destroyed. His angel saw fit to that. There be no need fer tears now, only celebration, fer Jack be with Jesus."

Jacob wiped the tears from his face and tried to focus on Shawn's description of Jack being with Jesus. "Thank you," he mumbled. "It's difficult to think about what you can't see." Jacob looked at the sky where the angel had vanished and again thought of how he had spoken to his friend the last time he had seen him. "Shawn, have you seen Rabbi Lazarus today?"

"Nay, I've not been a seein' him fer a few days now," Shawn explained. "I be hearin' something about him needin' to do something, but wasn't able to be a speakin' 'bout it."

Jacob nodded his head as he and the other Veritas made their way down the hill. When Jacob reached the inner meadow where Sarge teaches sword skills, he saw Lamech and Sarge talking. Jacob tried to get closer to hear what they were talking about because their demeanor and posture was looking like they were hiding something. Jacob caught the end of the conversation when Sarge bowed and said, "Thank you, Master." Lamech paused for a moment and looked at the swords hanging in the nearby rosewood rack, as if he wanted to pick one up, but continued his walk to the front gates.

Jacob approached Sarge trying not to look nosey. "It's okay, Jacob," said Sarge. "I knew you were looking at us, but what we were talking about wasn't for your ears. Not yet anyway."

"You're friends with Lamech?" asked Jacob.

"Much more than friends, my young Verita. He was my teacher."

"Lamech taught you the sword?" Jacob was all the more curious.

"Indeed. If you want to be the best, you need to learn from the best," explained Sarge.

"But I thought you said that Rabbi Lazarus was the best swordsman in the world."

"What I said was that Lazarus was the best man with the sword." Sarge picked up his sword and began sharpening its blade with a stone. "The one you see leaving Heldago right now is the best creature, man or animal, with a sword.

Lamech has forgotten more about the sword than I will ever know. He's taught all the great ones. Yes, even Rabbi Lazarus."

"But he doesn't carry a sword or use one anymore?" Jacob pulled his sword out, called forth its blade, and sat next to Sarge and began to sharpen his blade with a stone.

"He doesn't need to carry a sword any longer, nor does he see fit to do so. Some things happened years ago when I was a young Elder that made him lay his sword down. But, he doesn't need to hold a sword to teach. What he has to give in information and skills is far greater than he could ever show you."

"You saw him use the sword?" Jacob was intrigued and his imagination flew into thoughts of the horsorian using his six arms in battle. Jacob loved the sword; its history and learning new techniques were always a priority for him when he was at Heldago. It was a great connection for Jacob—a way to escape the pressures of the world. Ever since the first class he had with Sarge, Jacob had nurtured a love, reverence, and oneness with the blade.

Sarge grinned. "Oh yeah, I saw him use the sword. One time, I saw him take on 12 Tenebras. When he was done, he didn't have a scratch, and not one Tenebra had his head attached. He can walk on his rear two hands and use a sword in each of his other four. With one blade or four, he's virtually unstoppable."

Jacob continued sharpening his sword as his mind continued thinking of Lamech and his sword skills. Jacob pictured the horsorian taking on countless enemies with precision and accuracy. His thoughts drifted into what could have happened so long ago that made Lamech give up his sword. Unknowingly, using his imagination was a great escape to keep Jacob's mind off of the funeral.

Time quickly passed that night with not many classes being held because of the funeral. Jacob found time to go to the chapel for prayer and meditation. He knew the upcoming trip to Canada's Oak Island was going to be dangerous, but he didn't want another one of his friends to get hurt or killed. He decided he wouldn't tell anyone about the trip. Besides, he was growing more worried about who the conspirator amongst the Veritas could be. Someone had obviously tipped off Lucifer's evil followers for them to know about the Newport Tower location. *If I keep the secret between only Bina and me, then the traitor will not be able to find me or be able to tell Lucifer's followers where I am,* he thought.

After prayer, Jacob left for home.

# CHAPTER 24

# OAK ISLAND

Like most American children, Christmas was Jacob's favorite time of the year. With no school, the anticipation of gifts, eating lots of tasty treats, and celebrating Jesus's birthday, it was easy to be excited. Unfortunately, the death of Jacob's friend had made him somewhat disheartened, even during the joyous time of Christmas, but his mind, heart, and soul had felt clear of the gloom he had felt at Thanksgiving ever since the Prophet Elijah had hit him with some kind of power at the Garden Gethsemane, so he did look forward to Christmas again. He felt that his new found clarity and renewed spirit would help in his attempt to make the holidays easier for his mother, too. His one Christmas wish was that both she and he found the ability to celebrate Christmas joyfully without his father.

After deciding that they would go to Oak Island, Jacob and Bina had discussed going there on Christmas Day, because they figured that would be the best day to have few people, if anyone, on the island.

With some last minute shopping and decorating of the house, Christmas day came quickly for Jacob and Bina.

Earlier in the month, Bina's parents had invited Jacob and his mom, Sarah, over for a Christmas lunch. They knew that Sarah and Jacob didn't have any other relatives in the area, so they felt obliged to have them over.

After opening some gifts on Christmas morning, Sarah

began cooking her specialty dish for lunch. She had agreed to prepare her family's recipe for apple baked bean casserole, and like most women, she was nervous for others to try it. "Jacob, take a bite of this," she said, nervously holding the spoon full of her bean concoction.

Jacob took a bite and his eyes lit up from the mixture of salt and sweetness that had just hit his tongue. "That's amazing, mom!" Jacob struggled to speak with the food still filling his mouth.

"Oh you think so?" asked Sarah. "I hope the Feldmans like it."

"That is truly amazing. Why don't you make that like every week?"

Sarah giggled. "It's for only special occasions. The recipe was taught to me when I was your age by your grandmother, and I suppose one of these holidays it will be time for me to teach you, too." She paused for a moment thinking of the great family memories she shared with her father and mother during holidays. Sarah sighed and walked out of the kitchen to check her hair in the bathroom.

Jacob peeked around the kitchen wall to make sure his mom was out of sight. He tiptoed back over to the delicious dish. He quietly and slowly stuck his spoon back in the casserole and raised it to his lips. Now, it's been fabled for centuries that mothers have an extra pair of hidden eyes in the back of their heads, but what's even more amazing is their intuition, especially where their children are concerned. "Jacob! Jacob Jerlow! You put that spoon down right now, young man!" she yelled from the bathroom. "You save that dish for our friends."

Jacob groaned and returned the spoonful to its origin.

Jacob and Sarah carefully loaded up their rusty old car with their prized dish and left for Bina's house. "Screech!" the brakes squealed loudly as they pulled in the Feldmans' driveway. Window drapes could be seen down the block opened by curious neighbors, looking toward the loud noise.

Jacob exited the car and quickly jogged to the front door, hoping to be seen by as few people as possible.

"Welcome! Merry Christmas! Come in," said Bina's father, Levi as he opened the front door. "Here, let me take that dish for you, Sarah."

As politely as possible, Sarah declined. "Oh, thank you, but I've got it okay." She feared that in careless hands her work of art would make its way onto the floor.

Jacob and Bina went into the backyard to talk about the new gifts they had received, and, of course, they discussed the trip while their parents visited and set the table.

While preparing to sit down at the table to eat, a knock was heard at the front door. "Are you expecting more company?" asked Sarah.

"Hmm, not sure on that," Rebecca smiled. "Say, I need to go grab the turkey platter would you get the door for me?"

"Certainly." Sarah went to the front door.

Jacob heard the front door open, but there wasn't a sound. He became worried. Jacob stormed to his feet and rushed to the front door. There in the doorway, where he had feared to find some Tenebra menace, he saw his mom in the arms of Granddad. Sarah was crying, joyfully. The Feldmans had secretly contacted Sarah's dad and asked him if he could attend the Christmas lunch. He had gladly accepted.

"Well, if ya are gonna get all weepy, and don't want me around, I can head out," Granddad joked.

"No! No! Stay!" Sarah exclaimed. She pulled her dad into the house and closed the door quickly as if Granddad Ben might actually try to sneak out.

Jacob was excited to see his grandfather again. He rushed over to a welcomed bear hug. "How's my grandson been?" asked Granddad.

"Great. Especially now that you're here!"

"I'm sorry. It's been far too long, especially, for you, my

daughter!" Granddad teared up, looking his daughter in the eyes. When he looked at her, a rush of memories of his little princess in ponytails began overflowing his thoughts. "Can you ever forgive a stupid old man?"

"I forgave you years ago, dad," Sarah explained. "Now, there will be no more talk of this. Today, is a joyous day, a day to celebrate. A day to be thankful, and I'm most thankful that my dad is here with me."

Rebecca, Levi, and Bina finally came into the room and greeted their new guest. They had purposefully left Jacob, Sarah, and her father alone for a more private reunion.

"Sorry, Bina, I didn't bring any of your favorite rabbit stew with me," Granddad Ben teased warmly. He had taken a special shining to his grandson's friend when she had visited the previous summer. "It's not like I didn't try though. Darn fools at the airport confiscated it. They said it was fer security. Something about no liquids on an airplane cuz of safety, but I think they got a whiff of my specialty and took it to fill their bellies. Took my favorite crock pot and all."

Rebecca and Levi laughed because they thought it was just a cute story or joke, but Bina and Jacob giggled because they knew it was nothing but the truth.

"Speakin' of specialties." Granddad stuck his nose a little higher into the air. "I know that smell. I could never forget that smell. I smell your mother's apple baked bean casserole."

Sarah smiled. "You sure do, dad."

The families and friends sat down for lunch and after a heartfelt prayer did what every red blooded American does on holidays—gorged themselves. Turkey, ham, mashed potatoes, cranberries, stuffing, and, of course, the apple baked bean casserole were all a huge success. In addition, yes, to her delight, Sarah's dish was the favorite.

No sooner had Granddad finished his plate than was he asleep on the recliner in the living room. Levi was soon to follow, as Sarah and Rebecca enjoyed each other's company while washing up dishes. It wasn't like it was a chore for the women. It was more of a means of communication — like a root beer and ice cream, or a hot dog over an open fire.

After receiving permission to go for a walk, Jacob and Bina grabbed a few supplies and stuffed them in a backpack. Bina had the idea the previous day that they should wear their swimsuits under their clothes, just in case they had to go into the water, so they both had put those on that morning.

Jacob knew how dangerous this adventure would be, so he gave his mom a hug and kiss before leaving. He needed to make sure that if it were the last time he saw her, it would be treasured. Jacob really didn't want to go after Granddad had shown up unexpectedly, but deep down he knew it was the only way. He was the hope for all that was good in the world. He changed his thoughts of fear and worry over to thoughts of courage and honor. He saw what he had to do as a privilege – in essence a service to God.

When Jacob and Bina got into the trees where no one could see them Jacob opened the Dalet doorway to Oak Island. They looked at each other to give one another confidence and assurance, and they leaped into the doorway. Upon exiting on the other side, Jacob and Bina were first caught by the smell of the salt air and fish. They were in a forest area of the island and couldn't hear any signs of people. Being that it was Christmas Day, Jacob and Bina had imagined that the island would be barren.

"All right, we're here," said Bina. "The clue on the stone said, 'It's through His salvation that you find entry.' We need to find something that will lead us to its meaning."

Jacob and Bina started walking on the 140-acre island and soon came upon the signs that labeled the Money Pit and its treasure seekers' history. The large wooden painted signs told of the first digs in the mysterious hole, how the stone was found, and eventually the trap that was sprung that filled the hole with water. The two adventurers climbed over the fence that protected the hole from intruders and paced around the pit to look for clues.

"I don't see anything here, Bina," said Jacob. "Honestly, the more I think about it, I think from the history of this place that this hole was just a diversion. The history says when the boy found this pit in 1795 he saw an old dilapidated block and tackle still hanging from the tree above the pit. If someone was going to hide a treasure, why would they leave an important clue like that in plain sight? The block and tackle, the wooden beams every ten feet down in the hole, the stone that no one could translate—I mean, it just all sounds like a diversion."

"You're right, Jacob. I never thought of it like that. Maybe the pit was just a means to keep people puzzled. In my reading, I learned that one of the groups of treasure hunters poured red dye in the water of the pit. I printed out a map of the island, and on it, I marked the seven locations that they reported seeing the red dye from the pit flowing out into the ocean." Bina pulled the map out for Jacob to see.

"Let's go look at each one of these sites and see if anything stands out in relation to our written clue," Jacob instructed.

First, they went to the two locations on the south side of the island where dye was seen and found nothing. When they came to their third location, which was on the north side of the island, they came across some recent disturbance in the ground. An excavator had cleared some earth away from seven white stones.

Bina was curious. She climbed up a nearby tree to look at the stones from above. "Jacob, the stones are laid out in the shape of a cross!" she shouted. Bina jumped down and ran over to the nearest stone. "Check the stones for any kind of a marking."

The first stone Jacob investigated showed no signs, but when he came to the center stone, where the two lines of the cross converged, he found an etching. "Bina!" he shouted. "Come here!" Bina sprinted over. "You see this?" Jacob pointed at the rock.

"Yes, it is shaped like a funny U," said Bina. "But, it doesn't look like it's been carved into the stone; it looks like natural wear or weathering of the stone."

"To you it may look like that, but to me it appears to be a symbol. In angelic this character depicts the head of something or the leader."

Bina's eyes grew larger. "So our clue from the stone that said, 'It's through His salvation that you find entry,' was referring to this cross. Of course, that's it! It must refer to Jesus's salvation through His death on the cross. This cross tells us we are in the right place." She pulled her map out from her pocket. "The treasure hunters reported that they found red dye come out of that small cove right there on the island." Bina pointed toward a small inlet and then traced the cross with the same finger. "And look, the cross points directly to that spot."

Jacob and Bina ran over to the small inlet. Some of the larger rocks just off the shore were breaking the waves that were approaching, making the water less aggressive in the area. They walked up and down the shoreline looking for any other clue but found nothing.

"I think we're going to have to go out into the water and look further," said Jacob.

Bina agreed. They both shed their clothes and hid them under a tree. The brisk, December ocean wind caused them to shiver miserably as Jacob tied a piece of rope around his waist and attached his sword so that it wouldn't fall off. They knew the water was going to be freezing, but there was no other way. They waded out into the ice cold water looking for a clue.

"We have to act fast, Jacob, or we'll start to suffer from hypothermia." Bina bit her shivering lip.

Jacob stumbled over a rock in the water that grabbed his

attention. The water was clear enough to see the stone, but it was covered by moss and algae. Jacob picked up the sharpest stone he could find and began to rub the growth off of the stone. He noticed that under the natural growth was an inscription of the words "40 paces" in angelic, along with an arrow pointing the direction. "This stone says to walk 40 paces this way!" he shouted through chattering teeth – the freezing water was affecting them much more quickly than either of them had originally guessed.

Bina ran as fast as she could while treading the water. Both of the adventurers' skin was beginning to turn blue from the cold. They needed to act quickly before they froze. Jacob began counting his steps while Bina followed. As they walked away from the island, the water slowly got deeper, and by the time they were at step 35, the water was up to Jacob's chest and Bina's neck. Jacob took his 40th step, expecting solid ground beneath his step, but there wasn't. His foot stepped into a hole. Jacob fell beneath the water's surface out of sight. Bina panicked. "Jacob!" she screamed.

Jacob resurfaced a few moments later next to Bina. "There's a hole there," he joked.

"Very funny!"

"When I fell under the water, I saw the hole. I peeked my head in and couldn't see anything. It was really dark."

Bina was scared, but she tried not to show it. It would have been difficult to tell if she were shivering in fear due to how much she shivered due to the cold anyway. "I'll follow you in," she said, her words vibrating with her shivering.

Jacob nodded. "I'll make a light power come from my hand to shine the way. Stay close to me."

Jacob and Bina took in a few deep breaths and went under water towards the hole. Jacob cast a power from his hand and lit up the cavern. The hole was narrow, but it gave plenty of room to swim. They crawled along the rocks using their hands and feet or swam when appropriate. Just when they were ready to head back because they needed air, they came upon a fork in the passage with two tunnels ahead.

They stopped for a moment, not knowing which to enter. Bina noticed some of the red dye that the treasure hunters had dumped in the Money Pit stained on the rocks of the tunnel on the right. She motioned to Jacob to not go that way. She knew that was a trap that led to the Money Pit, so they entered the tunnel on their left and swam ahead. Soon, when they thought they couldn't swim another foot without surfacing for air, they saw Jacob's light reflecting back at him. Something shiny ahead was reflecting the light.

The tunnel led upward slightly, and then, the water ended in an opening above them. Jacob and Bina popped their heads above the water and gasped heavily for air. Bina began violently coughing in a reflex to expel water from her throat that she had accidentally inhaled in her haste to breathe.

"Are you all right?" asked Jacob.

Bina nodded. "I'm okay," she struggled to say after a few more coughs and rapid shivering.

They regained their bearings after receiving some much-needed oxygen and noticed that the walls were laden with blocks of gold. It was the treasure that had reflected the light back at them.

"We've found it!" said Jacob excitedly through his chattering teeth. "We've found the treasure that no one has ever been able to find!"

A series of roughly hewn steps in the rock led the two adventurers out of the icy water and into the even more frigid air. They were shivering violently and knew they needed to warm themselves as quickly as possible. Stacked next to one of the walls was a pile of old timber, and next to it, was a stone circle that had been used as a fire pit many years ago.

Jacob threw some of the wood into the pit and sent a fire power from his hand, lighting the wood on fire. Jacob and Bina knelt next to the fire and warmed themselves. As they regained feeling in their numb bodies and their strength, they stared at the stockpile of gold that surrounded them.

"Well, if I ever need some extra college money, I know where I coming," Jacob joked.

The smoke from the fire rose up a ventilation shaft that had been drilled through the solid rock above to the outside. The network of underground tunnels and shafts were ingeniously constructed. A group of people had gone through considerable extremes to protect the gold treasure and the clue to the Garden of Eden.

However, the gold at the entrance was just to keep a would-be treasure hunter happy enough to leave without searching any further. Jacob and Bina didn't know it, but if they would have taken a brick of gold from one of the walls, it would have set off a catastrophic series of traps that would have collapsed all of the tunnels — permanently burying any clue to the Garden of Eden and them. This trap was set for anyone that was greedy and thought of money above all else. If they were not of pure heart and not worthy to possess the hidden secret in the tunnels, they would take the gold and, unknowingly, destroy the biggest treasure hidden within.

After warming up for some time, allowing their measly swimsuits to dry, Jacob grabbed one of the longer pieces of wood and lit one end on fire to use as a torch. He looked back at Bina and asked, "Are you ready?"

Bina stood up and smiled. "Let's do it."

"Before we head out, I want to try something we have been learning in our powers class," Jacob said tentatively. "I have only just started to learn this power, but I don't think we will survive this cold in just our swim suits. You game?"

Bina nodded a little nervously, but she had already started shivering again, so her desire to be warm outweighed any fear of Jacob's amateurish use of his angelic powers.

"Okay, we will have to walk hand-in-hand because the

power will have to transfer from me into you," Jacob explained as he held out his hand for Bina's. "Let me know if you get too warm."

"Too warm?" Bina asked and chuckled. "I don't think I can get too warm right now. We should have planned for this a bit better or you should have thought of this power before we dove into that hole outside."

Jacob smiled because Bina was always able to make him feel better. He focused his mind on being warm and allowed the power to fill him from his center outward.

"Whoa!" Bina gasped as she felt a sudden warmth spill into her hand and move through her arm into her entire body.

"You okay?" Jacob asked quickly, concerned that he may have overdone it.

"Ooooh, yes, I am wonderful," Bina said. "You definitely should have thought of this before we entered the ocean outside."

Jacob laughed and reminded her that he had to concentrate on the power every few minutes in order to keep the warmth flowing through them. He asked her to keep an eye out for anything unusual while they moved through the tunnel because he might be focused on the power. Bina readily agreed. She would rather be warm and in charge of keeping an eye out than suffering hypothermia.

As they walked through the tunnel that was hewed in the solid stone and earth, they noticed pick ax and shovel scrapes in the wall, which were all that remained as a reminder of the years that it must have taken to remove so much rock and earth with rudimentary implements. Every few steps, they would be reminded again of the history by tripping over the shattered remains of an old excavating tool. The tunnel was no more than seven feet tall and three feet wide.

The ground was surprisingly dry, but every few feet there would be a slight dripping from the ceiling that would land on their heads. At some points, Jacob felt claustrophobic, but seeing Bina behind him helped to alleviate those fears. They both started to shiver again as the cold of winter in Nova Scotia seeped into their bodies, which were protected by swimsuits only, so Jacob took a moment or two to concentrate on warming them with his power. The cold was hard to ignore, but the excitement of finding the next clue to the Garden of Eden warmed them from within as they stumbled on into the darkness lit only by the makeshift torch that Jacob held before them.

They came to the end of the first tunnel and had to make another decision because before them stood two more tunnels. The one on the left was lined with gold and jewels, and the one on the right had nothing on its walls but dirt and rock.

"Do we follow the tunnel of gold and riches or the one with no wealth?" asked Bina.

"It seems to be a test," said Jacob. "My heart tells me to stay away from the treasure. I think it's meant to tempt and divert us from what we are truly seeking."

Bina agreed. They cleared some of the spider webs from the entrance to the tunnel on the right and continued forward. Soon, they came to the end of that tunnel and came upon the entrances to three tunnels. The one in the middle, again, was lined with jewels and gold, but the ones on the right and left were barren.

"Okay. If we are going to keep our same path of not following the gold, which one do we choose now?" asked Bina.

Jacob approached the tunnels and held his torch up to the walls, searching for a clue. He had lost attention on the piece of lit wood that had served as a torch, and it was nearly burning his hand. Bina searched the ground and found another thin piece of timber to ignite as Jacob dropped what little remained of the first torch to the floor.

"I don't see any clue to know which tunnel to take," said

Jacob. "I think we're going to have to guess."

"Well, we always try to do the right thing, so let's try the right one." Bina chuckled.

Jacob nodded in agreement and took Bina by the hand once again. He led her slowly as they entered the tunnel. About ten feet into the tunnel, a sudden draft of wind hit them from below. It was like someone or something blew air from their mouth. The fire died on the torch in the midst of the draft. It was pitch black. They couldn't see their own hand in front of their face. Bina squeezed Jacob's hand and bit her tongue to not scream.

Just as he was about to throw the power of fire on to the wood to reignite it, Jacob stopped when he heard the sound of cracking wood, coming from underneath their feet. "Don't move!" Jacob shouted. Though neither of them could see in the pitch black of the tunnel, they suddenly realized that they were standing on an old platform of rotten timber that was likely a trap. In fact, the platform covered a deep pit of razor sharp rocks. "We're standing on some kind of a booby trap. It's the only thing that makes sense with that sudden draft from under us and the sound of breaking wood, and I bet the timbers are pretty old," Jacob explained.

"I guess we chose the wrong tunnel, huh?" Bina tried to lighten the mood.

Almost as if in response to Bina's poor joke, the wood below made an awful cracking sound of impending doom.

"Just don't move," Jacob ordered. "It's holding our weight right now, but if we take another step or move too fast, it's going to break and who knows how far we will fall."

The cold and inky darkness didn't help relieve the stressful situation at all.

"Okay, Bina, we're going to be all right," Jacob comforted. He could feel Bina's hand shaking in his. "Here's what we're going to do, I'm going to use the Valoria power that will lift us both up into the air. But, when I do that, it's going to send a force downward, shattering the wooden beams beneath us. We have to time it just right. When I say 'three', we'll jump back the same way we came from. Okay?"

"Umm...okay. Yes, we can do this." Bina cringed in anticipation.

Jacob grabbed Bina's hand a little tighter. "Ready...ONE – TWO – THREE!" On three, he threw the Valoria power downward, shattering the wood beneath them just as he predicted; at the same time, Bina and Jacob jumped into the air backward towards the tunnel's entrance. In that moment of being in the air, Jacob and Bina looked below, and the light coming through the rocks below showed a most certain death if they would have fallen. Their momentum carried them backward and to the ground. Jacob fell on Bina, bruising her ribs, but they were alive. Even in her extreme pain and the cold, Bina hugged Jacob with all her strength.

The awkward moment of them hugging was quickly broken, and they arose to their feet. Their eyes finally adjusted to the darkness somewhat, so they stood at the edge of the booby trap and stared down into the pit where they almost had fallen to certain death upon the razor-sharp rocks that they could just make out in the darkness. They turned and hurried out of that tunnel back to where they started at the three-way fork of the tunnels. They had lost their makeshift torch in the booby trap, so Jacob called forth a fireball into his hand and held it out to see more clearly. "All right then, I say we take the tunnel on the left." Jacob joked.

"Agreed!" Bina responded and gripped Jacob's hand tightly. "And, Jacob, could you do that power thing and warm us up a bit? I don't know if it was that near miss or our rolling on this cave's cold stone floor, but I'm starting to shiver from my bones out."

Jacob focused his mind again on calling forth warmth from his very center and filling up to his extremities. He knew he had been successful when he no longer heard Bina's teeth chattering. "Let's move on," he said as he gripped her hand tightly and started down the left tunnel branch.

They cautiously entered the tunnel, examining the floor carefully before taking each step to avoid a repeat of the recent death-defying excitement, and soon, they came to a dead end. A stone wall was all that was in front of them. "There's got to be more," said Jacob. "This can't be a dead end for us."

A voice came into Jacob's head and instructed, "Speak the words that you found."

"Okay, I'll try," said Jacob.

"You'll try what?" asked Bina.

"I'm going to try what I was told."

"And what were you told?" Bina was totally puzzled.

"Oh, never mind." Jacob thought of the inscription on the stone that was found in the Money Pit, and spoke the words in angelic, "It's through His salvation that you find entry."

A rumbling was heard in the stone wall in front of them, and the rock split in two. There was just enough room to squeeze through the fracture to the other side. Jacob and Bina excitedly maneuvered through the narrow passage and found a beautifully carved crucifix hanging on the wall. At the foot of the cross was a kneeling station for prayer.

Jacob and Bina approached the holy site with reverence and knelt at the station to give thanks to God. When they knelt, words appeared on the cross that could only be read from the humble kneeling position. The words were written in Old English and read:

> "We, the chosen, select few of the Knights Templar, with the guidance of the keeper of the Garden of Eden, do deliver this treasure to you, for you have been found worthy to hold such an honor. From this day forth, our society

will be humbled and dissolve itself but will make itself anew and keep our secrets hidden through a new order. Now, good and faithful servant go to the wall of the Holy city and face death. There you will find what it is you seek."

Jacob and Bina stood up. With the flame in Jacob's hand still flickering, he lit the candles that were on pillars around the room. As the room lit up, they could see hundreds of Knights Templar skeletons still dressed in their distinctive white mantles with a red cross, seated around the room. After building the tunnel system, the majority of the knights had trapped themselves in the room to keep watch over the holy secret. The sight of the ancient soldiers sent chills down Jacob and Bina's backs that were even more pronounced than the goosebumps and shivers from the cold.

# CHAPTER 25

# THE GREATEST GIFT

Jacob and Bina made their way back through the tunnel system and to the water's entrance. "We shouldn't have any more surprises this Christmas Day, Bina," said Jacob. "I didn't tell a soul that we were coming here. So there shouldn't be any way that the Tenebras or Lucifer's servants or minions could find us here."

These were well-received words for Bina. She had never said anything, but she had experienced enough life threatening adventure and death in the past six months for two lifetimes. The two friends eased themselves into the frigid water and took a deep breath in for the upcoming under water swim. Just as they had entered, they exited the secret tunnel. They emerged from the cold ocean with a gasp of welcomed air to their lungs. They ran to their clothes and backpack as quickly as possible to dry and warm themselves. After using towels to thoroughly dry themselves, Jacob used his warming power to dry their swimsuits so that they would not make their clothes wet, which would only make the winter air that much more dangerous.

After dressing, Bina had to go to the bathroom, so she walked to the trees to find a more private, hidden spot. It had been over five minutes since Bina had excused herself, so Jacob grew concerned. He walked to the area he had seen

Bina vanish into the trees and yelled, "Bina! Is everything okay?"

There was no response. Fear overcame Jacob, and he sprinted into the trees. He stumbled over something and looked back at his footsteps. He saw an arm lying on the ground sticking out from behind a tree. "Bina!" he shouted.

Jacob ran over to the exposed hand and arm and saw that it was his friend. Bina was knocked out and not responding. Jacob felt her pulse and was relieved to feel her heart beating. He looked at the back of Bina's head and saw her hair was soaked in blood. Someone had struck her on the head from behind. Jacob looked left and right, up and down, and everywhere for her attacker, but he couldn't see anyone.

"Jacob," said an unfamiliar voice from the trees. "You have served me well. You are growing and maturing just as I planned."

"Who are you?" Jacob yelled. "Show yourself!"

"Now, Jacob, haven't you known me for this long and still you can't recognize me?"

"Lucifer, is that you? You say I've served you?" asked Jacob as he rose and stepped defiantly toward the voice, drawing his sword and calling forth its blade. "I serve God alone!"

The man laughed as dark clouds moved in front of the setting sun, cutting out any light that was making its way to the island. The winds increased, lightning flashed in the sky, and thunder rumbled loudly. "Haven't you heard? A man cannot serve two masters."

"What? What are you talking about? I serve God alone!" Jacob shouted angrily again, raising his sword toward the darkening skies above.

The man's laugh faded into the trees. Jacob was furious and confused.

"Well, Jacob Jerlow, it's time," said a different voice from behind him.

Jacob spun around once more and held his sword in

readiness. He saw that it was Prince Muammar.

"You've found the next clue to the garden, and now it's time for you to stop playing games and tell us what you know," Muammar said confidently.

"I'll never tell you anything!"

Prince Muammar's four armed bodyguard stepped from behind a tree to Muammar's right, holding a bloodstained club in his hand. He was apparently the one who had hit Bina, knocking her unconscious. Bodach easily snatched Bina from the ground and held her up. Prince Muammar drew his sword from his side and held its blade at Bina's throat. "Tell us, or she dies!" Muammar hissed threateningly.

Jacob's anger and confusion worsened as terror engulfed his emotions at the sight of the Tenebra leader's blade at his best friend's throat. Memories of Ramiro and Jack flashed before his eyes as another bolt of lightning streaked across the sky. He would do anything for Bina, but could he give away the world to save her life?

"All right," Jacob said resignedly, his sword arm dropping helplessly to his side. "The next clue is in the –"

"Stop!" a man yelled from the opposite direction. "Don't you tell these evil creatures a thing!"

Jacob spun quickly to see his powers teacher, the Elder Verita, Don. Jacob was shocked to see him. Even though Don had showed kindness to Jacob at Heldago since his harsh Bethal testing, there were still suspicions of Don being the traitor running in the back of his mind.

"Sorry I'm late, Jacob, but I have made up for my tardiness by bringing some friends." Don pointed.

From the trees on both sides of Don emerged Shawn, Sarge, Master Kang, and, just below them, Jacob could see how they got there — Yelkie. The magical gnome had been secretly following Jacob and knew where to find him from his conversations with Bina. When Yelkie saw the Tenebras hiding on the island, he had rushed back to Heldago, gathered the four teachers that were nearest, and brought them back to help Jacob.

Jacob turned back around and smiled at Prince Muammar. "So, here we are again. Good versus evil."

The prince laughed diabolically. "You think I came unprepared?" He nodded his head to the left and right. At least fifty Tenebras began to emerge from the forest, and more were arriving each passing moment. Prince Muammar was not going to be defeated as he was in Italy. The Veritas were surrounded and greatly outnumbered. "Give up now. Give us the secret, and we'll let you live," said the Tenebras' leader. "I'll let HER live," he hissed as he ran his sword's blade against Bina's throat, drawing forth a trickle of blood.

Sarge had been in similar situations throughout his years against the Tenebras and knew the prince didn't mean a word he said. He wasn't about to let Jacob second guess himself. "Cowards!" Sarge forced the word through his clenched teeth. He pulled his sword from his belt and made the blade appear. "If we are to die, let us die for God's kingdom!" he shouted. Veins popped from his arms as he gripped his sword tightly.

Sarge ran at the Tenebras and began slicing through their lines. Master Kang, Shawn, and Don were close behind. The low light on the island was shattered as Don blasted his first blindingly bright power, instantly killing three Tenebras. The man was small in stature, but enormous in power.

The four Elders fought with ferocity as Jacob joined the fight. Jacob wasn't surprised when Felix appeared out of nowhere and was in his face slashing at his throat. "You're dead!" Felix shouted as Jacob parried his first slash. The two young Clevan-level enemies began to battle with their swords and powers.

Master Kang came eye to eye with the Tenebras' martial arts and body control teacher, Master Fu. The last time they had met each other face to face was at a Certatim hundreds of years ago. Still to this day, many Elders talk of how evenly matched the two were in the competition. Master Kang had won that match in the last few seconds. When they saw each other now, they put their swords back into their belts and bowed. They wanted a rematch.

"I've waited many years to see you again in battle," said Master Fu.

"Indeed. Let it be so," said Master Kang.

The two attacked with unmatched skill and grace, each searching for the other's weakness in hand to hand combat.

Shawn was well rehearsed in battle as of late and was having his way with four young Tenebras, who thought they had him cornered.

Prince Muammar and Bodach stood by and watched as they saw their numbers increase dramatically in moments. Tenebras and goblins kept filing in from each side of the battle. The Tenebras had captured a father and son gnome pair a few months prior without the Veritas knowing. The father was Elior, and his son's name was Dannon. The son was being held captive in Muerte Palace's dungeon while the father was forced to carry Tenebras to where they wished to go. Prince Muammar had placed a strong fearable cage spell on the chains that held the young gnome, so he couldn't transport himself to safety.

Elior wasn't a very strong willed gnome and did what the Tenebras wished, for fear of his son being killed. He was currently helping the Tenebras by transporting them from Muerte Palace to the island.

The Veritas battled ferociously and valiantly, but there were just too many of the enemy. Master Fu was helped when a Tenebra struck Master Kang in the back with a stone thrown with the telekinetic power. Master Kang was bleeding internally and quickly weakening. Sarge had killed seven Tenebras, but powers were being sent at him that were too numerous to deflect or counteract. Don had killed nine Tenebras, but was growing weak from all the energy he had exerted in such a short amount of time. Shawn had killed ten Tenebras, but the numbers surrounding him were more than any one man could defeat.

Soon, Jacob and the other Veritas were backed up and completely surrounded. The numbers were too great for them to handle. The Tenebras waited for the command of their leader to execute them.

"Now, give up, or die!" commanded Prince Muammar.

Then, a loud rumbling sound could be heard through the trees coming in their direction. The Veritas and Tenebras looked in the direction of the sound with curiosity. It sounded like a stampede of buffalo coming their way. Bursting through the trees were 12 Nephilim, led by their leader, King Enoch. They began swinging their large clubs, and Tenebras' heads began falling to the left and right. The large hairy creatures dwarfed the Tenebras in stature.

Yelkie had seen what Elior had been doing by bringing in the inordinate numbers of Tenebras, so he went to his brother, Yagmur, and the Nephilim and told them of Jacob's desperate situation. The king of the Nephilim didn't hesitate. Enoch remembered the debt he owed for Jacob's rescue of his daughter and his vow to help Jacob when he was in trouble. He quickly gathered 11 of his best soldiers for war and traveled in an instant to Oak Island with Yelkie and Yagmur's assistance.

The Veritas regained their strength and courage when they saw the help that had arrived. Together, the Nephilim and the Veritas fought side by side. Such a sight had not taken place for thousands of years. They began to push the Tenebras back, striking many of them dead. Prince Muammar's eyes grew fearful.

Just as the Tenebras were going to flee in retreat, a loud rumbling rolled through the ground, shaking everyone in what felt like an earthquake. Four mighty Powers-level demons burst forth from beneath the earth, sending earth, rocks, trees, and combatants flying in all directions. Lucifer had sent more reinforcements. The demons were so massive they even towered over the Nephilim. Their wings were black and decorated with human bones. The wind carried their foul stench of decay through the island, bringing the chill of death and evil to all that were near.

The tables had turned once more, and the Tenebras regained their confidence. They turned from their near retreat and attacked again with the aid of the four demons. Good and evil clashed in a bloody battle. Within the first moments of the Tenebras' renewed attack, two Nephilim lay dead on the ground.

Jacob's rage and anger were at a boiling point. His skin glowed yellow with the light of goodness and his eyes black with the fear of death. He released everything he had upon the enemy. Jacob's power emanated from him to such an extent, the very air around the island increased ten degrees. Tenebras began to fall, one after another from his fury. Felix saw Jacob's power and backed away terrified, remembering what had happened to Rico in Indianapolis.

Seeing how the tides of the battle were shifting precariously against them, Prince Muammar ordered Bodach to enter the fray. Bodach threw Bina's limp, unconscious body to the side like a rag doll, and she landed harshly, bouncing off the trunk of a tree that a badly aimed power had blown asunder. Her body just missed being impaled on the still smoldering jagged splinters of the trunk and came to rest upon its roots. Prince Muammar also joined the battle to help the other Tenebras. Prince Muammar and Bodach purposefully separated the embattled Veritas and Nephilim from Jacob while the four demons encircled him. One demon would fly down to strike from above while another would attack the young Verita from the ground. Jacob's skin boiled. He put all of his power into his sword, but his friends could see that the four demons were too much. Each of the Veritas struggled to break from their personal battles to help Jacob, but there were too many of the enemy to get through to help him.

The four demons closed in around Jacob and ensnared him with an old angelic curse that put a fearable cage power to shame. They grabbed his arms and threw him against a tree, his sword flying aimlessly into the underbrush nearby. The Nephilim and the Veritas were trapped as well. They were completely surrounded. They had no choice, but to drop their weapons in defeat.

"Now, tell me the secret or die." Prince Muammar stomped toward Jacob. Muammar's sword glistened with the blood of his most recent victim.

Jacob was just calming down, coming back to consciousness, and realizing the grave situation he and his friends were in. Each of the four demons shoved one of Jacob's limbs against the tree, painfully splaying him wide open. "Prince Muammar commands you to speak!" one demon growled.

The Archangel Michael perched in a nearby tree, waiting and watching the entire battle to see what would happen. His heart called out to his grandson. Michael wanted to help Jacob badly, but he had orders from Jesus not to attack. He couldn't betray his king. *But Lucifer has broken the rules by somehow sending his angels to Earth,* he thought angrily. *They are supposed to be only able to inhabit the body of a victim, not physically come and make direct contact like this. I'm sure Jesus would tell me to help these valiant, faithful defenders of righteousness in their time of need in these circumstances. I must help!*

Just as Archangel Michael was about to leap to the ground, a man entered the scene below. It was Rabbi Lazarus. Yelkie had narrowly escaped the battle, and he had been able to find the Verita Rabbi.

"Enough! Enough hate! Enough bloodshed! Enough!" Lazarus shouted as he walked boldly through the trees to the site of the battle.

"Oh, look who decided to show up," said Prince

Muammar sarcastically. "A little too late wouldn't you say, friend of Jesus? We've already won the battle."

Lazarus looked up into the tree where Archangel Michael waited and watched, and, for the first time in many years, Lazarus could see him. Lazarus recognized Michael as the angel who had come to him before World War II and told him not to interfere with the Jewish holocaust. Lazarus imperceptibly shook his head in a subtle gesture that told Michael not to interfere. Lazarus looked at Jacob and a tear rolled down his cheek. "Take me," he shouted as he turned his attention to Prince Muammar. "I offer myself as ransom. You may take me and do with me as you wish, if you let Jacob and these others go."

"No!" Jacob yelled. He remembered the mean words that he had last spoken to Lazarus, and he couldn't bear not being able to tell him he didn't mean any of it.

Prince Muammar smiled. "The leader of the Veritas would give himself over to his enemy in exchange for a handful of Veritas and a bunch of – *pitiful creatures* he barely knows?"

King Enoch growled at the obviously derogatory reference to the Nephilim.

"I will," said Lazarus, looking at the king of the Nephilim hearteningly.

"No! Don't do it!" Jacob shouted again in utter frustration and fear.

Prince Muammar looked at the demons to know what the answer would be from their Master. They all nodded the master's agreement to the proposal. "Fine, then! You for these others!" Prince Muammar grumbled in delight.

Bina, who had been thrown to the ground by Bodach some time ago, was just coming to. She shook her throbbing head, trying to regain her bearings, and when she saw the crowd of combatants and bodies strewn around the area, she started to crawl painfully toward the Veritas' side of the battleground – each motion causing stabs of pain from her previously bruised and now likely broken ribs to shoot through her body while the throbbing in her head made the world spin before her eyes.

"First, let them go, and then you can have me," said Lazarus. "They will all leave with no more fighting, once you have me."

"How do we know you won't trick us?" asked Prince Muammar his tone rising in suspicion.

"You have my word," said Lazarus. "You know I can never go against my word." A heavy, pronounced sorrow waivered in Lazarus's voice and the tears in his eyes cut Jacob to his very soul.

Prince Muammar waved his hands at his army signaling them to release the captives. Jacob fell from the grasps of the demons and ran to Lazarus. "You can't do this," he said urgently. "I never got to tell you I was sorry for what I said. I didn't mean any of those words. You've been like a father to me," Jacob sobbed in anger, guilt, and sorrow. "I love you."

Tears fell freely from Lazarus's eyes, coating his face as he hugged Jacob. "My boy, you owe me no apology. I forgave you the moment you spoke, for I knew it wasn't you, but what's inside of you." Lazarus gently pulled Jacob from the hug and held his face firmly in his hands, staring intently into Jacob's eyes as he spoke gently. "There is no greater gift in life one can give than to be able to give one's life to save another. It's what needs to be done. You must go on. If my life can be given to save God's plan, then so be it."

King Enoch and the Nephilim had very hardened hearts, especially towards the Veritas, but Lazarus's courageous sacrifice to save their lives softened their spirits. Their entire outlook on the Veritas and their cause to serve God were being remolded in those brief moments.

"Jacob, always know that I will be with you wherever you go," said Lazarus as he placed his hand over Jacob's heart. "These people may do with my body whatever they wish, but my spirit they will never be able to touch. Here…

take my sword for safe keeping." Lazarus passed his old withered cane into Jacob's hands. "Always remember, God will be with those that serve him. Now go. Go with the others and don't turn back. You will not want to see what they will do with me. Remember only the good memories." Lazarus released Jacob reluctantly and turned to the Veritas and the Nephilim. "All of you. It's time to leave. I gave my word that I would give myself over for your freedom, and you will not fight, so I would hope that all of you will honor the vow I have spoken."

Lazarus looked directly into the tear-filled eyes of his Veritas and then to King Enoch. The king of the Nephilim's heart had been changed by Lazarus's selfless act, and his face was overrun with emotion.

Behind Lazarus, the Tenebras were celebrating their capture of the leader of the Veritas. They had made an archway with their swords as they lined each side of a pathway waiting for Lazarus to walk beneath it toward Prince Muammar. The sight of the archway reminded Jacob of the one that the Veritas had made at Jack's funeral, and he fearfully wondered if this arch was for the funeral of his teacher, friend, mentor, and Rabbi. Lazarus slowly entered the archway of swords as the Tenebras spat upon and mocked him. Some grabbed whips they had hanging from their belts and cracked them across the back of the Verita leader.

Thoughts of Jesus's last hours on Earth and how he had been mocked, scourged, and beaten before his crucifixion flooded Lazarus's mind. He fell to his knees in agony when a leather whip laced with broken glass struck the back of his head.

Shawn grabbed Jacob around the shoulder and tried to get him to turn away as they left the area. "It be time, Jacob," he said.

The Veritas, Bina, and the Nephilim had all left the area mournfully with the help of Yelkie and Yagmur, but Jacob had to turn back; he needed to see his friend one last time.

Lazarus finally reached Prince Muammar. Bodach ripped Lazarus's robe from his back, exposing his whip-slashed and bleeding skin. Bodach threw Lazarus to the ground before his leader's feet. "You call yourself a leader?" chided Bodach. "Look at yourself."

Prince Muammar knelt down and lifted the bloodied face of his enemy. "When we are done with you, we will hunt down all the Veritas and slaughter every last one. Your precious Jacob Jerlow will have nowhere to hide, and I shall save him for last so that I might relish his screams for mercy. You and your God are finished!"

Lazarus looked back over his bloody shoulder at Jacob one last time. Their gazes met briefly, and then, Lazarus closed his eyes, turned back to Muammar, and bowed his head for what was to come. Prince Muammar gave the order, and the Tenebras surrounded their prisoner and began kicking, beating, and whipping him, their maniacal howls of bloodlust echoing across the island.

Jacob wanted to run to his friend's aid but remembered Lazarus's final order. Jacob turned and walked away crestfallen, guided by his friend Shawn. Jacob's heart was confused with anger and sadness. *Whatever this is that's inside of me, I will find,* he thought angrily. *And I will destroy it,* he vowed beneath his breath to all of his friends who had given their lives for him.

Lucifer was in the shadows watching as Shawn wrapped his arm around Jacob's shoulder and disappeared into the trees. "The seed has taken root, and all is coming to fruition," he whispered to himself pleased. As the sounds of Lazarus's beating rose to a crescendo, Lucifer's possessed body smiled wickedly, licking his lips as he turned to watch the celebration of his Tenebras' triumphant battle.

# ABOUT THE AUTHOR

Lance Peltier is a high school teacher in his day job. He enjoys spending time with his family and enjoying God's playground – the outdoors. Lance has a Bachelor's degree from the University of Nevada Las Vegas and a Master's degree from North Dakota State University. JACOB JERLOW: TO THE FOUR CORNERS OF THE EARTH was his first published book in the Jacob Jerlow series. JACOB JERLOW AND THE NEPHILIM is the second. Lance and his wife, Robin, live in North Dakota with their four children and two energetic labs.